John [illegible] Houston, Texas and brought up in Texas, New York and Northern California. On graduating from U.C. Berkeley, he did various jobs before becoming a full-time writer, including working as a singer in Europe, a bar tender in an Irish pub in San Francisco and associate director of the Jewish Homes for the Aging in Los Angeles. After doctors estimated he had two hours to live when he contracted meningitis, John Lescroart decided, on his return to health, to take the risk of writing full-time. Two years after that decision, his novel THE 13th JUROR hit the *New York Times* bestseller list and stayed on the *Publishers Weekly* bestseller list for three months.

John Lescroart lives in Northern California, with his architect wife and their two children.

Also by John Lescroart

Guilt
A Certain Justice
The 13th Juror
Hard Evidence
The Vig
Dead Irish

The Mercy Rule

John Lescroart

HEADLINE
FEATURE

First published in the UK in 1998
by HEADLINE BOOK PUBLISHING

First published in paperback in the UK in 1999
by HEADLINE BOOK PUBLISHING

A HEADLINE FEATURE paperback

10 9 8 7 6 5 4

ISBN 0 7472 5458 3

Typeset by Avon Dataset Ltd, Bidford-on-Avon, Warks

Printed and bound in Great Britain by
Mackays of Chatham plc, Chatham, Kent

HEADLINE BOOK PUBLISHING
A division of Hodder Headline PLC
338 Euston Road
London NW1 3BH

Acknowledgements

I owe thanks to a host of people who read the completed manuscript and to those who talked to me about their fields of expertise during the planning stages: Peter S. Dietrich, MD, MPH; Kay Schnieder of the Rush Alzheimer's Disease Center in Chicago; Mary Beth Stamps, RN, MSN, associate director, Alzheimer's Disease Center, UC, Davis; US Federal Judge William Shubb for his gracious assistance and introduction to the Ninth Circuit Court of Appeals; Terri Nafisi for her insights into life in and around the court; Bob Lindell for a fascinating tour and history of the federal courthouse in San Francisco; Al Markel of the San Francisco Fire Department; my uncle, John E. Lescroart.

Al Giannini of the San Francisco district attorney's office continues to be a brilliant analyst, a great friend and a true collaborator; his wife, Jan, kept the flame of the book alive when its author couldn't feel the heat. Don Matheson must be black and blue from everything I bounce off him. Peter J. Diedrich is always there for a fact, a name, a date, an obscure reference, or general background material.

William P. Wood and Richard Herman, Jr., supplied a last, big epiphany; Karen Kijewski and Max Byrd are tremendous and ongoing psychic resources.

Finally, thanks to Jackie Cantor, my editor, confidante, and friend. And to Barney Karpfinger, without whom not.

To J., J., and L.,
Champions All

Suffering is a fact of life; suffering is caused by attachment

The First and Second Noble Truths of Buddhism

Prologue

The past kept unraveling, tangled in an endless present. Afternoon sunlight slanted through the open window, warming the skin of the old man's face, throwing into bright relief the two-day gray stubble. Salvatore Russo reclined in an ancient Barcalounger that he'd pulled over to catch the rays. God knows, balmy weather was rare enough in San Francisco. You took it when you could.

He had his eyes closed, remembering another sun-dappled day. But to Sal it didn't feel as though he were remembering it. It was more immediate than that. He was living that long-ago moment all over again.

Helen Raessler was nineteen and the light shone off her honey-colored hair. She was lying on her back on the sand in a dune at Ocean Beach. Even now he could feel the warm sand. They were sheltered by the contours of the land, by the surrounding sedge.

In spite of the difference in their backgrounds Sal knew that Helen loved him. She loved his big hands – already heavily calloused from work and from baseball – and his thick hair and powerful chest. He was twenty-five.

No, he *is* twenty-five.

He pulls away from their kiss so that he can see her perfect face. He traces the line of her jaw with his workman's hand and she takes it and brings it down over her sweater to her breast. They've been seeing each other for a little more than a month, and the heat between them has scared him. He's been afraid to push her, physically, in any way. They haven't done even this yet.

They are kissing again and a sound escapes her throat. It is hunger. He can feel the swollen nipple under the fabric of the sweater. He realizes that she has purposely worn no bra. A gull screeches high overhead, the waves pound off in the distance over the dunes, the sun is hot on him.

And then his shirt is open and her smooth hand is under it, pinching at his nipple, drawing her nails down his side, his belly. He pulls away again to see her.

'It's okay,' he says. 'I'll stop.'

'No.'

His hand has found her and she nods.

Hurry. She pulls at his belt and gets it undone.

She wears only a short skirt and it is up near her waist now and he is on top of her, her panties moved to one side.

She arches once into him. There is a moment of resistance, but she pushes violently then – once – with a small cry, and he is in her and she sets him, and the world explodes in sensation.

Opening his eyes, he looked down, surprised and absurdly pleased with his erection.

Well, what do you know? he thought. Ain't dead yet.

But the thought, as they all seemed to, fled. As did the tumescence. His headache returned – the sharp, blinding pain. Frowning, he brought his hands to his temples and pressed with all his might.

There. Better. But, Lord, he could certainly do without that.

He looked around. The room was furnished in Salvation Army. Sal's lounger had bad springs and canted slightly to one side, but it was comfortable enough. Over the sagging green couch hung a piece of plywood upon which, sixteen years ago, Sal had watercolored his old fishing boat, the *Signing Bonus*. The grain of the wood showed through the faded paint, but in the right light – now, for instance – he could make out what he'd done.

There was a coffee table in front of the couch and a couple of pine end-tables, scarred with cigarette burns and water stains, on either side of it. The wall-to-wall carpeting was worn to its threads.

But Sal didn't need much, and he had more than most of the other people who lived in this building. A corner that got some sun. The place was small, okay, but had three legitimate rooms, this one and the kitchen and bedroom, plus its own bathroom. What the hell more did anybody need?

There was still most of a bottle of Old Crow next to a half-filled tumbler on the low table and Sal leaned forward, picked up the glass, and smelled to see what was in it. He didn't remember pouring any of the booze, but that's what it was, all right. He drank it off, a mouthful.

Something was nagging at him. What day was it? He ought to get up, check the calendar in the kitchen. He was supposed to be somewhere, but damned if he could remember.

He closed his eyes again. The sun.

On his face, making him squint against it. He's on the third-base side, a weekend day game at Candlestick, and everybody's shocked it's so nice out. Where's the wind? The whole family's down on the field – Helen's holding his hand and smiling, proud of their oldest, Graham, out in the middle of the diamond now, by the mound, getting his fifty-dollar U.S. savings bond for winning his age in the finals of the city's hit-and-throw contest. Kid's only eight and hits a hardball a hundred and fifty feet off a tee.

He's gonna be another DiMag – you wait and see.

Six-year-old Deb holds her mom's other hand and, embarrassed at being out in front of thirty thousand fans, holds on to her old man's leg at the same time. Her little brother, Georgie, begs himself a shoulder ride and now bounces up there, bumping his heels against his dad's chest, holds on to his hair with both hands, pulling. But it doesn't hurt. Nothing hurts.

Sal's got Helen and he's got the kids. His own boat. He's his own boss. The sun is shining on him.

But it's gotten cold. He should get up. Dusk was coming on and where's the day gone?

He walked over to the window and pulled it down against the breeze, sharp now. He could see the fog curling around Twin Peaks.

Straightening up, he stopped still, his head cocked to one side. 'God damn it!' He yelled it aloud and raced into the kitchen. The day was circled on his calendar. Friday!

Friday, you fool, he told himself. Business day. Customer day. Make-your-rent day. Keep your life together the one day you've got to!

'No, no, no!' Yelling at himself, stomping on the floor, furious. He swore again, violently, then kicked at the chair near the table, but it just sat there, obstinate. So he grabbed the back of it and sent it flying across the room, where it slammed into the cabinets, cutting new gouges into the pitted wood.

He left the chair where it was on the floor, then stood a long moment, forcing himself to calm down, to think.

This was one of the signs, wasn't it? He'd warned himself to be sure to recognize them when they got here, and now he wasn't going to go denying them. His mind was going to leave him someday – inevitably – and in the lucid moments he was clear on his strategy. He wasn't going to go out mumbling with shit in his diapers. He was going to die like a man.

He had the syringes, the morphine. He still knew where they were. Thank God for Graham – his one good son. The one good thing, when he looked back over it all.

He would call Graham. That's what he'd do.

He walked back through the living room. How had the window gotten closed? He was sure he'd been sitting in the chair and then he'd remembered it was Friday and he'd gone into the kitchen . . .

All right. The syringe. He remembered. He could still remember, God damn it.

But then he saw his watercolor and stopped again, lost in the lines he'd painted so long ago, trying to render his old boat. A foghorn sounded and he stared at the window again – the closed window. He stood in the center of the room, unmoving. He had been going somewhere specific. It would come to him.

Another minute, standing there, trying to remember. And another blinding stab of pain in his head.

Tears ran down his face.

The vials – the supply of morphine – were in the medicine cabinet with a couple of syringes, and he took the stuff out and laid it on the dresser next to his bed.

He went back to the kitchen. Somebody had knocked the chair over, but he'd get that in a minute. Or not. That wasn't what he'd come in here for.

He'd come in to check . . . something. Oh, there it was. The fluorescent orange sticker taped to the front of the refrigerator. Opening the freezer, he found the aluminum tube where he kept the doctor's Do Not Resuscitate form. It was still inside the tube, where it should be, where the paramedics would look for it. The form told whoever found him to let him alone, don't try to help him, don't hook him up to any damn machines.

He left the form in the freezer. In his bedroom again, he gathered the other paraphernalia and went back into the living room, where he laid it all out on the coffee table next to his bottle of Old Crow.

The window drew him to it. The thin ribbon of light over the fog. He sat himself on the couch and poured himself another couple of fingers of bourbon for courage.

He hadn't heard any approaching footsteps out in the hallway, but now someone was knocking on his door.

Suddenly he realized he must have called Graham after all. To save his life for this moment. It wasn't time for him to die yet. It was close, maybe, but it wasn't time.

He *had* called Graham – he remembered now – and his boy had come and they would find some way to work it all out until it really was time.

Dignity. That was all he wanted anymore. A little dignity. And perhaps a few more good days.

He got up to answer the door.

PART ONE

1

Dismas Hardy was enjoying a superb round of darts, closing in on what might become a personal best.

He was in his office on a Monday morning, throwing his 20-gram hand-tooled, custom-flighted tungsten beauties. He called the game '20-down' although it wasn't any kind of sanctioned affair. It had begun as simple practice – once around and down the board from '20' to bull's-eye. He'd turned the practice rounds into a game against himself.

His record was twenty-five throws. The best possible round was twenty-one, and now he was shooting at the '3' with his nineteenth dart. A twenty-two was still possible. Beating twenty-five was going to be a lock, assuming his concentration didn't get interrupted.

On his desk the telephone buzzed.

He'd worked downtown at an office on Sutter Street for nearly six years. The rest of the building was home to David Freeman & Associates, a law firm specializing in plaintiff's personal injury and criminal defense work. But Hardy wasn't one of Freeman's associates. Technically, he didn't work for Freeman at all, although lately almost all of his billable hours had come from a client his landlord had farmed out to him.

Hardy occupied the only office on the top floor of the building. Both literally and figuratively he was on his own.

He held on to his dart and threw an evil eye at the telephone behind him, which buzzed again. To throw now would be to miss. He sat back on the desk, punched a button. 'Yo.'

Freeman's receptionist, Phyllis, had grown to tolerate, perhaps even like, Hardy, although it was plain that she disapproved of his casual attitude. This was a law firm. Lawyers should answer their phone crisply, with authority and dignity. They shouldn't just pick up and say, 'Yo.'

He took an instant's pleasure in her sigh.

She lowered her voice. 'There's a man down here to see you. He doesn't have an appointment.' It was the same tone she would have used if the guest had stepped in something on the sidewalk. 'He says he knows you from' – a pause while she sought a suitable euphemism. She finally failed and had to come out with the hated truth – 'your bar. His name is Graham Russo.'

Hardy knew half a dozen Russos – it was a common name in San Francisco – but hearing that Graham from the Little Shamrock was downstairs, presumably in need of a lawyer's services, narrowed it down.

Hardy glanced at his wall calendar. It was Monday, May 12. Sighing, he put his precious dart down on his desk and told Phyllis to send Mr Russo right on up.

Hardy was standing at his door as Graham trudged up the stairs, a handsome, athletic young guy with the weight of this world on his shoulders. And at least one other world, Hardy knew, that had crashed and burned all around him.

They had met when Graham showed up for a beer at the Shamrock. Over the course of the night Hardy, moonlighting behind the bar, found out a lot about him. Graham, too, was an attorney, although he wasn't practicing right at the moment. The community had blackballed him.

Hardy had had his own run-ins with the legal bureaucracy and knew how devastating the ostracism could be. Hell, even when you were solidly within it, the law life itself was so unrelentingly adversarial that the whole world sometimes took on a hostile aspect.

So the two men had hit it off. Both men were estranged from the law in their own ways. Graham had stayed after last call, helped clean up. He was a sweet kid – maybe a little naive and idealistic, but his head seemed to be on straight. Hardy liked him.

Before the law Graham's world had been baseball. An All-American center fielder at USF during the late eighties, he'd batted .373 and had been drafted in the sixth round by the

Dodgers. He then played two years in the minor leagues, making it to Double-A San Antonio before he'd fouled a ball into his own left eye. That injury had hospitalized him for three weeks, and when he got out, his vision didn't come with him. And so with a lifetime pro average of .327, well on the way to the bigs, he'd had to give it all up.

Rootless and disheartened, he had enrolled in law school at Boalt Hall in Berkeley. Graduating at the top of his class, he beat out intense competition and got hired for a one-year term as a clerk with the Ninth Circuit Court of Appeals. But he only stayed six months.

In early 1994 – the year of the baseball strike – about two months after he passed the bar, he quit. He wanted, after all, to play baseball. So he went to Vero Beach, Florida, to try out as a replacement player for the Dodgers.

And he made the team.

At the Shamrock he'd made it clear to Hardy that he'd never have played as a scab. All along, all he'd wanted out of the deal was for the Dodgers to take another look at him. The fuzziness had disappeared from his vision; he was still in great shape. He thought he could shine in spring training, get cut as a replacement when they all did, but at least have a shot at the minors again.

And that's what happened. He started the '94 season with the Albuquerque Dukes, Triple A, farther along the path to the major leagues than he'd been seven years earlier.

But he couldn't find the damn curveball and the new shot at his baseball career, upon which he'd risked everything, lasted only six weeks. His average was .192 when he got cut outright. He hadn't had a hit in his last seven games. Hell, he told Hardy, he would have cut himself.

Graham had a lumberjack's shoulders and the long legs of a high hurdler. Under a wave of golden hair his square-jawed face was clean shaven. Today he wore a gray-blue sport coat over a royal-blue dress shirt, stonewashed jeans, cowboy boots.

He was leaning forward on the front of the upholstered chair in front of Hardy's desk, elbows on his knees. Hardy noticed the hands clasped in front of him – the kind of hands that, when he got older, people would call gnarled – workingman's hands, huge and somehow expressive.

Graham essayed a smile. 'I don't even know why I'm here, tell you the truth.'

Hardy's face creased. 'I often feel the same way myself.' He was sitting on the corner of his desk. 'Your dad?'

Graham nodded.

Salvatore Russo – Herb Caen's column had dubbed him Salmon Sal and the name had stuck – was recent news. Despondent over poor health, his aging body, and financial ruin, Sal had apparently killed himself last Friday by having a few cocktails, then injecting himself with morphine. He'd left a Do Not Resuscitate form for the paramedics, but he was already dead when they'd arrived.

To the public at large Sal was mostly unknown. But he was well known in San Francisco's legal community. Every Friday Sal would make the rounds of the city's law workshops in an old Ford pickup. Behind the Hall of Justice, where Hardy would see him, he'd park by the hydrant and sell salmon, abalone, sturgeon, caviar, and any other produce of the sea he happened to get his hands on. His customers included cops, federal, municipal, and superior-court judges, attorneys, federal marshals, sheriffs, and the staffs at both halls – Justice and City – and at the federal courthouse.

The truck appeared only one day a week, but since Sal's seafood was always fresher and a lot cheaper than at the markets, he apparently made enough to survive, notwithstanding the fact that he did it all illegally.

His salmon had their tails clipped, which meant they had been caught for sport and couldn't be sold. Abalone was the same story; private parties taking abalone for commercial sale had been outlawed for years. His winter-run chinooks had probably been harvested by Native Americans using gill nets. And yet year after year this stuff would appear in Sal's truckbed.

Salmon Sal had no retail license, but it didn't matter because he was connected. His childhood pals knew him from the days when Fisherman's Wharf was a place where men went down to the sea in boats. Now these boys were judges and police lieutenants and heads of departments. They were not going to bust him.

Sal might live on the edge of the law, but the establishment considered him one of the good guys – a character in his yellow scarves and hip boots, the unlit stogie chomped down to its last inch, the gallon bottles from which he dispensed red and white plonk in Dixie cups along with a steady stream of the most politically incorrect jokes to be found in San Francisco.

The day Hardy had met Sal, over a decade ago, he'd been with Abe Glitsky. Glitsky was half black and half Jewish and every inch of him scary looking – a hatchet face and a glowing scar through his lips, top to bottom. Sal had seen him, raised his voice. 'Hey, Abe, there's this black guy and this Jew sitting on the top of this building and they both fall off at the same time. Which one hits the ground first?'

'I don't know, Sal,' Glitsky answered, 'which one?'

'Who cares?'

Now Sal was dead and the newspapers had been rife with conjecture: early evidence indicated that someone had been in the room with him when he'd died. A chair knocked over in the kitchen. Angry sounds. Other evidence of struggle.

The police were calling the death suspicious. Maybe someone had helped Sal die – put him on an early flight.

'I didn't know Sal was your father,' Hardy said. 'Not until just now.'

'Yeah, well. I didn't exactly brag about him.' Graham took a breath and looked beyond Hardy, out the window. 'The funeral's tomorrow.'

When no more words came, Hardy prompted him. 'Are you in trouble?'

'No!' A little too quickly, too loud. Graham toned it down some. 'No, I don't think so. I don't know why I would be.'

Hardy waited some more.

'I mean, there's a lot happening all at once. The estate – although the word *estate* is a joke. Dad asked me to be his executor although we never got around to drawing up the will, so where does that leave it? Your guess is as good as mine.'

'You weren't close, you and your dad?'

Graham took a beat before he answered. 'Not very.'

Hardy thought the eye contact was a little overdone, but he let it go. He'd see where this all was leading. 'So you need help with the estate? What kind of help?'

'That's just it. I don't know what I need. I need help in general.' Graham hung his head and shook it, then looked back up. 'The cops have been around, asking questions.'

'What kind of questions?'

'Where was I on Friday? Did I know about my dad's condition? Like that. It was obvious where they were going.' Graham's blue eyes flashed briefly in anger, maybe frustration. 'How can they think I know anything about this? My dad killed himself for a lot of good reasons. The guy's disoriented, losing his mind. He's in awesome pain. I'd've done the same thing.'

'And what do the police think?'

'I don't know what they can be thinking.' Another pause. 'I hadn't seen him in a week. First I heard of it was Saturday night. Some homicide cop is at my place when I get home.'

'Where'd you get home from?'

'Ball game.' He raised his eyes again, spit out the next word. '*Soft*ball. We had a tournament in Santa Clara, got eliminated in the fourth game, so I got home early, around six.'

'So where were you Friday night?'

Graham spread his Rodin hands. 'I didn't kill my dad.'

'I didn't ask that. I asked about Friday night.'

He let out a breath, calming down. 'After work, home.'

'Alone?'

He smiled. 'Just like the movie. Home alone. I love that answer. The cop liked it, too, but for different reasons. I could tell.'

Hardy nodded. 'Cops can be tough to please.'

'I worked till nine-thirty . . .'

'What do you do, besides baseball?'

Graham corrected him. 'Softball.' A shrug. 'I've been working as a paramedic since . . . well, lately.'

'Okay. So you were riding in an ambulance Friday night?'

A nod. 'I got home around ten-fifteen. I knew I had some games the next day – five, if we went all the way. Wanted to get some rest. Went to sleep.'

'What time did you go in to work?'

'Around three, three-thirty. I punched in. They'll have a record of it.'

'And what time did they find your dad?'

'Around ten at night.' Graham didn't seem to have a problem with the timing, although to Hardy it invited some questions. If his memory served him, and it always did, Sal had apparently died between one and four o'clock in the afternoon. This was the issue Graham was skirting, which perhaps the police were considering if they were thinking about Graham after all. He would have had plenty of time between one o'clock and when he checked into work near three.

But the young man was going on. 'Judge Giotti, you know. Judge Giotti found him.'

'I read. What was he doing there?'

Graham shrugged. 'I just know what everybody knows – he'd finished having dinner downtown. He had a fish order in and Sal didn't show, so he thought he'd check the apartment, see if he was okay.'

'And why would the judge do that?'

The answer was unforced, Graham recounting old family history. 'They were friends. Used to be, anyway, in high school, then college. They played ball together.'

'Your father went to college?'

Graham nodded. 'It's weird, isn't it? Salmon Sal the college grad. Classic underachiever, that was Sal. Runs in the family.' He forced a smile, making a joke, but kept his hands clamped tightly together, leaning forward casually, elbows resting on his knees. His knuckles were white.

'So. Giotti?' Hardy asked. Graham cast his eyes to the floor. 'You weren't *his* clerk, were you?'

The head came back up. Graham said no. He'd clerked for Harold Draper, another federal judge with the Ninth Circuit.

'I guess what I'm asking,' Hardy continued, 'is whether you and Giotti – him being your dad's old pal and all – developed any kind of relationship while you were clerking.'

Graham took a moment, then shook his head. 'No. Giotti came by once after I got hired to say congratulations. But these judges don't have a life. I didn't even see him in the halls.'

'And how long did you work there?'

'Six months.'

Hardy slid from the desk and crossed to his window. 'Let me

be sure I've got it right,' he said. 'Draper hired you to become a clerk for the Ninth? How many clerks does he have?'

'Three.'

'For a year each?'

'Right. That's the term.'

Hardy thought so. He went on. 'When I was getting into practice right after the Civil War, a federal clerkship was considered the plum job of all time right out of law school. Is that still the case?'

This brought a small smile. 'Everybody seems to think so.'

'But you quit after six months so you could try out as a replacement player during the baseball strike?'

Graham sat back finally, unclenched his hands, spread them out. 'Arrogant, ungrateful wretch that I am.'

'So now everybody in the legal community thinks you're either disloyal or brain dead.'

'No, those are my *friends*.' Graham took a beat. 'Draper, for example, hates my guts. So does his wife, kids, dogs, the other two clerks, the secretaries – they all really, really hate me personally. Everybody else just wishes I'd die soon, as slowly and painfully as possible. Both.'

Hardy nodded. 'So Giotti didn't call *you* when he found your dad?'

Graham shook his head. 'I'd be the last person he'd call. You walk out on one of these guys, you're a traitor to the whole tribe. That's why I came to you – you're a lawyer who'll talk to me. I think you're the last one who will.'

'And you're worried about the police?'

A shrug. 'Not really. I don't know. I don't know what they're thinking.'

'I doubt they're thinking anything, Graham. They just like to be thorough and ask a lot of questions, which tends to make people nervous. This other stuff with your background might have made the rounds, so they might shake your tree a little harder, see if something falls out.'

'Nothing's going to fall out. My dad killed himself.'

2

'Well, maybe he didn't after all.'

Hardy was having lunch with Lieutenant Abraham Glitsky in a booth at Lou the Greek's, a subterranean bar/restaurant across the street from the Hall of Justice.

The place was humming with humanity today, and their booth was littered with the remains of their bowls and the fortune cookies that had come with their lunch special of tsatsiki-covered Hunan noodles – yogurt and garlic over sesame oil, pita bread on the side. Lou the Greek's wife was the cook, and she was Chinese, so the place always served polyglot lunches, many of them surprisingly edible, some not. Today wasn't too bad.

When Glitsky smiled, it almost never reached his eyes. This kept it from being the cheerful thing that smiles were often cracked up to be. The effect wasn't much enhanced by the thick scar through both his lips. Hardy knew that the scar had come from a boyhood accident on playbars, but Abe the tough cop liked to leave people with the impression that it had been acquired in a knife fight.

The two men had been friends since they'd walked a beat as cops together twenty-some years before. This was their first lunch in a couple of months. Hardy and Graham Russo had spent half an hour covering questions about Sal's 'estate': the old truck, some personal effects, thrift-shop clothes, a few hundred dollars. This discussion had left Hardy wondering what might really be going on, so he'd decided to call Abe.

It was one thing to speculate about what the police might be thinking. It was another – and altogether preferable – to get it from the source. Except, perhaps, when the information was unwelcome, as it was now. 'What do you mean, maybe Sal didn't kill himself?'

Glitsky kept the infuriating nonsmile in place. 'What words didn't you understand? None of them had too many letters.'

For which Hardy wasn't in the mood. He was happy enough to help Graham out with estate issues, but that was as far as it went. Although he had defended two murder cases in his time and won both of them, he had no intention of getting involved in another one. They invariably became too consuming, too personal, too agonizing.

And now Glitsky was hinting that Sal might not have been a suicide. 'It wasn't so much the words as the meaning, Abe. Did Sal kill himself or didn't he?'

Glitsky took his time, draining his teacup, before leaning across the booth, elbows on the table. 'The autopsy isn't in yet.' The humor vanished, mysterious as its appearance. 'You got a client?'

This was tricky. If someone had sought Hardy's help in connection with a homicide, then that very fact would be relevant in the investigation of the death. But Hardy didn't want to lie to his friend. He hadn't accepted anything like criminal defense work with Graham, so he shrugged. 'I'm helping one of the kids on the estate.'

'Which one?'

A smile. 'The executor's. Come on, Abe, what do you hear?'

Glitsky spread his hands on the table. 'What I hear is that there was trauma around the injection site.'

'Meaning?'

'Meaning maybe he didn't stick himself. Maybe he jerked, pulling away, something like that.'

'Which would mean what?'

'You know as well as me. I'm reserving judgment, waiting for Strout' – John Strout, the coroner – 'although the investigation, as they say, is continuing. As you know, we roll on homicides until Strout calls us off.'

Hardy sat back. Glitsky waited another moment, then gave in. 'Sal's got a DNR in his freezer, a sticker telling about it on his coffee table. He was somewhere between very sick and about to die. The death itself is pretty humane – booze and morphine. Ends the pain.'

'I didn't read about pain. I thought the story was he had

Alzheimer's.' Although Hardy knew that Graham had said his dad was in pain, he didn't think this was public knowledge.

Glitsky's eyes had turned inward. He reached for his empty teacup, sucked at it, put it back on the table.

Hardy was watching him. 'What?'

The two guys used a vast vocabulary of the unsaid, a shorthand of connection. Glitsky nodded. 'We got our first woman inspector in the detail, up from vice. Sarah Evans. Very sharp, good, solid person. She got teamed with Lanier and pulled the case.'

'And she doesn't think it looks like a suicide?'

'Your insight never lets up, does it?'

Hardy nodded genially. 'It's why people both love and fear me,' he said. 'So this Sarah Evans is hot for a righteous murder investigation, and you're afraid she might be seeing things that aren't there?'

This time Glitsky's smile bordered on the genuine. 'You got it all figured out. Why do you need me?'

'I don't. You're just such a blast to hang out with. But I'm right?'

'Let's say you're not all wrong.'

'But there was this trauma? Evans noticed the trauma?'

'And a couple of other things.'

Sarah Evans fancied herself a no-nonsense professional police person, and not too many people would disagree with her. After a decade of hard work she had conquered the perils of the job and the myriad sexual stereotypes of her superiors. Finally she'd attained her personal career goal and had been promoted to sergeant inspector of homicide.

She had spent the weekend working on the death of Sal Russo. From the outset something hadn't felt right about it to her. She'd sensed that Sal's apartment was trying to tell her something, though she knew how stupid that would sound if she verbalized it. She didn't know how to convey the idea to her partner, a veteran male named Marcel Lanier. (A redundancy, she realized, since *all* veteran homicide inspectors in San Francisco were male.)

Still, the chair in the kitchen in Sal Russo's apartment had been overturned, there were fresh chip marks in the counter.

Other things, impressions really, struck her: the bump under Sal's ear, the expression on the old man's face, so far removed from what she would call peaceful.

His position on the floor. Why should he be on the floor? she wondered. If he'd decided to kill himself, she thought he would probably have sat in the comfortable chair, given himself the shot, gone to sleep. But he'd been on the floor, curled fetally. It just didn't feel right, although she wasn't completely certain how things ought to feel.

Was feeling part of it at all? Or was it, as Lanier had already repeated too many times, more cut and dried? The evidence points here or doesn't point there and that's all there is to it.

The homicide detail was mandated to investigate any unnatural death until the coroner called them off, but Lanier had seen a lot more homicides than she had, and he thought this one was obviously a suicide. If they wanted to work the whole damn weekend, Lanier told her they could more productively spend their time interviewing witnesses from their other homicides. They had several, he'd reminded her. A domestic-violence homicide. A poor kid whose best friend's father had kept his loaded .45 in the unlocked drawer next to his bed. Some gangbangers shooting each other up. It wasn't as if there wasn't work to do.

But Sarah hadn't wanted the trail with Sal, if there was one, to go cold. Not until Strout's decision, anyway. So Marcel went out and interviewed the elder son, Graham, whose name had been supplied by Judge Giotti.

Sarah had spent all of her Saturday with the Crime Scene Investigations team at Sal's apartment, going through the closets and drawers and kitchen cabinets and cardboard boxes and garbage cans, finding more bits of what she was calling evidence – the large, rather substantial safe that lay on its back under the bed, the other syringes, more morphine, paper records. She asked the fingerprint expert to dust all of it, which he was inclined to do in any event.

There was more paper than she would have imagined – crammed under the mattress, in the cardboard file boxes next to Sal's dresser and along one wall, in the three wastebaskets. This was going to be a whole day's work by itself. But there was one sheet of paper in the wastebasket in the bathroom that particularly caught her attention. It contained a long column of numbers, three to a group. Obvious enough. She went over to where they'd pulled the safe out from under the bed and tried them all.

The last one, 16-8-27, worked. For all the good it did her. Except for an old leather belt the safe was empty.

By Sunday afternoon she'd read Lanier's interview with Graham. His story was that he and his dad hadn't gotten along. Salmon Sal had abandoned his entire family when Graham had been fifteen years old. It wasn't the kind of thing you forgot. Or forgave. Graham told Lanier that he didn't know where the morphine had come from. He'd been up to the old man's dump once or twice, sure. His father knew he had gotten a law degree and wanted him to help with his 'estate,' such as it was. But it wasn't as though they were friends.

Lanier had gotten the names of the rest of the family from Graham, and Sarah got lucky making some Sunday phone calls.

Debra, Sal's daughter, also hadn't seen much of her father, but she volunteered that she didn't have the impression that his estate was as worthless as Graham had implied. She told Sarah that her older brother was probably lying, or hiding something. Graham wasn't very trustworthy. Debra knew for a fact that Sal had had a baseball card collection from the early 1950s. He never would have gotten rid of that. Hadn't the cards, Debra asked, been in the apartment?

Sarah felt sure that there was something more Debra could have said about Graham, but in midconversation she seemed to think better of blabbing out all of her feelings to the police.

Which in itself was instructive.

The younger brother, George, was an officer at a downtown bank and didn't like the fact that he was involved in a police investigation on any level. He hadn't seen his father in years – in fact, he didn't even consider Sal his father. His stepfather, Leland Taylor, had raised him. George had formed the impression that he, Graham, and Debra might come into some money when the old man died, but he'd called Graham when he got word of Sal's death and Graham told him there wasn't any money.

Evans thought it interesting that George, like his sister, conveyed the impression that Graham was lying.

* * *

Hardy was serious about not wanting to handle any more murder cases.

He'd never bought into the ethic of his landlord, David Freeman, a truly *professional* defense attorney. Hardy did it for the money; Freeman's vision of life and the law accepted the necessity, and even the *rightness*, of defending bad people for heinous acts they had actually committed.

Hardy had been a cop for a couple of years after college and a hitch in Vietnam. After that he spent a few years as a prosecutor for the district attorney's office. When his first marriage broke up in the wake of the accidental death of his son, he took close to a dozen years off to tend bar and contemplate the universe through a haze of Guinness stout.

Eventually, the haze lifted. He became part owner of the Little Shamrock. He married again. Frannie was the younger sister of Moses, his partner in the Shamrock. He returned to the law – again as a prosecutor.

Office politics, not a philosophical change of heart, had driven him from the DA's office and a benevolent fate had delivered him to defense work. He had believed in the innocence of his first two clients, and his instincts had been right.

After that there were opportunities to get 'not guilty' verdicts for other clients, but this was not the same thing as the clients themselves being innocent.

Hardy wasn't going to defend criminals and use his glib Irish tongue to get them off on legerdemain, on legal technicalities. He did not feel any kinship with criminals, and didn't much care what societal influences had made them go bad. He didn't want to help keep them out of jail, even if it put bread on his table. Not that he didn't believe that defendants were entitled to the best defense the law allowed. Personally, though, he just wasn't going to provide it.

So his professional life had devolved into estate planning, business contracts, litigation. Occasionally, he'd take a fee for walking a client through the administrative maze of a DUI or shoplifting charge.

He often dreamed of dropping the pretense altogether, go back to his bar and pour drinks full-time – but that was another problem. The world was a different place than it had been before the kids.

In those days he and Frannie felt rich. They had money in the bank. Hardy's house was tiny but paid off. Every six months they got a profit-sharing check from the Shamrock in the five-thousand-dollar range that cleared their credit cards. He'd made some money on those first two murder cases. They'd been able to get by, comfortably, on three grand a month.

Now they needed nearly three times that. Home insurance, medical insurance, life insurance, saving for college (assuming his kids went), the loan payment for the house addition they'd built. Food, clothing, the occasional sortie into the nonchild world of restaurants and nightlife.

He couldn't afford to stop working at the law. Loving what you did was a luxury he couldn't permit himself anymore. Frannie was talking about going back to work next year when Vincent started first grade. This was an issue – they both knew she'd be lucky to break even on the day care they'd need.

Of course, there was a second option: she could go back to school in family counseling, incur another mound of debt, possibly position herself to make more money ('In *family counseling*?' Hardy would ask) so that in ten years . . .

This was the downsized American nineties. You tightened the belt and everybody pitched in and worked all the time and maybe someday your kids would have it only a little worse than you did now.

Hardy knew he wasn't ever going back to his little bar where he could get by on tips. He was going to keep his nose at his desk and bill a hundred and fifty hours every month – which meant he actually *worked* two hundred – until he died.

Adulthood. He was developing a theory that it might be one of the country's leading causes of death. Someone, he thought, ought to do a study.

Life was too short as it was. He wasn't doing any more murder cases.

He did, however, follow Glitsky back across Bryant Street and into the familiar unpleasantness of the Hall of Justice, a huge, square, faceless, blue-gray monstrosity. Its address, seven increasingly depressing blocks south of Market, did not begin to convey the light-years of distance between the Hall and the sophisticated center of culture that it served.

Since Hardy's last visit the huge glass-front doors had been backed by graffitied plywood – a less-than-inspired design solution, if part of the building's visual statement was to make the citizenry feel safe. A cattle chute led through a metal detector into the lobby.

At the elevator banks, frothing with vulgarity, Glitsky was stopped by a young Hispanic man who started talking to him about a case. The kid seemed to be an assistant DA, as Hardy had once been. Had he been that young?

Hardy contemplated as the elevators came and went. The DA's office had truly undergone a sea change if this youngster had made it to prosecuting homicides already. But he was talking to Glitsky, so that's what it had to be about. Glitsky wasn't exactly Mr Idle Chitchat.

Abe finally got around to introductions, pointing a finger around. 'New guy, Eric Franco. Old guy, Dismas Hardy. Hardy doesn't work here anymore. He's moved on to greener pastures. Private practice. Franco's got his first one eighty-seven' – a murder case – 'he's a little nervous.' From Glitsky this qualified as an oration.

The doors opened. The elevator was empty. They all moved. Eric took up the patter, at Hardy. 'You on a homicide here, talking to the lieutenant?'

Hardy shook his head. 'Social.' Followed it with, 'Hard to believe, I know.'

The doors opened on three and Hardy nearly got out from force of habit. This was the floor for the DA's office, where he once had worked. Glitsky and the homicide detail were on four. When the doors closed on Franco, Hardy looked over at Glitsky. 'How old is Eric?'

'I don't know. Twenty-five, thirty?'

'And he's pulled a murder?'

A shrug. 'Probably a no-brainer.'

'Still,' Hardy persisted, 'how many trials can he have done?'

The doors opened. 'I don't know, Diz. I didn't hire him. The DA hired him. You want his resume, it's downstairs. Check it out.' Without looking back he led the way down the hallway to the homicide detail.

Hardy followed, wondering how a man of Eric Franco's age and experience could have been assigned to try a murder case in superior court and be expected to win even a no-brainer.

'He's not, is the simple answer,' Glitsky said. 'It's politics.'

Hardy was standing in the doorless cubicle Glitsky used for an office. Outside in the detail, fourteen paired desks vied for floor space in the big open room. There were a couple of structural columns poking up here and there, festooned with wanted posters and yellowing memos, joined to watercoolers or coffee machines. Years before, forty square feet in the corner had been drywalled off and an 'office' created for the lieutenant. Some years after that the door had been removed for painting and never replaced.

Glitsky was behind his big, cluttered desk, catching up on paperwork. He'd had no objection to Hardy coming up to the detail to talk to inspectors Sarah Evans or Marcel Lanier – the Sal Russo investigating team – if they'd let him. If they didn't want to talk, they wouldn't be shy about letting him know. If they did, Hardy might get a hint about what Evans had found at the old fisherman's apartment that had set off her warning bells: Sal might not have been a suicide.

But both inspectors had been out in the field, so Hardy went down to the bathroom, then wandered back into Glitsky's space and asked again about the kid Franco and got told it was politics.

'Losing trials is politics?'

'You really ought to go down there' – meaning the DA's offices – 'it's a whole new world.' Glitsky put down his report. 'You're not going to leave me alone, are you? Let me get back to my work?'

Hardy clucked. 'I want to. I really do. I'm trying, even.'

'I'm confident you can do it.' The lieutenant picked up his report again. 'Get the door on the way out, would you?'

David Freeman was in his trademark brown rumpled suit and wrinkled rep tie. Sitting in the low leather couch in Hardy's office, smoking a cigar, his tattered brogues crossed over the rattan-and-glass coffee table, Freeman, the wealthy, famous landlord of the building, could have been mistaken for a destitute client. The man was retirement age or better, and sported tufts of white hair from the tops of his earlobes and eyebrows. Bald on top, round in the middle, liver spots wherever skin showed, he was still a force in the courtrooms of the city.

'The reason it's politics,' he was saying – Hardy had worried it all the way back to his office – 'is Sharron Pratt, our esteemed DA.'

Hardy knew the story of the election well enough. Pratt had beaten a reasonably popular incumbent named Alan Reston the preceding November. Although Reston was a Democrat, as nearly all elected officials in San Francisco had to be, and African-American to boot – potentially an even bigger plus – he was a career prosecutor. Many people in the city, including Hardy, found it ironic that what had done in Reston, running for the job of chief law-enforcement officer in the city, was his tough stance on crime.

Sure, the DA was supposed to prosecute people who'd done bad things, but Reston seemed unable to make the leap of faith that this didn't mean they were bad people. He thought they *were* bad people. He thought people who committed crimes ought to be punished, and punished hard.

Pratt, on the other hand, while she agreed that many criminals, indeed, had done bad things – murder, rape, burning kittens for Santeria rites – she did not agree that this necessarily made them bad people. They were misunderstood, surely, but she believed that with counseling and guidance, many of them could again become productive members of society.

Also, it hadn't helped that Reston, a black man, had been a supporter of Proposition 209, the California Civil Rights Initiative. He opposed affirmative action, believing that trial lawyers, like brain surgeons, for example, ought to be hired and retained because of their ability to do their jobs getting convictions at trial and putting criminals in jail.

When he'd come aboard, Reston looked around the office he ran and saw that there were a lot of women, some people of color, a lot of old white guys. The job was getting done. When there were new openings, he hired the best person from a diverse pool of applicants – black, white, male, female, Asian, Hispanic

– he didn't care. Pratt did care, though. And Pratt got elected.

'So this relates to how Eric Franco pulled a murder?'

'Pratt unloads all the old white guys, she's still stuck with the cases, so to prove her theory that anybody can do this work, she hires her quotas and willy-nilly assigns the cases, and her people lose and it doesn't matter. Eventually they might win.' Freeman raised his shoulders expansively. 'Who knows, it could happen. Almost everything happens sometimes.'

After he threw out Freeman, Hardy realized he'd blown nearly the whole day on Graham Russo's problems, satisfying his own curiosity, catching up with the bureaucracy, city politics. He shouldn't have done it – he couldn't really spare the time – but somehow it had gotten inside him.

But the piper would have to be paid.

Hardy did not work within the organization of David Freeman & Associates, but Freeman's overload was keeping him afloat. His life over the past six months had been dominated by a contractor's liability lawsuit with the Port of Oakland over the failure of a loading transom. A container-load of personal computers – ten tons and over $18 million worth – fell sixty-some feet before glancing off the deck of the ship that was to take the computers to Singapore for distribution to the Asian market then sank into the bay. The accident had caused over $5 million in additional damages to the ship and, of course, delayed delivery of everything else on board.

As tended to happen, the lawsuits proliferated. The Port of Oakland was contending that the computer hardware manufacturing company – Tryptech – had overloaded its container. *That* had caused the transom's failure. Other shippers who'd lost revenue on their own deliverables were lining up to sue both Tryptech and the Port. One of the workmen who'd been on deck at the time was claiming that he'd wrenched his back trying to avoid flying metal. He was seeking over a million dollars from one of the parties, whichever might be found at fault.

In the normal course of events a private practitioner like Hardy would never find himself involved in any of these lawsuits. The various litigants' insurance carriers would slug it out through their mega-law firms and eventually somebody would settle or win and the attorneys would make a lot of money regardless.

But in this case Tryptech's insurance carrier had refused to pay for its loss of computers because it had come to the conclusion that Tryptech had misrepresented the number of units in its transom. So the company's president, a silver-haired Los Altos smoothie named Dyson Brunel, had come to David Freeman. He needed his own personal lawyer representing his own interests outside of the insurance chain.

There was a potentially large settlement down the road, he believed, and Freeman stood to collect a third of it. Deciding that Brunel's lawsuit against the Port had reasonable merit, Freeman accepted the case on a contingency basis plus expenses, and had farmed it out to Hardy, paying him by the hour.

It was a good fit all around.

So Hardy spent the rest of the afternoon and into the early evening crunching numbers. Now Tryptech seemed to be playing a game with *him*, its own attorney, on the number of computers that had actually been in the container, which was still sitting under forty-five feet of water at Pier 17 in Oakland. It was beginning to appear to him that his clients had, in fact, overloaded their container.

But Tryptech would contend – and Hardy would have to argue if he wanted to keep getting paid – that this, even if true, didn't matter because the containers still weighed far less overloaded than the threshold strength of the transom . . .

And so on.

At eight o'clock Hardy packed it in, and it was dark by the time he finally found a parking space four blocks from his house. He was going to have to tear out his beautiful, tiny front lawn one day and put in some kind of parking structure. He could see it coming, the day he'd be getting home at ten-thirty, unable to find parking within a mile of his front door.

Instead, maybe he should give up his car. But that left the Muni, which was unthinkable. Even if the city bus system had worked, it wouldn't fit his haphazard schedule, and it didn't work anyway, so the point was moot. Urban living.

Maybe they'd have to move out of the city. That was it. Cash their little place in, move to the suburbs, spend half a million dollars on a three-bedroom, two-bath, in Millbrae, be the proud owner of his own garage.

Sighing, beat, lugging his fat lawyer's briefcase and feeling a hundred years old, he arrived at his gate and stopped to take in the feel, the look, of his home.

There was no denying it: he loved the place. It was the only free-standing house on a street that was otherwise crammed to the lot lines with three- and four-story apartments. He was irrationally taken with the postage-stamp lawn, the white picket fence, the little stoop where, on evenings when he had gotten home before dusk – almost never anymore – Frannie and the kids would be out waiting for him.

Now the lights were on, inviting. He picked up the faint strains of music coming from inside, pushed open the gate.

Abe Glitsky was a surprise, sitting on his kitchen counter, carefully picking nuts out of the bowl next to him. 'What are you doing here? You better have saved me some cashews.'

Hardy's wife, Frannie, came up against him – long red hair and green eyes that were shining with good humor and perhaps a little Chardonnay. She was wearing black Lycra running shorts, tennis shoes, and a green-and-white Oregon sweatshirt as she pecked at his cheek, slipped an arm around his waist. He gave her a hug and felt the quick reassuring pressure of her thigh against him.

'Abe was in the neighborhood with Orel,' she said, '—soccer at Lincoln Park. I said I expected you any minute, he should wait. Orel's back with the kids.'

Hardy heard the unmistakable child noise from the back of the house. Orel was Glitsky's youngest son – a twelve-year-old – and Hardy's two kids – nine and seven – worshiped him. Glitsky, digging at the bottom of the nut bowl, looked up. 'I'm afraid the cashews have vanished. I don't know where they could have gone to.'

'I asked them to stay for dinner,' Frannie said.

'He's already had it.' Hardy went over to the refrigerator. 'Did he drink all my beer too?'

Glitsky slid off the counter. 'I don't drink beer. In fact, I don't drink at all.'

Frannie was smiling at Glitsky. 'We know you don't drink, Abe. That's all right. We still like you.'

Hardy wheeled. 'How can you like a guy who eats all your cashews?' He opened a bottle of Sierra Nevada pale ale, took a sip, faced his friend. 'So what's up?'

As though they'd been discussing it all along, Glitsky reported, 'We got the autopsy back on Sal. I thought you'd want to hear. Strout's going with homicide/suicide equivocal.'

Frannie didn't like how this sounded. She put her wineglass on the counter and crossed her arms in front of her. 'What's this? What homicide?'

'Just a case,' Glitsky said, getting a pained glance from Hardy for his troubles.

'Abe's,' Hardy said. 'Not mine.'

'That's funny.' Frannie wasn't buying it. 'It seemed like it had something to do with you.'

'No. A client of mine, that's all. His dad. Estate case.'

'And that's why Abe was telling you about it? Abe the homicide cop?'

Hardy had another pull of his beer. He shrugged. 'One of life's little coincidences. My client's dad. It looked like he killed himself, but maybe somebody else did it. Doesn't have anything to do with my client, necessarily. Right, Abe?'

A straight-faced nod. 'Right. Not necessarily.'

Taking a beat, Frannie reached for her wineglass again. 'Not necessarily, that's good. That's a nice show of solidarity. I'm impressed.'

'Frannie doesn't want me to take on any more murders.'

'I gathered that.'

'She thinks homicide equivocal can mean murder.'

'Well, she's not all wrong there.'

Hardy came back to his wife, gave her his biggest phony grin. 'So, what's on for dinner?'

Glitsky was gone.

As it turned out, Frannie had cooked a delicious chicken breast entrée with white wine and cream and artichoke hearts over rice. The kids had dominated the table talk with gross-out jokes – 'What's green and goes backwards? Snot' – that kind of stuff, until the adults told the little darlings they could be excused. Abe's 'homicide equivocal' didn't get a chance to raise its head again.

But now, almost eleven o'clock, the kids finally in their beds, Hardy and Frannie stood in the center of the kitchen, surveying the wreckage of the dinner, the pans and dishes.

Hardy grabbed a sponge and turned on the hot water, started washing up. 'This is why when I die I'll be welcomed into heaven with fanfare and trumpets,' he said.

But singing her husband's praises wasn't on Frannie's agenda at the moment. She went back out into the dining room, brought in a load of dessert dishes, put them on the drain. Then she stopped and leaned against the counter. 'Okay. What about this client? What client?'

'Graham Russo.'

'I've never heard you mention him. When did he become your client? Is it a big estate?'

'Not really, and pretty recently, come to think of it,' Hardy said. 'Roughly this morning, in fact.'

'And his dad was murdered?'

Hardy turned the water off. 'He's not charged with the murder, if it was a murder. I'm just helping the guy, Frannie. He's a good kid. I know him from the Shamrock. He thinks the cops are hassling him.'

'He thinks Abe's hassling him? Abe doesn't hassle people.'

Hardy shook his head. 'No, not Abe. Abe's just pushing paper anymore. It's one of the new inspectors. Maybe.'

'So your client is under suspicion?'

'That may be a little strong. He's worried that it may get there. He needs his hand held, that's all. It's no big deal.'

She was silent, arms crossed again. After a minute she said, 'It's no big deal, but the head of the homicide department came by here especially to tell you about it as soon as the autopsy was finished?'

Hardy put the sponge all the way down. He turned to face her. 'I don't want another murder case, Frannie. I'd probably turn it down if it got to that. I don't have the time anyway. It just got my interest, that's all. There are some elements that might be slightly more fascinating than Tryptech's transom accident, if you can believe that. Graham's dad evidently had Alzheimer's. It looks like he killed himself, but it might have been an assisted suicide.'

'So maybe Graham did do it?'

'He says not. He wants help with the estate, that's all.'

'And you believe that?'

Hardy averted his eyes. 'I don't disbelieve it, not yet.'

Frannie nodded. 'Very strong,' she said. Her arms were still crossed. She sighed. 'He's going to get charged, and you're going to wind up defending him, aren't you?'

'No.'

'You promise?'

'Frannie, I couldn't defend him. First, I've got Tryptech, which is pretty full-time, you might have noticed. Next, Graham's got no money, certainly not close to what he'd need for a murder defense, even at my rock-bottom rates. If he gets charged, he'll take a public defender. It'd be a high-profile case – other defense sharks are going to swarm all around it.'

'I didn't hear a promise that you wouldn't take it.'

'It won't get to there.'

She sighed again. 'Famous last words.'

The autopsy report had been on Sarah's desk when she and Lanier had come in from the field at the end of the day. That made it official. She remained late at the office, catching up on paperwork, and was there when the fingerprint expert checked in with his report. Graham Russo's fingerprints were all over his father's apartment – on the safe, on the morphine vials, on the syringes. Graham had told Lanier that he didn't know how his father had come upon the morphine, had only been to the apartment 'once or twice.' Sarah's suspicions took a quantum leap forward.

If the coroner was saying it wasn't a definite suicide, then she and her partner would find out what it definitely was. And Sarah knew where they'd start. She figured they had probable cause to search Graham's residence, see what else they could turn up. The judge who signed the search warrant agreed with her.

3

Next to Hardy's bed the world began jangling all at once. He pulled himself up with a moan from what felt like world-record REM sleep and slapped at the alarm. There was a moment's silence, then another jangle.

'The phone too,' Frannie said.

Hardy grabbed at the receiver and noted the time on the digital clock – seven o'clock. 'Grand Central Station.'

'They just woke me up with a search warrant. What am I supposed to do now?'

'They've got a warrant?'

'I just said that.'

'Take it easy, Graham. You've got to let them in.'

'I already have.'

Hardy threw a glance out his bedroom window. A heavy fog had rolled in during the night. 'What are they looking for?'

'Just a second.' Graham sounded like he was reading from some official paper. 'Morphine vials, used or unused syringes, baseball cards, sports memorabilia, documents reflecting number combinations of safe or safety deposit box . . .'

'Why do they think you might have any of that stuff?'

'They won't tell me. They just showed me the warrant, not the affidavit. They're doing me a favor letting me call you.'

Hardy knew this was true, so it couldn't be too bad. Not yet. He hoped.

The police had rung Graham's doorbell at exactly seven o'clock, the earliest possible moment. Because it tended to bring to mind visions of jackbooted Nazis breaking down doors in the middle of the night, the police were prohibited from serving search warrants between ten P.M. and seven A.M. unless there was immediate danger that evidence would be destroyed, or the suspect would disappear, or something specific of that nature.

So the fact that they hadn't come in the middle of the night meant that this was probably a relatively routine search. On the other hand, ringing Graham's bell at the first allowable second was not a good sign.

Hardy let out a breath. 'Okay, you hang in there. Don't be hostile. Give me your address, I'll be right over.'

He swung out of bed. As he was pulling on his pants, Frannie spoke. 'That would be Graham Russo?' She was sitting up in bed, arms crossed over her chest. Children's sounds came from the rooms farther back.

'My psychic wife.'

'The one who has nothing to do with a murder case?'

Hardy smiled. 'That's him. They're hassling him, that's all. He's got some enemies downtown.'

'Evidently.'

'I've got to go, be there for him. Keep him calm.'

'I know you do. Don't worry about the kids, I'll get them fed and clothed and off to school.'

He gave her a look. 'I'll do it tomorrow. It'll be a trade, sharing those special parental moments.'

'But I do have a real idea,' she said.

'My favorite kind. Let's hear it.'

'On the way to his place, start thinking about a defense attorney you can recommend for him. David Freeman, maybe?'

'Maybe.' A pause. 'If he needs one.'

Hardy had his map out. He stopped for a minute to consult it at the corner of Stanyan and Parnassus. Graham's street was well hidden. He turned right, went a block, then hung a left onto a nearly vertical lane that he thought was the equal of any incline in the city. Street signs warned off trucks and delivery vehicles – too steep. Another sign informed him that this was not a through street. Whoever lived up here, Hardy thought, didn't want anybody else to know about it.

He checked his map again. With the fog he couldn't see more than a hundred feet up the hill. He wished he'd gotten directions to Graham's place instead of simply the address, but he was stuck now. Nothing to do but keep going. If he was lost, he'd find a phone.

He nosed his old Honda up the steep hill, ran into another 'Not a Through' street that snaked off to the right and took it, and then suddenly – miraculously – the fog was gone. He'd climbed right out of it.

Into, it seemed, a wonderland.

Edgewood Avenue was paved with red bricks, lined with custom gingerbread houses, bathed in bright morning sunlight. On either side of the street a variety of trees were in full white and pink blossom. He rolled down his window and heard birds chirping.

What was this place? Hardy had lived in San Francisco for nearly all of his adult life, and he'd never been here, never heard anyone mention it, although it was less than half a mile from the Little Shamrock.

He pulled over at an open space at the curb, farther up the hill, just about to the copse of pine and eucalyptus that marked the end of the amazing dead-end street. He stood a moment outside his car, marveling at the red bricks, at the scented air. The fog below was a blanket of thick billowing cotton. The red spires of the Golden Gate jabbed through it.

But beyond the fog, to the east, the downtown skyscrapers' windows twinkled in the morning sun. Ships were moving on the bay. Across the water Treasure Island seemed close enough to touch. A ribbon of traffic was moving on the freeways, coming in over the Oakland Bay Bridge.

He found the address at the end of a driveway, a front door cut into stucco where once, obviously, there had been a garage. Standing at the door, he paused a moment.

As soon as he knocked and entered Graham's converted-garage mother-in-law flat, he was going to fall into the role, representing the rights of his client. And then if the police did find anything, he would be hip deep in Graham's defense.

Could he extricate himself after that, even if he wanted to? All his protestations to the contrary, would he really want to get out?

He was aware that his pulse had quickened. It never did that when he contemplated the mounds of paperwork and number crunching with Tryptech that awaited him in the office. But he couldn't afford the luxury of loving his work, he told himself again. He had other priorities now. He was a grown-up.

Then there was some noise from inside, and he took in a breath and rapped on the door.

'Your client isn't cooperating, so we don't either.' Hardy wasn't through the door yet. Inspector Marcel Lanier, whom he'd known for years, wasn't letting him in. 'We're conducting a search. You're not entitled to be in here. It's simple.'

Hardy lowered his voice. 'How's he not cooperating?'

Lanier shrugged. 'My partner's got some questions. He said if he's a suspect, he'd like his lawyer present.'

'He's smart, that's why. That's his right.'

'Absolutely. I couldn't agree with you more. But it's not his right to have anybody present while we look around here. People have been known to take things. You wouldn't believe. So as soon as we finish up here, you can come on in and we'll all have a nice talk on the record.'

Hardy could see Graham – barefoot, in running shorts and tank top – sitting at the huge country table by the floor-to-ceiling window, louvered shades blocking most of the sun and view in the back of the long, narrow one-room apartment. Lanier's female partner was back talking with him.

It was a beautiful street, all right, but Hardy didn't want to stand out in it for the better part of the day. Lanier wasn't a bad guy. He'd just gotten his feathers ruffled. Hardy would have to talk to Graham about his behavior around the police. They could make life very difficult if you made them dislike you, even if you'd done nothing wrong.

'Is he under arrest?' Hardy asked.

'He's being detained.'

Hardy kept his patience. 'Let me talk to my client. You guys' being here freaked him out, that's all. I'll calm him down, maybe he'll have something to say, something you can use.' Hardy's face cracked. 'Come on, Marcel. If you do find something, you're not going to want to tell Glitsky you had a chance to talk to your suspect and didn't take it when it was easy.'

Lanier took a beat, then stepped back and motioned Hardy in. 'All right. Sit at the table and don't touch anything.'

* * *

Graham's apartment was spotless and orderly. Hardy thought it was a fantastic living space. There was the huge picture window that dominated the back wall. Graham had adjusted the shades, and over the fog the view of downtown and points east was world class. There was a dark hardwood floor, Oriental carpets. The furniture was a mix of Danish and antique – heavy woods and teak – that somehow achieved a balance.

The wall to Hardy's right was lined nearly to the ceiling with books. There was a tall wine rack nearly filled with expensive wines. Three tiny vertical windows above the shelves. The rest of the right wall, near the back of the house, was given over to a kitchen area, stove, overhead racks, good cookware.

The apartment radiated good taste. Graham Russo might be a jock, but there appeared to be a lot more to him than that. A further consideration raised its ugly head, though, and Hardy couldn't put it aside: a place like this, and the lifestyle that went with it – the wine alone, for example – cost some serious money, and Graham was, at best, underemployed. He wondered how his young client could afford to keep all this up.

But he'd find that out on his own time. For now, he was here to hold hands, and that's what he'd do. He asked permission to put on a pot of coffee and – another peace offering – offered it around.

He and Graham found themselves talking baseball at the table. Lanier was on the low leather couch on the left side of room, going through a stack of magazines, seeking stuff that might be tucked into them.

In her search for syringes and vials of morphine Sarah Evans had been looking through things in the bathroom, a small cubicle with a sink, shower, and toilet that had been patched onto the back corner of the room.

Hardy thought that Evans had a really wonderful, sincere smile. Like the Hispanic DA he'd met with Glitsky yesterday, she barely seemed old enough, in his eyes, to be a Girl Scout, much less a homicide inspector.

When Hardy poured the coffee, she came out and sat down with the men, smiled, and placed her pocket tape recorder on the table between them. Shoulder-length dark hair framed a freckled oval face, set off by widely spaced green eyes. A compact and athletic, very attractive body was evident under the utilitarian work-clothes. 'You don't mind?' she said, still smiling. 'Two birds with one stone.'

Graham knew the law. He knew that talking to a police officer during an official investigation was a very serious matter. He had called his attorney first thing because he hadn't wanted to be tricked.

But then, after he'd admitted the two officers into his apartment, he'd really *seen* Sergeant Evans. He fancied that she'd noticed him as well. They were about the same age. The law was one thing, he knew, but this was a pretty woman and he had had some experience with them. He had no doubt that he could charm her and get her on his side, in spite of what her job might be, her professional role.

This went beyond the law. It was only common sense to take advantage of the way people worked. He would be in control. Talking to her would be a smart move, although the book recommended against it.

Sometimes you just had to go on what you felt.

Hardy began, 'No. I'm sorry, but my client doesn't—'

'It's all right.' Graham held out his hand, stopping him. 'You said it, didn't you, Diz? I might as well cooperate. I don't have anything to hide.' He shrugged, casually looked over at Evans. 'Shoot, Inspector.' A broad smile. 'Not literally, of course.'

Sarah returned the smile and took a sip of her coffee. She appraised him for another longish moment, then looked down, gathering herself, tucking away the last hint of the smile.

All right.

She launched into the standard police interview intro for the transcriber, then began. 'When you talked to Inspector Lanier on Saturday, you said you didn't know your father had morphine at his apartment—'

'Wait a minute,' Hardy said again. 'I *really* have to object to this. You shouldn't answer that, Graham.'

But the boy had gotten himself relaxed. 'Diz, I want to explain.'

He focused on Inspector Evans. 'That's not exactly what I said. I said I didn't know how it got there.'

Lanier abruptly closed the magazine he was leafing through, shifted on the couch, said, 'Wait a minute.' His face clouded. 'No, all right.' He grabbed the next magazine on the pile.

Evans asked, 'But you knew it was there, the morphine?'

'Graham.' Hardy might be upsetting his client, but he had to speak up again. He really didn't want Graham saying any of this. It could not help him. As a lawyer Graham must know this. What was he thinking? Didn't Graham understand that this wasn't casual conversation? It was being recorded and would be transcribed and perhaps used against him. Maybe Hardy's getting inside wasn't going to be worth the cost, and that worried him even more. 'We can talk about this later, when we're alone.'

Graham ignored him, smiled at the pretty inspector. 'The morphine? I showed him how to give himself shots. He was in a lot of pain.'

The pain again. Graham kept bringing up the pain.

'What from?'

'I don't know.'

'You didn't ask?'

'No. My father wouldn't have told me. He would have said mind your own business. He didn't want anybody to pity him.'

'So you went up to your father's apartment and showed him how to administer these morphine injections to himself?'

'That's right.'

'Even though you weren't particularly close?'

Graham cast a glance at Hardy. Looking for approval? Hardy couldn't say. The horse was already a couple of acres from the barn and still running. Hardy had tried to stop Graham when it might have done some good. If his client reined himself in now, he would just look worse. So Hardy sipped his coffee and waited.

'Just because we weren't close, I didn't want the guy to suffer.' Graham shrugged. 'He asked me to show him. I showed him, but I didn't shoot him up. I knew what he was going to do.'

'And what was that?'

Graham wasn't blinking in the face of the questions. He leveled his gaze at her. 'What he *did* do. Kill himself.'

Hardy thought he'd convey a little relevant information that his client might not know. 'The autopsy came in last night, Graham,' he said. 'It didn't rule out homicide.'

Graham stopped his cup halfway to his mouth, put it down on the table, sat all the way back in his chair. 'Well, that's bullshit.'

Hardy nodded. 'Maybe, but it's why these guys are here.'

Graham leaned forward, elbow on the table, and looked right at Evans. Again, the expression struck Hardy as a little much. The old eye-to-eye for sincerity was, he suspected, no guarantee that the truth was next up. 'I didn't kill my father. He killed himself.'

Sarah Evans wasn't giving anything away. She nodded, moved the tape recorder slightly, sipped from her mug. 'So how often would you say you saw your father in the last six months?'

'I don't know. Six, eight times.'

'More than once a month, then?'

'He was getting senile. He had Alzheimer's, you know. He'd call me, then forget he called me. He didn't remember where he'd put things. I'd come up and find them.'

'The morphine?'

A pause. 'Sure, yeah.'

'What was the pain from?' she asked again. 'Who gave him the morphine?'

He smiled broadly this time. 'You already asked that.'

'And you said you didn't know.'

'That's right. Still don't.'

She shifted gears on him. 'Don't you work for an ambulance company?'

'I'm a paramedic. I ride in ambulances.'

'And you carry syringes and—'

Hardy couldn't sit still any longer. 'Excuse me, but Graham already said he didn't know where the morphine came from.'

'I know,' she said. 'But I'm asking now about the syringes.'

'It's the same—'

But Graham put a hand over Hardy's arm, stopping him. 'I may have brought some syringes, left some there. I wanted to make sure he had clean needles.'

In the silence that followed, Lanier turned another page of his magazine. Graham leaned across the table and adjusted the louvered blinds. The room lightened up by half again. It was a great day above the fog here on Edgewood.

Evans took another tack. 'You're the executor for your father. What do you know about the safe?'

Graham got to the bottom of his coffee mug. His eyes shifted out to the view, then back. 'Not much,' he said.

'What did your dad keep in it?'

'I doubt anything,' Graham said. 'He didn't have anything worth saving.'

'What about his baseball cards? Where did he keep them?'

'I don't know.'

'Don't you want to ask *what* baseball cards?'

'No. I know he had a collection once. I don't know what happened to it. Maybe it was in the safe. I don't know.'

But Evans was closing in on something, and Hardy wanted to get there first and head her off if he could. The questions were rattling Graham. 'Anybody want another cup?' he said.

No takers.

Hardy got up and went to the machine, but Evans kept right on. 'But you never – personally – saw inside the safe, or opened it, or anything like that?'

'No. I think the safe was just a prop. Sal liked to pretend he was doing great, he didn't need anybody, he had lots of money. But you saw where he lived.'

Lanier was leafing through the swimsuit edition of *Sports Illustrated*. Suddenly he held up a piece of paper, stationery from a Motel 6, and said, 'Hey.'

Dear Graham,

Whatever anybody else thinks, I am proud of you. I don't know what that means after all this time, but I am. I've been following you as best I could – the one hope I had left among my kids. Your mother doesn't make it any too easy, and you all made it clear enough you didn't want me around. Your mom, I guess, what she told you.

But I did keep an eye out. Your career in the minors, you know, and then law school. I know where Deb lives with that husband of hers, and Georgie. How'd they get so messed up? Me leaving. I suppose that was it.

Did your mom ever let on that I would call and ask about

you? No, I guess not. Every three months, four, I would, though. You ought to know that. That's how I found out about you quitting the law job, trying for baseball one last time.

I saw you play today. Two triples. Remember how we used to say you'd rather hit a triple than a homer any day? Most exciting offensive play in the game, am I right? So, anyway, plus you started that beautiful 3-6-4 double play. You owned the field, son, and I am so proud of you for trying baseball again.

That's all any of us can do, and few enough try, and I just wanted – whether it means anything – I just wanted to say good on you, doing what you were born to do. Somebody appreciated it.

While Hardy looked over the letter, a heavy silence hung in the room. Then Lanier took the page out of Hardy's hand. He looked down at it again, showing it to Evans. 'This last is in a different handwriting. Sixteen, eight, twenty-seven.'

'What's that?' Hardy asked. He felt sick that this was going on and, really, it was his fault, his stupid mistake. You simply don't let your client talk to the police, and he'd not only done that, he'd facilitated it. The fact that Graham wasn't telling them anything they couldn't find out for themselves mitigated his self-loathing, but only slightly.

Evans knew what the numbers were right away. 'That's the combination to Sal's safe. The one Graham here says he knows nothing about.'

It was after eleven o'clock.

Evans and Lanier weren't about to let Graham go into the bathroom and close the door behind him to take a shower, so he was still in the clothes he'd slept in.

Graham and Hardy still sat, mostly in silence, at the large table by the back window. The blinds were completely open by now and the city outside, with the fog gone, shimmered in the sunlight. Graham had slid open the window a few inches and a light breeze freshened the air from time to time, but it was mostly quiet and unpleasant.

From Hardy's perspective, the two inspectors – buoyed by

their discovery that Graham had a means of knowing the combination to Sal's safe – had increased the intensity of their search. Working as a team, they had begun again at the front door, working slowly, opening every book and drawer, lifting everything that wasn't nailed down, checking pockets of clothes in the closet, canisters in the kitchen.

They had to be getting near the end, Hardy thought, and if the letter was all they wound up finding, it wouldn't be too bad. Graham had even made the argument as soon as they'd found the letter: so what if he might at one time have known the combination to the safe? He didn't even remember the letter from his father had been stuck in the magazine. Did they honestly think he cared about the combination to the safe? He didn't even remember why he'd written it down. He just didn't know.

Hardy wished his client hadn't talked so much, but it appeared to be over now, and little real damage had been done. The two inspectors were back by the dining table with Graham and Hardy, having thoroughly searched from stern to, nearly, stem. Lanier had just pulled up a chair and opened the drawer to a small desk table next to the Murphy bed when Evans lifted a Skoal chewing tobacco can from the utensil drawer and shook, then opened, it.

'Six keys,' she said, raising her eyes to her partner. She lifted the plain metal ring, and jingled the keys.

Suddenly Graham was a deer caught in headlights. The moment passed as quickly as it had come, but to Hardy it was worrisome. There was real fear in his eyes. He'd been hiding something in plain view that he hadn't expected them to notice, or if they did notice, he hadn't expected them to connect it to anything. And now they had.

Sarah Evans turned back to Graham and dropped the ring onto the table. 'Let's play "Name the Keys." What do you say?'

He raised his shoulders, drummed his hands – *da da dum* – on the edge of the table. He gave her his big smile. 'I really don't have a clue. They're just keys. Everybody's got a container full of keys.' He reached over and picked up the ring. 'These two are duplicates for my car, I guess. This one is the dead bolt for here.'

Evans held up one of them. 'You got a safe deposit box? That's what this looks like. What bank are you with?'

The smile faded. From his seat at the small table across the room, Lanier turned and looked over at the silence.

Just as Hardy put his hand up to warn Graham not to answer, he blurted out, 'I don't know.'

Lanier tapped on the desk with something he'd extracted from the drawer. 'Checkbook here is from Wells Fargo. The branch isn't five blocks away. We get done here, we ride down and take a look. Maybe get a brand-new warrant.'

Inspector Sergeant Sarah Evans pulled a chair up and sat upon it. 'Graham,' she said, 'you're telling me you don't know if you have a safe deposit box? Is that what you're saying?'

Graham just didn't seem to get it – he was making some bantering noises at Evans, trying to make light of the situation here, keep things casual, apparently unable to envision himself as a man with handcuffs in his future.

Hardy had no idea what was in the safety deposit box, but judging from Graham's reaction, when he found out, it was going to be ugly.

Hardy put a hand on Graham's shoulder and stood up. The interview was over.

He was thoroughly disheartened. It had been a long and wasted morning. He hadn't done much for Graham Russo up until now, and he knew there wasn't anything he'd be able to do until this chapter had played itself out.

4

Mario Giotti sat at his regular table at Stagnola's on the Wharf. He sipped his iced tea and gazed with a studiedly placid expression down to the fishing boats moored outside his window. He was a well-known man in the city and he thought it important to maintain a dignified, serene persona in public. In any event, it was a gorgeous May morning, a Tuesday, and when he'd arrived at the restaurant, he'd apparently been in fine spirits.

And why not? He was a U.S. federal judge, appointed for life, and he lived in the best city in the world. A vibrant sixty-year-old, he kept his sparkplug of a body in terrific shape by either jogging or spending an hour a day at the workout room in the basement of the federal courthouse. With his steel-gray eyes, his unlined face, the prominent nose, he knew he cut a dignified figure.

Although just at this moment, he was struggling to control his expression. The judge's wife was late. He was peeved with her and didn't want to show it.

He hated to wait, always had. Fortunately, in his life nowadays, people most often waited for him, waited on him. He never had to stand in a line. He came into his courtroom and he had a staff that made damn sure that the day's business was ready to proceed upon his entrance. But he still had to wait for his wife. Always had, probably always would.

As he looked down at the fishing boats, a sigh escaped him. He wasn't even aware of it. Coming here to Stagnola's – which he did at least once a week when he wasn't traveling – wasn't so much a nostalgic experience as it was a return to his roots.

That's how he felt about the place. It was his true home, his psychic touchstone. For sixty-five years, over three generations, the building had been Giotti's Grotto.

The judge's great-grandfather had opened the first cioppino stand here in the middle of the Depression, and it had stayed within the family, adding onto itself, growing into a Fisherman's Wharf landmark, until Joey Stagnola had bought it from Mario's father, Bruno, in 1982.

Mario was the last male of the Giotti line. But he'd been a lawyer, with dreams of becoming a judge. He wasn't going to run a dago restaurant on the Wharf. His father, Bruno, understood – if he himself were young again and college educated, if he'd had the same options as his son, he'd do the same thing.

But Mario knew that secretly it had broken the old man's heart. He sold the restaurant to Stagnola and, six months later, sitting in a red booth by one of these back windows, had died here. (He had just finished an after-lunch Sambuca and the coroner found three coffee beans – good Italian restaurants served them floating in the aperitif for luck – in his mouth, unchewed.)

'More iced tea, Your Honor?'

Mauritio, the maître-d', had sent the youngster over to check the judge's glass. Mauritio always took good care of him.

Giotti gave his practiced, friendly nod to the white-jacketed waiter and the young man poured. The boy could have been him, forty-five years before, earnest and efficient, making sure the patrons were happy. He moved on to the next table and the judge sighed again.

'You don't look very cheerful. Is something wrong?'

Giotti hadn't even noticed his wife's approach. Pat Giotti was still a fine-looking woman, with an unlined, ageless face, high cheekbones, a graceful figure. He raised his face and she kissed him, then seated herself across the table, immediately reaching over and taking his hand, squeezing it. 'Sorry I'm late. Are you all right?'

His face animated itself. 'Just feeling old for a minute.'

'You're not old.'

'For a minute, I said.' He squeezed her hand. They had made love the night before and he was telling her he remembered very well. She was right, he wasn't old.

'Are you thinking about Sal?'

He shook his head. 'Actually, no. The waiter just reminded me of when I used to work here.' The judge looked down at the boats for a second. 'Maybe a little.'

She eyed him carefully, seemed satisfied, then reached for a roll and broke it. 'I'm sure it was for the best,' she said. 'Sal, I mean.'

'I'm sure it was,' he agreed. 'It's just . . .' His voice trailed off. 'I look down there at the moorings, I can almost see the *Signing Bonus*, see Sal waving up at me. It's hard to imagine him gone.'

'He'd lived his life, hon.'

'He was my age. I think that's part of it.'

'He was sick, remember? He was dying anyway. It just would have gotten worse. His suffering's over now.'

'I suppose so.'

'It isn't all bad. It's much better this way.'

'I know you're right.' He looked out the window. 'This was probably just the wrong table for today, being able to see down there. It brings back those memories.'

'But this is *our* table, Mario. They hold it for you, the judge's table.'

He squeezed her hand again. 'I'm just saying he was my friend. I miss him, that's all.'

'The idea of him, love, the idea. He wasn't the same friend at the end, you know that, don't you?'

'Of course.'

She met his eyes again, squeezed his hand.

'You must know that,' she said.

'I do know it, Pat. It's better all around. It's just not easy.'

The waiter came by and took their orders. Pat ordered a glass of Pinot Grigio to go with her scallops. The judge was having a crab Louis and his iced tea – of course, no wine. He was going back to court in the afternoon.

They sat in silence for a while, until her wine arrived. She took a taste, then put her glass down. 'Did you read this morning's paper? They're saying maybe it wasn't a suicide.'

'Maybe? It wasn't,' the judge said flatly.

The wine seemed to stick in Pat Giotti's throat. She took another sip to clear it. 'Why do you say that?'

The judge shrugged. 'It's got all the earmarks of an assisted suicide. Look at the morphine vials, the labels removed. Some medical person was there, helped him along. I had Annie' – his secretary – 'stop by at the Hall of Justice and pick up a copy of the autopsy this morning.'

'And?'

The judge thoughtfully tore a piece of his sourdough, then seemed to forget about it. 'The morphine dose wasn't that large. Acting alone, Sal would have probably done lots more to be sure. He had three more vials at his place he could have used. But whoever helped him put it right in the vein.'

'Which would not have been enough in the muscle?'

Giotti nodded. 'So it was a medical professional. At any rate, somebody who'd know that.' In spite of the topic the judge had to smile in admiration. 'You don't forget anything, do you? What was that, *Ellison*?'

His wife looked pleased at the compliment. Giotti was referring to a medical malpractice case he'd heard on appeal a few years back, *U.S.* v. *Ellison Pharmaceuticals*, where the doctor's decision to administer one of Ellison's drugs intravenously (IV), rather than intramuscularly (IM), had proved fatal to a patient. The doctor had tried to place the blame on the drug company, but the strategy hadn't worked; drugs injected directly into a vein had a great deal more effective potency than drugs administered IM, and Giotti had ruled that every doctor on the planet knew that, or ought to.

Pat Giotti, whose life revolved around her husband's, made it a point to read as many of his cases as she could. She didn't have a profession – hadn't worked since the earliest days of their marriage. She harbored a lingering fear that she and her husband might someday have nothing to talk about, so she kept up on the law as well as the trivia that each case provided.

Giotti sat back, letting go of his wife's hand as the waiter set their plates in front of them. 'One thing I'm sure of,' he said. 'We haven't heard the end of it, especially now they're saying it might not be a suicide.'

Pat Giotti put her fork down. 'They haven't done that, have they?'

'If it's not a suicide, it's some kind of murder. And murder means it gets investigated.'

'That may be the law, but they shouldn't do that. They ought to just leave it alone.'

He reached across the table and took her hand again. 'Who can say how much pain he was in? And even if he was, what if he wanted to endure it for some reason? What if it wasn't his decision to die just then, at that moment? That's the issue.'

That was her Mario, she thought, ever the judge. Always considering the issues, the law.

'That's why they want to find out who was there,' he said.

Hardy figured out how much time he'd spent outdoors on this beautiful day. He'd walked through the fog near his house this morning at a little after seven – call it four minutes to get to where he'd parked the night before. Then he'd stood outside Graham's house for a total of about two minutes, taking in the sunlight, birdsong, smell of blossoms, talking to Lanier. Thirty seconds walking back to his car at one-fifteen. Two minutes getting from the downtown garage to his office.

Now it was seven forty-five and the sun was a recent memory, the dusk just settling on the buildings around the office. Hardy stood at his window overlooking Sutter Street, his tie undone, coat off, eyes burning. Between Graham Russo and Tryptech, he'd already put in a thirteen-hour day and in that time he'd spent all but eight and a half minutes indoors.

The deposition with Terry Lowitz of the Port of Oakland had ended fifteen minutes ago. They'd had sandwiches brought up at five-thirty when it looked as though it was going to go on for another couple of hours. He'd called Frannie and told her he was going to be late. She was less than thrilled.

Lowitz was a maintenance supervisor whose skills as a raconteur were, Hardy thought, woefully inadequate. It had taken Hardy three tries to get the guy to put his name on the record properly. Mr Lowitz was of the general opinion that the Port of Oakland had never in its history allowed one machine of any kind to run for an instant without being in perfect repair, especially the loading transoms.

Over the course of five hours Hardy had brought up perhaps thirty examples of accidents at the Port, large or small, that might have been attributed to faulty equipment, but Mr Lowitz, when he answered intelligibly at all, had an alternate interpretation for every mishap. He was not going to lose his job by criticizing his employer. Ever.

Hardy walked back to his desk and, without thinking, picked up one of the three darts that lay upon it and flung it at the dartboard across the room. A nanosecond after he released it, he remembered that he was theoretically in the middle of a record round and was shooting for the '3.'

The dart hit smack in the middle of the '20,' David Freeman appeared in his doorway with a bottle of wine and some glasses, and the telephone rang.

He threw up his hands. 'Life,' he said, 'it happens all at once.'

Freeman would wait and the phone wouldn't, so he grabbed at it. 'Yo.'

'Hardy. Abe.'

'By God, I think it is. You sound just like yourself.'

'It's a disguise for people who think I'm somebody else.'

'So what's up? You're going to say Graham Russo.'

Freeman came over and put the glasses down on Hardy's desk, then lifted a haunch onto the corner of it.

Over the phone Hardy heard his prediction come true. 'I'm calling about Graham Russo.'

'I'm listening.'

'This is a courtesy call. You must have impressed Lanier and Evans with your manners. I asked them if they minded if I call you and they said no.'

'They're really quite perceptive individuals,' Hardy said, 'for police persons. So what about Graham?'

Glitsky told him.

Freeman repeated it, making sure he'd heard it right. 'Fifty thousand dollars in wrapped bills? Four complete sets of early-fifties baseball cards?'

'That's it.'

The old man drank off most of his glass of red wine. Hardy noticed the world outside his window, that night had completely fallen.

He looked at his watch. Eight-fourteen. He had to stop now, call it a day, get home. He'd get a call later if Graham got booked tonight, and he'd have to come down to the jail. He didn't feel he would survive without a little time off.

David Freeman, on the other hand, had no family or consuming interests outside of the law. He had lived this way for all of his adult life and now, after his own full day in court, he was settling down with a newly filled glass, enthralled with the details of yet another case. It never ended for Freeman – he never wanted it to. 'So it's not an assisted suicide after all?'

'What do you mean?'

'I mean fifty grand plus the cards, taken from the old man's safe. This is not what we call altruism. He offed the guy to get the money.'

Hardy waved that off. 'I don't think that happened, David. You've got to know him.'

'I don't need to know him if I've got the evidence. If the evidence says he did it, then he did it.'

'You always say that.'

'That's because it's always true.' Freeman had settled himself on the couch. He'd brought the bottle over and put it on the coffee table in front of him. He poured himself more wine, swirled it in his glass, sloshed it around in his mouth, the connoisseur. 'Why don't you take off your coat and stay awhile? Share this excellent claret with me. Take a break, for Christ's sake, you've been at it all day. This new case of yours has all the makings.'

Hardy threw another dart. The hell with the personal best game, he thought. He'd get it some other time. 'Believe it or not, spending another hour or two here in the middle of the night discussing a case I'm not even taking is not my idea of a break. I'm thinking about going home, saying hello to my wife before she leaves me, maybe kissing my kids good-night.'

Freeman pursed his lips with distaste. 'Aren't you curious about the money?'

'There's an explanation for the money.'

'That's my point. Don't you want to know what it is?'

'I'll catch it on the news.' He had walked around his desk and grabbed his suit coat from the back of his chair where he'd hung it, and now, on his way to the door, he was pulling it on. He stopped at the doorway and picked up his briefcase. 'You want to lock up and get the lights when you leave? The landlord here's a real tyrant.'

Freeman picked up his bottle and got himself to his feet. 'No, I'll go down to my office.'

His brown suit looked like he'd taken a shower with it on, then slept in it. There were half a dozen rusted dots around his shirt collar where he'd cut himself shaving. The tie could have been cut from a tablecloth at an Italian restaurant. He was half a head shorter than Hardy and thirty pounds heavier, all of it in the gut. Nevertheless, David Freeman – the eyes, the manic energy – was impressive, even intimidating.

He came to a halt abruptly in front of Hardy, seemed to consider for a moment, then poked a finger into his chest. 'You know, this life isn't dress rehearsal. If you've got a vision of what really happened with Sal Russo, the boy's got a right to hear it. You took him on, so you owe him that, however busy you think you are. And here's a free tip: you might try fitting in a little fun.'

'Like you do?'

'Exactly! Like I do. I have fun all the time.'

'You work all the time.'

Freeman lit up histrionically. 'I love my work! I don't do anything I don't want to do.'

'I hate to say this, David, but you don't have kids.'

The old man squinted up at him. 'Well, you do, so what?'

'So I don't do what I *want* to do anymore. I do what I *have* to do. That's my life. That's reality. I don't even think about what I want to do.'

Freeman remembered his glass of wine and took a hit of it. 'It was your choice having the kids, am I right?'

'Sure.'

'So it's your choice how you want to live with them.'

Hardy found himself getting a little hot. 'That's a fine and learned opinion, David, but you don't know what you're talking about.'

'You need this case, a murder case, something you can care about,' Freeman said. 'You're burning out.'

Hardy didn't need to hear this – it was too close to the truth. He hit the lights and closed the door behind them. 'Well, thanks for the input.'

The short corridor was dark and ended in a stairwell down which the two men walked in silence. On the second floor Phyllis, the receptionist, had her station – deserted now – in the center of a spacious and extravagantly appointed lobby. The main lights had been turned down. Dim recessed pinpoints in the ceiling kept the space from blackness, but only just. Freeman grumbled a good-night and was nearly to his office when Hardy stopped at the top of the main circular stairwell. He sighed and put down his briefcase. 'David.'

'Yeah.'

'*You* ought to take this Russo case.'

'I'll be honest with you. I would kill for this case.'

Hardy smiled in the gloom. 'You don't have to kill anybody. It's yours. I mean it. From right now Graham's your client. You can introduce yourself when they book him, which could happen in the next five minutes. If you hurry, you can beat him down to the jail.'

The old man wrestled with it for a few seconds. 'It's tempting, but I can't take it. He can't afford me.'

'Do it pro bono. He can't afford anybody, and it would be great advertising.'

'It's your case, Diz. He's your client.'

'I don't want him, David. Forget him not being able to afford me, I can't afford *him*.'

Freeman's voice cut into the darkness. 'You want my opinion, or probably you don't, you can't afford *not*. All I've heard from you for years now is how my clients – my *guilty* clients – they're the scum of the earth. They deserve the best defense the law allows, but it's not going to be Dismas Hardy who gives it to them. No, sir. You've got higher standards, right? You've got to *believe* in your clients, in their essential goodness. But you know, I've got news for you about the nature of humanity – it fails all the time. Good people do bad things. That's why we have the beautiful law.'

The old attorney moved a step closer, all wound up now. 'You think the work you're doing with Tryptech is cleaner than what I do. Well, my ass. Dyson Brunel is at best a liar and at worst a crook, and you don't seem to have any problem doing his grunt work for a fee.' Freeman lowered his voice even further, his anger building. 'Graham Russo walks in because he needs you, and you tell me he didn't kill his father for his money. You *believe* in him, don't you? But you won't help him. You can't afford to. All right, but spare me the rationalizations and the self-righteous bullshit from now on, would you? I don't have the time.'

Freeman whirled and stalked into his office, slamming the door closed behind him.

In his living room a line of tiny elephants marched tail to trunk in a caravan across the mantel above his fireplace. They were made of blown Venetian glass.

Frannie had seen them at Gump's and fallen in love, though she knew there was no way she would ever have them. They were too expensive, too fragile. An unnecessary luxury back when they'd had nothing. But Hardy had bought six of them for her and then one each year on their anniversary.

Now, finally home a little after nine o'clock, he stood in front of them, wondering if he could hear what they might be saying to him.

The elephants were part of their history. When they had decided to get married, he and Frannie had had many discussions about where they would live together. Finally she said she'd move out of her duplex into this house – *Hardy's* house. He thought the gift would begin to make the place her own home, and he'd been right. She rearranged the elephants every couple of days, circling them, lining them up, facing them all in one direction or another. Mood stones.

(Her brother, Moses, did the same thing – rearranged the elephants – almost every time he came to visit. Hardy thought it must be genetic.)

It was a night for shadows. The living room, as the lobby in his building had been, was dimly lit, in this case from one light over the telephone in the tiny sitting area off the dining room. The house was eerily quiet. It was a 'railroad-style' Victorian with a long hallway, living and dining rooms up front. In the back the house widened with the kitchen and, behind that, three bedrooms.

The kids were asleep and Frannie had gone to bed, apparently to sleep. He microwaved the leftovers of macaroni and cheese, mixing in a can of tuna for the protein, or taste, or something. At the dining-room table he started to review some of the Tryptech pages from his briefcase, but he didn't have the energy.

He poured an inch of Bushmills into one of the jelly glasses the kids used. Returning to the living room, he lit a fire and drank his drink. When it was finished, he showered and slid in beside his wife's possibly sleeping form.

The elephants were dancing in an amber glow.

A naked man stood in front of the dying embers, watching the beasts. There were fourteen of them, in a line, perhaps preparing to caravan. The wind howled outside.

Outside the fire's perimeter the night was pitch, and out of its shadow a woman appeared. She was dressed in something white and flowing. Red highlights shimmered in long hair, worn down. She was barefoot.

The man half turned, afraid to step toward her lest he stumble. Twice already he had free-poured Irish whiskey into the Tom and Jerry drinking glass, too thick to break.

'Are you coming back to bed?'

'I couldn't sleep.'

'I guessed that.' She laid a hand lightly on his shoulder. 'Don't hurt yourself.' A reference to the drinking. When he'd been younger, before this marriage or their children, he had a personal rule forbidding hard spirits in his house. Now he sometimes thought they could open a liquor store.

'I love these elephants,' he said. It appealed to him to see one of the strongest animals in the world rendered in the most fragile of substances. 'They look like they're dancing, don't they? Excited about going somewhere, doing something.'

'Come on back to bed,' she said. 'I'll rub your back.'

'What time is it?' he asked.

'Two. The kids'll be up in five hours, Dismas. It's going to seem like five minutes.'

His hand was around the glass, on the mantel over the fire. He was aware that he was leaning on it for balance.

Frannie was right. Tomorrow – another in the seemingly endless procession of them – would come too soon. Freeman was right too. He was burning out.

He sighed, left the half-empty glass where it was on the mantel, let her lead him back down the long hallway to their bedroom.

5

Hardy wasn't going to acknowledge the fatigue, the slight headache, the buzz behind his eyes. He had set his internal alarm for six- thirty, and it didn't fail him.

Of David Freeman's words the night before, the ones that had the most impact were those concerning the children – Hardy had chosen to have them, and he could choose how he lived with them.

He was failing there, with his kids, lost in some downward spiral he didn't quite understand. He wasn't taking any joy in them, in Frannie, in his life. Certainly not in his work. He didn't know if it was only a function of attitude, but he knew he'd recognized it at last.

Maybe all of that wasn't too far gone to reclaim.

He didn't even know any longer where his black pan was. The cast-iron fryer weighed ten pounds and was the only physical legacy of Hardy's parents, Joe and Iola, who'd died in a plane crash when he was nineteen. For years – all through his first marriage and second bachelorhood – he had cooked almost everything he ate in that pan.

He'd kept it perennially on his stove, shined until it looked more like hematite than iron. He never put any water in it, just scraped it with a spatula, wiped it down with salt, then rubbed it with a rag. Even when he used neither oil nor butter, nothing stuck to it. The pan had been one of his treasures. He told Frannie when they first got together that it was *the* symbol of who he was.

If that was true now, he thought, he was in trouble. He didn't know where it had gone. He had searched the kitchen and finally found the pan under his workbench on the landing that led down the stairs and out to their backyard. Sometime in the past few years – and he hadn't even noticed – Frannie had moved it out of the kitchen. He didn't cook at home anymore. He was always working. And the damn thing was too heavy for her to lift. She'd essentially thrown it out.

This morning Hardy didn't go through his routine: shower, dress in his suit and tie, coffee. Instead he pulled on his old jeans and a faded Cal Poly sweatshirt, slipped into his Top-Siders and, keeping quiet, first went in search of the black pan.

Twenty minutes later he had the French crepe batter made and the table set for breakfast at the kitchen table. He fixed a cup of coffee the way Frannie liked it, with real cream and two thirds of a spoonful of brown sugar, and brought it in to her, placing it beside the bed, waking her with a kiss on her cheek.

Rebecca – they called her the Beck – was Frannie's child by her first husband, but Hardy had adopted her as his own. Now the nine-year-old lay on her back, covers off, mouth open. Her brother, Vincent, was seven and had his own room at the very back of the house, but for the past several months he'd been sleeping on a futon on the floor of Beck's room. He was entirely covered by his comforter. Hardy stepped over him, sat on the side of the Beck's bed, and leaned over, hugging her. 'Maple syrup,' he whispered. 'Crepes.'

'Crepes!' She was immediately awake. Her arms came up around him and squeezed and then she squiggled free. 'Vincent!' she yelled. 'Daddy's making crepes.'

Vincent was up and on him before he knew what hit him. He was knocked backward, wrestled down onto the futon in a jumble of arms and legs and tumbling, kid-smell and laughter.

With a roar he grabbed at both of them, holding them to him, tickling whenever he could get a finger free. He caught a knee in the groin – a constant – and groaned, which the kids ignored as a matter of course.

Finally it stopped. His back was against the Beck's bed and the kids settled against him, one on each side. He heard the shower start in the bathroom and the alarm went off next to his bed. He patted the kids on their backs. 'Let's get some clothes on,' he said. 'Breakfast in five.'

'Four!' The Beck was up, moving for the bathroom.

'Three!' Vincent was right behind her, but not fast enough.

Hardy heard the door slam, then a crash as Vincent skidded into it. 'Dad! Beck slammed the door.' More pounding. 'Dad!'

Hardy got up. Crisis number one. He took a breath, preparing to mediate. His groin didn't hurt anymore.

And his headache was gone.

When he got in to work, there was a call on his answering machine. Graham had called from jail. Evans and Lanier had shown up at his place again at seven A.M. This time they arrested him for murder.

Her partner was interviewing people in another homicide that had occurred long before Sarah had made it to the detail, so she drew the solo assignment to Sal's place.

The apartment was still sealed off. It might have been the lowest of drudge work, but for some reason Sarah didn't mind. There was something compelling about this old man who sold fish and his family who hated him.

She let herself in and closed the door behind her. In the living room the Venetian blinds were up, the glass in the windows opaque with grime. Although the sun had been shining outside, inside there was little sense of it. She flicked the switch by the front door – the six-bulb chandelier that hung from the center of the ceiling made almost no difference. Four of its lights were burned out.

She took a couple of steps over to the sagging couch and sat on the front inches of it. Before her on the stained pine coffee table the fingerprinting powder was still visible, a thin film. Beyond the table was the lounge chair. She leaned forward, elbows on knees, templed her fingers in front of her mouth, and blew through them.

The profound stillness bored into her. Only gradually did she even become aware of the traffic sounds through the windows over Seventh Street. The air didn't move at all.

What must it have been like, she wondered, to have lived here, to be dying here? Murder cases, she was beginning to realize, were of a different quality from the other crimes she'd been working on over the years: the robberies, assaults, vandalisms, frauds. The act, of course, the murder itself, might have been as considered, as violent, as brutish, or as passionate as any of the other crimes, but its consequence struck a far more resonant chord.

Here was where a life story had ended.

The consciousness that had once impressed its features on this inanimate *stuff* – furniture, walls, kitchen appliances, the air itself – had been replaced, now, with a vacuum.

Finally she got up, crossed the living room, threw open a west-facing window. There was a breeze outside. She could sense it before it breached the window, and the sun did shine. But it was as though the room conspired to keep these elements out, at least for another few seconds.

Sarah, turning to take in the place where Sal Russo had lived and died, suddenly, and clearly, experienced Sal's presence hovering here, his ghost, almost as though it were a physical thing.

Who had he been, after all?

Finally, the breeze stirred a dust ball that had formed on one of the end tables, blowing it to the floor. She opened another window on another wall, moving to be moving. Maybe the answer to her question was somewhere among all the paper.

Ridiculous though it was, she couldn't shake the feeling that Sal Russo was trying, somehow, to communicate with her.

If she could only hear what he might be saying.

On the first pass she went through every scrap of paper that wasn't in some kind of a box. There was paper between the mattresses on his bed, in the kitchen cabinets, in the drawers of the end tables. She'd already discovered the paper with the safe combinations in the wastebasket in the bathroom, but there was more in the garbage in the kitchen. Under the threadbare living-room rug. Some of it was brown paper bag material, some was lined invoice paper, plain sheets of copy paper, anything that would hold an imprint, pencil or ink.

Almost every piece contained a first or last name or both. Telephone numbers, or parts of them. Addresses, Evans figured. A lot of legwork there, a ton of follow-up, but some of it, possibly, fruitful. She didn't mind work; that's what they paid her for.

But this collection of paper wasn't getting her any closer to the man. She'd been sitting on the couch, going through it all piece by piece, placing it in one of the oversized yellow envelopes she'd brought along. Now, the envelope bulging, she dropped it on the table, and stood again.

The chalked outline where his body had lain crumpled was still visible on the rug. Somehow she'd avoided even *seeing* it when she'd come in. Now she squatted over it, trying to fill in the picture. Her finger dragged over the rug. 'Come on, old man,' she whispered, '*talk* to me.'

Most of the boxes, she knew, were in the bedroom, which was behind the kitchen off to her right, but there was one here in the living room, in the corner along the wall that held the couch. Crouching there on the floor, she saw it. And again, it was as though it were for the first time.

What else, she wondered, had she missed?

Her eyes came to rest on the piece of plywood that hung over the couch. She'd noticed the painting before, but had assumed it was just an el cheapo mass-produced rendering that had come with the furnished apartment. It hadn't been varnished, and the paint had bleached out to the point where the grain of the plywood showed more than anything else.

But here, from her angle in the early afternoon light – the sun had deposited a rectangle of light onto the floor – the lines of the painting stood out. The depiction was recognizably Fisherman's Wharf, but without the postcard patina. She squinted up at it, then stood and moved closer. If Sal had done this – as the rusted brown initials *S.R.* in the lower right corner indicated – he had had talent.

The fishing boat in the foreground, the *Signing Bonus*, was obviously abandoned. Crab pots lay in disarray around it, both on its deck and the nearby pier. The portholes were all hollows of jagged glass, the railing had caved on itself. There were no people anywhere. No, there was one. She imagined she saw a lone figure, what appeared to be a child, sitting with hunched shoulders on the flying bridge, holding a broken fishing pole. Behind the boat the charred skeleton of a building smoldered on the Wharf.

She stood back and stared for another minute, realizing that what disturbed her – more than anything the painting showed – was the sensibility behind it. If he'd painted this, Sal Russo wasn't your typical fleabag derelict. He had a tortured soul, or had had one at one time.

Then, shaking herself from her reverie, she went over to the corner, got the heavy cardboard box, put it on the table and folded back the flaps that had been interlocked, something that clearly had been done many, many times.

She supposed she'd been expecting more debris, the same mishmash of receipts and scribblings, except older, that she'd already gone through and bagged. Instead, she found two battered three-ring binders and four hardcover books.

Taking out the books first, she placed them to one side – Bernard Malamud's *The Natural*; a well-thumbed Chapman's technical handbook for sailors called *Piloting*; an ancient book-club edition – leather bound, gold trimmed – of *Moby Dick*; and Albert Camus's *The Fall*.

The binders were another surprise. They were photo albums, organized and cared for. Sal had kept them out here in the living room where he could get to them, and Sarah would have bet a lot that he got them out often.

Feeling a bit like an intruder, she opened the first one. Pictures of a young man, very handsome, with a beautiful young woman, progressively pregnant. She knew the man must have been Sal, but couldn't very well reconcile it with the old man she had seen here on Friday.

Then the first baby picture – *Graham Joseph Russo* written under it in a strong male hand.

She flipped through the pages more quickly. Here was the fishing boat from the painting on the wall – but new and trimmed, a beaming Sal Russo at the helm. Then there were two more children. A smallish house, typical for the Sunset District.

Graham growing up, playing baseball. Sal playing accordion at parties, more fishing boat pictures on the Bay, at the Wharf. Another child, a girl, Debra. George. The wife appearing less and less. Then, suddenly, halfway through the binder, a mansion.

After that the binder was empty.

The sunlight rectangle on the floor had grown, and Sarah stood and stretched her back. In the kitchen she walked around the chair, which still lay on its side, left there by the investigations team. She poured herself a glass of water. The sun was very much a presence in here, the one window much cleaner than those in the living room, and with no blinds or drapes covering it. There were three mugs on the drain, dark liquid still in the bottom of two of them. An unwashed plate was on the table, knife and fork on it. These artifacts bothered her. If there had been any kind of real struggle in here, wouldn't something else have been disturbed?

Back in the living room she made a note to bring this up with Lanier, and reached for the second binder. Baseball, baseball, and more baseball. Despite herself Sarah sat back. She was going to enjoy this. Baseball was her game – she still played on her women's team once a week, year round.

As an only child and a girl, baseball had been the bond with her father, whom she still adored. Her parents had now retired and moved to Palm Springs, so she didn't see them often, but every time they talked, they still joked about their Giant-Dodger rivalry – Sarah was Giants all the way.

Her dad and mom had both been raised in Brooklyn before moving to California, and the blood in their veins, they said, ran Dodger blue. She'd have to tell them about Graham Russo, she decided – making their team as a replacement player. That's the kind of team the Dodgers were, she'd say – they hired murderers. Her dad would love that.

This album started way farther back. Here were black-and-white pictures of a very young Sal Russo. She double-checked to make sure this wasn't Graham, but no, it was his father, in his own youth – always in uniform, always with a mitt or a bat. The first press clippings: Sal Russo throws no-hitter and hits two home runs in Little League opener. Freshman makes varsity at Balboa High. All-city high school team. All-state at USF.

She turned the photo of the college team sideways. There was Sal in the second row, next to Mario Giotti, the judge who'd found him on Friday. Amazing, she thought, the ties.

After the story of Sal's bonus-signing with the Orioles, there were two blank pages. Then the stories about Graham began, the same kind of stuff they'd written about his father. Little League, Pony League, high school, college, the Dodgers' farms.

Finally, abruptly, the yellowing newsprint ended and the paper turned white – these were the recent articles from Graham's aborted return. Even down to the box scores from spring training in Vero Beach, Sal seemed to have recorded everything about the baseball career of the son she had arrested for his murder this morning.

Closing the binder on her lap, she was still sitting back in the couch, her eyes stinging. All right, she thought. Maybe Sal had spoken to her, but she wasn't at all sure what it was she'd heard. Above all, she couldn't figure out how someone who had begun with such promise, as Sal had, blessed with musical, artistic, and athletic talent, with a personality, a beautiful wife, a healthy and attractive family – how could that have all gone away? How did he end up here? Could it all have been economics?

She didn't believe it. Sure, business failure could destroy a person's soul; she'd seen that often enough. But this wasn't any simple bankruptcy. Sal wasn't broke, by any means. He paid his rent, had a going business that supported him, even if it was illegal. He was a survivor. Plus, he had money stashed away, lots of money. And the bills were wrapped and bank-stamped, dated seventeen years before. What did that mean?

Something cataclysmic must have happened. Whatever it was had destroyed him, and now she couldn't help but wonder if it had finally killed him as well. And what did that mean about his son, who was now in jail because of her?

Maybe the answer was somewhere in the boxes back in the bedroom. She put the second binder next to its mate on the table and stretched again. She'd been here an hour and a half and had done almost no real police work. She'd better get on it.

But she was at eye level with that painting once again. It reeled her in and held her for another moment. Could that be a baseball mitt – that smudge – next to the fishing boy? (If it was, in fact, a boy fishing.) Was there something else she was missing? Was she missing anything at all?

She didn't know. The other boxes weren't going away. She'd better get to them. With a last glance at the painting she headed back to the bedroom.

At one-thirty that afternoon, just as Sarah was getting to Sal Russo's place, Hardy waited for the guard to open the door to Visiting Room B in San Francisco's jail. It was a relatively new building directly behind the Hall of Justice, only open for business for the past year or so. The new attorney visiting rooms were a good deal larger than those in the old jail had been, but the size didn't make much difference. In spite of its nickname among law enforcement personnel – the Glamour Slammer – it still wasn't anyplace you wanted to be.

They hadn't brought Graham down yet. Hardy asked the guard to leave the door open and walked the six steps over to the window. Six whole steps – the place was extravagant in its roominess! And the window, though glass block, was a definite improvement.

In the old jail the visiting rooms had essentially been closets, six by eight feet, with no ventilation and one overhead light bulb. A table and three wooden chairs took up all the space. Through a square pane of wire-reinforced glass set into the wall, you could see inmates and guards passing in the jail's corridor. The inmates would slam the window every once in a while as you talked to your client.

Hardy didn't think that could happen here. No prisoners walked down this hallway. The corridor outside was a kind of catwalk around the administrative rooms and holding cells, and with the glass block there was a lot of light, especially on a sunny day like this one. It wasn't exactly cheery, but it wasn't a dungeon either.

He turned away from the window, preparing himself. It was always a jolt, the initial meeting behind bars of a person you'd known in civilian life.

In a couple of minutes Graham Russo was going to walk in here and he wasn't going to look the same. He was going to be in an orange jumpsuit, perhaps shackled. Some small piece of his soul was going to be gone. That would make Graham different in some fundamental way, and Hardy didn't want to see it.

He put his hands in his pockets and waited.

They'd started out sitting across the table from each other, but Hardy was up and pacing now. Graham's story had changed in another, and particularly unsettling, way. He seemed to be having trouble believing that Sergeant Evans had actually arrested him.

'I never thought she'd do that.'

'Why not? She's a cop. That's what they do.'

'Yeah, but . . .' He paused, considering his words.

'But what?'

Coming out with it. 'I was playing a little head game with her. I thought she'd bought it. I didn't think she'd keep looking. Not at me. Not after I opened up and cooperated.'

'But you didn't tell the truth.'

Graham shrugged. 'I guessed wrong.'

'About what?'

'About whether she cared about the truth, I guess. I thought she'd believe *me*, not the words so much.'

This was close enough to how Hardy felt to make him feel uncomfortable. 'So what about now?'

'What about now?'

'You and me, the truth, all that silly stuff.'

'I haven't lied to you.'

'As a matter of fact, you did. You said you weren't close to your father.'

'But I'd already told the police that. I . . . it didn't seem like a big thing. I wanted you to help me out, and if I came across as inconsistent, you'd doubt me from the git-go. I screwed up, I guess. I'm sorry.'

Hardy closed his eyes for a moment. 'Okay, so let's get clear on this. Despite what you told me and the police – the police two times – you *were* close to your father?'

Graham nodded. 'I figured it would be easier to just say I wasn't.'

'Easier how?'

'That's obvious, isn't it? What everyone would think.'

Hardy stopped pacing. 'You know what Mark Twain said? He said the best part about telling the truth is you don't have to remember when you lied.'

'I know. All this just came at me, Diz. I didn't have any time to think about it. I said I'm sorry.'

'I'm sorry too.' Hardy wanted to get it straight. 'So you were afraid that if you admitted you and your father had reconciled, people would draw the conclusion that you helped him kill himself?'

'Yeah.'

'But you didn't? Help him kill himself?'

Graham had his huge hands folded on the table. He looked down at them, then back up at Hardy. 'No. I've told you that.'

Hardy came up to the table, laid a palm down on it. 'Okay, you told me that. But at this point, how am I supposed to know when you're telling the truth?'

'This one isn't a lie.'

'You didn't kill your father?'

'No.'

'You didn't help him kill himself? Talk him through it? Sit there with him? Any of that? Because if you did, it's going to make a big difference. We've got a whole 'nother ball game.'

'No, I didn't do that.'

'You weren't there on Friday at all?'

Again, the maddening hesitation.

'Graham?' Hardy slammed the table and his client jerked backward. 'Jesus, what's to think about? You were there or you weren't.'

'I was thinking about something else.'

'Don't. Keep your mind on what I'm asking you about. You think you can do that?'

Hardy pulled his chair out again and sat in it. 'Okay.' He modulated his voice. He wasn't here to rebuke his client, but he had to get a handle on the truth. 'Okay, Graham, let's talk a minute about you and me. You're a lawyer, so you know this stuff, but when you hired me the other day, I became your attorney. After that, anything we say to each other is privileged. Like now. Clear?'

'Right.'

'So I've got to know what happened with you and your dad. All of it. I'll take it with me to my grave, but I've got to know so I can help you.'

Graham slid his chair back a few inches and folded his arms across his chest, his sculpted face impassive. His eyes scanned the room, came back to Hardy. 'How long am I going to be here?' he finally asked.

The abrupt segue – frustrating as it might be – was no surprise. Hardy's experience with people who unexpectedly found themselves in jail was that their attention span lost a lot of linkage. 'I don't know.'

This was the exact truth. In spite of Glitsky's warning the previous evening, nobody had arrested Graham until this morning. Evans and Lanier had discovered the safe-deposit money late in the afternoon – too late, according to Glitsky, to go to the district attorney and get an arrest warrant.

Then, last night Graham had neither been home nor at his paramedic job. Concerned that he might flee, the two inspectors had arrested him without a warrant when he opened his door to say hello. So the DA wasn't yet involved in the case, and this meant that the exact charge – beyond simple murder – had yet to be determined.

Hardy went on with the explanation. 'Your arraignment is tomorrow and we can't get bail set until then, so you're here at least overnight. Assuming I can get you reasonable bail, which maybe I can't, you could be out tomorrow.' He paused. 'And if they're not going for special circumstances.'

This got Graham's complete attention. 'What do you mean?' The fingers spiked at his hair. 'Jesus Christ, what are you talking about?'

'I'm talking about murder for profit or during a robbery. That's specials.'

'I didn't—' He stopped. 'What robbery?'

Keeping it matter-of-fact, Hardy told him. 'Fifty thousand dollars in cash. Another twenty or thirty in mint-condition baseball cards. That's a lot of money, Graham. You kill somebody, you take their stuff or their money. That's robbery.'

Arms crossed again, Graham was chewing his cheek.

'So from an outsider's point of view, including the inspectors who arrested you, and not to mention yours truly, let's see how it looks. You make – what? – fifteen bucks an hour as a paramedic.'

'Give or take.'

'And you live in the nicest neighborhood in the city – what's your rent up there?'

Graham sighed deeply, answered reluctantly. 'Fifteen.'

'Okay, your rent is fifteen hundred dollars in this place a judge would probably salivate over. You've got beautiful furniture, more fine wine than you can drink in a month, what kind of car do you drive?'

'Beemer.'

Another fifty grand, Hardy thought. He should have guessed. 'I don't suppose it's paid for.'

'You're kidding, right?'

'So what's the hit on that?'

'Six hundred eighty.'

The hard numbers didn't matter so much – of course there would be other expenses, probably moving Graham's monthly nut up into the range of four to five thousand dollars. He wasn't making this riding in an ambulance.

'So the picture, Graham, is that you quit your incredible job as a federal law clerk, then you got laid off by the Dodgers, now you work part time. You see a question developing here?'

Graham came forward, elbows on the table. He pulled at the neck of his jumpsuit. 'I get at least fifty a game. That's if we lose. A hundred if we win. Bonuses in tournaments, for home runs, like that. Last Saturday I made four hundred.' He must have read Hardy's blank look. 'For softball,' he explained.

'Who pays you to play softball?'

'Craig Ising.'

'Who is?'

'Some rich guy, he owns the Hornets. That's my team.' Hardy still wasn't seeing it. Graham went on patiently. 'When I made the big club, during the strike, there were a couple of articles in the papers about us – the replacement players – and Ising kept his eyes open and waited. When the Dodgers cut me and I got back home, he looked me up.'

Hardy heard the words, but felt he was missing some crucial point. 'We're talking slo-pitch softball? You're saying there's a professional league?'

'No. It's all under the table. It's all gambling. These rich guys stack the teams and bet on the games.'

'How much do they bet?'

Graham shrugged. 'I don't know for sure. I hear numbers. Ten grand, twenty. Per game.'

Hardy was shaking his head. 'You're kidding me.'

'I don't think so. It's big business. The hitch is, I can't declare any of the money – no taxes, no nothing.'

'So how much do you really make?'

Attorney-client privilege or not, Graham didn't want to say. 'I don't know. Some weeks I play three games, tournaments on weekends.'

'And how many games are in a tournament?'

'Usually five if you go all the way.'

Hardy was scribbling some numbers on his legal pad. 'A grand a week?' he asked.

Another shrug. 'Sometimes.' Then, suddenly, he spoke with the first real urgency Hardy had heard. 'But this can't come out. They get me for tax evasion, they'll yank my bar card. I'll *really* never work again.'

'They get you for murder, that'll be the least of your problems.' This was inarguable, but Graham leaned back in his chair, pondering it. 'I thought you didn't want to be a lawyer anyway.'

'Come on, Diz. Why do you think I went to law school? Of course I want to be a lawyer.'

'But you—'

'I just wanted one last chance to play ball. I figured I'd play a few years, make my millions, then go back and practice law. Then imagine my surprise when I came back to the city and found I wasn't hirable. Good old Judge Draper had blackballed me, called everybody he knew, though of course he denies it.'

'You asked him?'

'I didn't have to. The word got out. I'm untouchable.' Another scan of the room. 'And now this.'

'Couldn't Giotti help you? He was a friend of your father's. Wouldn't he . . . ?'

But Graham was shaking his head before Hardy could finish. 'No chance. Federal judges hang together. You've got to understand that I *quit* these guys, quit the court, rejected their whole lives. They're never going to forgive me. Maybe I could find some work in Alaska, but I'm dead in this town. I've looked, believe me. I must have sent out five hundred resumes. I'm in the top of my class at Boalt. Not even an interview.'

'So why didn't you move to Alaska?'

The maddening hesitation suddenly reappeared. 'I might,' he said at last. The ambiguity seemed intentional. Whether he meant 'I might have except for . . .' or 'I might now someday,' Hardy couldn't say. But either way, for Hardy the light came on. 'Your father. He needed you. That's why you came back and stayed on.'

But immediately Hardy regretted what he'd said – he might have given his client an idea.

Graham stood up, got to the wall, and stood facing the window. Finally, he spoke without turning. 'I don't know. I really don't know. I didn't plan it. It just happened. He wrote me the letter – the one you saw yesterday – and I got in touch with him, and we just' – a pause – 'I just . . .'

Graham was silent so long that Hardy rose and crossed over to him. It shocked him to see tears, but in spite of himself, or wanting to, he wasn't sure he believed them. Not anymore. Graham had already been too duplicitous. His admission about trying to charm Sarah. Maybe now he was playing for his attorney's sympathy. Hardy put a hand on his client's shoulder and felt the tension break, the shoulders give.

Graham hung his head, the weight of holding it up apparently too much to bear. 'I loved him. He was my dad. He needed me.' His voice went down a notch. 'I needed him too.'

There was still the money.

Ten minutes later they were both back at the table. Hardy had been there for over an hour and had nothing substantive to show for it. He had to find out about the money.

'My dad wanted me to take it, to give it to somebody else. He didn't want anybody in the family to have it, didn't want it to be part of the estate.'

Hardy took that in. Like nearly everything else to come from the mouth of Graham Russo, the response raised more questions than it answered. 'Who did he want to give it to?'

'The children of a woman named Joan Singleterry.'

'Okay,' Hardy said. 'I'll bite. Who's she?'

'I don't know.'

'Didn't your father tell you?'

'He started. Then the phone rang. When I brought it up again when he came back, he looks at me like I'm from Mars. No memory. Just not there. That's the way he got.'

'And you didn't press him?'

Graham spread his palms. 'That was my dad. He wouldn't tell me, even if he remembered that he wanted me to know.'

'The time he did mention her – what was that story?'

He shrugged. 'He didn't know where she lived, but he wanted me to find her after he was dead and give her the money.'

'So he knew he was going to be dead?'

'He knew he was going to kill himself, sure.' Graham held up a hand. 'I know what that sounds like, but it's the truth.'

'Why wouldn't I believe it's the truth?' Hardy asked with heavy irony. 'This happens all the time. Some guy's father gives him fifty grand to give to somebody he doesn't know.' Hardy leaned across the table, punched up his voice. 'Listen up, Graham, you've got to start telling me something I can believe pretty soon or I'm going to be out of here.'

'This is the truth, Diz. I don't know, maybe he had some kids with this woman a long time ago and—'

'Where'd he get the money?'

'I don't know that either.'

Hardy slapped the table, shouted. 'Jesus! What about the baseball cards? What did he want you to do with them, put 'em in a fucking time capsule?'

It was the moment to leave – this anger wasn't going anywhere productive. Hardy got his voice back under control, gathered his pen and his legal pad, stood up. 'Let me tell you what this looks like, Graham. This looks like you killed your dad and stole fifty thousand dollars from him and you just didn't have the chance – yet – to launder the money, or do whatever it is you do with that much cash. And cash seems to be your thing. I'm not saying that this is what I think' – although Hardy was perilously close to believing just that – 'but this is what it's going to look and sound like to everybody who hears it. And if it looks, smells, and tastes like it, guess what?'

No reply.

Hardy took a breath. 'Now, I'm still your lawyer and I'm going to listen to what you say, and if you want to change your mind, I'm not going to hold it against you and we'll go on from there. But these are losing cards. This is a terrible hand.'

Graham looked up. 'It's what happened.'

'Well, if that's true, Graham,' Hardy replied, 'this has not been your lucky week.'

6

When the DA, Sharron Pratt, got the news that Graham Russo had been arrested without a warrant issued by her office, she angrily demanded that Glitsky report to her. She thought the police had seriously overstepped their bounds, particularly in this case where the larger issues surrounding assisted suicide needed to be thoroughly aired and debated. 'I don't understand,' Pratt was saying, 'why you didn't come to me first, Lieutenant. Why did you just arrest him?'

'We think he's committed a murder.' Glitsky didn't yet understand Pratt's anger, for while it was true that the police often came to the DA to get a warrant for an arrest, it was nearly as common to have inspectors make the arrest first. This tended to keep suspects from disappearing. 'But look, ma'am, if you want, you can just dismiss the case.'

'That's what you'd like, isn't it, Lieutenant?'

'No, ma'am. But it's your right.'

'Don't try to con me, Lieutenant. That's just what you want. If you'd come for a warrant for this boy's arrest, you knew I would have turned you down, but now that you've arrested him first, you've focused the issue, putting me on the spot.'

Hands clamped behind her back, Pratt wore her half-moon glasses midway down her aristocratic nose. She looked over them.

Pratt was not Glitsky's boss, and he didn't much care how she felt about him, but he was trying to do his job, and considered his reply carefully before he gave it. 'It was a timing issue,' Glitsky said. 'There was plenty of evidence to arrest, but if you want to play political football . . .'

Pratt's eyes glared. Her nostrils flared. 'Don't you *dare* accuse me of playing politics with a man's life. Your people made a mistake arresting this man.'

Glitsky couldn't stop himself. 'You know that the arresting inspector was a woman, don't you?'

It slowed her for a moment. 'That's not the issue,' she snapped. 'I don't care who arrested him. The point is we – this office – had not made a decision to prosecute. You knew we weren't ready to issue a warrant, so you went ahead without one.'

'I didn't know that. Why would I even think it? Your office prosecutes homicides. What's to know?'

Pratt nodded, as though Glitsky had confirmed something for her. She moved over to her desk, where the Russo file sat in its manila folder. 'I'm going to bring this up with the mayor and the Board of Supervisors, Lieutenant. This police vendetta to discredit me, it has to stop.'

'And why are we having this vendetta again?' Glitsky asked. 'I forget.'

'Because I believe – and I'm *right* – that some of the things that you call crimes are simply not wrong, and I'm not going to prosecute them.'

'I don't call them crimes – the legislature does.'

Pratt was shaking her head. 'I don't care what's on the books. The books are wrong. People are being hounded by you police, the city's resources are being squandered by your harassment of prostitutes, casual marijuana users—'

'Murderers?'

She leveled a finger at him. 'That's *exactly* my point. Based on the evidence I've seen here' – the finger went down to the folder – 'I don't think Graham Russo is a murderer.'

'You don't think he killed his father?'

'No, I *do* think he killed his father.' She slapped her palm down on the desk. '*Of course* he killed his father, technically speaking,' she said. 'Do you think I'm stupid?'

Deciding it would be wiser to sidestep a direct answer to that, Glitsky took a beat, tilted his head, ladled on the sincerity. 'Then I really am missing something here. What's the problem with us arresting him if you think he did it?'

Sighing heavily, Pratt pulled her chair over and sat down. 'What I'm saying, Lieutenant, is that though technically this could have been a homicide—'

Glitsky interrupted. 'Strout called it a homicide,' he said, 'so it's a homicide.'

But she was shaking her head. 'Regardless of that, it wasn't a murder.'

'No? Then what was it?'

'An assisted suicide.'

'Which is illegal.'

'But not wrong. In fact it was *right*. The boy did the humane thing and it was probably the most difficult decision of his life. And you want to try him for murder?'

'No. I arrested him for breaking a law. That's my job.'

'That's not true. Your job is to process warrants through this office. *We* make the decision as to whether we're going to charge a crime.' All the way back in her chair, she pointed again, up at him, eyes flashing. 'You police *knew* this office would make that distinction. So you circumvented me. You've been doing this kind of thing ever since I came on here. Can it be that you really think I don't see it?'

Glitsky stepped over to a grouping of wing chairs at the side of the room and pulled one around, sitting on it. He pointed at the file, adopted a conversational tone. 'You said you read this. So I'm curious – how do you rule out murder?'

'I start with the Constitution, Lieutenant, by presuming the man innocent.' When he didn't comment, she continued with her own perfectly plausible theory on Sal Russo's death: it was a mercy killing.

'So you're saying that from now on, in cases like this the DA decides we don't need a jury trial to get at the facts? And what do we call this, the mercy rule?' Pratt glared at him – it was no use arguing legal theory with her. He decided to return to the evidence. 'Okay, then, what about the money?'

'His father gave it to him. He loved him. He was still estranged from his other children. Apparently they hated him. Why would he want them to share his money?'

'Then why didn't Graham just admit it? Why did he lie about everything we asked him?'

'He was cornered. He didn't see a way to get out, so he panicked. People do it all the time.'

'All right. How about the trauma to the head?'

‘He could have fallen down and knocked his head anytime before he died.’

Glitsky fell silent. There were many other evidentiary points, but he knew that Pratt would have an explanation for how each of them fit her own theory. And, in fact, she might be right. The truth might be exactly what Pratt thought it was.

But Glitsky believed that it shouldn’t be her call. It should go to trial, to a jury. That was how the system worked.

The DA sat back in her chair, fingers at her lips. ‘You know . . . Abe . . . I would think you’d be a little more sensitive to this issue. Didn’t your wife suffer terribly?’

His scar tightened through his lips. ‘I didn’t kill my wife. I didn’t help kill her.’

She came forward in her chair. ‘I didn’t say that. But she must have been in great pain.’

Glitsky, too, was on the front six inches of his chair. ‘She was taking drugs. She said they helped. She wanted to live as long as she could. She didn’t want to die.’

‘But what if she had wanted to die, Abe? Wouldn’t you have helped her? Wouldn’t you have wanted to?’

‘Of course I would have wanted to. I probably would have.’

‘And yet you don’t believe that’s what happened here, with Graham Russo and his father? You think what he did was wrong.’

He hung his head. Arguing with Pratt was like trying to move a cloud by pushing on it. ‘No,’ he said with all the patience he could muster, ‘I think what he did was illegal.’

She must have thought she’d convinced him. She put her elbows on the desk and spread her palms as though releasing a little bird she had between them. ‘Then the law should be changed.’

David Freeman’s associates called his conference room the Solarium. Under a glass-and-steel enclosure, rubber trees, ficus, lemons proliferated. Visible through the forest, outside, was an enclosed and landscaped courtyard, and this added to the greenhouse feel.

Dismas Hardy sat under the foliage at an elliptical mahogany table with Michelle Tinker. Demure to the point of shyness, Michelle possessed what Hardy knew to be a brilliant legal mind

– far more focused, he thought, than his own. Freeman kept her on because, even though she was tongue tied before juries, she had a seemingly boundless aptitude for work and minutiae. And that's exactly what Hardy had told Freeman he needed after he'd come in this morning.

He was going to be working with Graham Russo, and that case was going to take some significant portion of the time he was now giving to Tryptech. Would Freeman mind letting him borrow a workhorse who would take off some of the Tryptech load? Freeman, not very convincing hiding his pleasure at Hardy's decision to take the criminal case, had been glad to comply.

Michelle had both an accounting and a law degree. In her mid-thirties, she was married with no children. Once you got beyond the shyness, she was friendly and well spoken, totally professional. Hardy knew Dyson Brunel would get along well with her, and she jumped at the invitation to assist with Tryptech. The lawsuit was all numbers and paper – she'd never see a jury, possibly not even a judge.

It was nearly five o'clock and Hardy had been getting her up to speed for the better part of two hours, outlining the issues, trying to acquaint her with the players. If Michelle's questions were any indication, she seemed to have absorbed most of it.

His files were in cardboard boxes that he'd carried with him down to the Solarium. Michelle was going to be reading them over the next several days. This was authorized full-time billing.

'So what about your role?'

Hardy smiled. 'I'll keep my finger in, but I've got other commitments, and this thing has been eating up all my time – it's way too much for one person to handle.'

'But you'll still be on it? I'm reporting to you, not David?'

Hardy nodded. 'The buck still stops here.'

'Where?'

They turned to see Freeman, just back from court, a sartorial mess as usual, standing in the doorway. 'Where does the buck stop? With you? You stealing my associates?'

Hardy nodded. 'As we discussed. Michelle's going to help me out with Tryptech. She said she had the time.'

Out of force of habit Freeman glared at them both, but then he focused on Michelle and his look softened. 'Watch this man,' he said, 'he's unorthodox and dangerous.'

Freeman reached into his breast pocket and extracted a cigar. Thoughtfully, he bit off the end, spit the tip into his hand, and deposited it into one of the potted plants. Finally, he spoke to Hardy. 'When's the last time you saw Graham Russo?'

'After lunch,' Hardy replied. 'Couple of hours ago in jail. Why?'

Freeman was famous for his dramatic flair in the courtroom. He played it out now, lighting his cigar, taking his time, exhaling a long plume. 'Nobody's called you?'

Hardy didn't like the sound of this. 'No, nobody's called me. Quit the games, David, what's going on? Is Graham all right?' He was up out of his chair.

'I'd say he's probably better than the last time you saw him. The word at the Hall was they were letting him go. I'd've thought somebody would've called you.'

'In a startling development today, District Attorney Sharron Pratt has announced in a special press briefing that she has declined to file charges against Graham Russo, the lawyer and former federal court clerk who'd been arrested in the apparent assisted suicide of his father, Sal.'

Hardy sat in the Little Shamrock at the far end of the bar, watching the television above it. It was still light outside the wide front windows, though traffic had thinned out on Lincoln Boulevard. Frannie would be here soon to meet him for the sacred and traditional Date Night – nearly every Wednesday since they'd been married. They would most often meet at the Shamrock – Hardy would drive halfway home, Frannie would cab it halfway downtown – and go someplace for dinner, maybe a movie, some live music.

Hardy sipped his stout and glanced up again at the tube.

Pratt's face filled the screen, the six-second sound bite all the pols lived for. 'I've read the file on this case and the autopsy revealed an advanced, irreversible brain tumor. Mr Russo was in great pain with no hope of recovery, and whoever helped ease him from this mortal coil should be congratulated, not prosecuted.'

Frannie was suddenly at his elbow, a married kiss on the

cheek, pulling up the stool next to him as the television reeled her in.

The pretty young newscaster was continuing. 'Right-to-die groups across the country have already begun applauding the DA's action, while police officials here in the city refused to comment on Graham Russo's arrest or subsequent release. Russo's attorney, Dismas Hardy, who denied his client had killed anybody, said Mr Russo had no plans to sue the city for false arrest, so that *may* be the end of this episode, but sources at the Hall of Justice say they wouldn't be too sure of that.'

'That would be you,' Frannie said. 'Dismas Hardy, not the sources at the Hall of Justice.'

'That's me,' he agreed. 'Fame and glory.'

But the story wasn't over. The screen widened to include the Serious Anchor. 'One thing seems certain, though, Donna – the district attorney's controversial decision will inflame the already heated national debate over assisted suicide.'

'That's a good bet, Phil. This was a political broadside by Sharron Pratt. No doubt of it. It's going to have ripple effect.'

Phil nodded sagely and met the camera's eye. 'And meanwhile, our Bay Area Action News team has learned that the state attorney general's office has not ruled out its own investigation into Sal Russo's death. Graham Russo is a free man tonight, but who can say for how long?'

'Who indeed, Phil?'

Hardy stood and went around behind the bar. He reached up and turned off the television. 'How can there be so many idiots? Where do they come from?'

'How'd you get Graham out of jail so fast?' Frannie asked.

So it didn't look as though the old TV-as-cultural-nemesis distraction was going to work with his wife tonight. He'd have to develop a new technique. 'I didn't,' Hardy replied. 'He just got out. Pratt let him go. What are you drinking?'

Frannie was white-wining, and Hardy waved Alan off and poured it himself while he was behind the bar. He went to the jukebox and put on Van Morrison. 'Moondance' was thirty years old and still sounded to Hardy as though it had been recorded yesterday.

He pulled up next to Frannie. A better kiss. 'Okay,' he said, looking at his watch, 'it is seven oh four and we are officially on a date. Now, for the record, I didn't do anything with Graham Russo. Well, that's not true. I talked to him in jail. How were the kids today?'

'Notice the clever way he tries to change the subject.' Frannie sipped her wine. He had to admit it, she was good, sticking right to the subject at hand. 'The kids were fine. Nobody broke any bones. They had two fights after school, one less than usual. Do you think you and I ought to talk about Graham Russo? I thought if he went to jail you were out of it.'

'I did too.' Hardy tipped his glass up. 'Then he went to jail.' A shrug. 'I couldn't just drop him.'

'No, you wouldn't be able to do that.' Frannie sighed. 'So how did he get out? You really had nothing to do with it?'

'*Nada*. Pratt just let him go. You heard Donna and Phil, so it's got to be true. It was political.'

'I also heard the case wasn't over.'

'That may also be true. In fact, I'm pretty sure of it. But I'm not certain he killed his father at all.'

Frannie put her glass down. 'I thought he did. I thought that was a given.'

'You're not alone.'

'So what did happen?'

'I don't know. I get the impression he might be protecting some doctor, somebody he knows. Maybe one of his family. He's adamant he didn't kill his dad or help him kill himself.'

She reached over and covered his hand with hers. 'But, Dismas, don't all clients say that, especially at first?'

'Yeah,' he admitted. 'Still . . .'

'Still you want to believe him.'

He shrugged. 'I don't know. I'm intrigued, I guess.' Suddenly, he snapped his fingers and jumped up.

'What?' Frannie asked.

He was behind the bar, rummaging. 'Something I just remembered,' he said, pulling out the phone book, opening it on the bar.

'Who are you looking for?'

He ran a finger down the page. 'Singleterry,' he said. 'There's only four of them. No Joan, though.' He told Frannie about the money, about Graham's explanation, where Sal had wanted it to go. 'Do you mind if I make a call or two? You have another glass of wine? The phone's right up front there, you can watch me the whole time.'

'A thrill a minute,' she said. 'Dismas, are we on a date? Are you working now?' But she touched his hand again. 'It's all right. Go.'

In five minutes he was back, frowning.

'What?'

'Two of them were home and both of them said I was the second person asking about Joan in the last three days. They didn't know any Joan.'

'Okay?'

'Which means that Graham had called looking for her. Which means maybe he didn't make up the story about the money.'

'And what does that mean?'

'I don't know, Fran. It might mean he was telling the truth.'

Sarah Evans gave herself an hour to sulk about Graham Russo's release. It bothered her that she'd gone to all the trouble of investigating and then arresting him, and then the DA had simply let him go. She could fume for the rest of her life if she wanted. But she reminded herself it was only one case in what she hoped would be her long career. And she had done her job. No one had found any fault with her.

The rest of it – Pratt's decision, the AG's response – all of that was out of her control.

It wasn't going to ruin her life, or even her night.

In fact, part of her was almost relieved. She'd thought Graham Russo was about the most attractive man she'd ever met and she hated to think that someone so good looking could be evil inside. That was superficial of her, she knew, and there were a million examples to the contrary, but before she and Marcel had started finding things at Graham's apartment, she almost allowed herself to feel some kind of connection with the suspect. They were about the same age. He was a lawyer and, like her, a jock.

She had felt his eyes on her. Stupid, but it had been there. It was the first time she'd felt that kind of easy attraction in five years or more. More.

But – a cop to her bones – she wasn't above using that attraction to get Graham to open up to her, as she'd done at his place. She could smile and feign enthrallment with his every word, and what made it work was that it wasn't *all* acting.

And maybe, when she thought about it, it had been as Pratt had thought – Graham helping his father out of his misery. If that had been the case, Sarah didn't necessarily have a problem with it. She had doctor friends who'd told her about pulling the plug at the request of anguished relatives of suffering patients. She didn't think the practice ought to be institutionalized, lest it be abused, but she understood it privately.

Or maybe Graham hadn't been any part of it. Even Strout's autopsy, she had to admit, called the death suicide/homicide equivocal. In other words, Sal *might have* killed himself. The forensic evidence didn't rule out that possibility. In any event, it was behind her now, and she wasn't going to think about it, not tonight. Her softball team had a game.

She lived alone in a two-bedroom over a grocery store on the corner of Balboa and Fifteenth Avenue. When she opened the door, she stopped on her landing, loving the unusual – in San Francisco, almost unheard of – feel of a warm night. It was great to be in the yellow nylon Blazers shirt, the dark-green shorts, the yellow knee socks. She yanked the gold baseball cap with the green *B* down over her hair, pulled her ponytail through the adjusting slot in the back.

Forget the cop world. She was thirty-two years old, in great shape. She had the job she wanted and had worked for, but it didn't rule her every waking moment. She knew it might, though, if she didn't have other interests.

That was one of the reasons she played serious, organized women's softball. It relieved the stress. It also guaranteed that she maintained her separate existence outside of the world defined by the Hall of Justice.

She caught a glimpse of herself in the grocery window as she passed it on the way to her car. She looked about eighteen. Life was good. The ball was going to carry a mile.

7

'Oh, Graham, thank God you're all right!'

His mother, Helen, rushed down the steps of the Manor in the exclusive Seacliff neighborhood on the northwest rim of San Francisco. He was only halfway up the slate walkway that bisected the enormous sloping lawn, and she ran down to greet him in the warm evening. She barely came up to his neck, but held his shoulders in her hands and pressed her cheek against his chest, a hug.

He put his arms around her and waited. The door to the Manor still hung open, but no one else appeared.

The skin on his mother's face was as smooth as marble. Though he knew that several cosmetic surgeries stretched it to its limits, the results so far were seamless; she looked a decade younger than her age. This, Graham knew, was fortunate given the person she was married to, the role she played.

Helen had always attracted men, with her wide-set blue eyes, high cheekbones, cornsilk hair. Now, in the warm dusk, dressed in tailored pants and a scoop-necked blue cotton blouse, she could have been Graham's girlfriend, not his mother. Beyond a doubt, on the outside she was a beautiful woman, as befitted Leland Taylor's trophy wife.

He wondered if the mom she used to be when she was with Sal, when he'd adored her, before their lives had changed – he wondered if she had looked the same. In his memory her face had had a different quality back then, a softness. It wasn't the one he was looking at now.

She pulled away and gazed up at him, a hand softly up to his cheek. 'You look tired, Graham. They didn't hurt you down there, did they?'

'It wasn't even a day, Mom. In and out.'

'We would have come to see you – to the jail, I mean – but we didn't know how you . . . we thought your lawyer would tell us something, but we never heard from him at all. I don't think we know him, Dismas Hardy, do we? What kind of name is that, Dismas? But it *was* a mistake, after all, wasn't it?'

He leaned over and kissed her. 'It was all a mistake,' he said. He met her eyes. 'All of it, Mom. Every bit. I didn't kill Sal. I didn't help him die.'

A brief flash of perfect teeth. She took his arm and started steering him up the walkway. 'Of course you didn't. Now come on up. The family needs to talk about this. I'm so glad you could come right over.'

After Hardy had dropped Graham back at his apartment, he'd played back his mother's message. It was the last of a half dozen on his answering machine – she'd called after his release had made the news. He'd taken a quick shower to wash away the jail. Within twenty minutes he'd been on his way to the Manor.

But the message had given him the impression only that his mother had been worried about him. She wanted to see him to make sure he was all right. Apparently, though, this was a misreading. 'The whole family's here?'

So his mother's real purpose in running out to greet him, he realized, was to warn him what to expect when he entered the house, calm him down if he exploded. This was how it had always worked. He was the hothead, the emotional one. Most of the time Mom could neutralize him before he raised his voice or caused anyone to feel any embarrassment, the two cardinal sins in Leland Taylor's home.

'We decided earlier today to get together, Graham, after they'd arrested you.' Holding his arm – protectively? to restrain him? – she stopped walking and looked up at him. 'We thought we needed a strategy on how to deal with this, this whole situation.'

Graham recognized his stepfather's involvement in this move. Leland Taylor probably strategized before he washed his hands.

'Present a united front, you know.'

'To who?'

But his mother continued, ignoring the question. 'And then when you got out—'

'You were all naturally so relieved . . .'

'Graham. Of course we were. Don't be like that.'

'I hope Leland didn't lose any business over the scandal. But, oh, that's right then, why would he? My last name's different. Nobody would have to know. That's what this meeting's about, isn't it? Keeping a lid on it.'

'No.' His mother had been given her marching orders and she was a soldier. No wavering. 'Emphatically not, Graham. We were worried about you.'

'Which explains why everybody rushed on down to jail to see how they could help.'

Exasperated, his mother shook his head. 'I've already explained that.' She stopped one last time at the foot of the stairs that led up to the grand double-doored entrance. 'Please don't be difficult, Graham. Try to understand.'

He looked down at his mother's face. Was it ravished or ravishing beauty? He could no longer tell. Of course, there were no worry lines. Lasers had erased them. He did think – hope? — he read some concern in her eyes, but he couldn't tell for sure if it was for him or the mission upon which she had been dispatched, and which seemed now to be tottering on the brink of failure.

Helen Taylor's husband's family money came from banking. Roland Taylor had founded Baywest Bank in the late forties. Leland senior carried the torch for three decades through the late fifties and had passed it to his only son by the early eighties. Over the years the bank had merged and gobbled and steadily grown.

For a San Francisco entity it was remarkably conservative. The bank did not prefer to lend money to new or small businesses. It did not have a woman or person of color beyond middle management. It did not run touchy-feely ads on the television and had an all but open disdain for, as George called it, the 'passbook crowd.'

No, Baywest was most comfortable with institutional lending, financing deals cut by men who wore suits at all times during the business day, belonged to exclusive country clubs, traded secrets behind closed doors. The bank knew a lot of secrets. And now Leland junior was at the helm. His stepson, George Russo, though only twenty-seven years old, was a first vice-president.

Through French doors, the formal dining room at the Manor was a couple of elegant steps down from the music room. Neither Leland nor Helen played, but this hadn't stopped them from purchasing the nine-foot Steinway grand and customizing it with a digital box that played classical music at the flip of a switch. After it had been installed, the couple had discovered that the natural sound of the piano was a little loud for dinner music, so they'd added the French doors to muffle it somewhat.

Now the piano was silent, but the doors were closed anyway. Leland Taylor did not want any staff to be privy to family discussions. Knowledge might be power, he'd often say, but secrecy thrills the soul.

The dining room was round as a plate, the cherry table within it an elongated oval that easily seated eighteen. Tonight, with the unusually beautiful weather, Leland ordered the drapes pulled back. Through the wraparound windows this afforded a view that extended from the Farallon Islands, clearly visible twenty-seven nautical miles off the Golden Gate, all the way around the city to the Bay Bridge and the coast range beyond. Only a few degrees to the right of due north, the spires of the Golden Gate Bridge seemed to float over the headland.

But no one in the room showed any interest in the view.

At the end of the table closest to the music room, Leland Taylor sat next to his wife. They weren't, after all, having dinner, although coffee had been set out, some cookies. Leland was dressed in a dark charcoal suit, a red-and-blue rep tie. He always wore a plain white dress shirt. ('A white shirt says you're the boss.') Graham thought of him as six generations of British inbreeding, and this wasn't too inaccurate. He was tall and lean, with watery blue eyes, a thickish upper lip, skin reminiscent of pink crepe.

A couple of chairs down to Leland's right – not, God forbid, directly next to anyone – Graham's sister, Debra, and her husband, Brendan McCoury, tried and pretty much failed to act nonchalant in the face of all this opulence. Debra had grown up here, but her life situation had changed. This was nothing like home anymore.

Brendan had what a portion of the world – although not Leland's – would call a good job as an electrical contractor. Debra was a veterinarian's assistant. Because she was a woman –

not a particularly stunning or charismatic one at that – to Leland she essentially did not exist. Her presence, and especially Brendan's, was suffered because in Leland's view this qualified as family business and Debra technically belonged.

George, like his older brother, Graham, was a big man, well put together. In his three-piece gabardine he commanded the far end of the table, drinking Heineken from a chilled Pilsner glass. Two more bottles were on ice in a small designer cooler on the table next to him.

The entire left-hand side of the table was Graham's. 'As a matter of fact,' he was answering Leland's opening question, 'it must be pretty obvious that I didn't know this arrest was coming. Otherwise, I would have called you all and set up something like this to go over the estate.'

'Yes, the estate.' Leland kept a sneer off his face, but Graham heard it. 'We were surprised to learn of the fifty thousand dollars, Graham. How did Sal get that kind of money? Surely not selling fish. That's what I'd be interested to know.'

'It's not coming to any of us, so what difference does it make?'

'What are you talking about, not coming to us?' This was George. He spoke quietly, but nobody was fooled. 'It gets divided three ways if there's no will. I looked it up. And there wasn't a will, was there?'

Graham had resolved to stay calm. He picked up one of the cookies and took a bite to slow himself down. 'Not as such, but there—'

'Excuse me,' Leland interrupted mildly, 'but if there was no will, Graham, how is it that you are the executor?'

Debra interrupted *him*. 'I read it was wrapped.' Debra was holding her husband's hand out on the table. Living in the shadow of her stunning, social-climbing mother, she had long ago decided not to compete and now, at twenty-nine, was not so much unattractive as unadorned. She wore no makeup of any kind. Her hair had once shone like Helen's, but she'd elected not to dye it, and now it was a drab strawberry-blond. She was also five months pregnant and her face had broken out. 'What does that mean, wrapped? Where did Sal get wrapped bills? And what were you planning to do with the baseball cards? Steal them too?'

Graham nodded across the table at his sister. 'Yeah, Deb. I

was going to steal them. I was trying to screw everybody.'

'Just like usual,' George said.

Graham turned down the table, a dangerous smile in place. 'Fuck you.'

Leland tapped the table for order. 'Now, now. Let's keep it civil, can we?'

'Sure,' Graham said. His hand was shaking and the coffee threatened to overspill the rim of his cup. He carefully put it down in the saucer. 'You know, guys, I haven't had my all-time best day, spending it as I did in jail accused of murdering my father. Then I come here and we play dump on Graham. But I'll tell you what. You can all go to hell. I don't need this abuse.'

From the time he'd been a child, when Graham got angry enough, tears came to his eyes. He wasn't going to have that happen now, or at least he wasn't going to let his siblings see it. Trying to maintain some dignity, though, he wasn't about to bolt from the table either. Focusing on the ceiling, he was blinking hard, pushing back his chair, when his mother suddenly spoke sharply, stopping him.

'For God's sake. Children, stop. Sit down, Graham! Please. Sit down. You're right. We're all just a little overwrought. You know that. It's been a very emotional time.'

An uneasy silence.

Leland took over again, the voice of reason. 'Your mother's right, all of you. It's been a difficult week all around.' He cast harsh glances at Debra and George, shutting them up. 'No one means to accuse you of anything, Graham. But we have some questions and I'm sure that you have answers. We don't mean to grill you, but they do seem important, don't they?'

Graham had moved back up to the table. He'd folded his hands in front of him. He was unaware of it, but his knuckles burned white from the pressure. 'You know, Leland, frankly, they don't. Frankly,' he repeated, 'I can't understand why Georgie here—'

'George,' his younger brother corrected him.

'Sure,' Graham said. 'George. Why *George* here cares at all about fifty thousand dollars, or even a third of it, which he's not going to get anyway because Dad wanted it to go to someone else.'

'Well, that's one of the questions,' Leland retorted. 'Who did your father want this money to go to?'

Down at his end George did his Leland impression, slapping the table three times. 'First, I think I'd rather talk about why I shouldn't care about seventeen thousand dollars. That's a lot of money.'

Graham threw him a withering look. 'What do you make a year, George – one thirty, one fifty?'

'What difference does that make?'

'It makes a difference how much you need seventeen thousand dollars.'

'Yeah, that's the way you think, all right, but it's not a question of how much I need it. That's completely irrelevant. The issue is that it's mine, whether I need it or not.'

Graham had that dangerous smile again. 'You know, Georgie, you're turning into a fine banker. And it's not yours anyway.'

Petulantly, his sister spoke up again. 'Well, regardless of George, *we* need it. It's a lot of money to us.'

Next to Debra, Brendan stiffened. If there was one thing Graham knew about Debra's husband – and he knew more than he wanted to – it was that Brendan didn't want or need anybody's help, financial or otherwise, ever. He was a man and he did it his way, on his own, no matter what. 'We're doing all right,' he insisted. 'We don't need it.'

'We do *too*, Bren!'

'Don't argue with me,' McCoury said. He appeared to be fighting the urge to strike her.

But Leland wasn't going to referee marital disputes. He tapped the table again. 'Excuse me, Debra. I don't think Graham has given us Sal's intentions here regarding this money.'

'Excuse *me*, Leland' – George again, the mimic – 'but Sal's intentions don't matter. If he didn't write a will, Graham can do whatever he wants with his third, but Debra and I get ours. That's the law and he knows it.'

Outside, the sun had gone down and a mother-of-pearl sky was fast going dark. Graham's patience – not his strong suit to begin with – was at an end. He couldn't imagine that his father's money would make even the slightest difference to George's life. Debra's, perhaps, for a short time.

His eyes swept the table quickly. This was his nuclear family. More, after Sal's death, it was every relative he knew on earth, and he felt no connection to any of them.

How had they all come to this? he wondered. What had made the family go so wrong?

Maybe there had never been any hope for them, he thought. Maybe the incompatibility ran so deep, it was structural.

For as long as he could remember, the conflict between Sal and Helen had been apparent. When he'd been very young, Graham hadn't been able to understand the causes of it, but even to the young boy there had been an obvious discrepancy simply in the way his mother and father *were* – in their very natures, it seemed – fundamental problems that went deeper than mere differences in the way they did things.

Sal was a second-generation Italian who grew up speaking the language in his home. He loved working with his hands, painting, fixing things, drinking, fishing, being with the guys, telling dirty jokes, and laughing out loud. He played party songs on his accordion. Darkly handsome with a wicked smile, Sal exuded physical confidence. He hugged even his male friends, kissed his wife in public, pinched her ass from time to time.

He was also a talented athlete. Like his son Graham after him, he had been signed to play baseball out of college; the Baltimore Orioles had given him a signing bonus of $35,000. Like his son – as with the great majority of players – he never made the big leagues. At Helen's urging, though, he'd saved his bonus, and had used it to buy his boat.

Helen had been raised on a different cultural plane. Her parents, Richard and Elizabeth (emphatically *not* Dick and Betsy) Raessler, were well-known jewelers. Helen had gone to Town School, the most prestigious private school in the city. She grew up in fine restaurants, at the opera, theater, symphonies, museums. She was a fine equestrienne – British style – and an outstanding cook.

By the time she was eighteen, she'd been to Europe with her parents five times, to the Far East twice. She met Leland Taylor while they both were in high school, and her parents considered him the perfect match for her, although believing they both should wait until a more seemly age.

Richard and Elizabeth had been torn by Helen's desire to attend Lone Mountain College, an independent institution but, informally, the women's adjunct to the University of San Francisco. They would have much preferred one of the eastern women's colleges – Vassar, Brown – for cultural as well as protective reasons. Lone Mountain was run by nuns and, the Raesslers suspected, those crafty Jesuits.

Plus, Catholics were a much more rowdy group than Helen was used to.

On the other hand, Lone Mountain was close by. Their girl would be at hand and they could keep an eye on her. They would just have to keep her insulated from the riffraff, some of the working-class young men from across the street at USF.

And of course Helen went and fell in love with one of them.

It was 1965 and Helen was a freshman. Sal was finishing his senior year after a hitch in Vietnam, so to Helen he also possessed that indefinable cachet of the 'older man' – she was eighteen to his twenty-five.

To say that Richard and Elizabeth were not pleased would be a considerable understatement. When she became pregnant at the end of that first summer, before she and Sal were even officially engaged, they counseled their daughter to get an abortion.

But Helen and Sal wouldn't have that. They were in love, they would get married and raise their family. When she eloped with the jock fisherman, the Raesslers cut their daughter off.

The slow thaw in relations between the families began at the birth of Graham, a name that, like George and Debra, did not exactly sing with Sal's Italian heritage. It had been Richard's father's name, and Helen persuaded Sal that they should present it – their first child's name – to her parents as a type of peace offering. Reluctantly, he'd agreed, although the peace never really extended to Sal.

A creeping bribery began. Elizabeth would buy nice clothes for the children and deliver them during the day, when she wouldn't have to see their father.

Clothes, shoes, Christmas gifts, bicycles. Finally, Richard and Elizabeth wanted their grandchildren to grow up in a safe neighborhood, with the right kind of playmates. They weren't trying to influence their daughter against her husband. No, it wasn't anything like that. Sal would grow to be comfortable in Seacliff. They would put the down payment on a suitable place and Sal and Helen would make the monthly payments. It wasn't a loan or charity. They were sharing equity, that was all. It was a partnership.

Sal hated all of this, but he told himself he couldn't blame Helen if her parents remained important to her. He let it go on, thinking it a compromise. He was being reasonable, forgiving. It wasn't so divisive.

Sal was wrong.

By the time Graham was old enough to notice, the difference in his parents was pronounced. Six days a week, before the sun was up, Sal was off fishing in the *Signing Bonus*. On Sundays he'd play some kind of sports with Graham and Georgie, except when the weather was prohibitive. On those days he'd go out to the garage and paint or drink or both.

In the meanwhile Helen had begun to see her parents more often. The clothes and other gifts had become a way of life. She would often meet her mother for lunch. Sometimes a childhood girlfriend of Helen's would be invited – always a fashionable young woman married to her doctor or lawyer or accountant – or banker. Leland Taylor might show up and say hello, might inquire after her children.

Sal drew the line at accepting cash money from the Raesslers, but the pressure never let up. He kept thinking that if he could just get ahead on his own, he'd have the legs on which to take a stand. As it was, though, times were always tight. Proud and house poor, Sal could barely keep up with the monthly payments on the Manor.

By the time Graham was thirteen, the foundations of the marriage had begun to erode, but the collapse of the whole structure, when he was fifteen, happened with a jarring suddenness. From Graham's perspective, one day Sal stopped going to work and the next he was gone from their lives. Completely cut off, as though he'd died.

In less than a year Helen had married again. To spare the children the trauma of another relocation, of more changes and domestic upheaval, Leland Taylor had moved into the Manor.

Perhaps finally, Graham thought, any real reconciliation between the Russo and the Raessler genes was hopeless. The schism was too profound. He was a Russo all the way, Sal's kid. Debra and George were Helen's.

Frustrated and angry, Graham pushed his coffee cup away from him, sharply blew out a breath. 'I'd like a show of hands,' he said. 'Does anybody here care at all that Sal Russo died last Friday? That *your father* is dead. Has that made an impression on anybody here?'

Across the table Debra's lip trembled at the question, while down at the far end George leaned forward. 'Oh, please. Yeah, we're heartbroken, can't you see? He was such a great dad, always there when you needed him.'

'Shut up, George,' Debra said. 'Don't talk about him like that.'

'Why not?' He raised his voice. 'Why the hell not?' The younger brother stood up, nearly knocking his chair over behind him. His eyes were bright with anger. 'You want us to feel bad that he died? I'll tell you what – I feel good about it. Relieved. Do you have any idea the hell he's put Mom through these last few months?'

Helen held up a hand to stop George, but nothing was stopping George, not now. 'You don't know anything about that, do you, Graham? All this late-in-the-day touchy-feely nonsense about dear old Dad, and you don't have a clue the torture he was putting your own mother through.'

'No. I didn't know that. What—?'

Leland was firmer than Helen had been. He rapped sharply on the table. 'We don't need to speak of that, George. It's over now. It did no lasting harm.'

'What didn't?'

George's blood was up. He sneered at his older brother. 'As if you care.'

'I might if you'd tell me what it is.'

'Dad came by here, that's what. He was threatening Mom—'

'I don't believe that. That's not true.'

Leland again. 'George.'

But the young man couldn't be stopped. 'You think anybody

believes this deathbed conversion of yours, Graham? You think all of us don't see right through it?'

Leland tapped the table and said, 'Son, please,' but he might have saved his breath.

George was advancing toward Graham, who was out of his own chair now. 'You know and I know – hell, we all know – he was a lousy father and husband and human being. He *deserted* us, Graham, all of us, maybe it slipped your mind. What happened was you found out he had some money. And after you blew off your law career, you knew you weren't getting any more out of Leland, didn't you? You thought you'd squeeze some cash out of old Sal. Wasn't that it?'

George had closed to within two feet of Graham. His face had gone red. Suddenly he was on him, pushing at him, backing him up, shouting, spittle flying from his lips. 'Tell me that wasn't it, you lying son of bitch! Tell me it wasn't—'

Graham pushed back, hard. His brother's leg caught the side of a chair. Graham, pressing his advantage, pushed again, and George went down.

Everyone else was up as Graham whirled around, a hand out in warning. No one should come any closer. George was on his feet again, glaring.

Graham held them all back. His breath was coming in gasps. He took a last look around the table, at his family. Then, half running, the tears threatening to break again, he was past his mother and stepfather, up the steps through the French doors, and gone.

The Blazers had formed a line in the infield. Sarah Evans, who'd run in from left field after the last out, was at the end of the line. 'Good game,' she repeated as each of the Wombats came by her, slapping palms. And they said it back to her. It was a ritual, a nod to sportsmanship – they played hard, sure, but everyone realized it was just a game. You congratulated the other team on a good one and then you went home.

The dugout area was a bench behind a low fence, and the Blazers filed into it to grab their bats and equipment bags and clear out for the next team. Sarah, recounting the highlights of the game with some of the other women, suddenly stopped talking and focused on Graham Russo standing behind the fence in his Big Dog T-shirt and Giants hat. Staring at her.

Grabbing her bag – she had her gun in it – she walked out of the dugout and around the fence, up to him.

He smiled easily. 'I thought that was you. I was pretty sure, actually.'

'Did you follow me here?'

The question seemed to surprise him. 'No.'

'How did you know I was here, then?'

She wished her heart would stop its pounding. She could feel the light nylon fabric of her jersey pulsing to its rhythm.

'I didn't,' he said. 'I grabbed a burger at the beach and came here to watch a few games, take my mind off some things.'

'Yeah, I'll bet.'

He broke another smile. 'I was cooped up inside most of the day, maybe you heard. It was such a nice night, I thought I'd sit outside awhile. I got a six-pack back in the stands, if you feel like a beer. Watch the late game.'

She shook her head. 'I don't think so. I don't think we ought to be seeing each other. If you think you're scaring me showing up here, you're wrong. It's a bad idea, stalking a cop. I'll put you back in jail so fast, you'll forget you ever got out. I hope you're hearing me.'

A couple of her teammates were passing them on the way to the parking lot. They heard the sharp tone and stopped. 'Everything all right, Sarah?'

'Sure. Fine.' She turned back to Graham. 'You stay away from me,' she said quietly. Then, to her teammates, 'Wait up, I'm coming.'

There were four softball diamonds, one in each corner of the enormous field. Sarah's game had been on #2, closest to the parking lot, and she could sit in her car and see Graham clearly in the stands – ten rows of raised benches – behind home plate.

With her windows down she watched him for twenty minutes. He appeared to be engrossed in the game, occasionally drinking from his can of beer. At least, she told herself, he hadn't made any move to follow her out to the parking lot. She thought his plan might have been to let her get a head start, then light out after her. But he hadn't even glanced after her when she'd left. He'd gone back to watch the next games as he'd said he was going to. Maybe he was telling the truth.

Which didn't mean he hadn't followed her here. He might have already found out what he wanted – where she lived and played. On the other hand, she told herself, his own explanation made sense. He'd been in jail all day and the city possibly wouldn't have a nicer night for the rest of the nineties.

She opened her car door and grabbed her equipment bag. Pulling a light warm-up jacket on over her jersey, she crossed the dark space between the parking lot and the stands.

She stood awhile longer, watching him. He was sitting forward, hunched over, his elbows on his knees, his hands dwarfing the can of beer he held between them. His T-shirt stretched itself tightly over the muscles of his back.

The DA had let him go. He wasn't charged with anything. She could go down and sit with him and there would be no grounds for any professional complaint. She rationalized another half-lie for herself – that he might make a verbal slip with some beer inside him and say something incriminating. She was still in cop mode, working. That's why she was staying around, why it was defensible to go talk with him.

On the field a young man hit a ball well over three hundred feet, outside the circle of the diamond's lights. Graham was on his feet, following the trajectory, his face alight with excitement, lost in the moment. It was a child's look – unguarded, simple, innocent, pure. A doubt flashed briefly in her consciousness: could someone who had committed a murder summon such an expression? She didn't think so.

She'd changed out of her cleats and now wore running shoes, which made no noise as she walked down the benches. She sat down next to him.

'Okay, I'll have that beer.'

He glanced over, his face showing nothing. Casually, he reached under him and pulled up a can, popping the top, handing it to her. 'You see that hit?' he asked.

She tipped the can. 'That letter from your dad,' she said, 'you were playing pro baseball?'

He didn't answer right away. On the field the shortstop went deep into the hole for a ground ball, flipped it back to second, then on to first for a double play. It ended the half inning.

Graham finished up his beer. 'I thought I could hook on as a replacement during the strike. I couldn't.' He risked a look at her. 'I really didn't follow you,' he said. 'This is where I come sometimes, that's all. Then I saw you, watched you play a little. I figured, what the hell, we're both here, I might as well say hello. It didn't occur to me you'd think I'd followed you.'

'But I arrested you.'

Graham nodded, a smile tugging at his lips. 'I did notice that.'

'Most people,' she said, 'you arrest them, they don't like you anymore.'

'But then they let me go. They're not charging me. So you and me, we're both citizens.'

'I don't think so, not exactly. I'm still a cop. You're still a suspect.'

He chewed on that for a beat, then shrugged it off. 'Well, guess what? I myself am an officer of the court. And P.S., I didn't kill my father.' He indicated the field. 'You play pretty good, Sergeant. I saw your triple.'

She found herself loosening up. 'Most exciting offensive play in the game.'

'So my dad said.'

'You still think so?'

'Sure.'

'Me too.'

'Well, there.' Graham pulled another beer from underneath his seat, popped the top. 'Something else we've got in common. You want another one?'

She'd nearly finished the first. Sarah had never been much of a drinker, and she was already feeling the slow warmth of even so little alcohol beginning to spread. 'I'd better not,' she said. 'I've got to be going. Work starts early.'

'I remember,' he said.

She hesitated another couple of seconds, taken aback by his ready acquiescence, surprised at the act of will it took for her to stand. 'Thanks for the beer,' she said.

He nodded. She'd gone off a couple of steps when he stopped her. 'Sergeant Evans?'

She turned.

'What's your first name?'

Her face clouded, then suddenly cleared. She shook her head, laughing at herself, then met his eyes. 'Sarah.'

'Sarah,' he repeated. His smile seemed completely genuine. Endearing. 'I love that name.'

Back in her car, she checked her face in the rearview mirror. She felt absurdly pleased with herself and wondered if it showed. So what? Graham Russo liked her name. Big deal.

The warmth had spread. She told herself it was the alcohol. She'd better be careful driving home.

PART TWO

8

Great rivers may begin with a tiny trickle, but the creation of an avalanche does not occur in the same way, where one snowflake adheres to another and the growing mass slowly coalesces until it simply begins to fall over itself. No, an avalanche just *happens* – all at once the side of a mountain gives way, coming loose with explosive force, unstoppable and indiscriminate, rearranging the landscape of everything in the path of its inanimate will.

By two A.M. on Thursday morning, less than eight hours after Graham Russo's release from jail, the momentum of the avalanche had pushed every other issue in San Francisco off the political map. By that hour the early-morning edition of the *San Francisco Chronicle* was coming off the press with the banner headline: 'Mercy Killing Debate Rips City, State Offices.' The long story merely scratched at the surface of the many fronts on which the battle had erupted simultaneously.

The mayor supported the district attorney. San Francisco had always been in the forefront of social awareness. Sharron Pratt had done the right thing. People shouldn't be forced to live in unrelenting pain. Where was the quality in a life like that? If a person chose to take his or her own life to end their suffering, they had the right to do so, and the people who helped them were not murderers. They were heroes.

Dan Rigby, the city's chief of police, was outraged. This was the latest and most serious example of the DA's utter disdain for the police who kept the city safe. His officers had acted correctly in arresting a homicide suspect. There was no evidence that the death of Sal Russo had been anything but a murder in the course of a robbery.

But even if it had been an assisted suicide, 'The DA is elected to enforce the laws, not make them. I shudder to wonder what other kinds of homicides Ms Pratt is going to decide are not crimes.'

Dean Powell, the state attorney general, was studying the case, refusing to disclose, or foreclose, any of his options. Art Drysdale, formerly of the DA's office (and fired by Pratt) and now with the state attorney general, would only comment that 'as a matter of law it's unambiguous that we have jurisdictional responsibility. We're not going to let murders go unpunished in San Francisco.'

The Board of Supervisors called an emergency session for late in the evening, and declared by a 9 to 2 majority that San Francisco should be a 'right-to-die' haven – the country needed a humanitarian city that would become a mecca for the terminally ill and hopelessly suffering.

The Catholics and the Protestants wasted no time squaring off. Archbishop James Flaherty reiterated the stand of the Catholic Church on any form of euthanasia. God took His children when it was His time. Jesus himself had suffered horribly, Flaherty said, and that he had allowed himself to do so was meant clearly to serve as an example to all of humanity: suffering was part of life. It had a purpose. It ennobled and strengthened the spirit, especially when offered up to the glory of God.

The archbishop ended his remarks with a not-so-subtle dig at the mayor's stand on 'quality of life.' 'Life is a sacred thing unto itself,' he said. 'A quality life is a life lived in the service of God, not in the pursuit of comfort.'

At first light, from the altar of Grace Cathedral on Nob Hill, with the huge AIDS mosaic on the floor, and AIDS blankets hung from the rafters, the Right Reverend Cecil Dunsmuir fired his own broadside back at Flaherty to his own bank of cameras.

'Anyone who could extol the virtue of suffering ought to spend more time with our AIDS community. Here he will find great caring, great love, great sacrifice, and great nobility in the face of death. But the end of pain is a blessing from God, and administering to that end is the true meaning of Christianity.'

Police had to be called to a meeting of a previously planned antiabortion protest group at an Elks Hall in Potrero Heights when differences on the morality of mercy killing erupted into a melee among the activists.

Barbara Brandt was an attractive woman in her late thirties who made her living as a Sacramento lobbyist. As the state's chairperson of the Hemlock Society, the national right-to-die organization, Brandt saw Graham Russo's picture on the front page of *The Sacramento Bee* – young and movie-star handsome – and, after reading the story, realized that here was this year's poster boy for major fund-raising.

She looked up Graham's number in the telephone book and was a bit surprised when he picked up on the second ring.

'I'm really not interested in talking about it,' he told her after a couple of minutes. 'I'm a lawyer, you know. If I break the law, they'll yank my bar card. I've already had enough problems with my career.'

'But you did the right thing,' Brandt persisted.

'You don't know what I did.'

'Yes, I do,' she said. 'I know just what you did. I'm on your side.'

But it wasn't any use. He wasn't budging. After he hung up, she considered it for several minutes. She'd heard enough to know the truth. Graham's law career would be over before it had begun if he admitted he'd helped kill his dad.

But he'd done the right thing; he'd already committed his civil disobedience. All he needed now, Brandt thought, was the courage to admit what he'd done. And she thought she could help him find a way to do just that.

The public television station made a controversial decision to change their early Thursday-morning programming. Entitled *Just Let Me Die,* the show later won television's Humanitas Award and an Emmy for Best Local Documentary. It was a grueling and poignant half hour of hastily assembled and edited file videotape of suffering hospital and nursing-home patients – AI sufferers, cancer victims, other terminally patients of both sexes, all ages, creeds, and colors – and all conscious enough to voice their desire to die.

* * *

'This is Hank Travers with Bay Area Action News. I'm standing outside the offices of the California state attorney general's office in San Francisco, and with me is Assistant Attorney General Gil Soma. Mr Soma, can you tell us whether the state has decided to bring charges against Mr Russo?'

Soma was a talking head. 'We need to carefully review all the evidence, of course. But the law, and my office, believes that the deliberate killing of another human being is usually a crime.'

There was an avid glint in his eyes that belied the apparent objectivity. Clearly, Soma wanted the head of Graham Russo.

And just as obviously, Hank Travers recognized this. 'Is it true that you and Mr Russo used to work together?'

The camera angle widened. Soma was the picture of the fighting young attorney. The cameras were out on the street and a freshening breeze was playing with his tie, messing with his hair. He ignored these distractions, giving all his attention to Hank. 'It's a matter of record that we were both clerks for Federal Judge Harold Draper. Beyond that I can't comment.'

The camera moved in for a close-up. Hank's voice came over Gil Soma's intense glare. 'But you know a different Graham Russo, don't you? The man behind the outward appearance? And you believe he would have killed his father for fifty thousand dollars?'

'No comment.'

Travers tried a last time. 'But in your opinion he's the kind of person who *could* have done it?'

Soma kept it straight. 'We're looking at the evidence. That's all I can tell you.' But he continued nodding into the camera, and the message came across loud and clear: Soma despised Graham Russo. He was going to take him down if he could.

9

Glitsky had Evans and Lanier in a borrowed office in the vice detail down the hallway from homicide. It was important that the office have a door that could be closed, and Glitsky's cubicle did not provide that particular amenity. The situation regarding the continuing investigation into Sal Russo's death was unusual and volatile.

He was taking them through the game plan. When he had finished his first pass, Evans raised a hand and the lieutenant, atypically, took on an amused expression. 'We're not in school here, Sarah, you can just speak up.'

She folded her arms back across her chest. 'I've got just one question: what are we supposed to do that we didn't do last time when they let him go?'

Glitsky nodded; it was a good question. 'Not much, to tell you the truth. Same stuff, just more of it.'

Marcel Lanier had been around long enough that he got the gist of it the first time. He was sitting in a comfortable chair next to his partner and he looked over at her. 'Everybody has their guards down, Sarah. Witnesses think there won't be any charges, so what they saw or heard might not be so threatening. People might open up. The investigation is still open. That's really what Abe's saying.'

'That's it.' Glitsky was all agreement.

'But Russo is still our suspect?' Especially after last night this was not welcome news.

'Best and only. He did it.' Lanier was ready to hit the streets. Glitsky had delivered the message. Time to go to work. But Sarah was still in her chair, arms still crossed over her chest.

'Is something wrong, Sarah?' Glitsky asked her.

She shook her head. 'I don't know. Yeah, something.' They

waited. 'I don't think he did it,' she said at last. 'I think we were wrong.'

Lanier began sputtering something, but Glitsky stopped him with a gesture. He set a haunch on the corner of the desk. 'I'm listening.'

'I don't know,' she repeated. 'I'm just not sure.'

'What's changed since yesterday?' Glitsky asked.

'A couple of things.' She hesitated, then came out with it. 'I talked to him.'

'When?'

She told them about the meeting at the softball diamond, leaving out her personal reaction. 'He came up to me.' Not precisely true but, she thought, close enough. She was positive he'd been about to approach her when she saw him staring at her. 'I don't think he would have done that if he'd killed his father.'

'Sure he would have.' This was Lanier's territory. He'd interacted with a hundred murderers in his career and had not a doubt that he had the psychology down. Whatever it might be, he'd already seen it twice. 'That's exactly the kind of shit these assholes try to run on us. We let him out of jail, so he's untouchable. He wants to know what we know. He's sucking up to you, Sarah, trying to get under your skin.'

She didn't believe it. 'It wasn't like that.'

Glitsky: 'What was it like?'

'There's wasn't any sucking up. He barely mentioned it.'

Lanier leaned in toward her. 'I bet it did sneak its clever little way into the conversation, though, didn't it?'

She shrugged. 'He just said he didn't do it. An afterthought.'

Lanier had seen that too. 'Ahh, the subtle approach. He barely brings it up after he's been arrested and spent the day in jail?' The psychology of that failed Marcel's litmus test, and he wanted his partner to know it. 'If *you*'d just spent your first day in jail and met the person who'd put you there, don't you think it might be kind of the main thing on your mind? Wouldn't you want to talk about it just a tiny bit?'

'Marcel, I think she gets the point.' Glitsky came back to Sarah. 'You said there were a couple of things. What was the other one?'

Her eyes fixed on each of the men in turn. 'I thought about

this all night, reread over the file. We don't really have anything that puts him there.'

Glitsky nodded. This, too, was a valid point. 'That's why Drysdale wants the investigation to proceed. He says he needs more to get a conviction.'

'You mean we shouldn't have arrested him last time?'

'Now, wait a minute!' Lanier wasn't about to accept that analysis. 'The guy had already hired a lawyer—'

'Not in itself a crime,' Glitsky pointed out.

'Sure, sure, but still . . .' Lanier knew what cops knew, and that was that innocent people – if there were any – didn't tend to bring their lawyers into the picture until they were charged, until they finally understood that they were in trouble. He continued. 'Basically, we got an unemployed, selfish kid with a million-dollar lifestyle who needed the money and saw an easy way to take it.'

'So it's all the money?'

'Absolutely. He had the safe combination at his place. That puts him at his old man's.'

'Then why didn't he just pick up the safe deposit key while we were searching his place, put it in his pocket? We wouldn't ever have found it.'

Lanier shrugged. 'I give up. Maybe he thought we'd catch him if he tried. Maybe he didn't believe we'd be so thorough. I'm not saying the guy's a professional hit man. Maybe he was just nervous.'

'If it was all about the money, he would have done something to hide it.' She was shaking her head. 'It would have been so easy. He couldn't *not* have done it.'

The old bromide – that killers needed to tell somebody about what they'd done – wasn't all false. 'He wanted us to find it. Call it a type of confession.'

'He wouldn't feel the need to confess if it was an act of mercy, if he felt he'd done the right thing.'

Lanier shook his head. 'Uh-uh. This wasn't any assisted suicide either. This was murder. That bump under the ear—'

'Which Strout said could have happened hours before.'

'No no no. Our boy Graham cold-cocked him from behind with the whiskey bottle, gave him a veinful of morphine, cleaned out the safe, and tiptoed home through the tulips.'

'So if Sal was cold-cocked, lying still on the ground, and Graham gives shots every day of his life, why was there trauma around the injection site? Why wasn't it a clean little poke?'

'I don't know. Maybe he was scared. He was hurrying. Maybe there was an earthquake. The needle was broke. Maybe he missed the vein. My doctor does every time.'

But Glitsky had listened to enough arguing. 'All right, all right. This doesn't matter. I think you had plenty to arrest Russo yesterday. If you keep looking, maybe you'll find more. You're authorized to keep looking, that's all. Make it tight. If the AG wants to move on him, we'll bring in Graham again. If the evidence points to somebody else, we'll go after them. Sarah, you got anybody else you're thinking about?'

She said she didn't, 'But Sal still might have killed himself, right? The autopsy didn't rule that out.'

Glitsky nodded. 'That's true.' He pushed himself off the desk. The meeting was over. 'And that is precisely the reason that God in Her infinite wisdom invented the jury system.' He spread his hands, as though blessing them. 'Which, fortunately, never fails.'

'Well, at least we had a nice summer, didn't we?'

Lanier had his jacket buttoned all the way up, his head down in his collar. Next to him Evans, her hands tucked into her own jacket, squinted into the face of the wind and the dust it was kicking up. 'Where did this come from?' she asked. They were both walking fast. 'It just *can't* be this cold.'

After their meeting with Glitsky, they'd driven the half mile from the Hall up Seventh Street and pulled into Stevenson Alley, a narrow and grimy, if schizophrenic, line of asphalt and garbage a half block south of the always exotic bus station.

The north side of Stevenson was lined with the backs and delivery doors of the ancient medium-rise buildings of retail businesses that were struggling to survive on Market Street. Of the few structures whose fronts faced the alley, the most prominent was the Lions (no apostrophe) Arms apartment building, where Sal Russo had lived and died in corner room 304. Stenciled in fading black paint onto the side of the building were the words *Daily, Weekly Rates*.

For most of the past decade the south side of Stevenson had fit in with the run-down ambience of the neighborhood – an open sore of a construction site while the Old Post Office Building was being renovated. Recently, though, that work had been completed.

The Postal Service now had its own new home out at Rincon Annex, and the building's other tenant – the Ninth Circuit Federal Court of Appeals – had taken it over. The federal courthouse now loomed fresh and imposing, a massive and elegant structure between Stevenson Alley and Mission Street.

Lanier and Evans didn't notice any of it. As they stepped around the homeless man camped, sleeping now, in one of the back doorways, all they saw on the south side of the alley, the courthouse side, was a solid gray wall, already sprayed with graffiti, topped with coils of razor wire. It wouldn't have mattered to the two inspectors if the Taj Mahal had been across the way; the Lions Arms didn't pick up any reflected majesty from its surroundings. It was a flophouse, pure and simple.

The uniforms had canvassed the Lions Arms when Sal's body had been found, but after dark were prime hours for a certain class of people who made their living on the street – lots of tenants hadn't been home.

So Sarah and Lanier were back, planning to knock on more doors. Normally, inspectors don't like to work alone in this kind of environment, but it was midday and they could get more done if they split up. Both were aware that they probably should have gotten back to this sooner, but in the crush of other priorities it had had to wait.

To accommodate a relatively spacious lobby and mailbox area – the building dated from a more gracious era – there were only four units on the first floor, and Sarah began knocking on them. The upper three stories had eight units each.

Lanier mounted the stairs that began in the back of the lobby and took the second floor. He was going to start at 204, directly below Sal's apartment, at the front of the building. He wasn't even there when Sarah appeared on his landing. 'Nobody home on the first floor. I'll start on three.'

The name in the slot next to the door said Blue, and Blue was coal-black. She was vaguely familiar by sight to Lanier – he had probably seen her around the Hall after she'd been busted for prostitution, for there was no question about her profession.

After Lanier identified himself through the door, there was the sound of some movement inside. She must have been expecting a customer, Lanier thought. Probably was putting away some novelty items, maybe a bong. The door eventually opened. She'd opened the window, but the room still smelled strongly of marijuana and, somewhat less so, of musk. Blue was tucking a red teddy-bear top into a pair of skintight black denims.

She stood in the open doorway, not asking him in. He showed her his badge. And then she surprised him. 'This be about Sal, upstairs?' Lanier said it was and she nodded. 'I thought you be by sooner. I almost call you 'cept I don't call cops. Sal was okay.'

'You knew him?'

She shook her head. 'Not real good. We talk a few times in the lobby, sometimes out the alley there. He brung me up some fresh salmon sometimes. I love salmon.' Her eyes got wistful. 'It was so sad, him dying. You find who killed him?'

Out of habit and caution Lanier did not answer questions put to him by witnesses. Instead, he talked to her for a moment, realized he might have something, and pulled out the tape recorder he almost hadn't bothered to bring along.

After intoning the standard introduction for the transcriber, he came back at her. 'Did you see or hear anything on last Friday, May ninth, that made you believe Sal Russo had been killed?'

'I didn't know killed at the time, but somebody be up in Sal's place with him. I hear the door open, then' – she indicated over her head – 'the ceiling creaks, somebody else there.'

'And where were you?'

'Here, in my apartment. And then some other noises.'

'What kind of noises were they?'

'Like he fell down. Like some scraping furniture.' She looked up. 'This place, you know, the walls pretty thin, not 'zactly soundproof.'

But Lanier was going to keep her at it. 'So you heard this noise, some furniture scraping on the floor?'

That wasn't precisely right. 'Wasn't like anything pushing, more like something fell, hit against it or something, and it scraped. Then he kind of moaned and yelled, "No," bunch of times.'

'No?'

'Yeah, like he was in pain or something. But pleading, like? The saddest sound.'

'Did you hear anybody else, any other voices?'

'Yeah, two voices. Sal and somebody else.'

'Male, female?'

'Male. Having some argument, it sounded like.'

'This was before Sal moaned? Before the furniture scraped?'

Blue closed her eyes, her face a study. 'Before.' But there was an uncertainty.

'What?'

'Nothing. It was just before.'

'And then, after the moan, what? Anything else?'

She took a moment, closing her eyes again, making sure. 'No, just that. Then the door opened and closed again a few minutes later, and then it be quiet.'

'So what did you do?'

The question seemed to spook her. She looked down, then at a place somewhere over Lanier's shoulder. 'I did go up, but later. No one answered.'

Lanier almost got sarcastic with her – dead people generally didn't answer doors too well. But he kept his tone neutral. 'Yeah, Blue, but you heard this noise that sounded like Sal might be in trouble while you were right here underneath him. You said you guys were friends—'

'I didn't say we were friends. Not exactly friends. I knew him a little. He seem like a good guy, that's all.'

'Okay, so why didn't you go up and see him while you still might have been able to help?'

Again, that look over his shoulder.

'Blue?'

'I couldn't.' She paused and sighed. 'Somebody was here, sleeping afterward, you know. I couldn't get up.'

10

Dismas Hardy remained unaware of developing events for the whole day, until nearly nine o'clock Thursday evening. He had awakened at six and met Michelle at David's Deli for a breakfast meeting an hour later. They were going down to Palo Alto – forty-some miles south – to meet with Dyson Brunel, Tryptech's CEO, to introduce Michelle and discuss some of the substantive issues related to the lawsuit.

Hardy hadn't taken the time to even glance at a newspaper. From his perspective the Graham Russo case was still smoldering, but the immediate fire had been put out. Hardy was going to have his hands full anyway, bringing Michelle up to speed on this litigation, continuing with his daily work. He figured that Graham was going to be in his life sometime in the future, but for now it was important to will Graham onto a back burner, impending murder charge or not.

It was easier said than done. Over lunch the conversation between Michelle, Brunel, and Hardy had come around to the surveillance equipment in use at the Port of Oakland. Perhaps, Michelle suggested, there was some video record of malfeasance, some smoking gun locked in the video camera at one of the security checkpoints. There was no record anyone had looked into that possibility.

Graham's bank! Hardy had thought. Video records at the bank could prove, perhaps, that Graham hadn't gone there with his father's money after Friday. That would mean that, whatever else might have happened, he didn't kill Sal so that he could get at the safe. It would get any murder charge out of the range of special circumstances.

Once the idea about videotapes at the bank came to him, the rest of the day was an agony of detail and protocol. Hardy couldn't shake the feeling that even during this apparent hiatus, his inability to get out of Tryptech's office might be costing Graham Russo years of his freedom. Hardy'd let himself be lulled by the media attention around the idea that the death of Sal Russo had been an assisted suicide. That was, after all, the express reason that Sharron Pratt had declined to file charges.

But – the realization came to him in a bolt – if the attorney general was going to play hardball politics and bring a charge against Graham Russo, it wasn't likely to be for less than first-degree murder.

Still, Hardy couldn't very well leave his bread-and-butter corporate client and his brand-new associate together and tell them to just catch up on things. He had to sell Brunel on Michelle's skills and competence, simultaneously giving her a chance to show off what she had – miraculously – mastered in such a short time.

As if that weren't enough, he also felt they needed to conduct some real business, going over deposition testimony he'd taken in the past couple of weeks, squeezing hard data from the elusive Brunel. The three of them and some of Tryptech's staff remained at it until after seven.

Then Hardy decided to stop by his own office downtown and check his messages. From the pile of slips and first four phone calls on his answering machine, all from reporters, it was immediately obvious that the Russo case had gone ballistic.

Making his delay more crucial.

He tried calling Graham at home – by now it was nine-thirty – and no one answered, not even the machine. Hardy reasoned that if his own tangential connection to the case had produced today's volume of mail and phone calls, then Graham must have been absolutely inundated by the flood. No doubt he was lying low.

He didn't get home until eleven-thirty, and Frannie was by then asleep. His dinner was on the dining-room table, cold.

This morning, out in the Avenues, where Hardy lived, it was more than mere fog. It was wet as rain, although for some reason the droplets didn't fall, just hung in the air. The temperature was in the low forties and a bitter wind whipped his coat as he approached his car.

Things at home were not good.

He thought he remembered telling Frannie yesterday that he wouldn't be home for dinner. He had *never* planned to be home for dinner last night. If he had told her, though, she didn't remember it, and in all honesty he wasn't completely certain that he had.

Though he ached with every bone in his body to be out of the house – he needed a court order and then he needed to get to Graham's bank – he also knew he had better wait and talk to Frannie when she got back from taking the kids to school.

Which he had done.

Now, driving downtown through the soup, he wasn't sure if he was happy or not that his wife wasn't a nag. If she'd only yelled at him, he could have responded in kind or worked himself up a froth of righteous indignation that she didn't appreciate all the hours he was putting in so that he could support the family, and all by himself, he need hardly remind her.

It was a grueling responsibility – the daily grind. But it was his job, and he was sorry if once in a very great while he had to miss a goddamn dinner. Some wives actually understood this.

That's what he would have said if she'd come back in on the warpath.

But if she had lost her temper at any time last night, she'd found it by the time she talked to him this morning. She wasn't mad, and this threw him, as she knew it would, back on himself.

Was this the way it was always going to be? She simply wanted to know, so she'd be able to deal with it. So she could be a better mom to the kids. (She didn't say, 'in the absence of a father figure,' but he heard it.)

So he tried a few clichés – 'Life is complicated.' 'We have different roles we're trying to juggle.' 'This is just a busy time' – but he'd ended up by apologizing. He'd try to communicate better in the future. She was right: something had to change.

Well, he thought, something already had. He'd brought on Michelle to help with Tryptech. He'd more or less committed to Graham Russo's defense. This case intrigued him as corporate litigation never would. There was no passion for him in business law and it took all of his time, wasting him for anything else – like his family. It made him feel old.

He might – no, he *would* – wind up working the same kind of hours for Graham Russo, but it would be in the service of something he believed in. Maybe, at forty-five, he was finally getting down to the core of who he was.

The car behind him honked and he moved forward, then pulled over to the side of Geary Street, letting the traffic flow past him.

This was the way he always reacted when he began caring too much: he went on autopilot and ran from it. There was too much to lose. It wasn't safe.

It was what he'd done after his son had died during his first marriage, when he was twenty-seven. Something in him decided he wouldn't survive looking over into the chasm. He closed up and went to sleep.

He and Jane had gotten divorced, he'd quit the law entirely, and for nearly ten years he'd tended bar at the Shamrock. Drinking a lot, but rarely getting drunk. Functioning quite well, thank you, but keeping any feeling on a short tether. Sleepwalking.

Then, suddenly, Frannie. Realizing that the essence of him had nearly dried up and would surely blow away if he didn't risk part of it, he'd started over. Fatherhood, again. Criminal law, again. Caring too much again.

What if he lost all this now, or even any part of it?

No, he couldn't let that happen. He was at his limit of risk tolerance. It was too dangerous; it was a matter of his survival, he had to pull back.

And that's what he'd done: gotten back to sleepwalking. Functioning, keeping too busy. He was on the run, avoiding the only kind of work he found fulfilling, maintaining a low level of interaction with his family.

It stunned him – he'd become afraid. Of change, of failure in his job, of caring too much at home.

It had to stop, he thought. He had to wake himself up. What was the point of protecting the essentials in your life – your talents, your family, your friends – if you never took the time to enjoy them? If you were already dead?

Superior Court Judge Leo Chomorro, a brush-cut, swarthy block of well-tailored muscle, was in his chambers, playing chess with his computer. He had blocked out six days for a murder trial in his courtroom, and this morning one of Pratt's young wunderkind had forgotten to subpoena the witness he had planned to call at the start of the day. So Chomorro had a morning off, not that this had put him in an especially good humor. On the other hand, one of Hardy's trials had been in Chomorro's courtroom, and there was no evidence that *anything* put him in a good humor. Nevertheless, he was the only available judge this morning, and Hardy needed him.

He kept it short: he'd like the judge to sign a court order to look at the surveillance videotapes from Graham Russo's bank. He explained why he needed it.

'Why don't you use a subpoena?' the judge asked him.

'I can't. There's no case pending.'

'So what jurisdiction do I have to issue this order? Who am I to tell the bank what to do? I can't issue an order any more than you can issue a subpoena.'

'Your Honor.' Hardy laid on the respect. 'The bank doesn't care about the tape. All they need is paper to cover themselves. If you sign this, no one will ever object. If you don't, important evidence in this case could be lost because the police don't want to preserve it.'

Chomorro snorted. 'They shouldn't care either way.'

Hardy nodded. '*Should* is the operative word there, Judge.'

'You think this one's going to get hot, don't you?'

Another nod. 'It's smoldering already. That's why I need the order now. I don't know how long they save the tapes. If it's a week, maybe I'm already too late. I need last Friday's.'

Chomorro reviewed the order that Hardy had printed out from the word processor in his office.

> 'To: CUSTODIAN OF RECORDS, Wells Fargo Bank, Haight Street Branch.
>
> 'GOOD CAUSE APPEARING THEREFORE, you are hereby ORDERED, upon receipt of reasonable payment therefore, to surrender to Dismas Hardy, counsel of record for Graham Russo, copies of surveillance videotape film for the dates May 9–13, inclusive.'

Below the date was a line for the judge to sign, and this he did, looking up when he was finished, handing over the paper. 'I haven't seen you around here in a while, Mr Hardy. You been on vacation?'

Hardy kept it light. 'Just waiting for the right case.'

Chomorro nodded. 'Looks like you found it.'

Graham had his telephone and answering machines unplugged, but in New York on Thursday afternoon a senior editor at *Time* – Michael Cerrone – convinced his boss that the Russo story in San Francisco was a potential cover. On Friday at one-twenty, shivering in the wind and fog – even up on Edgewood – Cerrone knocked on Graham's door and introduced himself. He had his photographer with him.

'*Time* magazine?' Graham said. 'You're kidding me.'

Cerrone had seen this response before in people whom fame had sledgehammered. He proffered his credentials.

'This is so unreal,' Graham said. 'Here I just come home from getting laid off and now you want to take my picture for *Time* magazine?'

Cerrone wasn't much older than Graham, though he looked even younger, with dark hair to his shoulders and an open, inviting smile. In jeans, hiking boots, and a bright blue parka, he was the farthest thing imaginable from a threatening big-city media type. He showed his teeth, grinning. 'Hey, I know it's not *Rolling Stone*, but I'll buy you a beer.' Then, more seriously, 'Who laid you off? How come?'

Graham explained it. His employers had no complaints about his work, but due to all the publicity, they'd gotten several phone calls. Potential customers didn't seem all that thrilled with the idea that their sick patients would be riding in an ambulance with a paramedic who might help them end their suffering. After all this blew over, the ambulance company might reconsider bringing Graham back on, but until then . . .

'That sucks,' Cerrone said sympathetically. 'Don't you want to tell your side of it? You'll never get a better chance.'

Graham Russo thought about it for a couple of seconds, then told Cerrone he might as well come on in out of the cold, bring his photographer in with him.

* * *

The manager of the Wells Fargo branch – a cooperative woman named Peggy Reygosa – was inclined to comply promptly with Hardy's court order. She wasn't about to let go of the originals, however, but arranged with the bank's custodian to make copies for Hardy. Yes, of course she'd tell him to be extremely careful not to erase the originals until he'd checked over the copies.

In her corner cubicle Ms Reygosa assured Hardy that the front entrance to the bank, where the video camera was mounted, was the only way into and out of the building, even for employees. She called in her custodian and asked him to get to work copying the tapes right away. 'But if you wanted to see when Mr Russo last accessed his box, you should also check the sign-in form. Nobody gets inside their box without signing in.'

'Even if they have their own key?'

She shook her head. 'No. It takes two keys – yours and ours – and your signature. The inspectors who were in on Tuesday, they've already made a copy of the sign-in sheet. Would you like to see it?'

Bleary eyed, feeling stupid and finessed – he really was out of practice – Hardy told the manager that it would be nice. She got up and returned a couple of minutes later.

It wasn't much of a formal document, just an oversized page with the bank's logo on the top, vertical lines intersecting the signature and date lines below, so that each signatory had an individual box. A bank officer had a stamp, which was initialed in the first box, then there was the date, then the signature, and finally the time.

Ms Reygosa came around to peruse the sheet over Hardy's shoulder. On the line above Graham's every box had been filled in. Hardy couldn't make out the name – Ben something – but he'd accessed his box on 5/8, which was Thursday, at 4:40 P.M. A bank officer with the initials A.L. – 'That's Alison Li' – had signed Ben in.

On Graham's line, Li had initialed her stamp again, but beside that there was only a signature, no time or date. 'How did this happen?' Hardy asked. 'What does this mean?'

It was evidently the first time that Ms Reygosa had studied the document. She straightened up, surprising Hardy by laying a hand on his shoulder, and told him she'd be right back.

While she was gone, he went back to the list. Below Graham, order had once again been restored. On 5/10 – Saturday, he realized – at nine-fifteen, a Pam Barr had signed in. In all there were eight lines below Graham's through Tuesday night. But there were no names at all for Friday.

He put his hands to his eyes and rubbed them, wondering why nothing was easy. When he looked up again, Ms Reygosa was back with a diminutive, terrified young Asian woman. 'Alison' – the peppy friendliness had disappeared – 'this is Mr Hardy, and I'd like you to explain to him how Mr Russo signed in for his safe deposit box without either a time or a date.'

Hardy smiled, trying to put her at ease, but it didn't seem to work. She stared at the sheet for what seemed an eternity. 'I remember this. I *reminded* him about the date and time.'

Hardy kept his voice neutral. 'But you didn't see him write them in?'

'Obviously, no. As you can see, he didn't.' She threw a glance at Ms Reygosa, stammered to Hardy, 'We stamp, you know, after we check the signature, then go into the room with the customer, with our key.'

'And the customer writes the date and time?'

'Sometimes. Sometimes I do it.'

'But neither of you did on this occasion?'

She indicated the sheet. 'As you see,' she repeated. 'Mr Russo, he was in a hurry. He signed and I remember I even said not to forget to put the time, and he smiled like he does, said he'd get it on the way out. He'd remember. But he didn't, and I must have gotten busy, so I guess neither did I. It seemed like he was anxious to get inside, like he was nervous. He had a briefcase with him.'

I'd be nervous, too, Hardy thought, if I were carrying around fifty thousand dollars in cash. But Hardy had no desire to keep cross-examining the woman. He didn't want to antagonize her, since if Graham did go to trial, which he considered all but certain, he would be questioning her then. 'Do you remember what day this was, Ms Li, Thursday or Friday? You said it was near the end of the day. Do you remember the time?'

She was biting her lip, thinking hard. Finally, it seemed to come to her. 'It was the afternoon. Thursday or Friday, though, I can't be sure.'

Hardy pointed down at the sign-in document again. 'Do you remember if it was right after this man, Ben somebody, came in? You signed him in, too, at twenty minutes to five.'

She pondered for another long moment. In his desperation Hardy gave her a hint. 'No one else signed in on Friday. Mr Russo would have been the only one that day. Does that seem right?'

The poor woman was on the verge of tears. Another glance at her boss, Ms Reygosa, didn't help. Alison was trying to give Hardy the information he wanted, give him the right answer, but she didn't know exactly what it was.

Hardy pressed further. 'You said you thought it was the afternoon, Alison. Did it feel like it was after three o'clock? Mr Russo went to work at three on Friday.'

Suddenly her face cleared, and she let out the deep breath she'd been all but holding for five minutes. 'Oh, yes, then, it must have been Thursday afternoon. Thursday, I'm sure of it. Near the end of the day.' She pointed down at the sheet. 'Maybe we should write it in now that we know?'

Since the inspectors had already copied the original of this document, Hardy – gently – allowed as how that might not be an inspired idea. They should just leave it as it was.

Hardy's errand at the bank had, he thought, been supremely worth it.

As it turned out, the Haight Street branch did erase their tapes on a ten-day cycle. Hardy got his copies and spent most of the rest of the afternoon watching television in his living room, the front door of the bank as people came and went. After getting his bearings he got so he could fast-forward until someone appeared in the doorway, stop the tape, determine it wasn't Graham, and move on. In this way he got through viewing three days of the most boring video he'd ever watched in a little over five hours.

Perhaps it wasn't conclusive, but at least once he'd seen his copies, he had a good argument that Graham Russo hadn't entered this bank from the time of his father's death on Friday until he was arrested on Wednesday morning. If a jury believed this, then it *would* indicate that Graham did not kill his father to get the money. He already had the money and the baseball cards before his father was dead.

During the same viewing period, Hardy'd had no trouble identifying Evans and Lanier when they'd come in to check the safe deposit box.

Glitsky, Assistant AG Art Drysdale, and San Francisco coroner John Strout sat around the latter's desk in his office behind the morgue. All around them Strout's collection of murder weapons under glass, from medieval torture devices to guns and knives, lent a humorous, macabre air to their surroundings, but the three men weren't joking now. Between them they had assembled the foundations for hundreds of murder cases, and yet their respective roles were not necessarily complementary.

Glitsky and Drysdale – the cop and the prosecutor – viewed themselves as true allies. They found *and interpreted* evidence with the mutual goal of proving that a particular person had committed a crime. They did different work, but it was toward the same end.

Strout, on the other hand, jealously guarded his independence and his objectivity. He was a scientist. If his discoveries helped Glitsky and Drysdale – and they often did – then so be it. But he had no ax to grind. He did not consider himself a lawman, an officer of the court, anything like that. His job was to rule on cause of death. Speculation did not enter into it, nor did politics. If he didn't know, he said he didn't know, and vice versa.

At this moment, behind his desk, Strout's normally unflappable Southern style was being put to the test. Drysdale had decided he wanted to be sure he had Strout's support in calling the homicide of Sal Russo a murder, and he'd enlisted Glitsky to come down as moral support.

'Now, Art, that's just simply not going to happen. I am not *about* to change an opinion without different evidence, and to be honest with you, I'm just a bit offended that you thought I might.'

But Drysdale had his game face on. Dean Powell – the attorney general – had told him what he wanted in the best of all worlds, and if it were gettable, Drysdale was going to get it. Strout's feelings would heal. 'You've already called it a homicide, John—'

Strout was holding a hand up. 'Well, that's just plum inaccurate, Art. I did not say it was a homicide. I called it a suicide equivocal/homicide, which is not the same thing. It means I can't say for sure that Russo didn't kill himself.'

'Mr Powell thinks that's splitting hairs.'

Strout removed his wire-rimmed spectacles. 'Well, Mr Powell can hire himself another pathologist and get himself another opinion, but he's already got mine, and it's stayin' the way it is.'

Glitsky thought he would try to calm the waters. 'You know Art doesn't mean to insult you, John. He's asking if there's anywhere this can bend, that's all. Okay, it *could have been* suicide – we accept that—'

'Well, thank you all to hell, Lieutenant.'

Glitsky ignored him. 'But isn't there anything that militates against it? Makes it a little more likely somebody killed him?'

'The bump, for example.' Drysdale had studied the autopsy report carefully. He had years of experience, and to him it read like a murder. Someone had whacked Sal to knock him out, then administered the fatal dose of morphine. It was open and shut.

Unfortunately, other scenarios were possible. Maybe not as probable, but medically feasible. It made him short tempered.

Strout kept his glasses off, but sat back in his chair, elbows on its arms. 'The bump was caused, as I mentioned, by a blow to the head, which is not inconsistent with the deceased banging it on the table as he fell down.'

Drysdale didn't buy that at all. 'That would have meant he fell backwards, John. How could he fall backwards unless somebody pushed him? There was no hair on the table. He didn't hit the table. He got hit by the whiskey bottle.'

Strout made a gesture at Glitsky, who reluctantly spoke up. 'The bump didn't even bleed, Art. It's not inconsistent that it didn't take any hair—'

Betrayed by his ally, Drysdale bit out the words. 'Not inconsistent, not inconsistent! You fellas got a tape loop going down here?'

Strout impatiently explained some more. 'There was sufficient edema – which, as both of you know, is swelling – to allow for the flow of blood for a half hour or more.' He turned his palms up. 'He was alive, Art. The blow to the head didn't kill him. I can't even say for sure it knocked him out. If it did, it wasn't for more than a few seconds.'

'Long enough to give him the shot.'

Strout shrugged. 'I can't say. Maybe.'

Drysdale's face had gone red, and he sat back in his chair, unbuttoned his shirt, pulled at his tie. In his own office he let off tension by juggling baseballs, but there wasn't anything to juggle here except hand grenades, and he wasn't going to go grabbing at them. For all he knew, they were live.

There was a short silence, broken by the screech of rubber and colliding metal on the freeway outside Strout's window. All the men got up to gawk. The coroner raised the blinds. They couldn't see the freeway through the fog, and it was less than fifty yards away.

They all stayed standing by the window. Nothing had been said, but the anger, somehow, had dissipated.

'Y'all just plain aren't gonna prove it *couldn't* have been suicide,' Strout began. 'I've heard you say it a hundred times, Abe. You can't prove a negative. It might be y'all want to concentrate on why it *could* have been a homicide.'

'I'm listening,' Drysdale said.

Strout ticked off reasons on his fingers. 'One, he'd never used the site before, the inside of his wrist. Two, his blood alcohol was point one oh – pretty drunk – hittin' the vein on the first try was dang good shootin'. Three, the needle wasn't in him. It was sitting on the table there. Isn't that right, Abe?'

Glitsky nodded in agreement and Drysdale asked what the last fact meant.

'It means Sal Russo shot himself up and remained conscious long enough to withdraw the needle. Except you got eight or more milligrams of morphine goin' IV, on top of a point one oh alcohol, most people, time they got the plunger all the way down, they're at least in shock. The needle might fall out when consciousness went, but it don't get itself put neatly back on the table. The cap doesn't get itself put back on the syringe, that's for damn sure.'

Drysdale chewed on it for a moment. 'If I'm on a jury, those three taken together, that's beyond reasonable doubt.'

'I don't know,' Strout replied, true to form. 'It might be, but it don't have to be, which is what I said all along.'

11

The photographer had left to develop his film. Fearing they'd be interrupted if they stayed on Edgewood, Graham and Michael Cerrone had spent the afternoon and evening at Modena, an upscale Italian deli on Clement Street, sharing two bottles of ten-year-old Gold Label Ruffino Chianti. Now they were no longer strangers. In seven hours Cerrone felt he'd captured the soul of his subject on tape.

Cerrone had come out to California with high expectations – a cover, after all, was not a daily occurrence, even for a senior editor. But the interview had exceeded his hopes by far, both in scope and in human drama.

The story had everything: Russo's background as a bonus athlete cut down in his prime by injury, a brilliant law student, a clerkship with a federal judge. Then chucking it all to give his dream one last try, only to fail again; and only, in turn, to have that noble effort ostracize him from the legal community. And now there was the fallout from the murder charge that had been summarily dropped: even his part-time employer wouldn't keep Graham on.

But Cerrone thought the personal side was even more compelling. Although it was nowhere on the public record, he learned that privately Gil Soma wanted Graham's head on a platter. The state prosecutor had been Graham's office mate at the federal courthouse. Graham had told him that in Soma's eyes he was far worse than a mere murderer – he was a traitor, to be hunted and brought down.

On the other side was the picture of a talented and sensitive hero, reconciling, after years, with his father, who then became terminally ill. Graham had confided to Cerrone that over the past two difficult years, his father had been the only person who'd accepted him, who loved him. The only person keeping Graham from being utterly alone.

Of course he'd taken care of him. Though he didn't admit to knowing the source of the morphine, he had often given him his shots.

Cerrone fell short of getting the coup, the confession, but what he had was almost better – it played into his 'hook' perfectly. The issue of the week was going to be assisted suicide – the agony of the decisions confronting everyone stepping through this emotional minefield. Cerrone would write his story so that the conclusion was obvious.

Graham had done the right thing. His father wanted to end his life, but he needed support, someone to hold his hand; at the last moment he was afraid of being alone. He would choose his own time, but Graham, his dutiful, perhaps prodigal, son, would help him if need be.

This, Cerrone was sure, was what had happened. And the beauty and pathos of it was that there was no way that Graham could own up to what he'd done, not if he ever wanted to work again.

After her morning meeting with Glitsky, Sarah's turmoil increased by the hour. By sunset, when she parked down the street from Graham's place, she was a wreck. Twice during the day Marcel had wanted to come up here to Edgewood, find Graham, push a few of his buttons, see what popped up. Sarah told him they ought to wait, get more on him, bide their time. In reality she wanted to keep Marcel out of it, to go see Graham again by herself. This was dangerous on many levels, she knew, and unprofessional on all of them, but she was going to do it anyway.

For the first time in her career she wasn't sure she was after the right person. Suddenly, after last night's really meaningless discussion at the ballpark, she'd lost her cop's simple take on Graham Russo. He'd become mostly a human being, not mostly a suspect.

And worse, he was a human being she could be attracted to, *was already* attracted to. It was wise to acknowledge that, keep it in front of her.

She knew it was a bad situation, untenable really. She ought to take herself off the case. Her objectivity was shot.

But what if that apparent objectivity led her and Marcel to the wrong conclusion? They might, for the second time, arrest the wrong man – a black mark on each of their careers, a possible false-arrest lawsuit, to say nothing of the grief to Graham. This is what she wanted to avoid, why she wanted to see Graham without her partner hovering.

She'd talk to Graham and get it clear to her own satisfaction, lay this ambivalence to rest. He was either a murder suspect or not. She had to know for herself. Then she could do her job.

That was all it was. She was just making sure, taking that extra step, being a good cop. That's what she told herself.

But there was one other problem: she found she couldn't shake a kind of simmering anger at Graham for having put her in this position. Was he manipulating her, or trying to? Who was this guy? He shouldn't have come up to her at the ballpark. They were enemies, on opposite sides. What was that all about? Arrogance, as Marcel contended? Or was Graham simply, as he'd appeared, a sweet guy who held nothing against the woman who'd arrested him, had wanted no more than to tell her that he knew she was only doing her job? No hard feelings.

She just didn't know. It was personal somehow, and it shouldn't have ever gotten to there. It made her mad.

She was going to find out who he was.

Graham and another man stood talking out in the street in front of his place. It was full dusk and the fog had thinned up here on the hill, though the wind still gusted fitfully, shaking fistfuls of blossoms, snowlike, from the trees around them.

Sarah walked up, dressed for business in a blue suit as she'd been all day. 'Hello, Graham.'

He turned to look at her. She thought she saw something welcoming in his face, though it disappeared instantly.

She kept moving toward him. 'Your father called you twice on Friday morning. What did you two talk about?'

It tore at her heart to see something go out of Graham's shoulders, but he recovered quickly, bringing his companion into it. 'This is my favorite cop, Sergeant Evans. Sarah, Mike Cerrone. He's a reporter.'

The reporter put out his hand, and she took it. 'You're not with the *Chronicle*.' Sarah knew the locals, and this guy wasn't one of them.

'*Time,*' he answered.

'My, how the word do get around.'

In truth, she'd been expecting something like this. The shop talk at the Hall was about how big this had gotten in a hurry. And now *Time*.

'You boys been drinking?' she asked. To Cerrone: 'I could call you a cab. Here in the Wild West it's considered bad form to drink and drive.'

Graham had his grin back. 'What did I tell you? She is some pistol. Don't let her sweet looks fool you.'

'I don't think they were going to,' Cerrone said. He never took his eyes from her. In fact, Graham had mentioned her, but only in passing. Now it seemed to Cerrone – an instinct – that there was something more here, or might be. More story. An attractive female investigator coming up alone to interview him at night? 'How 'bout coffee instead? Go inside, kill an hour, get sober.'

'Coffee just makes you wide-awake drunk.'

'I don't think I'm drunk.'

'Nobody thinks they're drunk. That's kind of the problem.'

'Hey!' Graham said, getting their attention. 'What's with you guys? *I* think I'm drunk, how about that? I'll make coffee.'

Evans looked at him levelly. 'If you invite me in without a warrant . . .'

But Graham had already turned, heading for his door. 'What a hardass,' he said. 'I'm going in, I'm freezing. You can come or don't, I don't care.'

Cerrone, in a mock gallant gesture, indicated Evans should precede him. She did.

Nobody was in a hurry to get down to business. Graham had put on the coffee, then some music – Celine Dion's *French Album*. Cerrone hated it. Didn't Graham have any Alanis Morissette? Evans was somehow relieved that Graham didn't. She didn't want to think he had that much affinity for rage. In the end he put on Chris Isaak's *Baja Sessions*, came back to the table. Sarah finally asked him again about his father's phone calls on the morning of his death.

Graham sighed wearily. 'Okay, we talked twice on Friday.'

'What did you talk about?'

Graham drank some of his coffee, then seemed to remember something. 'Are you recording this? Not that it matters. With Mike here I've been recording all day. How many tapes we go through today, Mike?'

'Five.'

Sarah processed that, then got out her own recorder. 'The electronic age, you gotta love it.' Her face dimpled prettily. 'Thanks for reminding me.' She gave her introduction, and asked again.

'We talked about his pain mostly.' He paused and stared out at the blackness. 'Actually' – his voice took on a husky edge – 'Sal and me, we had the same discussion twice. The first one kind of went away. Maybe the second one, too, I don't know.' He shrugged. 'It was one of his bad days.'

Sarah found that she had to blink. This response – 'It was one of his bad days' – was Graham's first real reference to the day-to-day fact of Sal's condition. In her concentration on the son she'd nearly forgotten the father.

With difficulty she found the thread and picked it up again. 'Your father called you seventeen times in the past month, Graham.'

He nodded. 'Something like that, I guess.'

'So what did he want you to do?'

The huskiness remained in his voice. He'd obviously been drinking. His defenses were down. She was sure this was honest and raw emotion, an open wound. 'I don't know what he wanted that day. It wasn't one thing – it varied. He was dying, you understand? He'd wake up and not know where he was. He was scared. He needed his hand held. He just wanted to talk to somebody. Take your pick, Sergeant. He counted on me.'

At the opposite end of the table Cerrone was an irritant. God only knew what impression this interrogation was making on him. But Sarah had a tipsy and emotional Graham talking voluntarily. The opportunity had to be taken if she was to get what she needed.

Cerrone stared at her disapprovingly, but she ignored him. 'All right, he counted on you. And what did you do, that day, after the second call?'

Graham sipped at his coffee. He put the cup down and brought his hand to his face, rubbing at his jawline as though it had gone numb. When he spoke, his voice was flat. 'It wasn't just a bad day. It had been a *terrible* couple of weeks, just terrible. Everything was going downhill – the pain, the forgetting, all the sudden, way worse than it had been. I don't know what happened, if the tumor affected the Alzheimer's somehow. I don't know what it was. But something had changed. Something was going to have to be done.'

'Did you know what?'

Graham shook his head. 'When we first got back together, we'd talked a little about having to put him in a home someday. Back then he'd gotten lost a few times, but the disease wasn't very advanced. He was functioning pretty well. I think he went to see somebody, some doctor, to get diagnosed, but chickened out before they could run all the tests. He didn't want to know for sure, didn't want to face that he had it. But he knew.'

'And what did he think about being in a home?'

'There was no way. He wasn't going to end his life as a vegetable. He made me promise I'd kill him first.'

'And did you do that? Promise that?'

Cerrone leaned forward. 'Graham?'

The trance was broken. Momentarily. 'What?'

'I'm sure the sergeant meant to inform you that you don't have to answer any of this. That you can have your lawyer here.'

The alcohol was a definite if subtle presence. Graham reached over and patted the reporter on the arm. 'Hey, it's cool, Mike. It's cool. Sarah's not here to bust me' – he turned to her – 'are you?'

Their eyes met, held. Finally Sarah broke it off. 'I'm just trying to get to the truth, Graham. I'm trying to find out what happened. You just told me you promised your dad you would kill him . . . ?'

'*If*.' Graham held up a finger. 'There was a big if.'

'And what was that?'

'If the Alzheimer's snuck up on him, and suddenly his brain wasn't there. That was when I was going to do it.'

'How?'

'I don't know. I hadn't figured that yet. Or even if I was really going to. We hadn't got there. He was still functioning. But then he started getting the headaches and we found out about the tumor . . .'

'How did you find out about that?'

Graham's eyes went to Cerrone for a moment, then to Sarah. 'This is starting to sound like an interrogation, you know that?'

Sarah tried to bluff it. 'We're just talking, Graham.'

He motioned to the tape recorder. 'With that thing running? You're telling me you won't use anything on there?'

She shook her head. 'No, I can't tell you that.'

'So this is an official visit after all?'

Again, the eyes. 'What else would it be?'

'I don't know,' he said. 'A guy can hope.' He paused for a longish moment. 'Sure, Sal went to a doctor, I guess.'

'Do you know who?'

Another pause, longer this time. Graham sighed heavily and lowered his head, shaking it like a tired dog. 'You want to go off the record?'

She considered, then shook her head. 'I can't do that. I'm investigating your father's death, Graham. If you know something about it, you can tell me. Do you know the doctor your father consulted or not?'

Graham's eyes moved to the tape recorder. 'On the record I don't know. He went alone. I didn't live with him, you know. He had a life.'

'Did he tell you how he paid for this doctor? Didn't you talk about money?'

Graham shrugged. 'He told me about the cancer, that they couldn't operate, it was going to kill him. Then the whole question of putting him in a home kind of became moot. He wasn't going to get old as some shell in a wheelchair. He wasn't going to get old at all.'

The simple truth of this fact struck them all dumb. The CD even chose this moment to pause between cuts. Finally, Graham shrugged. 'Anyway, as I said, the last couple of weeks it got worse.'

But Sarah, now, wasn't quite ready to move on. Something

else was eating at her. 'The last time we talked on the record,' she said, 'you didn't know what was causing your father all this pain. Now you *did* know. Do I have that right?'

'Yeah. I knew. It was the cancer, the tumor.'

'But you didn't tell me then?'

Bad though it sounded, the rationale was obvious enough to Graham. 'I also told you we didn't see much of each other.' He broke a grin. 'Come on, Sarah, I was trying to be consistent and you caught me anyway.'

'And you still say you don't know where the morphine came from?'

'That's right.' He pushed his chair back. 'Hey, can we stop this already? I'm going to open some more wine. You want a little wine? A glass of beer? Mike?'

Sarah declined, and Mike said he had to go. He had a plane at an obscene hour the next morning. The three of them walked to the door, and Graham opened it, shook Mike's hand, told him good luck. Sarah hung back as Mike crossed the street and started walking downhill toward his car.

Sarah stood crammed next to Graham in the doorway. It seemed to her that every cell in her body was attuned to his proximity. Yet it also felt as though he was daring her not to move. He put an arm on the doorsill just over her shoulder, then put some weight on the arm – all but leaning on her. 'Are you really leaving?' he asked her.

She told herself that he wasn't completely sober. His inhibitions were lowered and, okay, he found her attractive. For the moment he'd forgotten that she was a cop. That was all it was. And she would be damned if she was going to duck away. Raising her head, she was looking up into his eyes.

Bad idea. Whether or not it betrayed her true feelings, she'd better blink. Otherwise, their superficially professional relationship was about to develop an overt new element. And if she thought she had troubles up to now . . .

She swung under his arm, outside onto the driveway. 'All right, Graham,' she said, 'if you'll just answer three quick questions, I promise I won't bother you anymore.' She broke a conciliatory smile. 'Tonight.'

'Then afterward you'll have a glass of wine with me?'

She shook her head. 'I can't. I'm on duty.'

'So go off duty,' he said. 'Ask your three questions, then declare your workday over.' His eyes never left her face.

This time she met his gaze. 'First, I want to be clear. You did, in fact, give your father morphine shots from time to time?'

He nodded. 'I said that.'

Actually, he hadn't said that, Sarah knew, but he'd been speaking so freely and he'd had enough to drink that she wasn't surprised that he didn't remember exactly what he had admitted. But he was telling the truth now. 'How often?'

'Is that the second question?'

She thought about it, and decided it could be. 'Yeah.'

'Couple of times a week, if I was there. He didn't like to shoot himself up. Okay, what's the third question?'

'After the two calls on Friday morning, when your dad called you in great pain, why didn't you go over there to help him?'

This last hurdle didn't slow Graham at all. He brought his arm down off the door, took a step toward her. 'Well, tell you the truth, that's what I did.' Spreading his hands, he grinned sheepishly. 'And guess what?' he asked. 'The old fart had gone out. He wasn't even there.'

Shaken with the import of what she'd heard – not only had Graham been at Sal's on Friday, he had often administered morphine to his father – she was nearly back to her car when she stopped herself up short and swore.

Her tape recorder was still on Graham's table!

She'd gotten up with the two guys to make sure Michael Cerrone of *Time* was good and gone before she attempted to ask her half-drunk suspect her last three questions. Then she'd ducked *outside* to escape the awful chemistry, asked her questions, and all but run away.

What a fool she was.

It had been less than five minutes, but the window slits high on the side wall had already gone dark. Knocking on the door, she heard no sound from within. Maybe he'd gone to sleep already, passed out. Or, more likely, she thought, he'd had it with reporters and the police. Whoever it was, he didn't want any. She knocked again, softly. 'Graham,' she whispered, 'it's me. Sarah.'

Sergeant! she reminded herself. She was here not as Sarah, but as *Sergeant* Evans.

After a minute she heard movement. The light over her head came on. When the door opened, Graham seemed somehow diminished. His expression, she felt, made every attempt to welcome her, but she couldn't miss the labor behind it. His eyes were exhausted, suddenly heavy lidded. 'I thought you were having another glass of wine,' she said.

All of Graham's glibness was gone. It was as though he'd fallen into a deep sleep and been rudely awakened. 'I think I'm about done for today. You gone off duty?' But the question wasn't inviting.

She pointed ambiguously behind him. 'I left my recorder on your table.'

He nodded and hit the light switch next to the door, stepping back to let her pass. The recorder was where she had left it, still spinning. She flicked it off and walked back to the door, where Graham had remained, waiting for her.

Outside again, she hesitated one last moment, looking up at him. 'Well, thanks for opening for me.'

'Sure, anytime,' he said. The door closed on her before she could turn away, and she wasn't three steps down the street when the overhead light went out.

For herself, she had her answer. This man had loved his father. There were still outstanding questions about the wrapped bills, the baseball cards. Graham had all but admitted he knew more and would tell her if she would go off the record, but she couldn't do that. Whatever else might be true, he hadn't killed Sal for his money.

Coming up here alone had served a purpose: she now believed that Graham had revealed who he really was, to her, to Sarah. But *Sergeant* Evans, homicide inspector, realized with a pang of anguish that the cost had been dear. She'd helped him dig himself further into an ever-deepening hole.

12

Hardy was in his backyard, a long and relatively narrow strip of grass bordered by Frannie's rose gardens. On either side apartment buildings rose to four stories. But directly behind to the east there was a clear view all the way to downtown. Also, beginning in about mid-April, when the sun contrived to shine, the path of it cut between the apartments, making a warm and cozy enclosure.

Now, tending to the barbecue, scraping the grill down, waiting for the coals to turn, Hardy was nearly recharged for the new week. Glitsky and his young son were coming over for dinner. So was Frannie's brother, Moses McGuire, and his wife, Susan, and their baby, Jason.

It was late afternoon on Sunday and both the weather and the mood around the house had warmed a little from the deep-freeze late in the week. And here in the backyard the house shielded most of the breeze off the ocean.

The other center of chill – Frannie – came down the back stairs with a large covered Tupperware container. Hardy watched her as she put it on the picnic table that was up against the house. She stood still a moment, then set her shoulders and deliberately walked the half-dozen steps over to her husband, leaning into him and putting one arm around his waist.

'Whatever you decide is all right, you know. It doesn't matter to me as long as we're in it together.'

He brought her in to him. 'Sometimes it doesn't seem like that,' he said. 'I thought you were pretty clear about no more murder cases.'

'That's what you told me *you* wanted, remember, so I got used to the idea, but I don't really care. It doesn't matter to me if you're a dog catcher if that's what you want to be, if that's what makes you happy.' She moved away a step so she could look at him. 'You're the one with all the angst, Dismas. I know what I'm doing.'

'It burns you out,' he said. 'The kids all the time.'

'No, it doesn't. Well, a little. But so what? That's not your problem. It's what I'm doing. If my husband were happier, life would be perfect. If *you* were happier with the kids . . .'

Hardy let out a breath. 'I love the kids, Fran, but—'

'There's always a *but*, Dismas. There shouldn't be a *but*. It's not the kids. It's not me or your job. It's your attitude.' She walked up and placed a quick kiss on his lips. 'Don't worry,' she said. 'Be happy. Sing the song. Check it out.'

Abe Glitsky sat straddling the picnic bench at the table by the house. He sat forward, elbows on his knees, his hands around a glass of iced tea. Hardy was lifting the lid from the kettle cooker, checking the chicken.

'You're not supposed to keep lifting the lid. It won't cook right. There's nothing worse than uncooked chicken.'

Hardy threw him a withering look, took a pull at his beer. 'Global warming is way worse,' he said. 'Acid rain. Hemorrhoid commercials. I can think of a hundred things.' He leveled the tongs at the grill. 'You don't lift the lid, how do you turn the chicken?'

'Once,' Glitsky said. 'You lift it once, turn the chicken, put the lid back on, come back in a half hour, it's done. That's why they invented this kind of barbecue, as a matter of fact. Brilliant scientists working around the clock to save you from the necessity of having to watch your chicken every minute.'

'That's my personality,' Hardy said. 'I need to watch things, stay in control. And a good thing I do too.'

Glitsky stood up and walked over. 'You could turn them now, for example. They look about done on the bottom. Then you could sit down and enjoy your beer without interruption.'

Hardy took a minute, poking and jabbing, then started turning the pieces. 'I'm not doing this because you said so. Independently, they look done to me too.'

'Half done,' Glitsky corrected.

Hardy took his beer back over to the bench, and sat down.

'Okay, now I'm enjoying my beer without interruption. By the way, what do you hear about Graham Russo?'

'By the way, huh?'

A nod. 'At your very own suggestion I sit myself down to take a moment of leisure, and what should pop into my brain unaided but the thought of my client.'

Glitsky took a seat at the other end of the bench, straddling it again. 'And here I allowed myself to hope that your wife had invited me over again because she enjoyed my company so much last time.'

'Maybe that too,' Hardy said, 'mysterious as that may be to the rest of us. But while you're here . . .'

'While I'm here, seriously, I'm not talking about it.'

Hardy had heard this kind of denial before in a dozen different guises, and usually it went away of its own accord. He wouldn't have to push. His friend would get around to telling him, off the record, or he wouldn't.

Hardy brought his bottle to his mouth, started to get up to check the chicken again, caught himself, and sat back down. 'So, how about them Giants?'

But the lieutenant was shaking his head. 'I don't think I can tell you anything this time, Diz. There is some serious juice around this one.'

'Powell?'

Glitsky shrugged. Hardy didn't even have to ask. He knew Powell had decided to prosecute the case. The question was when.

But he wasn't going to get that by asking directly. 'Did you know about the wife?' Hardy asked. 'Or did you read about it in the paper?'

In this morning's paper a reporter had discovered from reading recent police incident reports that Leland and Helen Taylor had summoned the authorities to the Seacliff palace known as the Manor three times in the past six weeks.

The first two times, it seems, Sal Russo had come by and knocked on the door. When Helen had opened it, he'd simply walked in, making himself at home – Helen's home was his home, wasn't it? wasn't she his wife? – helping himself to whiskey, becoming verbally abusive, refusing to leave.

The third time, Sal had let himself in through an open servants' entrance in the back, helped himself again to a couple of drinks, gone upstairs to where Helen was napping, and lain down next to and begun fondling her, demanding his conjugal rights.

In each case police had taken Sal to a local mental-health facility and booked him as a 'danger to himself and others.' The third time he was held for two hours and released. The first two times he hadn't stayed that long.

Glitsky nodded. 'Yeah, we heard about that on Saturday.'

'And you were looking into it as a possible motive for Sal's murder? Get another suspect in the loop?'

'Nice try. No comment.'

Sal Russo waited patiently on one of the plastic yellow chairs in the sunlight that streamed through the lobby door of the social welfare detention center. He had Graham coming down in a couple of minutes to take him back home. He'd surprised this social worker here – Don. Not only did the old man know who he was, he knew his son's telephone number.

'Hey, Sal,' Don called to him.

He opened his eyes. 'What?'

'You want to tell me why you keep breaking into your old house?' Don thought he could trick Sal into giving an answer that would incriminate himself, so they could maybe send him to jail. But Sal knew his game. Don wasn't fooling him.

'Sometimes I miss my wife. That a crime?'

'Except she's not your wife anymore.'

'We said till death do us part. I remember that clear enough, sonny. I'm trying to get her back.'

'Still, maybe it upsets her family now, don't you think? You do it again, they might try to lock you up.'

'Helen wouldn't lock me up. Don't you worry about it. What I got on her, she wouldn't dare.' He closed his eyes and faced the sun for another minute, a peaceful look settling over his features. 'She wasn't always Little Miss Proper, you know. We had ourselves some times. I reminded her today. Got her upset, I think. She doesn't want anybody to know.'

Sal suddenly brought his hand up and squeezed at his temples.

'You all right?' Don asked.

'Damn headache. I'm fine. We used to smoke a little dope, you

know. A few lines of cocaine once or twice. You think her Leland wants to hear about that? I don't think so. You think Leland knows she got arrested for shoplifting that time? You think that might bother him? Her Leland's a little too uptight to handle that news, isn't he?'

Don chuckled. 'And your wife had me thinking she didn't file a complaint because she didn't want to cause troubles for a harmless old man. You were blackmailing her, weren't you? You're not harmless at all, are you?'

Sal smiled. 'Not even a little,' he said.

Hardy got a better idea of the way the wind was blowing during dinner. It was still light outside, and the five adults were eating in the dining room while the kids ate their drumsticks in front of the video.

Susan Weiss was McGuire's wife. A cellist with the symphony, although she'd been on strike for a while now, she had an artistic temperament and spoke her mind freely. She knew all about the troubles with Glitsky's wife, Flo – that she had died a couple of years before after a prolonged battle with cancer. She couldn't understand how a man – 'even a cop' – who'd been through that experience could be opposed to ending the suffering of someone else who was in the same place.

'I'm not.' Glitsky put the evil eye on Hardy, as though his friend had somehow prompted Susan, then did his best to answer her, his voice under tight control. 'Even if I'm a cop, I'm not opposed to the idea of assisted suicide. But I think it ought to be more private, *much* more private than – than what we are seeing sometimes.'

'What do you mean, private?'

'I mean between the involved parties and no one else. Private.'

'How about doctor-assisted suicide? Kevorkian, all these guys. I hear half the doctors in the city do it all the time.'

'And this means?'

'Well, if you're going after Sal Russo's kid, shouldn't you also be going after these doctors? Isn't it the same thing?'

Glitsky appeared to be having trouble swallowing. He was the only adult at the table drinking water and now he took his glass and drank from it. 'No, it's not.'

'How's it different?'

Cornered, Glitsky let out a quick breath. 'It's different because somebody killed Sal Russo. *Murdered* him, and not out of mercy . . .'

'I don't think so,' Hardy said.

Seated between his wife and his sister, Moses McGuire had been relatively quiet throughout the meal. An Irish brawler, a doctor of philosophy turned bartender, Moses usually tended to be a presence. But he'd sat without comment on this discussion up to now, drinking steadily from his glass of Scotch.

McGuire knew that Glitsky and Hardy were friends. Moses also considered himself Hardy's *best* friend. This did not mean that Glitsky and McGuire were especially close. Now McGuire laid a proprietary hand on his wife's arm. 'Didn't the dead guy, Sal, didn't he have cancer?'

Glitsky nodded again. 'Yeah.'

'Inoperable, from what I hear? Right?'

Susan popped in. 'So how can you write off the idea that somebody helped him kill himself, that *that's* what he wanted?'

'We don't just write it off, Susan.' Glitsky was still striving for the patient tone. 'We collect evidence, see what it looks like, go from there.'

But McGuire was now warming to the argument, or from the Scotch, one of the two. 'You're going to have to go a hell of a long way from there to get around the fact that the guy was dying in a couple of weeks, anyway. Why in the world would somebody want to kill him?'

Frannie joined in, answering for the lieutenant. 'Abe's going to say it was money. Graham had a lot of his dad's money – fifty thousand dollars.'

'So what?' Susan said. 'That means he killed him?'

'No,' Abe replied, 'it means he might have. That's all we're looking at.'

Hardy spoke up. 'The reason he had the money was in case his dad had to go into a home.'

Though he knew Graham's story about the children of Joan Singleterry, he wasn't at all certain that he believed it. In any case, he didn't want to muddy the waters, and he'd come up with his own theory over the past day or two. He thought it had a more credible ring. 'His dad had it in a safe under his bed and Graham didn't think that was the most brilliant idea . . .'

Glitsky turned to Hardy. 'He tell you that?'

'He didn't have to.'

'I wonder why didn't he tell us?'

'Abe.' Frannie put down her fork. 'We don't mean to pick on you, but this just doesn't make sense. Susan's right. This kind of thing is happening every day. Why are you going after this boy?'

Glitsky clipped it out. 'Because he lied about everything we asked him. Lying makes us law-enforcement types suspicious.'

'But it was all of a piece, Abe.' Hardy, the voice of reason. 'Graham's already blackballed for legal work in town, he was afraid he'd lose his bar card if it came out he helped kill his dad, even with the best of intentions.'

Frannie picked it up. 'So he made up the story that he and his dad didn't see each other. He didn't think you guys would look so hard.'

'So it sounds like he didn't lie a lot.' Susan joined the chorus. 'He just told one lie and then had to make up a bunch of other stuff to support that one.'

A ghost of a smile flickering around his mouth, Glitsky sat back and crossed his arms. 'Just bad luck we happened to catch him at the big one, huh?' He came forward and picked up his fork. 'Maybe it's just me, but does anybody else think it's funny that he still had the money after his father was dead, then kind of forgot to tell his family about it?'

'Maybe he was going to,' Susan said. 'Maybe he just didn't have time yet, you arrested him so fast.'

'Maybe. More bad luck.' Glitsky's voice dripped with sarcasm. 'Graham Russo,' he said, 'the original bad-luck kid.'

Playing up front in mixed doubles, and standing too close to the net, Mario Giotti didn't even see the vicious forehand his opponent launched at his head.

One second he was on his toes, poised for a volley, following the flight of the ball his wife had just returned, and the next moment he was on the ground, flat on his back, the wind knocked out of him, conscious only of pain.

Sunday evening, and they were playing indoors at the

Mountain View Racquet Club, located on the crest of the escarpment in Pacific Heights, where Divisadero Street began its cascade down from Broadway to Lombard – eight hundred vertical feet in six blocks.

The judge was aware of people gathered over him, then his head on his wife's thigh. Someone brought over a white towel, then another one – wet and cool. He had an impression of blood, blotches of red on white in his vision, the brassy taste in the back of his throat.

Pat was taking control, as she always did. After satisfying herself that it was true, she assured one and all that Giotti was fine. She came down close and whispered into his ear. 'It's all right,' she assured him, 'you're okay.' She wiped the wet towel over his face again, gently.

Then they were up, he and Pat, walking together. The judge held the stained, wet towel to his face, aware of the stares of the other patrons. Their opponents, another couple a decade younger than they were, tagged along – extras, without any role – a few steps behind them. Giotti felt the sturdiness of his wife's shoulders, the weight they could bear. 'Just lean on me,' she said. He noticed some streaks of red on her short tennis skirt.

By the time they got to the juice bar, his breath was returning. He felt sure that his nose was broken, but the pressure he'd applied with the towel seemed to have stanched the flow of blood. The other couple – Joe and Dana – insisted on buying something, and Pat ordered large bottles of water for them both. They went off together, stricken and solemn.

Giotti watched after them. 'What's he think, we're in the goddamn French Open? This is supposed to be a friendly little workout, and we get Agassi and Evert. What is this shit?'

'Shh.' Pat put a hand on his knee, leaning in toward him, whispering. 'Somebody might hear, Mario.'

'Let 'em,' he snapped back at her, but his eyes, following hers, surveyed the nearby tables. No one was within earshot. He turned back to her. 'This public court nonsense. They should have installed one at the courthouse. You know your opponents. They know you. You can be civilized.'

The judge worked and had his chambers in the newly redone U.S. courthouse, the building that had gone unnoticed by Lanier and Evans two days before. The recent renovation, over eight years and at a cost of nearly $100 million, had restored the building to its original opulence, and that was saying something. Nicknamed the Federal Palace, it was widely considered, after the Library of Congress, to be the most beautiful government building in the United States.

The Palace had originally been built by Italian artisans. Completed just in time for San Francisco's Great Earthquake of 1906, it had miraculously survived that catastrophe because the postal clerks who worked in the new building at the time had refused to leave, choosing instead to fight the fires that threatened it.

Now the elegant interior of the place – marble walls and frescoed ceilings – had a modern infrastructure. It was newly wired for computer terminals in nearly every room. Over the objections of many of the judges, including Giotti, who felt that the courts should be open and accessible to the people without hindrance, security was tight. Video cameras hovered at each entrance, with a bank of television screens overseen by uniformed deputies at a central command post by the front doors. Downstairs, a private, indoor parking area for the judges led to an equally private workout room and gym for the staff.

But no tennis courts, for which Giotti had lobbied strenuously. According to the experts there hadn't been room.

This was an opportunity for the judge to remember it, and he continued raving at his wife, although quietly, to be sure. 'We should join a private club.'

'No, we can't do that, Mario. We've discussed it. Let's leave that now.'

'No. I don't agree.'

Her eyes narrowed in resolve and her fingers tightened on his leg, just above his knee, a warning. Pat was a powerhouse, physically strong and mentally tough. The monitor of the judge's behavior outside of the court, the guardian of his precious reputation. He rarely disagreed with her judgment in these areas, but today he did. 'People can be discreet,' he said. 'We don't need to make friends, have private dinners. But the class of people—'

'Don't use that word, please.'

A frustrated expression. 'You know what I mean.'

'And I also know we can't refer to it. Ever.'

So Giotti went back to his original complaint. 'A hundred million dollars and they couldn't figure out a way to put a court in the basement. I solve more difficult problems three times a week. Fucking bureaucrats.'

Pat was by now reassured that her husband couldn't be heard, but his profanity when angry still was a source of frustration. Her fingers tightened around Giotti's leg again. It made her crazy – he didn't seem to realize who he was sometimes. Or, more truthfully, he seemed to want to forget that a federal judge was not an ordinary citizen. All of them breathed rarefied air and were accountable on a different level.

And her husband particularly – a centrist Democrat – had to be ever vigilant. There were rumors that he was in line for the Supreme Court at the next vacancy. Surely, he'd earned it: the lifetime of sagacious decisions, published majority opinions, brilliant dissents, the millions of travel miles as he flew the circuit, the sacrifice of abandoning all their old friends, all of the city's rich social life, on the altar of judicial purity.

But that last wasn't unique to the Giottis. To avoid any appearance of conflict of interest, and because of the awesome responsibility of the issues they must daily decide, most, if not all, federal judges wound up cutting off their preappointment relationships – both business and personal. That was part and parcel of the life of the federal judge, and those who didn't know it at their appointment soon found out, sometimes to their great dismay and disappointment.

Even despair.

They couldn't have friendships in the usual meaning of the word. It wasn't so much that people couldn't be trusted. No, it was more that if he served long enough – and the job was a lifetime appointment – sooner or later a federal judge would be called upon to make a decision that would impact nearly everyone he had ever known.

A casual friendship, an innocent prejudice, a personal comment, an inappropriate liaison, too great an attachment even to a son or a daughter, or a wife – any of these could sully the sacred objectivity of the law.

Pat Giotti knew that this was why all the federal judges were such a family. And in that artificial and ethereal family, where there were few real friendships and little outside influence, reputation was all.

Of course, she knew, Mario's profanity wasn't going to lose him his job, but it might lower the judge in the eyes of even one citizen, and Pat Giotti, bred to the culture of the Ninth Circuit, would not abide that. She, too, had made great sacrifices to further her husband's career – her own friendships, her fun, the intimacy of their four children, her youth. Sometimes, she thought in her dark moments, her very life.

But these thoughts passed. They couldn't be allowed. It had all been worth it. Mario Giotti was a federal judge now. He was someday, with luck, going to the Supreme Court, perhaps as its chief justice, the culmination of their every dream, the goal for which they had never ceased laboring. Together.

The couple had come back and the man was blathering on. 'I'm just so sorry,' Joe was saying. 'I get too competitive. I shouldn't have—'

'Don't be silly,' Pat interrupted. 'Spirit of the game. You don't play if you don't want to win, isn't that right, Mario?'

The judge pulled the towel down from the bridge of his nose. His eyes were mild, the smile benign. 'It's one of the absolute truths, Joe.' He took a long sip of the bottled water. Then, 'Don't worry about me, I'm fine. Could've happened to anybody.'

Helen Taylor reclined in the oversized marble bathtub, soaking in scented oils. The disastrous meeting with Graham on Friday night had exhausted the family. After her children had gone, she and Leland went out to a late supper at the Ritz-Carlton and afterward, keeping the unpleasantness at bay, they'd danced at the Top of the Mark. The rest of the weekend had been given over to society events. They'd had no private time to talk. Until now.

Leland knocked at the bathroom door and she told him to come in, which he did, taking a seat in the brocaded wing chair that graced the wall opposite the bath. Crossing one leg over the other, he leaned back, enjoying the sight of his wife in the water. He was wearing the pants to one of his Savile Row suits, a white shirt and dark blue tie, black shoes, black socks with garters.

Inhaling through his nose, he seemed to have suddenly encountered an off scent. His voice had a reedy tone, highly pitched and phlegmy. 'I suppose we're going to have to pay for Graham's defense, aren't we?'

Helen took a moment before answering. 'I keep hoping they're not going to arrest him again.'

'No.' Leland was certain. 'It's a matter of time, but they will. I wouldn't squander my hope there.'

His wife sighed and moved. The water lapped gently once or twice. 'Then I suppose we must. Pay his attorneys, I mean. I know he can't.'

The phantom scent wasn't getting any better. Leland held his chin high, turning his head from one side to the other, as if trying to place it. 'We'll have to keep it from George.' He paused. 'Perhaps it should be a loan this time. A real loan.'

'Through the bank? If it's through the bank, it would be impossible to keep from George.'

Her husband was shaking his head no. 'I was thinking of a personal loan. We could—'

But another thought had crowded in, and Helen interrupted. 'You don't really think he'll go to jail, do you?'

'I don't know, Helen. If he did kill his father for the money—'

'Graham couldn't have done that, Leland. It's impossible. That's not who he is. He might have helped him die, but it wasn't for money.'

Her husband raised his eyebrows, a parlor trick of impressive eloquence. He lived in a world entirely circumscribed by money, and believed that to a substantial degree *everything* was connected to it. But there was no need to make this point to his wife, and he moved along. 'I'm thinking, though – back to the loan now – that if he *doesn't* get convicted, we might be able to get some reasonable behavior out of the boy, at least until the debt was retired.'

'But if he does? Get convicted, I mean.'

'I suppose then he'll have rather a more difficult time paying us back.' Leland seemed to savor the thought. 'But that isn't really the issue. When we paid for his law school – a mistake, as it turns out—'

'Maybe it won't turn out to be eventually.'

But there was no sign he heard her. 'Law school, if you recall, supposedly wasn't the money either.' He held a palm up to forestall any interruption. 'I'm only saying that if it had been a loan instead of a gift with no strings, if he'd felt the monthly burden of paying off a debt, he might have thought twice about quitting his job.'

'No, he wouldn't have. He thought he'd be stepping up, playing in the major leagues, making multiples of his clerk's salary at the court. That was the whole problem. He probably wouldn't take a loan anyway, knowing he couldn't guarantee paying it back.'

'So what's this attorney of his working for?'

Helen shifted again, sitting up. Slipping the net from her hair, she shook it out and it fell gleaming – dyed, but gleaming – to her shoulders. Her breasts were buoyant at the water's surface. 'I don't know. Advertising, maybe. I imagine there'll be a lot of publicity.'

'Of course. There always is.' From Leland's expression the bad smell was back. 'Well, there'll be time to decide. This assisted-suicide angle looks promising. Perhaps a jury will clear him on that score.'

'But that would still ruin him,' his mother said. 'He couldn't ever work in the law again, and I do think that eventually he intended to do just that.'

'Don't entertain these false hopes, Helen. He's out of the law – that's already come to pass.' He uncrossed his legs and came forward in the chair, a great deal more urgency in his body language. He cleared his throat, his voice taking on a deeper pitch. 'Now, I must tell you, I am worried about George.'

'Yes,' she said simply. Her younger son's reaction to Graham had been wildly disproportionate as well as out of character. If George had any trademark, it was generally his *lack* of emotion, not his susceptibility to it. 'That really wasn't like him.'

'I wondered if he'd talked to you.'

Her pretty face held a thoughtful frown. 'About what?'

'That Friday. Anything that might have happened that Friday.'

She shook her head. 'No. Not to me.'

'Because, you know, he wasn't at the bank.'

Her eyes narrowed; apparently this was news to her. She slid back down, slightly, into the comforting water. 'When wasn't he at the bank?'

Leland stroked his upper lip. 'I don't have it precisely fixed, but it seems between about eleven and two.'

'Did you ask him?'

'I did. But you know George. He said he must have been at a client's, he couldn't remember exactly. If it was important, he'd double-check. But he hasn't gotten back to me. I wondered if he'd mentioned anything to you.'

'No. Nothing, Leland. Honestly, nothing.' She let out a sigh, watching as her husband resumed his old posture, his back rigid against the wing chair, one leg crossed over the other. 'You don't think he went to see his father?'

'I'm afraid I think it's quite possible. I don't like to think it, but it's almost as though I see it happening.'

Helen shook her head. 'We shouldn't have had him come over when Sal was here. That last time.'

But Leland brushed that off. 'Well, what we should or shouldn't have done is beside the point now. He did come. And in this one area, protecting you from Sal—'

'I know. I think it was just he never got over the hurt. He continued to believe that anyone who could inflict such pain couldn't be harmless.'

'Maybe, at base, Sal wasn't harmless after all.'

'No.' She was certain. 'He was.' She reached a hand out over the marble, and her husband took it. 'He wasn't like you, Leland. He really was a simple person. He wouldn't ever have hurt me. He was sick and confused, that's all.'

The tableau froze for a long moment. At last the banker's eyes came back into focus. 'I just wonder if George realized that. That we'd taken steps. Maybe if we had in fact filed charges—'

But Helen was firm. 'There was no need, Leland. We did inform the social agencies. They would be getting around to him. This wasn't a continual stalking, just an episode—'

'Several actually.'

'Three. Only three. But the point is that there wasn't really any urgency. And these things always take time. There was no further danger – in fact, there hadn't been any danger all along. Sal would just flip into the past. I *know* George realized that.'

'I hope so,' Leland said. 'But I'm not at all so sure.'

13

On Monday morning, early, Hardy was in his office with Michelle, one of them on either end of the couch, folders and copies of briefs on the low table in front of them.

'You know where we get the term *straight from the horse's mouth*?' Michelle looked up from some paper she'd been reading as though Hardy had broken into Sanskrit. 'It relates, it relates.'

Small talk wasn't Michelle's long suit, but she had already learned that this was how her new boss liked to break up his work, so she sat back and listened.

'No, this is important. We're talking one of the major philosophical questions that plagued the early Middle Ages – right up there with "How many angels can dance on the head of a pin?" '

'What was?'

'How many teeth a horse had.'

'You're kidding me.'

Hardy was having a difficult time believing that Michelle – with the possible exception of David Freeman the most highly developed brain in the office – was ignorant of this fact. But then, he'd seen enough intellectual myopia that it didn't shock him anymore. Here in the Age of Specialization if you held a double major in law and accounting, you weren't expected to master any *context*. Any *history*. That was irrelevant junk for the most part.

But Hardy thought it wouldn't kill her to know an oddball fact or two that wasn't strictly related to the case at hand. 'I'm not kidding. They argued about it all the time.'

'Who would argue about that?'

'Philosophers and theologians, most of whom, I think, would have been lawyers in today's world.'

'So why didn't they just count them?' She made a face at him, wondering if he was teasing her. 'Are you making this up?'

'No, I swear I'm not. It's true. Okay, Michelle, you got the right answer, but you're ahead of my story. Listen. These guys would sit around the old monastery, convinced that there was a Platonic ideal number of teeth in the perfect horse. They evidently debated this thorny problem for decades.'

'These were not rocket scientists,' Michelle said.

Hardy wondered if she realized they were talking about a time before there were rockets, or scientists, for that matter. 'No, but these were intelligent men.'

'No women?'

'I doubt it. I'd be surprised. This was a guy thing.'

'No wonder,' Michelle said.

'Well, anyway,' Hardy continued, 'one day a monk who was far ahead of his time decided on the revolutionary approach of going out, finding a horse, and counting the teeth in its mouth.'

'And that settled it.'

'Well, not exactly. I gather it took maybe a hundred years or so before everybody agreed that this was an acceptable way to get an answer to a question like this. Anyway,' he pressed on in the face of Michelle's sublime tolerance, 'that's where we get the expression.'

'Great,' she said dryly. 'That's fascinating. Really.'

The judge in the Tryptech case had just taken on the modern role of the monk who'd counted all those teeth. First thing this morning, Michelle had called Hardy at home with the news that they had been served with a cross-complaint. The Port of Oakland had evidently decided to press the charge that Tryptech had overloaded their container. Further, a judge had decided that Tryptech had the burden of proof as to how many computers were actally in the container. An affidavit from some shipping guy wasn't going to do it.

Tryptech – through Hardy – had been making the argument that the container hadn't been overloaded. He had presented the bill of lading, which, in theory, 'proved' the actual number of computers inside the container. Additionally, the computers were insured and therefore it would obviously be counterproductive for the company to claim *fewer* than had actually been there, since they were being paid for every one that had been lost.

Of course, Hardy knew it wouldn't take a genius to realize that the monetary difference between say, two hundred extra computers at a thousand dollars each, and the millions the company stood to lose if the Port of Oakland won the lawsuit, was fabulously insignificant. Now the thing would have to be lifted from the bottom of the Bay, so that the computers within could be counted.

But pulling up the container would cost a bundle, and their client had told them he didn't have a bundle on hand in cash just now.

The name of the game was delay, and Hardy had been successful in putting off this problem for nearly five months. However, now that the judge had decided, it was going to happen. The dredging fee of one hundred and sixty-five thousand dollars might not be unreasonable in light of the potential size of the damage award, but Brunel was saying it was blood from a turnip.

Hardy didn't know how he could delay any longer. Tryptech would have to figure out some way to come up with the money.

'Actually' – Michelle was more comfortable now that they were back to business – 'I see a way that we can use this to our advantage. We should be able to string this along for a while.'

'Okay, hit me,' Hardy said.

'Take it out to bid. We'll of course comply with the ruling, but unless the Port wants to take on some – no, *all* – of the expense, I think we can argue that it's only fair that we solicit bids from competing dredging firms, get the best possible price. Who could argue with that?'

Hardy had to admire her. Say what he would about the values of his own classical training, he had to admit that in the here and now Michelle was a godsend. Competing bids would buy them another few months at least, and anything could happen in a couple of months.

Maybe, Hardy fantasized, he could convince Brunel to hire a team of scuba divers to locate the container in deep secrecy by night and put in some extra units, the presence of which Brunel continued to assert.

'How would you like to handle the details?' he asked her.

She had already gathered the paperwork and put it atop the stack of briefs they still had to discuss. 'That's what I'm here for.'

* * *

Before the 'horse's mouth' issue had intervened, the morning routine at home had been anything but. Today's drama was the mystery of how every toothbrush in the house had disappeared.

Upon some pretty hefty cross-examination, Rebecca and Vincent had confessed that maybe they remembered that yesterday Orel Glitsky might have thought of another use for them and they'd played some game in the backyard, or mostly in the backyard, they thought. There were fences and forts involved.

And Jason, their little nephew – 'and he's still a baby, Dad,' Rebecca reminded him – had played with the toothbrushes too. But both of his kids were *sure,* they were *positive,* that if somehow they *had* taken all the toothbrushes, which wasn't very likely, but if they had, then they had put them back right afterward.

After finishing up the morning's strategy-and-review session with Michelle, he'd walked three blocks in the breezy forenoon and picked up half a dozen fresh *bao* – sticky buns filled with *hoisin* and plum and barbecued sauces and stuffed with various roasted meats – pork, chicken, duck. All by itself, he thought, the ready availability of hot-out-of-the-oven *bao* was reason enough to live in San Francisco.

He was in the greenhouse Solarium, alone, the *bao* a still-fragrant and comforting memory, the morning *Chronicle* open on the table in front of him. He hadn't forgotten anything about his talk last night with Abe Glitsky. (Maybe Glitsky had stolen the toothbrushes! Aha! That was it. Even if it wasn't, he could accuse him of it and have some fun.)

It had become pretty clear in the talk at the table that Glitsky thought Sal had been killed and, more, that Graham had murdered him. And if that was the case, then Glitsky knew more than Hardy did.

He scanned the paper, but there was nothing particularly new and exciting there. The weekend hadn't provided any startling revelations. Even DA Pratt and AG Powell had maintained what one article called a 'wary silence.' Thirty-one doctors took out a full-page advertisement announcing that they had helped patients kill themselves, but this, Hardy knew, wasn't going to have any direct impact on the Graham Russo case.

So what did Glitsky know?

Pulling the ten-button conference-room phone over to him, he started to call the homicide detail, but hung up. If the lieutenant hadn't talked to him sixteen hours ago, he wasn't going to start now. Nothing had changed on that front.

Suddenly, that old horse's mouth yawed open before him again. 'Idiot,' he said to himself, shaking his head.

A miracle, Graham was home and picked up his telephone. But the first words out of his mouth – that he'd spent more time chatting with Sarah Evans – cut short Hardy's happiness that he'd reached his client. 'You're making this up, aren't you, Graham?' he said. 'Please tell me you're making this up.'

'No. I'm not. It was really good.'

'It was really good,' Hardy repeated. 'That's nice. I'm happy for you.'

'It wasn't like what you're thinking,' Graham protested.

Hardy could picture him, sitting framed in his splendid back window, looking out over the city, having a cup of his terrific Kona coffee, perhaps savoring a fresh croissant, bought with who knows what money. Maybe, Hardy thought, living up there in fairy-tale land colored one's view of the rest of the world.

In any case, Graham was in serious need of a reality check. 'What wasn't it like? You tell me. How it *could* be different from what I'm thinking? Even in the best of all worlds, what other interpretation could there possibly be?'

'If Sarah was going to arrest me, Diz, she would have done it already. She just wanted to know.'

'We're talking *Sergeant* Evans of the homicide detail, is that right? Suddenly, she's Sarah now? Are you guys going out together, staying in, what? It would help if I knew.'

'Nothing, Diz. Nothing like that.'

'She just wanted to know the truth?'

'Right.'

'And the *Time* guy, what about him?'

'He was a good guy.'

Hardy could envision the shrug, the nonchalance. He knew he was getting geared up here, and he didn't think it would hurt his client any to realize it. 'Graham, it's this reporter's *job* to be a good guy and get you to like him so you'll open up and tell him the story he needs to write. It's not personal.'

'No.' Graham was convinced. 'This was different. Really. It was great to get to lay some of it out finally.'

Hardy had both of his elbows on the table, the receiver cradled against one ear, his head held up with the other one. There wasn't any sense in going further with this. It was time to shift to damage control, if that was going to be possible. He forced some modulation into his voice. 'So what did you tell your friend Sarah this time? I hope parts of it were close to the last version.'

He heard an amused chuckle. 'It's just the obvious stuff. Nothing to worry about.'

'Obvious?'

'You know.'

'I don't, really. Why don't you humor me?'

'Well, the truth about my dad and me. I mean, of course I helped him out. Once it was clear that we'd kind of patched things up, the rest of it just followed.'

'What "rest," though? That's what I'm trying to get at.'

A pause. 'That I'd given him morphine a bunch of times. But not that day,' he added.

'You told Sergeant Evans that?'

'Yeah.' Another hesitation, longer. 'And that I'd gone by there, on Friday. By Sal's. But he hadn't been home.'

At almost precisely the same moment State Attorney General Dean Powell was reaching his own decision. He'd quietly come down from Sacramento early in the morning and spent the morning with Drysdale and Gil Soma. Now they were finishing their lunch at a back table in Jack's – one of the city's finest and oldest restaurants. An elderly waiter in a tuxedo was pouring coffee all round. The white linen had been cleared of crumbs.

Powell originally hailed from San Francisco. Before his election he'd been a senior attorney in the DA's office. His habit of combing his long white hair with his fingers had been the subject of dozens of caricatures, and he was doing this as he spoke to Soma. 'I think we're close to settled on the basics, but I must confess, Gil, I've got a reservation or two about your involvement. You ever put on a murder trial before?'

Powell, of course, knew the answer to this. He was impressed with Soma's credentials and, more, his passion, but if the young man couldn't stand up to the pressure of his boss's informal interrogation now, he'd melt in the crucible of a special-circumstances-case courtroom. Better to find out sooner.

Soma brought a napkin to his lips, but didn't waste any time with the motion. He wasn't stalling. 'No, sir, but I can win this case.'

'As a murder one?'

'It is a murder one. This morning's police reports lock that up. This wasn't any assisted suicide.'

Powell nodded. 'I buy that, Gil. It's critical, though, that we have the right man.' He leaned over the table, combed his hair back again, then pointed a finger at Soma. 'You hate this Graham Russo, don't you? It's personal, isn't it?'

Soma glanced over at his mentor, Art Drysdale, who was stirring his coffee. No help there. 'I don't like him, sir, that's true.'

'And you're sure you're not seeing what you want to see here? You've thought about this a lot?'

Now Soma did reach for his coffee. Powell thought this a well-rehearsed move. The question appeared to call for thought and even if Soma had considered every possible ramification of it, he would take a formulaic pause. Placing the cup carefully into the center of its saucer, Soma brought in Drysdale for a beat, then proceeded. 'The original case – the DA's here in the city – had several holes. The money alone wasn't really enough, and we knew that, which was why we waited. Since then we've discovered that there was a fight, that Graham Russo was there – he's admitted it . . .'

Drysdale finally spoke up. 'That's a little squirrely.'

But Soma didn't think so. 'It's evidently not on the tape, but Glitsky guarantees we've got Evans's testimony. She'll swear to it.'

'Then we're back to "he said, but she said." '

Powell interrupted. 'Art, play devil's advocate a little later. I want to hear what we've got altogether.' He gestured back to Soma.

'Okay, we've got the fight. We put Graham there. We've got the morphine, plus syringes from a box traced to his ambulance company. We got a fistful of his lies on the record. We've got his financial position, which is horrible, and which leads us back to the money. We've got means, opportunity, and motive. It's classic, sir. He did it and we can prove it.'

On Soma's left Drysdale cleared his throat. He wanted in.

'Art?' Powell asked.

'I agree with everything Gil's said here, but if we're talking specials . . .'

'We are.' Powell was solid with this decision.

'Okay, then the options we've got are LWOP' – this was life in prison without the possibility of parole – 'or death. Gil, you're telling me you're comfortable asking the state to put your old office mate to death?'

This, finally, stopped the posturing. Some of Soma's spark went away. 'I don't know,' he said, taking in both of his superiors. 'To be honest, I don't think so. I don't think we should ask for death.'

Powell nodded. This was the right answer. Soma was passionate, but not blinded by hatred, a critical distinction.

'I wouldn't either,' Drysdale said, 'but we might wave it around early on, see if something shakes loose.'

Soma shrugged. 'I can do that.'

'And no other suspects? Real? Imagined? Implied?' Powell wasn't getting into this without having it locked up. He hadn't gotten where he was by going high profile and losing. Drysdale passed the question over to Soma with a look. 'We're still checking some of his fisherman contacts. He poached for a living, but the volumes are tiny. A hundred, two hundred bucks. I don't see anyone killing him for it.'

'The family,' Drysdale prompted.

'Oh, yeah. Sal – the victim – he broke into the family house three times in the past few months. Nobody seemed to get too upset, though. They didn't file criminal charges. Just wanted to help him get some assistance.'

Okay, Powell was thinking. The loopholes are closing up. 'And it was definitely not a suicide? I don't want to have that come back and bite us.'

Drydale took this one. 'I don't think they'll even make the argument, but Strout's got some pretty good stuff for us. Nobody thinks Sal killed himself. That didn't happen.'

A silence descended for a moment. Powell raised his eyes. 'Dismas Hardy's doing the defense?'

'Yes, sir.' Soma knew the story as well as he knew his name. Three years before, in the last major case Powell had prosecuted before moving to the state capital, Dismas Hardy had pulled a rabbit from a hat and beaten him after a jury had both convicted his suspect *and* sentenced her to death. It was no secret that the AG longed for payback.

'All right,' Powell said at last. 'Let's go get him.'

Drysdale tapped the table with a fingertip, getting their attention one last time. 'I suggest, with all respect, Dean, it might be wiser to wait another couple of days. Graham's not going anywhere. Make it fat.'

This was jargon from Powell's earliest days with the DA – FAT was the acronym they'd all used back then for making a watertight case. Frog's-ass tight – FAT.

Powell gave it another second's thought, then nodded. 'All right,' he said. 'That's probably smart. But let's tie this sucker down by Thursday, Friday at the latest.'

He was looking directly at Soma, and the young attorney simply nodded. 'Done,' he said.

He'd been the head of homicide now for nearly two years, and Glitsky felt he was growing into the job, taking bold steps to improve conditions and performance. This morning, for example, after he'd trotted down to vice again with Lanier and Evans so they could enjoy the privacy of an office with a door, he'd come back to homicide and pulled a tape measure from one of the drawers in his desk.

After carefully measuring the size of the hole in his wall where the door should have been – in fact, used to be until it was removed one day for painting and never returned – he called a local hardware store and found that doors were not some kind of embargoed item. The salesperson to whom he'd spoken had seemed somewhat amused that Glitksy didn't realize that doors were available on a regular basis almost anywhere.

Upon reflection the lieutenant realized that he should have known this from his own life, but he also knew that when you worked in a bureaucracy, simple tasks had a way of becoming herculean, difficult tasks impossible. He'd filled out four requisition forms from building maintenance requesting a new door, and in two years hadn't yet gotten even one answer.

Eventually, he'd come to accept that a new door wasn't ever going to appear. And then, suddenly, the bolt of inspiration had struck him this morning: he could just order his own door! Take up a collection among his inspectors. The salesperson assured him he could have the door installed by Friday – painted, fitted, hung.

Miraculous!

Now it was midafternoon and Lanier and Evans were back. It was Glitsky's second meeting with them today. The first one, down behind the closed door in vice, had been to bring the lieutenant up to date with a recap of their weekend's activities. At this confab he'd learned of the apparent fight in Sal's apartment. He was also pleased with Evans's discoveries about Graham Russo – the morphine, the visit to Sal's on the day of the murder. He wasn't so thrilled about her technical blunder with the tape recorder, but what could he do?

That first meeting had been to prepare Glitsky for his nine o'clock with Drysdale, who'd be passing along all of his information to Dean Powell. Evidently that meeting had gone fairly well, because after lunch Drysdale had called again.

Powell had been disposed to proceed immediately with the arrest of Graham Russo, Drysdale said, but he had convinced the attorney general that a few more days might be productive, might lock the case up FAT. He gave Glitsky some marching orders.

And now – the second meeting – the lieutenant planned to pass these along to the troops. Gil Soma had been sent along – Drysdale probably trying to make the new kid feel part of a team.

They were all crammed in Glitsky's office, the lieutenant at his desk, Soma in the doorway. Evans stood at ease behind one of the chairs facing his desk. Lanier was more relaxed, propped on the corner of the desk, cracking and eating peanuts, dropping the shells in the wastebasket. Mostly.

But first Glitsky was killing a couple of minutes, loosening up the audience, crowing in his low-key way about his proactive move regarding the door.

He had just finished outlining his bureaucracy theory and it rang a bell with Lanier. 'Reminds me of one time back when I walked a beat, they were having this trade show. At the Holiday Inn, I think. One of those hotels. Anyway, guys in one of the booths were just freaking out. Couldn't get all these logos and lights and stuff to go on. So they called us cops over, right? I take a look and there's this plug on the ground and I ask 'em, "This the plug?" and they say, "Yeah, but the union rep came by and told us not to touch it." So I give 'em the look, plug the sucker in, the place lights up like a Christmas tree. I give 'em my badge number, tell them if anybody asks, they didn't touch it, have a nice day.'

'That's perfect,' Glitsky said. 'Exactly what I mean. You think the door might really be in here by Friday? I don't know what this office will feel like, it's been so long . . .'

Against the back wall Evans coughed politely. 'Are we going back down to vice?' she asked.

Glitsky caught her drift. 'Okay, you're right, it's probably not as fascinating to you all as it is to me.' He straightened up in his chair. 'No, I think we'll stay here.' He included the young attorney. 'This okay with you, Gil? There's nothing to hide about this.'

The two inspectors glanced at each other. 'About what?' Lanier asked.

'About what, Gil?' Glitsky repeated.

Soma was pumped up from his personal meeting with the attorney general. His tailored dark suit seemed to hang like a tent on a thin frame. Glitsky had sat down because he didn't want to tower over Soma.

But what the young man lacked in physique, he made up for in intensity. Nodding at the lieutenant, he began. 'The AG likes everything you've both done up to now. We've got plenty of evidence to convict. But for the next few days he thinks a change of emphasis might be productive.'

'To what?' Lanier asked.

'To everybody but Graham Russo.'

A moment of silence. Lanier cracked a peanut. 'But Graham did it.'

Soma nodded. 'I know that. But Dean Powell wants to turn over a few more rocks, that's all. You've both undoubtedly noticed this one's a political bomb. We want to head off any accusation that we're going after Graham for politics. Show that there's no rush to judgment.' He altered his tone, lightening it. 'He just wants to make sure.'

Glitsky leaned back and his chair creaked. Lanier swung his leg and his heel kept knocking into Glitsky's desk – *bump, bump, bump*. Deep and hollow sounding. 'These interviews,' Soma went on. 'Do you tape all of them?'

Lanier threw a glance at Glitsky, who was silent, sitting back, arms crossed, listening. 'Maybe we *should* have gone to vice,' Lanier said.

Evans moved forward. The young attorney had moved more into the room and had lowered his voice. She didn't want to miss anything. 'Why would we need to go to vice?' she asked.

But her partner was a veteran cop. He knew what was coming and didn't wait for Soma before he butted in. 'You don't want us to create any paper. Is that what you're saying?'

The young attorney nodded. 'That would probably be more convenient.'

'What are you guys talking about?'

With a nod Soma tossed it back to Lanier. 'Discovery.'

'Okay,' Evans said, 'I give up. What about discovery?'

'The prosecution's got to give everything to the defense, right? Everything they get. So if we go finding alternative suspects and reasonable evidence, guess what? The defense gets to bring them all up in front of the jury, so they can make up their mind.'

'Essentially,' Soma added, 'Mr Powell doesn't want us to help the defense by providing them with other suspects a jury might get confused about. So you talk to these people—'

'What people, though?'

A shrug. 'The rest of the family, where Sal got his fish, who got him the morphine if it wasn't Graham, like that.'

Lanier: 'But we don't run tape, we don't take notes.'

Soma: 'Right. Basically, you tell us what you find, but you don't create discovery.'

'And as an extra special treat,' Lanier added to Sarah, 'you didn't hear it here.'

Sarah all but glared at the inscrutable Glitsky, hoping that he'd speak up. He didn't.

'But—'

Soma stopped her. '*Except*, of course, if someone really starts to look like a suspect.' He added hastily, 'But if you think you've got something, talk to us before you write it up.'

Silence.

'We wouldn't want to create false impressions . . .' He trailed off lamely.

In the small room Sarah again became aware of the bump of her partner's heel. He cracked another peanut. She moved around and sat in the chair in front of her lieutenant's desk. This type of discussion was all new to her, and it wasn't settling well. Soma and Lanier must have realized it, as a glance passed between them, and Lanier took the ball.

'I think Mr Soma's just talking about the preliminary interviews, Sarah. We get anything that sets off a charge, we come back and do the soup-to-nuts version. Is that it?'

'But you won't,' Soma said, 'because Graham did it, right?'

'Right.' Lanier was with the program, ready to be rolling again. 'You just want to avoid making a case for the defense. We got it.'

Sarah wanted to make it crystal clear. 'But we are, in fact, looking for another suspect. Isn't that true?'

'Absolutely,' Soma said. 'If somebody jumps up at you, we put Graham on hold and go after the new guy. But there isn't going to be any new guy. Look, Sergeant, you and your partner here found Graham out of a universe of potentials, right?'

'Right.'

'So he's the man. This is just some CYA for the AG. We're beating the bushes, backfilling, making sure we haven't missed a bet. Any righteous evidence, I promise you, we cough it up.' Sarah obviously still didn't like it, and Soma moved to cut her off. 'We're not subverting anything here. We're not asking you to.'

Finally Glitsky's chair squeaked again. He came forward, the scar white through his lips, a pulse visible at his temple. All eyes went to him. 'I'm going to pretend I didn't hear any of this,' he whispered. He turned his wrathful gaze to Soma. 'I don't know how you boys do things in other jurisdictions, but this department writes up everything. That's our job. We find what there is to find, all of it.'

Soma had blanched. 'I didn't mean—'

His voice still low and taut, Glitsky sounded meaner than he looked, and Evans thought that was a physical impossibility. 'I know what you meant. I heard you all the way out. And I'm telling the sergeants here that they are going to do it by the book. Every time. Everybody we talk to. That covers our ass. It covers your ass. Everybody stays clean.'

He shook his head, calming down by degrees, still at Soma. 'Listen. What do you think happens if some defense attorney notices we haven't interviewed anybody except the suspect? You think this might raise an eyebrow somewhere? What if they find we talked to somebody and "forgot" to tell them? Think that's a problem? I do. I've seen it happen. No. Our position is that if there's anybody else to look for, we're looking for them. We don't find 'em, there's no other leads, that's why the case is strong.' He met the eyes of all three of them, one at time, slowly. 'Just so we're clear. Everybody on the same bus here?'

Nods all around.

In under a minute they'd all filed out. He decided then and there: he would pay out of his own pocket if he had to for a door to close behind them.

14

After his inspectors had gone, Glitsky was drinking a cup of tea, filling out a requisition form for the door. That, he decided, would be his first offensive sally. Stamping URGENT in red ink on the slip, he put his tea down and was taking the slip outside to post in the building mail when he ran into Dismas Hardy in the hallway, coming down in his direction.

'All right,' Hardy said, anger all over him. 'What did you do with them?'

'What?'

'My toothbrushes, that's what. Every single toothbrush in my whole house.'

'What did *I* do with your toothbrushes?'

'Right. They were there yesterday when you came over. This morning they were gone. Ruined my placid morning, upset my domestic tranquillity, which is explicitly guaranteed by the Constitution. The preamble. Right up in the front there, after "We, the People." '

Glitsky stood still for a moment. Then he nodded, said, 'Excuse me,' and went to post his requisition slip.

When he came back into his office, his friend had settled himself down at his desk, feet up, eating peanuts.

'What do you think?' he asked. 'If I took away the peanuts, would anyone ever again come into my office?'

Hardy gave the room a once-over. 'I doubt it. As a popular destination it's a little flat, don't you think? How come nobody's ever here anymore? You notice that? Look out there – the place is a ghost town.'

Glitsky glanced back over his shoulder. 'An hour ago we had to call in crowd control. I don't know. Everybody's out working. They come in here to write reports. Why are you here?'

The feet came down. 'Because through secret sources I have discovered what you already knew yesterday when you wouldn't talk to me about Graham Russo.'

'Which was?'

'He was at his father's place. He shot him up with morphine all the time.'

'Did I know that yesterday? I don't think I knew that, if I do, until this morning.'

'You knew something, though. More than you had last week. You were convinced you had a murder.'

Glitsky moved into the room. 'No comment.'

'Has it gone to the grand jury yet? Tell me that.'

'No comment.' Then, 'Sal had a fight.'

Hardy gave them a minute, then shook his head. 'Not with Graham.'

'If you say so, and you probably will at the trial.'

Glitsky had just told him what he wanted to know: there was going to be a trial. There was no point in arguing the merits. With the combination of Graham's presence at Sal's *and* the fight, added to the lies and the money, there was a case the attorney general could prosecute, even if the district attorney would not. The lieutenant had one more remark, however. 'Whoever did it, Diz, this was a murder. You mind if I sit in my chair?'

Hardy got up and they did a little dance moving around each other. Glitsky looked up at him. 'Why don't I think you came all the way down here just to have some peanuts?'

'I needed to know if you had a smoking gun before I did anything else.'

Glitsky considered this. 'No comment.' He flashed his terrible smile. 'What else brought you down to our little garden spot?'

'No comment.' Hardy smiled back. 'Gosh, we've turned into some great conversationalists here in our middle years, haven't we?' He hesitated, about to say something else, then thought better of it. He checked his watch. 'Lord, how time flies. Thanks for the peanuts. Later.'

Hardy had tried to make the appointment with Sharron Pratt's chief assistant, Claude Clark, soon after he'd hung up with Graham. His client might choose to deny it, but Hardy knew that after his admissions to Sergeant Evans, big trouble was brewing. He had a wild idea that might head it off at the pass.

Clark already had a reputation as a trim and officious bully. In his late thirties, he sported a sandy buzz haircut, a clipped mustache with goatee, and an openly fey style that he would exaggerate around people whom he suspected of homophobia.

He had the power now; he controlled access to the district attorney and was very effective at conveying the feeling that if you wanted to see her, then you could very politely kiss his ass. Pratt liked to pretend that she was sensitive to people, that she *cared* about their personal feelings, and keeping Clark near by to do her hatchet work was, she believed, good politics.

The chief assistant dismissed Hardy's request to meet with Pratt as ridiculous. The district attorney did not take meetings with defense attorneys on little or no notice. She might be able to set aside some time for him in several weeks if he put his request in writing.

Thinking, It's bad luck to diss the Diz, Hardy put on the press. 'I'd appreciate it if you'd just tell her I'd like five minutes. It's about the Sal Russo case. It hasn't gone away. I've got some information that might help her.'

'Why don't you just brief me and I'll pass it along to her?'

'I'll tell you what,' Hardy had said. 'I'll just call my good buddy Jeff Elliot over at the *Chronicle*. You know Jeff? Hell of a reporter, writes the "CityTalk" column. Gets his teeth in and never lets go. Sharron can read about it in the morning. Take care now.'

In ten minutes he got the call. Pratt could set aside a few minutes if Hardy could be at the Hall at four o'clock, sharp.

The DA set the rules of engagement. She reigned from her chair, protected and isolated from supplicants behind an expansive slab of polished hardwood. Claude Clark hovered by the windows. Hardy hadn't been in this room since he'd been fired five years before by the late Christopher Locke. He had been ushered to his spot front and center.

'Mr Hardy' – she nodded – 'nice to meet you, though of course I know you by reputation.' Hardy doubted whether this was true, but made the appropriate face. 'I understand you've got some information for me.'

He nodded, getting right to it. 'Yes, ma'am. Graham Russo talked to the police over the weekend. He admitted that he'd been to his father's and that he'd injected him with morphine.'

She sat forward. 'He admitted he killed him?'

'No. I'm sorry. He admitted that he'd *earlier* injected him with morphine. The point is, he's contradicted his original story again. Also, apparently there was a struggle.'

'The chair?' she asked. Then shook her head. 'We've already seen that. That's no proof of a struggle.'

'They have a witness.' He saw her eyes narrow. She was following him closely. 'In any event, I'm convinced that they now have a case. The AG is going to make an arrest.'

She nodded. 'I had assumed they would. Powell wants to make some bones. He won't win. Assisted suicide shouldn't be charged as homicide, and every jury that gets picked in *this* city is going to agree with me. But what does this have to do with you? Or me?'

'I want you to arrest him again.'

Her eyes went down to slits, then opened as an admiring smile formed. 'Let me see if I get your meaning here.'

She understood it perfectly. She would simply pull the rug out from under the attorney general. If she charged Graham in Sal's death, then cut a deal with his attorney, then under double jeopardy, Graham could never be brought to trial again for the same crime.

She locked him in her gaze again. 'You're afraid Powell's going to charge murder one with specials here, aren't you?'

Hardy nodded. 'Yep.'

'And you're sure he's not indicted the son yet?'

Thinking of Glitsky, Hardy felt a tug of guilt. They'd played the 'no comment' game, but Hardy knew that if they hadn't been friends off the court, Glitsky wouldn't even have spoken to him. In fact, Glitsky had as much as confided that the case hadn't yet been to the grand jury, and now he was telling that to Pratt. It bothered him to do this to Abe; he should have thought about where it might go before he'd come in here, but he'd been psyched on his strategic brilliance, and now was the time. He had to go ahead. 'No indictment. That's what I hear.'

'So what's your offer?'

'You charge him tomorrow morning, early. If the grand jury indicts first, we're dead. I bring Graham down and the next day we plead manslaughter. The deal is probation. No time. Community service negotiable.'

'And your client's on board with this?'

He didn't really see how Graham could disagree. He'd called him back after their early talk to propose it to him but again, maddeningly, there'd been no answer, not even a machine. But Hardy would get to Graham before the morning if he had to camp on his front step. He nodded. 'He will be.'

This response, though, brought Pratt up short. 'You don't have your client's approval for this?'

'I wanted to get your take on it first. If you weren't interested, what was the point?'

Pratt obviously thought this was bass-ackwards – as indeed it was. But the idea itself played beautifully into her hands. As a vehicle for votes she could ride it for miles. Still, 'I won't move forward on this until I've heard from you.'

'I understand that.'

She nodded once. 'Claude, give Mr Hardy one of my cards with my home number. Mr Hardy, I'll expect to hear from you.'

Since the business day was nearly over, Hardy drove directly from the Hall of Justice. Graham was home and cracked a bottle of beer for each of them, suggesting that they walk up and have their talk outside at the top of the Interior Park Belt, which marked the end of Edgewood.

They were sitting on a low brick wall, looking down the canyon at the lush eucalyptus-scented greenery. The microclimate was putting on a show for them; there wasn't even a light breeze, and the temperature was pushing eighty. Hardy had left his coat in his car, had removed his tie. Graham was barefoot, in khaki shorts and a mesh jersey.

'I never asked. You play ball this weekend?' Hardy thought he'd ease into the real reason for his visit. Get some dialogue happening before he dropped the bomb.

'Luckily.' Graham pulled at his beer. 'I told you I got fired from the ambulance company, didn't I?'

Though Hardy wasn't happy to hear this, it wasn't any surprise.

Things were going to get a lot worse for Graham, and anything that helped him realize it was to the good. 'You make some money?'

A sidelong look. 'Is this a subtle intro to the fees discussion?'

Hardy smiled. 'Don't worry, I'll send you a bill eventually. No, I just wondered how you were getting along.'

'Sorry, I'm a jerk lately. Yeah, we played a tournament down in Hayward yesterday. Five games, went all the way.' He made some dismissive gesture. 'I pulled down two grand.'

'In one day?'

'Five games. The second game we got a bonus of a thousand bucks on the mercy rule. That's how it works.'

'Two grand a day?'

'Best case, if we win. If we'd have lost the first game, I would have made fifty dollars, so we're motivated to win. The mercy rule helps.'

'What's the mercy rule?'

Graham looked at Hardy as though he'd just stopped by from Mars. 'If a team's ahead by ten runs, that's the game, they call off the slaughter. It's called the mercy rule. The way the sponsors bet, they get double, sometimes more, if the game's mercy-ruled. The players get a bonus.'

'That happen a lot?'

'Team full of ringers like us? Yeah, I'd say.'

'So the guy who sponsors your team – what's his name?'

'Ising. Craig Ising.'

'So Craig Ising paid your team ten grand in one day?'

Shrugging, Graham gave it a minute. 'I guess so, something like that.'

Hardy whistled. 'What did he win? Betting.'

'More than that,' Graham said. 'These guys, they don't get out of bed for ten grand.' But this subject, clearly, was making him uncomfortable. He bought his bottle up, took a drink. 'So? Something tells me you didn't come up here to talk softball. You get some more news?'

'Well, actually, I did.' There really wasn't going to be any way to sugarcoat it, so Hardy didn't try.

Graham listened patiently, shaking his head. 'They're not going to arrest me again,' he said easily when Hardy had finished.

'Sarah's not going to arrest me. She likes me. I like her. She's cool.'

'She's a cop,' Hardy said. 'She's using the fact that you think she's cool – that maybe there's a buzz between you two, you talk to her – she's using that to take you down.'

'That would really surprise me,' he said. 'When she came by here Saturday night, that wasn't business.'

'So what was it, a date?'

Graham laughed at that. 'Almost. Not quite, but we might have got there.'

Hardy shook his head. 'Why is it, Graham, that you're the only person in the city who doesn't think you're going to get arrested? You ever ask yourself that?'

Graham shrugged, sipped his beer. 'They already took their shot with me, Diz. What's in it for them doing it again?'

'It's not the same people. How about that?' He stood up and walked a few steps away. He was thinking that after all he should have come here with the appearance of panic. Maybe that would have gotten his client's attention, made him realize the seriousness of his situation. But he hadn't wanted to scare him off. He'd wanted to keep him talking, not to reject the plea-bargain plan out of hand, out of defensiveness.

Well, there was nothing for it now. Hardy had to make his case. He turned back. 'Look, Graham, here's the situation. You're going to be arrested again in a couple of days, certainly by the end of the week. You're going to get charged with first-degree murder, maybe even special-circumstances murder. This is going to happen. Even if it's not your Sergeant Evans, and I think it is, *somebody* is going to get this done. It's too big an issue. It's not going to go away.'

He didn't win him over, but at least the confident smile vanished. 'All right. Let's say that happens. Let's just say. Then we're just where we were last week anyway, right? We duke it out.'

'That's one approach. But I've got a better one.'

He came back to the low fence, handed his untouched bottle of beer to Graham, and laid it all out – his deal with Pratt, the whole strategy. When he'd finished, he waited, watching his client's face.

It wore a dead sober expression now, conjuring with the possibilities. He blew out heavily, shook his head at something, craned his neck. 'But I'd have to say I did it,' he said at last.

'But you wouldn't serve any time. Nobody could come back and get you for it. It would be over. The deal's already cut, Graham. Pratt's bought it.'

'It's a good attorney move, I'll give you that.'

Hardy tried a light touch. 'Afterward, you could even call up Sergeant Evans again, ask her out.'

'But' – maddeningly, seemingly unable to leave it alone, Graham played his refrain – 'I'd have to say I did it.'

There was no evading this. 'Yeah, you would.'

'But what if I didn't?'

'It doesn't matter,' Hardy said, surprised by how much he sounded like a defense lawyer. *It didn't matter if he committed the crime? What was he saying?* But he pushed at it. 'It's just a legal issue.'

'And I'd be off? That would be the end of it?'

Hardy had him on the verge – he could feel it. Now was the moment. He had to close the deal. 'You might get a couple or three years probation, but, Graham, listen to me. You're just starting out in the business world. There's a lot more to do than be a lawyer. I am a lawyer and I know. It's ninety-nine percent drudge and the rest is kissing your client's—'

This brought a smile. 'Like now, with me? You're kissing my ass? Somehow it doesn't feel like you're kissing my ass.'

'This is an exception. What I'm saying is you could do anything. You don't need your bar card. You don't need to be a lawyer any more than you needed to be a baseball player. They're just jobs.'

Finally, a heartfelt note. 'But I'm *good,* Diz. I made law review. I got the clerk job with Draper. *Nobody* gets that job except the best.'

Hardy was shaking his head. 'So you've got a good brain. Use it on something else. And if you don't, you're looking at prison, Graham. We're not talking your second or third choice in your career goals, we're talking years out of your life. Prison. Hard time.'

For nearly a full minute that seemed like an hour, Hardy

waited. Birds chirped in the foliage around them, but otherwise the stillness was complete. At last Graham shook his head. 'I'm sorry. I know you put a lot of thought into this, but I didn't kill my dad. I can't say that I did.'

Hardy, his stomach tight, wished Graham could simply leave it that he hadn't killed Sal, instead of always adding that he couldn't *say* he had. He gave it a last try. 'We don't have to call it *killing* him, Graham. We can say—'

'No! Listen to me! I am not going to say I killed him.'

Hardy listened to the birds chirp for another moment, then gradually stood up. 'I've got to tell Pratt your answer by the morning,' he said.

'You've got my answer. My father killed himself. He left the DNR tag for the medics. He did it. That's what happened.'

15

A large percentage of Marcel Lanier's working life outside of the office was spent in and around the city's various slums and housing projects. Poverty being the wet nurse to so many crimes, this was the usual beat and homicide cops soon grew accustomed to it. Occasionally, though, the work took him on a different tour.

So while Sarah Evans was working phones at the Hall of Justice, punching the numbers that Sal Russo had written on his scraps of paper, playing connect-the-dots with the names, Lanier thought he'd grab this opportunity to take a different, more direct, approach. In spite of Glitsky's explicit instructions Lanier forgot his tape recorder.

He knew that Danny Tosca held down the end of the bar most nights at Gino & Carlo's. The place had been in its North Beach location forever. This was where the authentic old Italian heart of the city beat most strongly, and Danny Tosca was in some sense its unofficial pacemaker. Now in his early fifties, cue-ball bald, casually dressed in a dark sport coat, burgundy shirt, tasseled loafers, Tosca was – ostensibly – in real estate. And in fact, many of the businesses in the neighborhood made their rent checks out to his company, which brokered for the actual property owners.

Danny Tosca had never been indicted or arrested. As far as Lanier knew, he'd never even had a parking ticket, although if he had gotten one, it would have been taken care of before the ink on it had dried.

He occupied a unique niche in the sense that he did not appear to believe in physical force. He would be the first to admit that he had a knack for persuasion and negotiation, for locating the pressure point, and wasn't averse to accepting commissions from grateful clients. He simply took a proprietary interest in his community and, like Lanier, viewed himself as one of the many checks and balances in the city by which order was maintained.

He was enjoying his inevitable demitasse of espresso when Lanier pulled up a stool and said hello.

Tosca gave every appearance of being glad to see the inspector, nodding at the bartender to set him up with whatever he'd like. Marcel had a Frangelica in a pony glass on the bar in front of him before his seat had gotten warm. The two men chatted about the beautiful night, the warm spell, the Giants, who were on television above the bar, losing to the Dodgers.

Finally, Marcel deemed the moment propitious. 'That was a shame about Sal Russo,' he said. 'I guess he'd been sick a long time, though.'

Tosca sipped his espresso, waved at a couple who'd just come through the door, came back to Lanier. 'Maybe it was better. The son, what he did.'

'You think it was, Dan?'

A shrug. 'That's what the papers say.'

Lanier nodded, taking his time. 'You see Sal recently?'

'You know, here and there.'

'And how'd he seem? In a lot of pain?'

'He don't show it, you know. Doesn't mean it isn't there.'

'And what if it wasn't about his pain? How about if it was something else?'

Lanier could see that Tosca didn't expect this. The question slowed him. He fiddled with a sugar cube, turning it around and around on the bar. Lanier leaned in closer. 'Somebody killed him, Dan. We don't know why. If it wasn't the kid, we'd like to know it before we arrest him again.'

'You're saying it was business?'

'I'm saying I don't know. Maybe somebody does. I'm wondering if there wasn't something else in the fish.' Meaning drugs. If the illegal fish sales – condoned as they were – were a cover, if Sal had in fact been a mule for some major dealers, there might be a motive.

But Tosca was shaking his head. 'That didn't happen,' he said flatly. 'He sold fish. Good fish too.'

'A lot of it?'

Tosca eyed him carefully. 'One day a week.'

'Not exactly what I asked.'

The twirling had moved from the sugar cube to the cup itself. 'I don't think he cleared two hundred a week. What he needed to survive. There wasn't any loan to welsh on. This was cash business – he paid when he picked up.'

'Okay, but the suppliers? Some of them turn volume, am I right?'

Tosca thought a beat. 'You're asking was Sal blackmailing somebody, getting some payoff? If they didn't pay, maybe he'd fink to Fish and Game? Why would he do that? More money? What would he need more money for?'

Lanier shrugged. 'Suddenly he needed morphine?'

Although not particularly convincing to Tosca, this was at least an answer. He chewed his cheek for a minute, popped a sugar cube into his mouth, and chewed some more. 'Okay, there's one guy,' he said. 'I'll see what I can find out.'

'If you give me his name,' Lanier said, 'I can go see him tonight.' At Tosca's glare, he explained. 'We're on deadline here, Danny. Sooner would be better.'

The glare abated. Tosca patted Lanier's hand on the bar. 'I hear you, Marcel. I'll see what I can find out.'

Sarah was almost beginning to think Sal Russo had sat in his room for hours, making up names and telephone numbers. Certainly, not one number she reached in the first hour admitted to knowing him, or had any idea what her call could be about. She reasoned that there must be a password she didn't know, or everybody knew that Sal Russo was the subject of a murder investigation. Either way, the well was dry.

Until she got to the name Finer. Disheartened and ready to call it a day, she listened to five rings and was about to hang up when a weary voice answered. 'Who's this? What time is it?'

'Mr Finer?'

A deep sigh. Exhaustion. '*Doctor* Finer. And I'm not on call. This isn't right. I haven't slept in two days. How'd you get this number?'

'From Sal Russo.'

'I don't know any Sal Russo.'

'Dr Finer, wait a minute. This is Sergeant Evans with San

Francisco homicide. Sal Russo's been murdered.'

She wondered if he'd hung up anyway. There was nothing but air in her ear. Then another sigh.

'Homicide? Who's been murdered?'

She gave him an abbreviated version and at the end of it, he seemed to have broken a bit through the fatigue. 'Did I treat this man? I'm sorry, but I'm interning at County. It's not like I have patients the way you're thinking. What did he have?'

'Cancer. A brain tumor,' she said, 'and Alzheimer's.'

'And you got my number at his house?'

'That's right.'

'Well, then, I might have seen him. But I'll tell you, it wasn't recently. I've been in the ER for the past six months and if he wasn't bleeding, I didn't treat him.'

'He wasn't bleeding. But it might have been before that. I don't know when it was. I've got your name and phone number on an old crumpled piece of paper and that's all I know.'

She heard, 'I've got to get some sleep.' Then, 'What was your name again?'

'Evans.'

'All right, Evans, hold on. It might be a minute. Russo?'

'Sal Russo,' she said.

It was more like five minutes, but Sarah was content to wait. At least she had someone trying to find something related to Sal Russo. It was better than punching phone numbers and getting nothing.

Finally, he was back. 'If he had this number, I must have seen him here.' This didn't mean anything to Sarah, but he was going on. 'Salvatore Russo? He'd be near sixty now, right?'

'That was him.'

'All right.' Finer was obviously reading his notes. 'He came into the public clinic on his own and was referred to me. I was doing primary care. Said he'd gotten lost twice in the last couple of months, just suddenly couldn't figure out where he was. He was worried he might have AD.'

'AD?'

'Alzheimer's. So anyway, let's see, hold on.' She waited and heard paper flipping. 'Yeah, I scheduled him for blood chemistry and a thyroid panel, but he didn't show. Then he had another episode – this was four months later – and we tried it again, the blood tests.'

'Is that how you diagnose Alzheimer's? Blood tests?'

'No. First you eliminate other possible causes of dementia – third-stage syphilis, for example. There isn't any diagnostic genetic test for AD. We're talking a whole battery of this and that until they get to imaging, and even then the diagnosis, especially at the early stage, is uncertain.'

'But you did diagnose Sal?'

He made sure, answering slowly. 'No. He stopped coming. We never got to the MRI. He didn't want to know for sure, maybe he got scared.'

'Of knowing?'

'Some of that, I'm sure. I don't know, maybe I made some mistakes. I've got a note here – he wanted to know what would happen if we got to a diagnosis.'

'What would happen?'

'Well, I'm mandated to report to the DMV, for example. If somebody's got advance dementia, you don't want—'

'No, I see that.'

'Also, this was him, not me, but I've got it here where he said he didn't want to get to be a burden on anybody. He'd kill himself before that happened.'

'He said that?'

'Yeah. But then . . . you know, this is hard to deal with. He didn't want to get any closer to it, especially if he thought it would be his duty or something to kill himself if he had it. He'd rather not know about it for sure.'

'That makes sense,' Evans said. She tried another tack. 'So you didn't prescribe anything for him?'

'No. We hadn't gotten anywhere, really.'

'Do you remember him at all, personally?'

A pause, then a sigh. 'These last couple of years, I often don't remember my name. I'm on autopilot. Supposedly it's going to make me a better doctor someday.'

Sarah felt for the man. 'I won't keep you much longer, Doctor. It wasn't you who prescribed a DNR tag for him, then?'

'Don't resuscitate? No. Did he finally kill himself, if he had a DNR and cancer? I thought you said somebody killed him.'

'We think so. We're trying to make sure. Here's the last question: you're a doctor and you couldn't diagnose Alzheimer's only a couple of years ago. Could it have progressed far enough by now that he was somehow incompetent to live alone?'

Finer gave it some thought. 'I can't say for sure. It could. It varies. He could be going in and out of dementia with more frequency and still live a semi-normal life if he had help. Of course there's no cure. It just keeps getting worse. You know,' Finer concluded, 'if he had the DNR, that's a pretty good argument he wanted to die.'

'I know,' she replied. 'We're trying to figure it out. Thanks for your help, Doctor. I'll let you get back to sleep.'

The Hardy family was having a renaissance. They'd all eaten dinner together – an unusual occurrence over the past few months. Supposedly, that had been due to their father's work schedule, but today he'd put in nearly as many productive hours as he usually did. This time, though, he'd made it a point to come home when he finished. After they ate, they had sprawled with popcorn on the living-room floor, playing a marathon tournament of Chinese checkers.

When he'd gone to tuck them in for the last time, both kids put their arms around him, not wanting to let go. As he came out to the kitchen, his wife did the same thing. 'They miss you all the time. This is what they need. Once in a while I do too.'

He held her. 'I know. I'm going to try and keep doing this. Being around.'

'It's a concept,' she said. She moved closer against him. 'Were they asleep?'

'Asleep enough. We close the door and they won't hear a thing.'

Snuggled together, they were dozing to the news. At first Hardy didn't know if he'd dreamed or heard the name Graham Russo, but Frannie nudged him. 'Did you know about this?'

'What?'

But it had only been the teaser. They had to endure four commercials before the news came back on. 'While local police still won't comment on the apparent assisted suicide of Sal Russo ten days ago, saying only that the investigation is continuing, in Sacramento today, the chairperson of the Hemlock Society – a right-to-die group – came forward and said that Sal Russo's son, Graham, had spoken to her just minutes before he went to his father's apartment. For more on that story, live in Sacramento, here's . . .'

Hardy was sitting all the way forward. 'Oh, Lord, give me a break.'

Barbara Brandt, looking every inch the lobbyist, confidently met the eye of the camera. 'He was very emotional and upset, as anyone would be when it comes to the moment. I think he just wanted some assurance. It was natural.'

Off camera the reporter asked why Graham hadn't admitted this himself.

Brandt, understanding yet slightly disappointed in the nature of people, shook her head. 'We argued about it last weekend on the phone. This was heroic. The public has a right to know the truth. Sal and Graham Russo together had the courage to act, but Graham doesn't want to embody the issue. Well, it's too late for that now. I'm going public to let Graham know that he's not alone. The laws against assisted suicide and euthanasia must be changed.' She stared at the camera. 'Whatever the consequences, Graham, you did the right thing.'

Hardy hit the mute button. 'I don't believe this.'

Frannie, too, had come awake. 'What don't you believe?' she asked. 'That she came forward with this or what she's saying?'

'I don't know. Who is she? I never heard of her. Graham never mentioned her.' Hardy was shaking his head. 'But I'll tell you one thing for sure. Whoever she is, she just screwed him.'

16

At eight forty-five, Sarah opened the door to her apartment, thinking she should get herself a cat or a hamster or a goldfish – something alive to greet her when she came home.

She had stopped in at the corner grocery downstairs and bought an apple and a TV dinner that she called 'mean cuisine,' and now she took off her jacket, unstrapped her holster and hung it on a kitchen chair, unwrapped the food and put it in the microwave, went into the bathroom to take a quick shower.

Fifteen minutes later she had eaten and gotten dressed again in civilian clothes – blue jeans, tennis shoes, a white fisherman's sweater. She wasn't planning to go out, but it was too early for pajamas and her robe.

She made the conscious decision not to pursue any thoughts on the Russo case tonight. Her workday was done. Dr Finer had been the end of it. Well, almost. After that discussion she'd sat at her desk, fingering her paper scraps, conjuring her own image of who Sal had been.

Carrying her afghan in from the bedroom, she got herself settled in her chair and spent most of another hour finishing a paperback about Kat Colorado going on tour with a country singer in Nashville, saving the woman's life, of course, winning another one for the good guys.

Sarah liked these books about women private eyes, especially the quick-witted, smart-mouthed ones. She didn't fancy herself like them, but it was fun to live in their shoes for the space of a book, although they always got so personally involved. That wasn't like real police work.

She wasn't going to think about it.

She turned the television on to pick up the end of the Giants game. They had just come back in the bottom of the ninth and beaten the Dodgers. She thought she'd call her parents and rub it in a little. But they weren't home. She left a message, came back to her chair in front of the TV, sat down heavily. Her parents were always going out nowadays, having fun.

Three of her girlfriends and her little brother, Jerry, in Concord – three answering machines and one she woke up.

Okay, she told herself, it was just one of those nights.

But – the walls closing in, the droning television her only companion, she decided she'd go out for a walk, grab a cup of decaf at one of the places over on Clement, that's what she'd do. By then her mom and dad might be home and she could talk to them for a few minutes and then turn in.

She considered calling her partner; but no, she saw enough of Lanier, and socially he was not her idea of company. Besides, they would wind up talking about the case.

It was eating her up.

She felt an unseen pair of hands pushing down on her, holding her in the chair. She was not going to turn out like Sal Russo, she told herself. So what if she lived alone in an apartment not too dissimilar from his? What did that mean? Half the city – hell, half the people her age in cities all over the world – lived like this. Or worse, sometimes much worse. It didn't necessarily lead anywhere.

She wasn't anything like Sal. She wasn't going to wind up where he had. She was a success. By thirty-two she'd reached the peak of her profession.

The walls again. She hadn't gotten around to hanging any art. With her work she hadn't had time. And look, there *were* a couple of posters after all – the Monterey Aquarium, a saguaro cactus in a desert somewhere that reminded her of her parents – but they were both unframed, sagging from their tacks in the faded drywall.

She got up and took the five-step walk into the kitchen. It was neat enough, unlike Sal's. ('See?' she said to herself.) There were no dirty dishes piled anywhere. But the linoleum was peeling up in the corners. The table and chairs were thrift store, secondhand. Nice enough, but after thirty more years, she wondered what they'd look like, what they'd *feel* like, at that time to someone who was her age now.

But that was silly. Of course she'd move up, into something better. Now she was young and unattached. She didn't need any more. But Graham – damn him, coming back into her consciousness like this! – Graham's place wasn't at all like this, was it? It was elegant and fine. And he, too, was young and unattached.

In the door between kitchen and living room she surveyed her own place objectively, as if it were a crime scene, as if something had happened to her here, tonight, now.

The afghan had been tossed off, and lay half on the ancient wing chair, half on the woven throw rug. Everything in sight was well used: the homemade brick-and-board bookshelves with their dog-eared paperbacks and law-enforcement journals, the cassette player, the lion's-claw coffee table, pocked with rings from hot, cold, wet glasses placed directly on the wood.

The couch was frayed and worn, its once-bright red, gold, and green brocade now lackluster, nearly sepia. The three-bulb standing lamp behind the sofa threw almost no light; two bulbs needed to be replaced.

She was going out. All right. This was just a mood. If she didn't like her apartment, she'd change it soon. It had never bothered her before. She wasn't stuck with it forever. She'd just turn off the television . . .

'. . . Graham Russo, who was arrested, then released, last week for assisting at the suicide of his father . . .'

He was not home. The house was as dark as it had been the night before.

She'd parked at the bottom of the street, across from a streetlight under a canopy of trees. Now she stood leaning against the hood of her car, looking north, back toward her apartment, trying not to think.

Edgewood dropped off in a cliff. From where she stood, she could look down a hundred feet or so into the backyards and onto the roofs of the multi-story buildings below her, on Parnassus. In one of the upper windows – close enough to see clearly – two men were in a bed together, naked.

The chill had come up again, a brisk breeze out of the west, although with her fisherman's sweater, she wasn't cold. Still, she tightened her arms around herself. A stair street – Farnsworth –

fell off steeply to her right. In the wake of the *chik-chik-chik* of an owl flying overhead, she heard footsteps coming up the steps.

She'd left her apartment hurriedly, unarmed. Now she backed into the shadow of the canopy as the steps came up to her, paced and rhythmic, jogging.

Suddenly certain, she stepped out into the light as Graham got to the top of the steps. Seeing her, breathing hard, he stopped. His shoulders dropped and he shook his head as if she'd finally beaten him. Gathering another breath, he spread his hands, palms out. 'Am I under arrest?'

The thought was so far from her mind that she laughed out loud. 'What are you doing?'

It took a minute for him to figure out what she meant. 'Trying to stay in shape. Running off some of this' – he gestured ambiguously, took in another lungful of air – 'all this madness.' He was still panting. 'Those are some serious stairs. More than a hundred, I'd bet, but who's counting?' Then, focusing back on her, 'So if I'm not under arrest . . . ?'

She took a half step toward him. 'I guess I'm finally off duty. I thought you might have some of that wine left.'

They walked uphill, in the middle of the street, in silence.

Inside, he turned on the indirect track lights and opened the curtains to the view. Downtown and the East Bay shimmered down below them. 'I was going to take a shower,' he said, indicating the tiny booth that was his bathroom. 'There's no room to change in there.'

She swiveled in the chair, grabbed one of the magazines. 'I won't look.'

When he got out of the shower, he opened a bottle of red and poured them both a glass. They moved to opposite ends of the low leather couch. Graham was back in his uniform – barefoot, baggy running shorts, a T-shirt. Sarah, tennis shoes and all, had her legs curled under her.

Though Barbara Brandt's announcement that she'd counseled Graham in the minutes before he'd killed his father was the immediate catalyst that had gotten her out of her own apartment and up to here, Sarah felt no inclination to raise the subject. She'd told him she was off duty, and she was. Graham evidently hadn't yet even heard about it; he'd been out jogging to the beach and back, over an hour. The phone, she noticed, was unplugged.

She had no idea where the words came from. 'Your father painted,' she began, out of the blue.

The comment seemed to require an adjustment to Graham's mind-set. He shifted on the couch, averted his eyes. 'He did a lot of things. Are you still off duty?'

She had to smile at that. 'Yeah.'

'You want to talk about my father?'

She nodded. 'Looks like. I was at his place. It got a little bit inside me. So did he.'

Graham leaned down and put his wineglass on the floor, then stood again, crossing to the bookshelves. He turned. 'You know, when I got the letter, I hadn't talked to him in like fifteen years. He was at my high school graduation, just came up and said hello when my mom wasn't around. Congratulations. I had no idea what to say back. I think I just looked at him. All I really remember is it made me feel sick.'

'And that's the last time you saw him? I mean, before the letter?'

Graham shook his head no. 'That's what's funny. When I worked for Draper, I'd see him on Fridays all the time, out in his truck behind the courthouse. I'd stand at the window and watch him out in the alley. Everybody seemed to love him.'

'But you didn't go down?'

'I thought I hated him.' Still across the room from her, he pulled a kitchen chair over and straddled it. 'Even after the letter . . .' He stopped.

'I thought the letter was when you connected.'

He considered that for a beat. 'I saw him in Vero then, once. But it wasn't very good. I was a jerk. I think it's my truest talent, jerkhood.'

'I think it's jerkitude.' Then, realizing how that could be interpreted, she added, 'Not your truest talent. The word.'

He shrugged. 'Well, whatever you call it, there it was. So right after I read the letter, I decided I'd sucked it up enough. I should spill out how I felt. It would do me good. My dad had caused us all so much grief and I'd never told him how I felt about it, what he'd put us all through. So he writes me this, this beautiful letter, reaching out really, and somehow this cues me – sensitive guy that I am – that the time is right to go and beat up on the old man.'

'Literally? You hit him?'

'No. I might as well have. I told him he was a son of a bitch who had a hell of a nerve thinking he could make some kind of amends.'

Sarah didn't think Graham was aware that he'd stood up and begun pacing.

'As though he's going to somehow make up for leaving us, just walking out. In his dreams. What'd he think I was going to do, forgive him? Take him back with open arms? Get a life, Sal – but I'm not letting you back in mine! I don't want to make you feel better. Not now, not ever. I don't *care* how you feel. And we're not going to be friends, for Christ's sake. You think we can be friends? I hate you, man. Don't you fucking *get* it? I hate your guts!'

He was yelling by the end. Now, in the small room, the silence when he stopped left a vacuum. He was breathing hard, looking back at Sarah as though in panic. 'Yeah,' he said, 'I beat him up. I beat the hell out of him.'

She waited until he'd crossed to the kitchen sink and scooped a few handfuls of water into his face. 'Sorry,' he said.

'So what did he do? How did he react?'

He was leaning against the counter, his arms crossed over his chest, his massive shoulders slumped. 'He said I was right. He was crying. And you know what, I was *glad* he was crying. He said he was so sorry.' Graham blew out in frustration. 'And right in character, I told him sorry wasn't good enough. Sorry didn't make any damn difference anymore.'

In the pause she asked, 'And then what?'

'Then I left.'

'So how did you . . . ?'

'That was later,' he said.

There was an old hose in the alley where he parked his truck across from his apartment. It had been left behind by the construction crew at the federal courthouse, and Sal Russo had claimed it. He had it hooked to a spigot and was washing out the bed of his truck, which got tolerably rank by the end of Friday.

There wasn't any nozzle, but Sal was happy enough to control the spray with his thumb. It spit water back all over him, but he didn't care. His life was sea spume and fish smell. This was part of it.

He'd polished off the last mouthfuls of the gallon bottles of Carlo Rossi that his customers hadn't got to. He had the cigar butt in his teeth, chopping words off around it, half singing, half humming 'Sweet Betsy from Pike.' It was the middle of the summer, two or more hours of daylight left, and the wind was gusting up in front of him, blowing the spray back, soaking him by the second. Chomping down harder on his cigar, he grinned into the force of it, then turned to get another angle on the truck bed, flush out the scales.

Initially, he thought it was a premonition of one of his spells – a shadow in the center of the sun's glare, something about the shape so mnemonic, it felt like a haunting. Moving to one side, he squinted up into it. 'Graham?'

'Hey, Dad.'

Sal bent the hose over on itself, stopping the flow of water. He hadn't seen his son since that time in Vero, and that had been a stupid mistake. He had seen him play and then hadn't been able to stop himself. He thought enough time might have passed. Maybe Graham could understand. But he'd been wrong.

And now here he was again. 'What's goin' on? Your mother all right?' He couldn't imagine any other reason his son would come to see him – not after the last time. Helen, he thought, must have died and they send Graham to tell him.

'Mom's fine.' He shifted on his feet. 'I, uh, I came by to apologize. I'm sorry.'

The world took on a blurry edge for a beat, but Sal only blinked and nodded. 'Yeah, well, like I said, you were right.' He released his grip on the hose, pointed it vaguely at the truck. 'So how you doin'?'

His son didn't answer right away, which forced him to look. 'Not that great, to tell you the truth.'

Sal kept the water going. 'I saw they cut you.'

'I don't blame 'em,' he said. 'I sucked.' There was a set to the face, a tight control. He looked about to break. 'I'm too old. It's a kid's game. I was stupid, the whole thing was stupid.'

Sal nodded. 'Yeah, probably. If it's any consolation, it's in the blood. I'd a probably done the same thing, then got cut too. Bet that makes you feel better.'

A smile started, but went nowhere. 'Lots. Thanks.'

'Don't mention it. You hungry?' He squeezed off the water again, held it with one hand, and pulled a roll of bills out of his front pocket.

Sal had a regular spot at the U.S. Restaurant, a lone table that spearheaded the sidewalk at the narrowest point in the triangular building. The place was in the heart of North Beach and had been in its location half a block from Gino & Carlo's bar, essentially unchanged, for as long as Sal could remember. You still couldn't spend ten bucks on a meal there if you tried.

They were on their third carafe of red wine. The wineglass was a prop and Sal had his hands wrapped around his. A foot from them both, outside the glass, the tourist night was getting into swing, the lights coming up on the street.

'I don't know if there is a why anymore,' Sal was saying. 'Maybe there never was. I don't know.'

'But there had to be, Sal. You don't just . . .'

'Maybe you do. Maybe one day you wake up and you're a different person. You're going along and something happens and the whole vision you have of who you are – suddenly that whole thing just doesn't work anymore. So everything it was holding up comes crashing down around it.'

'What? Did Mom have an affair?'

Sal shook his head. 'It wasn't your mother. This was me. Who I was.' He lifted the prop and used it, buying some time. 'It wasn't anything as easy as an affair.'

'So what was it?' Sarah asked him.

By now it was nearly midnight, although neither of them was much aware of the time. They were facing each other, sitting cross-legged on the floor.

'To this day I don't know. He said I didn't realize how insecure a person my mother was – still is, if you want to know. No one who saw her out in the world would ever see that. Though we kids had seen it, of course, after we were older. The face-lifts now, the trappings. Stuff you don't need if you're together with yourself.'

Graham seemed embarrassed by the cheap psychology. He looked down at his hands. 'Anyway, she loved him. Their backgrounds might never mesh, they got uncomfortable doing each other's *things*, you know?'

'Like what?'

'Oh, Mom wouldn't go out on the boat. Sal wouldn't get dressed up for anything. It broke down to money – Mom was used to things you bought, Sal liked things you did. It was a pretty big difference.'

'But they got together?'

He nodded. 'They'd never be friends like some couples were, but he loved her and knew he could make her keep loving him.'

'He could *make* her?'

'That's what he said.'

'And how did he do that?'

'By being stronger than she was, having a stronger will.'

'And that made her love him?'

'Yeah, I think it might have.'

Sarah and Graham had never gotten around to drinking any of their wine – the glasses remained half filled on the hardwood by the couch. Graham was still trying to reason it through for himself, how it had happened with his father and mother.

So it wasn't the hour or the alcohol. Still, with no real intention of doing so, he was becoming more aware of the planes of Sarah's face, the soft bow of her lips, the way her hair fell across her cheek.

Sal's eyes danced with the memory. 'See? I knew who I was. I was happy in myself. I was a person – okay, a schlemiel like I still am, but I knew where I belonged, who I was. Your mother, she didn't. She was looking, always looking for something solid, always unsure of where the ground was.

'I think – no, hell, I know – that nothing in her parents' life got inside her. She'd gone to the schools and had the clothes and the fancy friends, but you know what? They didn't do it for her. Then when we got together, finally she was happy – not always thrilled

with the way we lived, with no money, none of that society junk, but she loved you kids.'

'And what about you? Did she still love you?'

His father leaned across the table and Graham could pick up the odor of fish, of cheap wine. But even with that, the old clothes and the stubble, the random fish scale on his skin, Sal remained a compelling figure. 'I told you. I made her.'

Graham rolled his eyes and his father laughed.

'That, too, but that wasn't what I was talking about.' Graham hadn't touched his spumoni ice cream and now it had melted into a waxy, pinkish-brown liquid in its small, tarnished metal bowl. Sal pulled it over in front of him and dipped a spoon. 'She'd get the doubts, you know. "Do we belong here?" "Maybe my parents are right." "Where are we going?" "Did I still love her the way I did when we started?" All the time.' He shook his head, sadly. 'All the goddamn time, Graham.

'And you know what I'd do?' He scooped up another spoonful of melted spumoni. 'I'd tell her I was sure. That this is really what she wanted, down in her soul. That the kids, the house, the worries – this was real life. It was the only thing that had ever made her happy. She knew that. And that I loved her, not because of anything except for who she was.'

He sat back, scratched at his face, pulled at the sides of his mouth. Finally speaking about this after all these years, to his oldest son, bringing it up again – the memory seemed to be battering him. 'It was just a constant battle, Graham. You can't imagine – the conflict between how she was raised and how she was living. It seemed like she always had one foot out the door, ready to go back. So I couldn't ever waver, couldn't show any doubt of my own, or she'd lose faith. If I stopped acting like I believed, then she couldn't go it on her own. It wasn't her dream at all, really. It depended on who I was.'

'And who were you?'

He sighed wearily and spoke with a huskiness that now betrayed the words. He had confidence in the memory. He knew who he'd been. 'I was Sal Russo. I'd never make a lot of money, never change the world, but I was as good a man as there was. I was strong, I worked hard, I didn't cheat. I loved your mother with all my heart. Simple stuff, but it was what she needed to hear, who she needed me to be. And it was true.'

'So what happened?'

He searched the crowded restaurant for a minute, hiding or searching for the answer. Letting out a deep breath, he shrugged. 'I lost my confidence, I guess. I couldn't pretend I was anybody special anymore.'

'But why?'

'Because I wasn't.'

It wasn't really an answer, but another, more pressing, question kept Graham from pursuing it. 'But what about us? Me? Deb? Georgie? How could you just leave us?' He reached across the table and put a hand on his father's arm. 'I'm not here to bust your chops on this. I'd just like to understand it, that's all.'

'I would, too, Graham. I'd go back and live every minute of that time over again if I could. I don't know how I could have done it. I want to blame your mother, but again, it was all me. I could have fought her.'

The implications here rocked Graham. The only story he'd ever heard was that his father didn't want to see his children anymore. And, indeed – apparently – he hadn't made any effort to. Not that Graham had heard of. 'What do you mean,' he asked, 'you could have fought Mom?'

They were out of props: wineglasses, ice cream, coffee cups. At the U.S. Restaurant steady customers could sit all day and night over a demitasse if they wanted. Nobody hustled them out.

Sal had his hands folded on the table, the knuckles gnarled and white with pressure. 'I don't know exactly how to say this, but when we broke up, when it stopped working, your mother . . . it meant she'd failed. She'd gone up against everything she was raised with, because I'd convinced her it was somehow truer, or nobler, better. Then when it didn't work, she had no choice, I think. She had to hate me. I had betrayed her. I was the devil.'

'You couldn't see us because of her?'

Sal didn't like that slant on it. It wasn't Helen's fault. It was his own. 'She got very protective of you. I had ruined her life. She wasn't going to let me ruin yours.'

'And you accepted that?'

He shook his head. 'I was at the bottom, Graham. I was worthless. I guess I thought she must be right. It was too hard. I *don't know. Every time I tried, she was in the way until finally I just gave up.'*

Graham's hand was still on his father's arm. He tightened down his grip. 'How could you do that?'

Sal's eyes leveled on his. 'I got hit pretty hard by a few of life's pitches, Graham. I guess I got afraid to come back to the plate. You know what I'm talking about?'

'I think I do,' he said. 'It's kind of how I feel. Why I thought I'd come look you up.'

They were outside now, where Hardy and Graham had sat late that afternoon. Though by now the temperature had dropped to the fifties, Graham was still barefoot, still wore his shorts, although he'd pulled on a warm-up jacket. Sarah leaned against a lightpost, hands in her pockets.

Graham was concluding. 'So that's when we became friends again. I was pretty low. I didn't know who else . . .' He let it hang, but it was clear enough. Graham felt – and from all accounts with some justification – that he'd alienated everyone in his world, too, and didn't know where to start to get back in. Maybe with his dad, who'd been there as well.

'I wish I'd known him, somehow,' she said.

'I'm glad I did, finally.' But the subject suddenly seemed too close, embarrassing him. 'He was great.'

'But that night, in North Beach, did he already have Alzheimer's then?'

Graham nodded. 'I know, that's a question. It didn't seem like it at all. He was like he'd always been. But the symptoms had started before. I found that out later, after we . . . after I became more involved with him. It was getting worse, of course, it doesn't get better, but he was still trying to live with it.'

It was a clean opportunity to get back to the pursuit of her investigation, but she no longer had the heart for it. 'So how sick was he at the end?'

'It wasn't the Alzheimer's,' Graham said. 'AD wasn't ever going to kill him. It wasn't going to get the time.' He shook off the thought. 'The funny thing is, you know, we were so much like each other. Firstborn kids, jocks, confident to a fault. Even now . . .' He stopped again.

'Even now what?'

'Even now, with everything that's happened with the clerkship and with baseball, with being unemployable, getting arrested, then fired – I still know who I am. I'm fine with me. It's everybody else's reaction that's a little hard to take.'

He wasn't whining. It was said so matter-of-factly that another person might have missed it altogether, and that would have been fine with Graham. But Sarah knew what he was saying: he had no close friends anymore, no one to share what went on in his soul. There had been Sal, his father, and now Sal was dead.

His smile wasn't a come-on; it was a question. 'It makes one cautious.'

Sarah smiled back. 'I'm a firstborn jock with attitude myself,' she said. 'Do you know the secret handshake?'

'I'm not sure I do.'

Moving off the lamppost, she took his hand, raised it open to her mouth, and, holding his gaze, licked his palm.

PART THREE

17

It was Friday in the third week of May. Hardy was at an outside table, alone, just finishing an order of mussels from a lunch at Plouf, a bistro on Belden Alley, smack in the middle of the financial district. Belden was a true downtown alley, perhaps a dozen feet wide, shaded except at high noon by the buildings on either side of it. The sun had just passed out of sight, and the slice of sky above the alley was bright blue.

Hardy had taken Frannie to Paris the previous summer, leaving the kids with Moses and Susan, for five too-short days. He hadn't been to France since just after his hitch in Vietnam, and going back had nearly broken his heart. He'd been a free man in Paris, the one Joni Mitchell had written her song about – unfettered and alive.

Well, the savory smells of great food cooking here on Belden didn't completely mask the underpinning aromas of fish and tobacco and urine. With those, plus the half-dozen French restaurants in the space of its one block, the place was Paris.

Sitting over his crock of mussel shells, Hardy had that feeling again. Not exactly unfettered, but alive. Energized by the tastes and smells and bustle around him, he was certain that very soon he was going to be back in the thick of what he was born to do, and it wasn't Tryptech. He'd looked in on Michelle back at the office, up to her elbows in paper, and had left for lunch with nary a trace of guilt.

There was one problem, though. He hadn't been able to reach Graham. Calls hadn't been answered. He'd left notes tacked to the front door on Edgewood. Nothing. His client had vanished without a trace. And given their disagreement over the plea bargain he'd struck with Pratt, Hardy wasn't a hundred percent sure that he still had a client at all. After what he'd been through adjusting his attitude and priorities, this was something he'd rather not consider.

'This seat taken?'

The familiar face belonged to Art Drysdale, who'd long ago been Hardy's mentor. Art had even rehired him to the district attorney's office, getting him back into the practice of the law after his decade-long self-imposed exile.

Since then their professional lives had put them in different corners, but Hardy had always liked Art and was glad to see him. The other guy with him, he didn't know. 'Have you met Gil Soma?'

The two shook hands. The lawyer club. It didn't have to be personal. Not yet, at least.

Hardy looked from one man to the other. 'The mussels are really great,' he said, smiling. 'Going on the assumption that you being here with me is a coincidence.'

Drysdale grabbed a leftover piece of bread and dipped it in Hardy's sauce – wine, parsley, garlic. 'Mostly. I did happen to call your office right after you'd left and Phyllis told me you were coming here.'

'She's very efficient.' Hardy had his poker face on. It was good practice. He'd been out of the game awhile.

'Then, since it was such a nice day and lunchtime to boot, we figured we'd take a walk, get out and enjoy the city.'

'Good idea.' He waited. Let them come out with it. It was what had brought them here.

They pulled chairs and got themselves arranged. 'Have you heard from your client today?' Drysdale finally asked.

'Which one, Art? I've got clients coming out of the woodwork. I can't keep track of them all.'

Soma didn't appreciate all this pirouetting. He snapped it out. 'The famous one. Graham Russo.'

'Oh, your buddy? Didn't you guys use to work together?'

'Till he stiffed us.' Soma was smiling, but Hardy was getting the feeling that it wasn't sincere.

Even before Barbara Brandt had entered the picture with her claim that she'd counseled Graham just before Sal's death, the case was developing a lot of momentum. Of course, it didn't hurt that Cerrone's article had indeed made the cover of *Time*.

Graham's handsome, guileless face had stared out at Hardy from every newsstand he'd passed on his way to lunch. The photographer had captured a vulnerable moment, and the tale it told was wrenching. Hardy thought the story was also probably true or mostly true – at least in some respects close to true. Unfortunately for his client, two out of three of those choices were disastrous.

But he got back to the point. 'Anyway, no, Art. I haven't heard from him. He's probably lying low. Maybe he left town. I think I would have.'

Soma jumped at this. 'Did you counsel him to do that? Where did he go?'

Hardy took in Soma for a beat, then turned to Drysdale. 'The reporters were getting on his nerves. Tell you the truth, they're getting on mine too.'

'Then you did talk to him?'

Resolutely mild, Hardy kept his eyes on Drysdale, which he knew was making Soma crazy. 'Did you read that little piece about me and Sharron, Art?'

Jeff Elliot's 'CityTalk' column this morning had alluded to Hardy's aborted plea bargain and Pratt's displeasure with the way things had turned out. Reading it at their kitchen table in the morning, Frannie had commented that her husband seemed to have a knack for alienating district attorneys. Hardy allowed as to how that was probably true. It wasn't the worst possible trait in a defense attorney.

To which Frannie had raised her eyebrows. Her husband was precise with his words, and if Dismas was calling himself a defense attorney right out loud, that's what he meant.

But Drysdale was nodding, smiling. Pratt, after all, had fired him recently enough that he still didn't wish her all the best. 'She shouldn't have leaked it before the deal was done,' he said. 'I'm afraid it made her look less than astute. Bumbling, in point of fact.' The wattage on the smile increased. 'Poor woman, my heart goes out to her, but I do think, Diz, it put you on her list.'

'I'll try to make it up to her.' Hardy, enjoying himself, finally turned to Soma. 'Anyway, to answer your question, Gil, Graham's been a little tough to reach. He hadn't been indicted. In her wisdom Ms Pratt let him go. He was a free man.' He smiled all around. 'It's a free country.'

Drysdale cut to it. 'He's been indicted now. And I expect you to surrender him.'

Though this was news, it was hardly unexpected, and Hardy took it calmly. 'What charge?'

'Murder one with specials.'

Expected or not – and it was the official confirmation of what Hardy had predicted – this wasn't good news. 'You can't be asking for death on this?'

'LWOP.' This was Soma, rapping the rap, trying out the sound of the jargon, pretending to be an old pro. Hardy wondered if Soma had given any thought to the reality of life in prison without the possibility of parole for someone very much like himself, as Graham was. If, in fact, Soma had given thought to much except getting high-profile cases and winning them. Hardy guessed not; the boy had all the signs of testosterone poisoning, which meant he wouldn't do it by the numbers.

Also, the case had a personal edge, which increased the odds – if Soma was smart, which also appeared to be the case – that he'd come up with some tricks in the courtroom.

But here in Belden Alley the attorneys for both sides of this highly publicized case were at the same table, informally, in some kind of free-form mode. From what they'd said, they hadn't found Graham yet to arrest him. Hardy knew Drysdale well, and thought he'd orchestrated this meeting for some specific purpose. Maybe get another plea in play.

Although – a zing of caution – maybe Art thought he could get information they didn't have while Hardy's guard was down. He'd find out. 'Either of you read the article in *Time*?'

Cerrone had done a masterful job of creating an impression without ever crossing the line into accusation. The Graham Russo case, he'd written, was a poignant *illustration* of the many ambiguities facing the country surrounding the entire problem of elderly care/assisted suicide/the right to die.

Woven into the fabric of the legal story of the arrest and subsequent release of Graham Russo was the relationship between him and his father, the desperation of Sal's condition, Graham's access to morphine and syringes. Reading the article, Hardy concluded that no reasonable person would assume that Graham had not helped his father die with dignity.

Hardy had his ear to the ground, and as far as he could tell, the article, coupled with Barbara Brandt's confession, had pretty much settled the question for the public. Even some of the legal public – Freeman, Michelle.

These two lawyers with him now, however, represented something entirely different. A waiter had come and taken their lunch orders and Hardy had decided on a cup of espresso, high octane. After it arrived, he slowly stirred in a spoonful of sugar. 'I've got to say, Art, this is a terrible call. If you read the article—' True to form, Soma butted in again.

'The article left out just a few things.'

'Yes it did.' Hardy was all agreement. 'And I know all about them – the money and the so-called struggle? But I'll tell you something: Graham didn't kill Sal for the money. You'll never be able to prove he did.' He found himself addressing Art again. 'Powell's got to know this, Art. It's damn near frivolous.'

'We did get the indictment.' Drysdale shrugged. 'The grand jury didn't think it was frivolous.'

Hardy sat back in his chair, amused. 'Wasn't it your very self, years ago, who assured me that if the prosecution asked nice enough, the grand jury would indict a ham sandwich?'

Drysdale nodded. 'I might have said something like that when I was but a callow youth, but I was wrong.' He grinned. 'Besides, the ham sandwich might have done it.'

'So remind me again, why are we having this discussion? You came down here looking for me, remember? Why didn't you just give me a call and tell me to bring in my man?'

Putting a hand over the arm of Soma, who looked equal parts ready to interrupt again and in sore need of a bathroom break, Drysdale leaned forward. 'Dean's made his point getting the indictment, Diz. He's upholding the law, Pratt isn't. I don't think this kid has to spend the rest of his life in jail.' He threw a quick glance at Soma, shutting him up.

'So what do you want?'

'You tell me. The word was you went to manslaughter, no time, with Pratt. I don't think Dean will go there, but he might bend down from the specials.'

But Hardy was shaking his head. 'My client didn't even cop to probation, Art. He says he didn't do it.'

'Although the entire country now thinks he did.'

Hardy spread his palms. 'Be that as it may. And even if that's true, even if some jury comes to that view, they won't see murder with specials. They'll see an assisted suicide.'

Finally, Soma could hold it no longer. 'Which *is* murder.'

Drysdale agreed. 'Forget the legal niceties, Diz. This was a murder. We can prove murder.'

'Which means Graham did it,' Soma blurted.

Hardy took a beat. 'That's an interesting legal theory,' he said.

'The point,' Drysdale went on, 'is this: you know Powell, Diz. He's not immune to public opinion . . .' This, Hardy thought, was surely one of the great understatements of Drysdale's career, but he let him go on. 'He doesn't necessarily want to try a case where sixty percent of his constituency thinks his suspect is a good guy who did the right thing.'

'But—'

Drysdale's hand went back to Soma's arm. '*But* Dean is convinced – and I agree – that this was a murder. You will, too, Diz, when you've seen all the discovery. So if you plead, it's win-win. Dean gets a *W* in his column for upholding the law, you get a *W* for pleading down. Pratt picks up an *L*.'

'I love the sports analogy,' Hardy said. 'So Graham gets time in the slammer? My guess is he'd call that one the big *L* for him. What do you think?'

'*L* for life is the big *L*,' Soma said. 'This would be lower case.'

'It's not going to happen,' Hardy replied, standing up, 'but I'll convey your kind offer to my client.'

If I can find him.

Shaking hands, he was effusively friendly. He told Art it was nice seeing him again. They ought to *plan* a lunch together sometime, catch up on their families, the changes in their jobs, old times.

Turning to the younger man, extending his hand, Hardy broke a practiced smile. 'It was nice to meet you, Mr Soma. I wish you luck in your career.'

The young man wasn't blind or stupid. He caught the dismissive tone and served one back to Hardy. 'We need to see

Russo by tomorrow. We don't mean the day after.'

Hardy nodded. 'Yes, sir. I guess I hear that message loud and clear. Thank you very much.'

An hour after Soma and Hardy exchanged their pleasantries, Marcel Lanier sat double-parked in front of the office of the attorney general on Fremont Street, drumming his hands on his steering wheel.

This was supposed to have taken five minutes – whip by here and get confirmation that Graham Russo was in the system. He'd sent Sarah up and she'd already been gone for twenty. Marcel sat with his driver's window down, eyes closed. It was a nice afternoon, smells of coffee roasting and diesel fumes – not altogether unpleasant.

He was half dozing until another cop pulled up behind him. Marcel flashed his badge and explained the situation and tried to go back to dozing. Until two minutes later when *another* traffic- and parking-enforcement meter-minder tapped him – hard! – on the elbow. 'Come on, now, move it along.'

Another flash of the buzzer, this one not as effective. 'I don't care about the badge, Inspector. You're blocking the street here. You gotta move it along.'

So Marcel, humoring this bozo, drove in a big circle, hoping Evans would be back down when he returned. But she wasn't, so he double-parked again in the same spot, closed his eyes again. It couldn't be long now, he told himself, it just couldn't be.

But it was long enough for a pair of indigents, one of them wearing a football helmet and the other pushing a stolen shopping cart loaded with recyclables, to stop at his window and ask him for money. Marcel revved the motor and took off again for another tour of the surrounding three blocks.

When he returned this time, he at least got the time to start drumming his fingers before Evans appeared, coming out of the building with the skinny young lawyer.

Lanier was watching the guy move. Soma had come all the way down from the third floor with Sarah Evans when all he needed to do was have his secretary check the computer? So *that's* what it was – Soma was hitting on her.

Leaning on the horn, he saw her wave, gesturing to him,

making excuses. As though she needed to explain to this dweeb that she was supposed to be doing her job. He rolled down the window on her side. 'Hey, Sarah!'

He didn't know what it had been – whether Soma had been overbearing, or he'd honked too often. Maybe it was PMS. You never knew. *He* was the one who'd had the frustrating twenty minutes out in the car, but now she was sulking, her elbow out her own window as they drove west, staring out away from him.

'You all right?' he asked.

'I'm fine.' *Except, of course, that the man I love is now a fugitive and the next time I see him I've got to arrest him.*

'That guy Soma bothering you?'

She shrugged, still not looking over.

The silence went on for another few blocks. Finally, Lanier spoke again. 'So what happened?'

'Nothing.'

'Well, nothing seems to have got you pretty upset.'

Now she turned. 'I'm not upset.'

'Right. That's right. You're always this way. Quiet and kind of moody.'

Another block. 'I told him he was making a mistake.'

'Who?' Lanier asked. 'About what?'

She flicked at the folder containing the file. 'Gil Soma. This thing.'

Marcel threw her a concerned look. 'The warrant? What's the matter with it?'

'Russo.'

'You back on that again? Give it a rest. He did it.'

'Oh, okay. Never mind.'

'Sarah.' Asking her to be reasonable.

'No, really. You think he did it, therefore he did it.'

'Who cares? It's Soma's problem. It's not our problem. We're just doing the delivery.'

'You're right. There's nothing to discuss.'

'Besides, he did it. Nobody else could have done it. We checked. Everybody else is clean. You read that *Time* story? That woman up in Sacramento? He did it.'

She was silent.

'What?'

'He helped his dad die to put him out of his misery, right?'

'Right.'

'So what about the struggle? What about the hooker downstairs, what she heard? The bump on the head?'

Marcel was nodding. 'That's what I mean. He did it.'

'For the money?'

'Sure.'

'But you just said it was assisted suicide.'

'Maybe it started that way, and the idea that when it was done he would have the money, maybe that kind of grew on him. Then he got started and panicked when the old man changed his mind. Anything could have happened, Sarah, but whatever it was, he was there. He did it. This stuff happens. I had a guy once killed his wife. Same thing.'

'She was sick?'

'Oh, yeah. Same thing. Wouldn't admit he did it.'

'Why not?'

'You're going to love this. Guy was like sixty years old. He didn't want his eighty-year-old mother to be mad at him.'

'What?'

'God's truth. You heard it here first. The mother didn't believe in the concept, so the son tried to fake it and make it look like a straight suicide, but he botched it all up.'

'Did he also try to make it look like a murder? Steal his wife's jewelry, anything like that?'

'No. But that would have just been going into more detail. He just wasn't as smart as this Russo guy, that's all. Same basic idea, though.'

'Well, thanks for making that clear.'

'Anytime. You think he'll be home?'

'Russo? I doubt it.'

Sarah didn't simply doubt that Graham wasn't at his home. She knew it for a fact. He'd been staying at her apartment since the long night they'd spent with each other after she'd licked his palm. Sarah's argument to herself (fatuous, and she knew it) was that Graham had not been under indictment at that time and was, in theory, a citizen who was to be presumed innocent. Now the indictment had come in and though it had been expected, like it or not it changed everything.

He saw it as soon as she walked through the door, closed it carefully behind her, kept her distance from him. For the last few days she'd entered the apartment and they'd fallen into each other's arms. He stood in the middle of the living room. 'What's the matter?' he asked. 'What's happened?'

'The matter is you got yourself indicted this morning by the grand jury. I'm not supposed to tell you that. I'm not supposed to be in love with you. I'm supposed to arrest you right now.'

He tried a tentative smile. 'You going to?'

'This isn't funny.'

'I don't think it's funny.'

'Then do me a favor. Don't laugh about it.'

'That ought to be easy. Not laughing, I mean.' He couldn't make himself move toward her. He could feel the aura from where he stood; she had to keep a distance between them. He wasn't going to push it. 'What do you want me to do, Sarah? I'll go if you want, leave here if it'll make it easier for you. Or you can take me in. Whatever you want.'

'Don't you understand? Shit. I don't want to take you in!' Her strong shoulders sagged. She bit at her lip. 'This is wrong. This is all so wrong.'

This time he did take a step toward her, but she held out a hand. 'Don't!'

He stopped, waited, spoke quietly. 'My dad and I, I didn't—'

She interrupted him. 'That's not the point, Graham.'

'So what is?'

'The point,' she said tightly, 'is that I'm a cop and you're indicted. If I was doing my job, I should have come here with Marcel in the middle of the afternoon, taken you downtown—'

'I'm not kidding you,' he said. 'I'll go. I'll go right now. I'll beat this, and then—'

'No! God damn it, no! We're not doing that.'

He waited. 'Then what?'

She slumped onto one of the kitchen chairs. 'I don't know. I don't have any idea.' She was about to cry.

'I'll give you a dollar if you let me come over and hug you.' He crossed the room, went down on a knee, and put his arms around her shoulders. 'Don't worry,' he said. 'It's going to be all right.'

'How?' She was shaking against him. 'What are we going to do? I can't see you. You can't even be here. If I don't take you in, I'm committing a felony myself. In fact, I am now. How can I commit a felony?'

'You're right, you can't,' he said. 'Look, I'll just turn myself in. I'll call Hardy, find out where he lives, show up at his house, and have him do it.'

'But I don't want to leave you to them, even to him. I want you to be here. This can't be the only time we're ever going to get. I can't, I just can't . . . I mean, we just started, and it's so good, Graham. It's so good. Don't you feel that?' Her cheeks were wet now and he wiped the tears gently away.

'We've had a few days,' he said. 'We'll hold on to them, how's that? We won't lose this.'

'You don't know that. Who knows how long you'll be in jail, with the trial, even if you win . . .'

'I'll win.'

She shook her head, sniffling. 'But what if you don't?'

'I will. Nobody's going to be able to prove I did anything wrong. I'll beat it. And however long it is, we'll get through it, okay?'

She shook her head again. 'I don't know. I don't know how we can, *if* we can.'

'We will. I promise. I've been looking for this for too long and now we've got it. I'm not letting you go, and that's all there is to it.'

Hardy was intensely unhappy with Graham's disappearance, but there wasn't anything he could do about it now. The police would probably find him first and Hardy would get a call from jail.

Meanwhile, he did have other clients who needed consistent, if perhaps low-level, effort. He tried to leave Friday afternoons open for the motions and correspondence that covered a decent part of the overhead of a small commercial practice like his own. He was just finishing up a memo for one of these clients, when he looked up and saw Abe Glitsky standing in his open doorway.

Momentarily startled, Hardy sat back. 'Now I know how you

must feel. People turning up in your office without any warning. Hey, wasn't today the day? Tell me your door's been installed.'

'It's in.' Glitsky nodded, but there was a set to his features. He wasn't here to talk about his door.

'What's the matter?'

The lieutenant took a step into the room. 'I tell you something in confidence as a friend, and you take it to the DA and try to make your own juice out of it, I feel kind of like you're a sack-of-shit lawyer instead of my old pal.'

Any profanity from Glitsky was unusual, but a directed vulgar insult was unheard of, serious. 'You want to come in? I'm sorry. I was wrong.'

Glitsky didn't move. 'I don't think I do. I'm just here with the message, so you'd know I knew.'

Dan Tosca was allowing himself to be treated to a nice dinner at Firenze by Night. Lanier had wanted the information sooner if he could have gotten it, and now, technically, it was too late; the attorney general had already got its indictment on Graham Russo, though he and his partner hadn't been able to serve the warrant.

Lanier didn't really think there would be anything with Sal Russo's business dealings that might complicate the investigation into his death. But, as it turned out, he was wrong.

Tosca was eating *coniglio con pancetta* – Lanier called it bunny and bacon – and Marcel was having spaghetti and meatballs. '. . . so I was surprised, mostly because I hadn't heard a word about it.'

'But it was a heart attack, you're sure?'

Tosca shrugged, pushing sauce around his plate with a piece of bread. 'Nobody's sure of anything, come right down to it, but Pio gets a pain in his chest, he goes to the hospital, he dies.'

'Pio?'

'Pio, yeah. Ermenigeldo Pio. He ran the fish operation.'

'For who?'

Tosca lowered his voice. 'It was his shop. He built it up.'

'And how big was it? Not just Russo's, the whole thing?'

'Dollar volume? Thirty, thirty-five.'

'A month?'

Tosca shrugged, agreeing. 'People like fish. Everybody's

worried about cholesterol. Me' – he pointed down at his plate – 'I like this. I don't worry about it.'

Marcel put his fork down. 'I don't feel good about Pio dying just now.'

A smile. 'I bet he don't either. And it's not now. It was last week.'

This really set off warning bells. Like all veteran cops Lanier set little store in coincidence. 'They do an autopsy?'

'Why? It was a heart attack. Guy's sixty-two. Probably didn't eat enough fish.' Tosca speared some meat. 'But you ask me, it's all genes anyway. You get your time, then you're dead.'

'You're a philosopher, aren't you, Dan?'

Another shrug. 'Part time. Look, if it makes you feel better, I can tell you, this has nothing to do with Sal Russo and his one truck of fish. Pio was doing *vans*, he's got a fleet. He's doing Half Moon Bay up to Tomales seven days a week.'

'So who's doing that now? Who's taking that over?'

Tosca's eyes twinkled. 'I don't think that's all settled yet.' He reached over the table and patted Lanier's arm. 'A vacuum like this comes up, there's always a little power struggle. It'll work itself out. But I guarantee you this has nothing to do with Sal Russo.'

If it was all fish, Lanier could believe that, even at the enormous volumes they were discussing. But if it was anything else . . . 'You would tell me if you'd run into drugs, wouldn't you?'

Tosca put his fork down. 'Marcel, this is not how dope is handled. You know this. You got your Koreans, your Vietnamese, the Chinatown tongs, your longhairs. Bunch of guinea *pescadores* go up against these hard-ons? I don't think so. Besides, I thought you told me you were arresting the boy, his son.'

'We are.'

'And wasn't there some magazine story he admitted it?'

'Yeah.'

Tosca spread his hands. 'So what's the problem?'

18

Sarah wasn't sure whether it had been her idea or Graham's, but somehow they'd decided they would spend a last weekend together, after which Graham would turn himself in.

But it wouldn't be in San Francisco, where the risk was too great. Sarah already felt so compromised that she barely considered what difference another day or two would make, especially over a weekend.

Graham had a Saturday tournament across the Bay. If his team won, he would have more money for his defense, which he would need. So at nine-fifteen Saturday morning they parked at the tournament site, a multidiamond complex in a valley surrounded by oak-strewn rolling green foothills. Graham was pulling his bat bag from his trunk when a trim man in a designer sweatsuit, gold chain, sunglasses, came jogging up. 'I can't believe it, I can't believe you're here.'

Graham turned. 'Hey, Craig, how you doin'?' A bounce of the shoulders. 'We got games, I'm here.' Graham's macho pose was kicking back in. Sarah saw little sign of the man she'd been with for the past week, for whom she was sacrificing everything. This untouchable athlete needed no one. It was an unsettling moment.

But this man, Craig, was going on. 'You're having some week, aren't you? I know some important people, let me tell you, and I don't know anybody who's ever been on the cover of *Time*.'

'It's just stuff around me,' Graham said. 'I'm here to play ball, that's all.' He put out his hand to include Sarah, bring her up to them. 'This is a friend of mine, Sarah Evans. Sarah, Craig Ising, our sponsor.'

Shaking hands with him, Sarah was struck by his relative youth. He wasn't much older than they were, certainly not over forty. From Graham's description of him – really from what she knew he must be worth – she had expected someone in his fifties, at least.

Half an hour later Sarah was eating a Sno-Kone, watching the teams warm up. Ising appeared from somewhere and sat next to her. 'So, you been seeing my star a long time?'

'Couple of weeks,' she said.

'You live in the city?'

'Yeah.' She glanced out the side of her sunglasses. 'How'd *you* find Graham?'

'I knew his dad.'

'Sal?'

'You knew him too?'

'Graham talks about him a lot.'

'Yeah. Hell of a funny guy. Was, I mean. Shame about that. He had some great jokes. Anyway, Graham was in Triple A and got cut, and Sal told me I ought to try him out. I'm glad I did. Kid's made me a bundle.'

'That's nice.'

'He's mature, you know, a leader.'

She smiled. 'I like him already, Craig. So what was it? You bought fish from Sal?'

'Naw.' He lowered his voice. 'He had protection, you know? He was good luck.'

Sarah felt the hairs rise on the back of her neck. 'What do you mean, protection?'

The game had started and the shortstop for the Hornets took a hit away from the first batter, going deep into the hole. When Ising sat down again, Sarah repeated her question.

'I'm just curious. Protection from what? This kind of thing fascinates me.'

Ising, impressing the pretty girl, unraveled the mystery for her. 'He was connected, I don't know. Somebody way up there. He looked like a bum and nobody touched him.'

'So how did you meet him?'

'One of my friends. I do a little betting, maybe Graham told you, these games, other things. So sometimes cash moves around downtown.'

'You're saying Sal carried this cash?'

He playfully hit her lightly on the knee. 'Hey, you got a knack for this, Sarah, I'm not kidding you. Yeah, you give Sal a paper bag and a bill and off he goes. He stopped lately. He must have known he was getting forgetful, didn't want to lose track of anybody's money.'

All those names, she was thinking, *all those numbers*. They weren't the people who supplied his fish to him. Could it be they were gamblers – high-stakes gamblers? 'Did Graham know about this?'

'I don't know, you ought to ask him. Hey, by the way.' He was fishing in his pockets for something and came out with a business card – his name and a number. 'Don't take this wrong, but it wasn't real clear. Are you and Graham an item?'

She shrugged. 'Close. Kind of.'

'Well' – he handed her the card – 'if it doesn't work out, give me a call. I have a pretty good time.'

'I can see that,' she said, smiling at him. 'I'll keep it in mind.'

Right after Hardy got up Saturday, he'd called Glitsky to apologize again and the nanny told him the lieutenant was busy. She didn't know when he'd be available. He asked her to make sure and give him the message that his friend Hardy was a horse's ass, but he wasn't sure she'd deliver it verbatim.

Then, while he was telephoning, he'd tried Graham Russo's home for the fun of it and gotten the expected result. Nothing.

Then Frannie reminded him that the kids had arranged for some school chums to come over and play, and Frannie was going to her Saturday jazzercize class, so Hardy was in charge.

She'd told him! Didn't he remember? Of course he did, he had told her, although this was a lie. He said he was just teasing her.

So for three hours Hardy had baby-sat. Although, as his wife never tired of telling him, he shouldn't think of it as baby-sitting. They were *his* children. He wasn't merely *watching* them. He was their father, responsible for their guidance and development.

Too true, he admitted every time this topic surfaced. He even believed it. But there were moments – as for example when five pre-ten-year-olds were playing some kind of parade game with every pillow, blanket, cushion, and stuffed animal in the entire house on the living-room floor – that his parental role seemed limited, more or less, to just baby-sitting. Neither his kids nor their friends really cried out to have old Dad guiding their development at that particular moment.

This was not to say there was not a great deal of crying out in general – and screaming and giggling and fighting and running around – and Hardy never for a moment doubted that if he wasn't in *baby-sitting* mode, they would destroy the house as surely and as efficiently as Vesuvius had destroyed Pompeii.

Finally, Frannie came home. Hardy, nearly insane with enduring the kid stuff, asked her if she minded if he took a little break. He'd be back in a while – going for a jog.

Until three years before Hardy had been religious about running a four-mile circle from his house on 34th Avenue, out to the beach, south as far as Lincoln, then back east along Lincoln to Park Presidio, up through Golden Gate Park, and back home.

Frannie warned him that maybe he should warm up for a week or so, get back in some aerobic condition before tackling four miles. To which he'd beaten his chest like Tarzan, getting a big laugh from the kids – their dad was funny – and told his wife he'd be home in forty-five minutes. He was still in shape.

He had never given the workout much thought; it had been part of his daily routine. Today, before he'd even made the fifteen or so downhill blocks to the beach, he was truly winded. But never one to let a little physical discomfort stand in his way, especially when he thought it could be overcome by an act of will, he turned south and kept jogging.

Frustrated by the burning in his lungs and leg muscles, he decided he'd just *show* his uncooperative body who was boss and run in the soft sand, not the hard pack by the breakers.

When he finally realized that the cramp that stopped him a mile farther on was not a fatal heart attack, he was in a real pickle. He hadn't brought either his wallet or keys.

So now, at the farthest possible point from his house, he was stopped in agony, without cab fare or ID. He was going to have to walk, or limp, home.

He'd better start walking. Getting back home wasn't going to be quick. It was sometime after noon and the wind off the ocean had picked up. His sweat glands worked fine, and the dampness of the sweats he wore made it even colder.

He wasn't going to make it home. He would die here, limping on the beach. The fine-blowing sand would imbed itself into his damp sweatsuit, his very pores, and turn to cement, and leave him permanently frozen in place.

He could see it clearly: generations hence, tourists would flock to San Francisco, to the binoculars at the Cliff House, and pay a quarter to look down the beach and marvel in wonder at the origins of the manlike form that had magically appeared one day in the late nineties, an eternal sandstone monument to middle-aged flabbiness and stupidity.

It took him nearly an hour and a half to get home from the beach. He had a bath, tried Glitsky and Graham again to no avail, got in a twenty-minute nap. He was going to survive, although the next few days might not be much fun.

That night, he and Rebecca were having their own 'date.' The word had a lot of emotional resonance in the family due to the traditional Wednesday 'Date Night.' They'd instituted something of the sort with their kids – Hardy with the Beck, Frannie with Vincent.

He and his daughter got to North Beach with time to kill before their dinner reservation, so they strolled the neighborhood together. The Beck's dress was a flounced floral print in pinks and greens. She wore black patent leather shoes and white tights. Holding hands, flushed with excitement to be in the grown-up world with her dad, Rebecca chattered her way through the tail end of Chinatown with its ducks hanging whole in the windows, its bushels of strange green vegetables and even stranger brown tubers on the sidewalks, its fish in tanks, live poultry in cages.

'Can we go in one?'

'Sure.'

In front of them a tiny Asian woman ordered something and the man behind the counter took a turtle from a tank and a cleaver from the butcher block, eviscerating and cleaning it as he would have any other foodstuff.

'I didn't know people ate turtles,' she whispered as they left.

Hardy bought an orchid from a street vendor and leaned down to arrange it under his daughter's hair band.

They quickly passed – Rebecca silent, holding Hardy's hand

tightly – through the gaudy tourist Saturday-night gauntlet of strip shows and adult theaters, the hawkers and gawkers and rubes from out of town, and then up Broadway by the tunnel to the quiet serenity of Alfred's.

At their banquette the Beck smiled at her father with an adoring radiance. Her strawberry-blond hair was pulled back off her broad, unlined forehead, usually hidden by bangs. It made her look three or four years older. Her manners were flawless.

'What a little doll!' 'Such a charming child!' 'You are one lucky man!' 'You must be so proud of her!'

The two of them – Rebecca was meant to hear – took the compliments in stride, modestly, graciously. 'Thanks.' 'She is a gem, isn't she?' 'I know – her dad is so proud of her.'

It was difficult to reconcile the sophisticated daughter who sat across from him now, dazzling the waiters and staff, with the jelly-covered dervish of the morning. But then Hardy realized it would be equally difficult to recognize the well-groomed man in the dark suit as the limping, teeth-chattering hunchback of Ocean Beach he'd been only a few hours ago.

'And for the lady?' the waiter asked.

She ordered a Shirley Temple in a martini glass to go with her father's Bombay. After the drinks arrived, they clinked their glasses. 'To you,' Hardy said. 'I'm so glad we do this.'

Rebecca looked down demurely. 'Me too.' She sipped and put the glass down carefully, then looked back up at him. 'Daddy? That man you're helping, why did he kill his father?'

Out of the mouths of babes, he thought.

'Well, I don't know if he did.'

'They said at school he did.'

'They did, huh?'

She nodded solemnly. 'Because he was sick – the dad, I mean. We had a big talk about it, if it was okay. They said he killed him because he was so sick, but I know I wouldn't want to kill you, even if you were sick. Then I wouldn't have you anymore.'

'No, that's true, you wouldn't.' Hardy searched for an approach. 'Have you been thinking about this a lot?'

She shrugged. 'A little. I mean, I know you're helping him, right? So you must think it's all right.'

'I don't think it's bad, hon, not necessarily. It depends on the person who's sick, I think, if he wants to die.'

'But that would mean he'd want to leave his son too.'

'Well' – Hardy rubbed at the table with his fingertip – 'not that he'd want to. But what if he was hurting all the time? What if I was? You wouldn't want me to spend my life suffering, would you?'

'But I wouldn't want you to *die*!'

He reached across the table and put his hand on top of hers. 'This is just something we're talking about, Beck. I'm not going to die, okay? We're talking about my client's dad, and he was old and really really sick. I think he wanted to die and he needed his son to help him. He couldn't trust anybody else to do it right.'

'Well, then, why is there going to be a trial if it was the right thing?'

'Because the law says it's wrong. But sometimes things that are against the law aren't really wrong. They're just against the law.' He heard himself uttering these words and wondered if he really believed them. When he'd been a prosecutor, the distinction wouldn't have mattered a fig to him. He wondered if he was beginning to even *think* like a defense attorney, and, for the millionth time, wasn't sure if he was comfortable with it.

But Rebecca, her face betraying every nuance of the quandary, hadn't lost the thread. 'Like what? What *isn't* wrong but *is* against the law?'

He searched his brain. 'Well, you know those places we passed coming here, with all those posters of naked women?'

'Yeah. That was gross.'

'It might be gross or whatever, but it's not against the law. It might not be the way you'd want to choose to live, to do that kind of stuff. You might even think it's *wrong*, but it's still not against the law.' He squeezed her hand. 'Are you sure you want to talk about this? Is this a little . . . serious?'

A frown. 'Dad-*dee*. I'm nine, you know. I think about a lot of things.'

'I know. I know you do.' He smiled at her, this justice-freak daughter of his with a passion for knowing what's right and what's wrong. And the example he'd just given her was backwards – something perhaps morally suspect but within the law. He wanted the opposite to make the point. 'Okay, let's start over.

Maybe I used the wrong word, like *wrong*, for instance. There's the law, right?'

'Right.'

'Okay. So the law is just a bunch of rules. That's all it is. Some good rules and some rules where it doesn't make too much sense that they even have the rule. The point is, though, good or bad, if you break one of the rules, you're going to get punished. That's another one of the rules.'

'Right.'

'But sometimes you break a rule – a law – because you think there's no reason for it, or it's just plain wrong. Now you're still going to get punished, because you can't allow people to just go breaking the rules, but maybe when you go to trial to get punished, people will realize that the law is dumb, and they'll change it.'

'Like what?'

Hardy thought a moment for a clean example. 'Well, like it used to be against the law for black people to sit on buses with white people.'

'I know, but that was just stupid.'

'Of course, but it was a law nevertheless, until this lady named Rosa Parks—'

'Oh, I know all about that. We learned that in school. She sat on the bus and they went on strike—'

'Yeah, well, and then they changed the law, and then it wasn't against the law for black people to sit on buses. It was the same *thing* – in this case a right thing – but one day it was against the law, and the next day it was okay. It wasn't the thing itself, it was the rule. Is this making any sense?'

'Sure. I get it completely.'

'Okay, I bet you do. Anyway, this thing with Graham – my client – it's a little like that example, but not exactly. I'm not sure the law about letting you kill your father or mother ought to be changed.'

'Why not?'

'Because then how do you decide for sure whether or not it's a good reason? If the person who's sick really wants it? Or even knows what's happening?' Hardy decided to test his martini, buy another few seconds to think. 'Or sometimes sick people are really hard to take care of, and maybe the people taking care of them get tired of it and just want the person to go away.'

'That would be horrible!'

'Well, yes, it would. But if there wasn't some law preventing it, it might happen. There's just all kinds of problems. It's really really complicated. But in this case what Graham did might not have been wrong. I think. I hope.'

She met his eyes. 'I know, Daddy, if you're helping him, he didn't do the wrong thing.'

Hardy had to laugh. 'You know that, huh?'

'Cross my heart.'

Graham and his father didn't only have Hallmark moments.

'Who do you think you are, telling your old man what to do?' Though it wasn't yet ten in the morning, Sal had been drinking. He took a feeble swing at his son, as though he were going to cuff him. 'I'm the dad here. You are just my *little snot-nosed kid and you do what I tell you, not the other way round.'*

Graham easily ducked away from the roundhouse, but that was the only thing that was going to be easy about this morning.

'We got an appointment, Sal. The doctor, you remember?'

'I ain't going to no doctor. I told you. They take my driver's license, what am I supposed to do for a living?'

Graham tried to remain patient. 'This is Dr Cutler, Sal, my friend. Not the other one – what's his name? – Finer.'

'They're all the same. Finer, Cutler. I don't care. I'm not going.' He had settled himself onto his couch, arms crossed, the picture of resistance. There was a flask on its side on the table in front of him and he grabbed it and swigged from it. 'You know how tired I am of getting poked at?'

'Yeah, I do, Dad.' Almost as tired as I am of all this, Graham thought. And Russ Cutler had told him the AD was only going to get worse unless this brain tumor turned out to be inoperable. Which – the good news – looked like the diagnosis.

Graham didn't think it was funny, but the irony didn't escape him. He'd brought Sal down to Russ Cutler for the Alzheimer's. Sal's eccentricity had suddenly become far less manageable. Graham had wanted an opinion whether his father should be left to live alone, or should be placed in the dreaded home. Would he even know it if he was?

Alzheimer's wasn't Cutler's specialty, but he knew enough. The disease began almost imperceptibly, with smaller losses of short-term memory gradually becoming larger, more all encompassing. The distant past began to assume a more immediate reality than the present.

For Graham the most heart-rending aspect of the situation was its apparently random appearance. Forgetfulness, then a reversion to normalcy, or near normalcy. You kept wanting to deny that it had reached a point of no return. You kept hoping.

Up until a couple of months ago he had spent lots of time with his father, making his fish rounds, playing cards, going to meals, taking walks – Graham trying to get his own reality into focus. What he was going to do with his life. Where, if anywhere, he fit in. And Sal had been great. His best friend. A wise, albeit vulgar, counselor, playmate, drinking buddy.

But then, all at once, Sal wouldn't be there in an almost literal sense. He wouldn't know who Graham was. 'Son, my ass! I haven't seen either of my sons in fifteen years. Who the hell are you trying to fool? What do you want out of me? You think you're going to get my money, you got another think coming.'

The hours Graham had spent camped in the stinking hallway of the Lions Arms, making sure Sal didn't go out when he was this way. It was killing Graham, never mind Sal.

So he'd gone to Russ and learned that this randomness was part of the progress of the disease, until finally the brain didn't appear to process anymore. Whether or not it did was impossible to say.

'And even then,' Russ had told him, 'you'll go into the nursing home to visit your dad one day. He hasn't said a meaningful word in six months and he'll look up and know you and say hi like it was yesterday, and maybe for him it was.'

But then they'd found the tumor and would be doing the tests on that. That was today, the first of these tests. The tumor, if it wasn't fatal, might be affecting the Alzheimer's, moving its schedule forward. Although that, too, wasn't more than informed conjecture. It was possible that arresting the tumor's growth might inhibit Sal's memory loss for a time.

'Come on, Dad. Dr Cutler's going to be waiting for us. He's a good guy.'

But Sal's eyes were closed now. He had collapsed to one side on the couch. His pants were wet at the crotch – either alcohol or urine.

God! Graham couldn't keep doing this for long. He wished the old man would have the good grace to go and die.

19

The ritual of a cup of coffee over the newspaper had fallen victim on most days to the mad rush of getting the kids washed, dressed, fed, teeth brushed, hair combed, lunches made, out the door to school. But Sundays still had some of that old charm.

Hardy and Frannie were still in their bed with the Sunday paper spread out all around them. They had their mugs of coffee. Last night, before he'd left North Beach with Rebecca, he stopped and picked up some cannoli and biscotti, and the crumbs in the sheets would have to be dealt with, but later.

Vincent and Rebecca hadn't slept in – on a weekend? don't be absurd – but for the moment were cooperating in building the world's largest Lego castle, both of them quiet and happy.

Hardy had cracked one of the windows two inches to let in some fresh air. Sunshine filled the whole room.

The telephone rang. The portable phone by their bed had disappeared, so someone was going to have to get up and answer at the kitchen extension. Frannie flashed a smile at Hardy. 'The walk might do you some good after your jog yesterday.' But she was up, answering it. Reappearing a moment later, she stood in the doorway, her hand up through her long red hair, one foot resting on the other one. 'It's Graham Russo,' she said.

It was also Bay to Breakers Sunday.

Every year upward of a hundred thousand people flock to the City by the Bay to run approximately seven miles from the Ferry Building on the Bay to Ocean Beach. Although only about one tenth of one percent of these people come to compete in any meaningful way, the event has evolved into a party of significant proportions.

There are running teams outfitted as caterpillars, barefoot teams, naked runners, participants who sprint for the first three blocks and then duck into bars to watch themselves on television, grandmothers, children, dogs, snakes, marching – no, jogging – bands. A party.

Graham Russo called Hardy from Jack London Square in Oakland. He told his attorney he'd gone into hiding for a few days to make some decisions, to consider his options.

Now it was time. If Hardy would like to take the Alameda ferry over and meet him, Graham was ready to turn himself in. They could talk strategy and Graham would answer Hardy's questions as they chugged back across the Bay.

As a plan it wouldn't have been bad on most days. But it left the race out of the equation. Hardy hadn't even gotten to his car when the crowds and traffic around his house told him something was going on.

After a minute's reflection – even before yesterday's painful reminder of his lack of conditioning, Hardy had never been a Bay to Breakers kind of guy – he realized what he was dealing with. He knew it was going to be iffy taking a ferry anywhere in the next several hours. Even getting to the Ferry *Building* was going to be a challenge.

But he tried. He'd told Graham he'd be there in an hour, maybe a little more, though he had been hoping for less. Clients about to turn themselves in on murder charges had been known to change their minds.

Since the route of the race was along the edge of Golden Gate Park, which was several blocks south of the main east-west corridor, Geary Boulevard, he thought he might have some hope of making it. He vaguely knew that the race began at about eight o'clock, and it wasn't yet ten. It was possible, he knew, that some of the participants still hadn't crossed the *starting* line; they queued up for miles along the Embarcadero before the gun that started the race. So maybe the outbound arteries wouldn't be clogged yet with people who'd finished and were leaving the city to go to their post-race parties.

And indeed, he got nearly to Van Ness, the western edge of downtown, before things stopped. Dead.

After ten minutes at one corner he got out of his car and

looked around him. The honking was in full blare. Lines of cars, glaring in the bright sunlight, stretched out in all directions. A river of humanity – waving, singing, high-fiving, having a great old time on that fabled runner's high, although few were actually running – flowed by. There was no place even to pull over and park, after which he could try to walk it. He wasn't going anywhere for at least a couple of hours.

Vincent had a birthday party to attend in the early afternoon, and while that went on, Frannie and Rebecca met her grandmother – Frannie's first husband's mother, Erin – for a picnic on the cliffs just outside the Legion of Honor. So no one was home to answer Graham's next couple of calls, though Hardy did hear them on his answering machine, progressively angry and frustrated, when he finally arrived back at the house a little after four.

He was somewhat angry and frustrated himself.

The last incoming ferry was at the dock in Alameda. Graham sat in a windbreaker next to his duffel bag on one of the pilings by the gangplank where it tied up.

Sarah, as she had when the last four boats had docked, hung back by the shops. When Graham's lawyer came up to him, she was planning to leave and go home. But they both agreed there was no sense in Graham waiting all afternoon alone until Hardy showed.

And now it looked like he wasn't going to. Sarah was really unhappy that Hardy hadn't found a way to get to Graham. What the hell kind of lawyer was he, anyway?

'He's a good guy,' he said. 'Something must have happened.'

'What could have happened?'

He shrugged. 'Maybe he was on an earlier ferry and we just missed each other.'

'With you sitting here on a piling that everybody has to walk past? No. You're visible. He wouldn't have missed you.'

A last group of passengers disembarked and started up the gangplank – four couples in their twenties and face paint, not sober, laughing a lot, wearing Bay to Breakers T-shirts over the body armor they'd evidently run in.

Graham and Sarah had spent the whole day here, saying

goodbye, preparing themselves for what was to come. Every time a ferry had arrived, the tension had overwhelmed them. Where was Hardy? What was going to happen to Graham now? To them? Everything else was invisible.

Now, suddenly, together, they both realized what they were looking at. 'Bay to Breakers,' Sarah said. 'Smart of us to pick today.'

Graham picked up his duffel bag. 'I think our timing's off.'

'That must be it.'

They were stopped in the middle of the Bay Bridge when she brought it up to him. It had been haunting her since she'd been so thoroughly uncharmed by Craig Ising the day before. She had to get it clear.

'You know, your friend Craig Ising—'

He interrupted her. 'He's not my friend. He pays me. That's our entire relationship.'

This, while gratifying, was not the point. 'Well, whatever he is, he told me your dad used to deliver money around the city for him and some other gamblers.'

'Yeah, he did. So what?'

'Don't get mad. I'm trying to get a handle on your father, that's all. Who he was.'

But Graham took offense at this tack. 'He lived on the fringe, Sarah, okay? He sold illegal fish, he might have run some money, so sue him.'

'I'm not saying—'

'Yes, you are. Maybe he wasn't a good citizen, but there's no way he did anything that hurt anybody. He's not so unlike his oldest son that way.'

'What way exactly?'

'You follow the rules, you play fair, and you get screwed anyway. It makes you lose faith in the sacred rules.' He lowered his voice. 'You're doing it here with me, Sarah, right now. The rules don't work sometimes. Then what do you do?'

'You don't break them, I know that. Or if you do,' she added, mostly for herself, 'when you're caught and punished, you don't whine about it.'

He looked over at her – the strong face, the set jaw. He reached across and put a hand on her leg. 'Hey,' he said gently. 'I shouldn't have put you in this. I'm sorry.'

She let out a breath. 'I put *myself* in this, Graham. If I didn't want to be here, I wouldn't be. And I know people break rules all the time and sometimes it seems justified. What I was trying to get to was Sal – if running this money around might have gotten him killed.'

Graham let out a sigh of his own. 'But he stopped a long time ago.'

'How long?'

'I don't know. Couple of years at least.'

'You're sure.'

'I think so, yeah. When he started forgetting more, he thought it wouldn't be safe.'

'Which is what I'm getting at.'

Graham pondered for a minute, his feet up on the dashboard. It was just dusk. The window on his side was open and the skyline was a sparkling jewel over the darkening water. 'He wouldn't have started up again. There was no reason to. He didn't need the money and it wasn't that much anyway. A hundred now and again. Not worth the risk he might forget and lose enough money for somebody to make them mad at him.'

'Maybe that somebody ran into him recently, last week even. Asked for a favor. One time. And he forgot. Or forgot that he would forget and said okay.'

'And then what?'

'I'm just thinking. It might be a motive, that's all.'

Graham put his hand on her leg. 'Sarah, we don't need a motive. He killed himself.'

She turned to him. 'Stop saying that, Graham! Please. Nobody believes that.'

'I do.'

She moved his hand off her. 'It's not true. That's why I don't believe it. I know what happened well enough now. I'm just trying to come up with some theories that might help your defense. This might be one of them.'

Another silence. Graham looked across at her. 'So what did happen that you're so sure of?'

'Graham. Come on.'

'No, really. I want to know.'

She took her eyes from the road. It didn't matter, they were barely creeping. 'What are you saying?' she finally asked.

'What are *you* saying?' he shot back at her. 'After all this time, after everything, you still think I killed Sal?'

'I'm saying somebody was there. If it was you, helping him, it wouldn't matter to me, Graham. That's what I'm saying.'

'It *would* matter to me! Jesus, Sarah, don't you believe anything I've told you?'

'Don't yell at me. Please don't yell at me.' She was afraid to look over at him again. Her eyes were glued to the road, hands tight on the wheel at ten and two. 'Because I'll tell you something,' she said. 'Somebody was there. Somebody did help him die. Or killed him.'

20

Abe Glitsky stood in the main doorway to the homicide detail, seemingly unable to move. His mouth opened and closed a few times, but no words came out.

It was the beginning of a new week and most of his inspectors were already in the big open room, sitting at their desks, drinking coffee while doing paperwork, going over their day's schedule, writing reports on witness interviews, taking notes on transcripts, busy busy busy. No one looked up.

Abe wasn't going to give anyone the satisfaction. He finally got his legs moving and walked into his office, closing the door quietly behind him. His door, installed and freshly varnished on Friday with a nice new-wood yellowish finish, wasn't yet completely covered with bumper stickers and wanted posters and shooting targets from the police range, but someone – or a team of trained professionals – had done a pretty good job getting to most of it. There was even a bullet hole. The centerpiece was a large picture of Bozo the clown with the international symbol for *no* through it.

Taking deep breaths, he sat at his desk. The room seemed smaller with the door closed. He couldn't see anybody outside the windows in the drywall. He had not been able to before the door was in, either, but he hadn't noticed.

Now he suddenly felt cut off from the detail. He steeled himself, and finally brought his eyes right. Inside, the door looked pretty much the same as it had on Friday, new and nicely varnished, except for where the bullet had splintered the wood around its exit hole.

He remembered that years before, during one or other of the endless labor disputes in which the city always seemed to be embroiled, some unknown and never apprehended officers had released chickens on a Friday night into the offices of Police Chief Dan Rigby. Apparently, some felt at that time that their chief was acting in a chickenshit manner, not standing up for the demands of his troops. It was a not-so-subtle but ultimately effective way to express their displeasure.

Glitsky didn't think there was anything like that going on here. The detail wasn't in the midst of any turmoil that he knew of. He got along with everybody.

Pratt, he thought. Her staff. But no, not here in the detail. Nobody who worked with her would have risked it.

This was just a practical joke. He didn't find it very funny, but he remembered that Rigby hadn't laughed all that much about the chickens either. In fact, Rigby's reaction had been so over the top that it had cost him some respect. Glitsky wasn't going to have that happen to him. He was going to remain cool and never mention it to a soul.

But he was as mad as he'd ever been.

Pushing back from the desk, he walked over and scratched away at the splintered wood. The hole went all the way through. Instinctively, he searched the opposite wall. There it was, up by the ceiling, the next place the bullet had hit. He couldn't believe that some idiot inspector, goofing off, would discharge a firearm in the building, even if it had been during the weekend when the odds of hitting someone with the bullet were marginally lower.

For just a second he toyed with the idea: maybe he could find the slug somewhere in the building and run ballistics on it and all the weapons of his inspectors. This might identify the shooter, whom he would then publicly humiliate, horribly torture, and then fire, not necessarily in that order. He crossed over to the hole. Sure enough, the slug had been pried out.

Of course, he realized, these were pros. Idiots, but professional idiots.

Whoever did it had customized themselves a light load of powder – probably not as light as they'd intended. But they'd given the matter some thought – and then dug the slug out and disposed of the evidence. Pros.

His telephone jarred him back to where he was. 'Glitsky.'

'Hardy.'

He was already angry enough, and now Hardy wanting to

banter his way back into his good graces. 'What do you want?'

'You get a message over the weekend?'

'Yeah. Great, you're sorry. I got that Friday, too, at your office, remember? Sorry's a big help. Is that it? I'm busy.'

A pause. 'That's not it. I'm bringing Graham Russo in this morning. I wanted to let you know.'

'That's really swell, thanks. I'll pass it along.'

He hung up, took another look at his very own bullet hole, then opened the door and went out into the detail.

Graham spent the night alone on Edgewood and called Hardy as soon as he got up, before sunrise. Ha, ha, yeah, that was funny, they agreed, the whole Bay to Breakers thing. Hardy picked him up on the way in to work.

Now they were in his office, on either end of the couch. The doors were closed behind them. Phyllis was holding calls, although Hardy had already phoned out to Glitsky. But the morning paper had contained yet another new story about his client. He wanted to ask Graham about it. Barbara Brandt, the Sacramento lobbyist, had taken a lie detector test for Sharron Pratt, saying that she'd spoken to Graham on the day Sal died. And she passed. Ostensibly, she was telling the truth.

'So what about that?' Hardy asked. 'She says she counseled you before you went over to your dad's. And you're telling me you don't know her.'

'You got it.' Graham, in slacks and a sport jacket, was shaking his head no. He seemed truly baffled. 'I have no idea where she's coming from, Diz. I never met her in my life. No, correct that, she called me once.'

Hardy was sitting with studied casualness, legs crossed, hands clasped on his lap. 'Graham, she took a lie detector test and passed it.'

'I don't care. I'll take one too. I don't know her. She's got to be some fruitcake.'

'She's a lobbyist in Sacramento.'

Graham smiled. 'I rest my case.'

Hardy's brow was etching itself a few new lines. 'You don't know her?' he repeated a last time. 'Then what—?'

'I don't know. Maybe it's some kind of publicity stunt.'

'But she did talk to you on the phone?'

Graham was showing his impatience. 'We didn't even get to what she wanted.' He shifted forward, elbows on knees. 'I still don't know what she wants. What does this get her?'

Hardy was wondering the same thing. 'You're on the cover of *Time*. It was a sympathetic article. Maybe she's on your coattails for her cause.'

Graham sat back. 'But the conclusions in *Time*, the way he made it all sound, it was all wrong.' This was what he'd argued about with Sarah, although he couldn't very well tell that to Hardy right now. 'I never went inside, Diz. I went over early, Sal wasn't home, I left. I didn't talk to any Barbara Brandt or anybody else. I'm not lying.'

There was real anguish in his voice, and Hardy was almost glad to hear it. Maybe Graham was at last starting to get some understanding of the predicament he was in. But there was still one last hurdle before Hardy could sign on for the duration, and they had to jump it now. 'Okay, Graham, you're not lying. That's good news. I believe you. But the bad news is I might not be able to stay on with this case.'

'That's not funny.'

'But it's true.'

Graham looked at him imploringly. He hung his head for a beat, looked back up. 'Why not?'

This was his least favorite part, but Hardy had to explain his position. 'As it stands now, you're into me for maybe four hundred dollars, two hours.'

'It's been more than that.'

Hardy waved off the objection. 'We're talking round figures. Four hundred gets us to here, but if I continue and we go to trial, then you get most of my time for most of a year.'

'Or else I take the public defender?'

'That's right. There's some good lawyers in that office. I could recommend—'

But Graham stopped him. 'So could I. I know those guys. They got fifty cases going all the time. I'd be one of them.'

Hardy didn't want to waste breath arguing it. Many public defenders were decent enough trial attorneys, but Graham was right. In general, workload remained a factor in quality of defense. But they couldn't sit here all day either. Hardy had already alerted Glitsky that he was bringing Graham to the Hall, and judging from the lieutenant's mood, he wouldn't put it past him to send a car down here and make the arrest in Hardy's office – a little object lesson in the etiquette of friendship.

'How about this?' Graham asked. 'You take me on for a small retainer – say a couple of grand – and after six weeks you tell the judge I'm busted, then the court appoints you to represent me, and it pays you.'

Hardy was shaking his head. 'No, I don't do that.'

'Yeah, I don't blame you. It's pretty sleazy.'

'So where does that leave us? You want a private attorney, you've got to pay for one. That's the way it works.'

'I know. You're right.' He pulled an envelope from the inside pocket of his sport coat. 'Deduct the four hundred I already owe you and that's eleven thousand, six hundred.'

Hardy flicked at the envelope a few times, then left it on the couch, got up, and walked over to the window. He hated this. There was a time, he knew, when he would have taken this case, literally, for nothing. He would have lived on beans and burgers and somehow made it work. But it wasn't only him now. He had a family that depended on him absolutely. He thought of Talleyrand's axiom that a married man with children will do anything for money.

Leaving aside the thornier question of where this money had come from, he turned back. 'I'm sorry, Graham. It's not close.'

'Not even as a retainer? I could sign a promissory note for the rest.'

'And what about if you're convicted? It's notoriously hard to make a good living in prison.' He didn't mean to be such a hard-ass, but he knew this was gentle compared to what Graham would be facing in the coming months.

'If you put my Beemer up for sale, you could probably clear another twenty-five. Sal's baseball cards, maybe another thirty.'

'Except that Sal's cards aren't yours. They're under seal.'

Since Graham was going to be charged with killing Sal for the money and the baseball cards, if he was convicted, those items would be permanently confiscated by the state. They were untouchable assets.

But Hardy badly wanted this case. He'd been living with it for a couple of weeks and he couldn't imagine letting it go now. He'd committed. Thirty-seven thousand dollars – twelve in the envelope and twenty-five from the BMW – wasn't going to cut it for a year's work in a murder trial, but it was a reasonable retainer under normal business conditions.

They'd just have to figure some other way. Hardy was convinced that Graham was doing his best to show good faith, although he really didn't want to think about the provenance of the cash in the envelope he was holding. It was probably money saved from his softball tournaments, maybe left over from his well-paying law job.

It broke the first law of the defense attorney, which is 'Get your payment up front', but Hardy did not care. As with all acts of faith it was irrational and in many ways unexplainable. It was just something he felt he had to do. 'All right, Graham,' he said, 'my fees are two hundred an hour, twice that at trial. You want to sign a note that you'll pay it all when this is over, no matter how it comes out?'

It was a no-brainer – maybe, Hardy thought, on both sides – and Graham gave it all the time it deserved. About a second. 'Yeah, I'll do that.'

Hardy put out his hand. 'Then you got yourself a lawyer.'

When Hardy returned to his office in the late afternoon, there was a call from Helen Taylor, Graham's mother – a cultured voice – saying she'd like to make an appointment at his earliest convenience to discuss the case.

'Of course we want to help Graham any way we can. Are we allowed to come and visit him at the jail? Where did he go this last week, do you know? When is he being . . . what's the word, arraigned?'

'That's the word. Tomorrow morning, nine A.M., but these things aren't very exact in terms of time,' he explained, understating considerably. 'If you're there at nine-thirty, Superior Court, Department Twenty-two, you won't miss it. We can meet after that.'

'I'll be there,' she said. 'My husband too.'

'Fine,' Hardy replied. 'I'll be the one in the suit standing next to your son.'

Lanier and Evans had spent the afternoon going door to door in Hunter's Point, questioning the residents who lived near one of the neighborhood's busiest intersections, wondering whether any of them had noticed the fusillade of eighty shots from at least three different weapons last Thursday night that had killed two teenagers and wounded four others, broken sixteen windows, and set off alarms in five of the street-front businesses.

Mostly, nobody had seen or heard a thing. Thursday? No, Thursday be pretty quiet most times.

Sarah had been in the game a long time, so this didn't surprise her. But it did make her angry. Between them, she and Marcel had located and interviewed a grand total of three witnesses who had seen the car drive up and fire randomly into the crowd gathered on the corner. But it had been dark, and there was no telling the make or model, or the color or size or sex of the driver or other occupants, if any.

'What really gets me' – Sarah was a few minutes into milk-shake therapy at the closest McDonald's – 'is they treat it like it's a natural disaster, some act of nature. Nobody's fault, it just happens.'

Since this was the essence of police work, it didn't seem to faze Marcel, who'd walked the walk through dozens of similar incidents. 'I don't know why they make these things so thick. I cannot get a drop out of this straw. You think if I went back and told 'em I was a cop, they'd add some milk or something?'

'Here's a wild concept, Marcel – you could use a spoon. See? Just like I'm doing. But doesn't it make you crazy?'

He put the shake down and lifted his shoulders. 'The thing is, Sarah, *nothing* that happens is anybody's fault. Things just happen to people. So you called it – it's a natural disaster.'

'But somebody did this, Marcel. Somebody drove up and shot these kids—'

'Hey, don't you go losing sleep over these poor kids. Somebody in that crowd had guns on 'em. That's a guarantee.'

'And so you shoot at the whole crowd?'

'And miss,' Marcel said. 'Don't forget that part. You are not a true gangbanger if you actually hit any part of the person you go to take out. You only hit bystanders. It's kind of like the unwritten rule. Maybe an inside joke. I'm not sure which. I'm going to go get a spoon.'

When he came back to the table, Sarah was staring at nothing, eyes glazed. Marcel slid in. 'What now?'

'Nothing.'

Lanier spooned some milkshake. 'Look, Sarah. You want some free advice? Probably not, but here it is. You can't worry so much. You take all this too seriously.'

'Thanks, but I wasn't thinking about this anymore. I'm thinking about Graham Russo.'

'That's exactly what I mean. Graham Russo is in jail. That means we're done with him until he goes to trial. What are you thinking about?'

Wondering how much she could say, she stirred at her shake. 'There's something going on we don't know. There has to be.'

'This is always true,' Lanier said. 'But a lot of what's going on doesn't have squat to do with our jobs.'

'This does. Look, they ask us to go find everything we can to make sure Russo's not the wrong guy and give us three days to do it? So we don't find it in three days it doesn't exist?'

Marcel was dipping his spoon, his brain reluctantly engaged. He nodded. 'Essentially.'

'Okay, now we're six days down the road. Tosca tells you about a power struggle that Sal's smack in the middle of, and I learn that there's at least some chance he was holding a big bag of cash on the day he's killed. So what do we do with this information? You're telling me you believe it doesn't relate?'

Lanier shrugged. 'Even if it does. So what?'

She just stared at him.

'Do you really think the attorney general of the state of California would bail on this now after sticking his neck so far out? There is no chance. I know Dean Powell. He used to work here. And Soma? Jesus. These guys could get an affidavit signed by two dozen eyewitnesses that Graham Russo was in New York for the week all around Sal's death and they'd say then he must have killed him by phone.'

Sarah sat back, drummed her fingers on the table. 'I think we ought to tell Abe. Cover ourselves, if nothing else.'

'And what's he going to do?' Lanier gave up on his milkshake, pushing it aside. 'Look, they got the grand jury to indict Russo already. He's in jail. Anything but a smoking gun in somebody else's hand – and maybe not even that – it's not going to matter. From now on the evidence talks.'

'Except what we've found since Friday—'

He was shaking his head. 'None of it's evidence. It's all "maybe" and "what if." '

'Sure, but there's a hell of a lot of it. Any other case we'd still be looking around, see what we found.'

'That's right.'

'Well?'

He took a moment. 'Well, this case we don't.' Lanier shrugged. 'That's the way it is.'

Sarah knew that, in general, Lanier was right. That was the way it was. They were in police work and it got ugly and intense. You took a position and you held it against the odds if you needed to. Above all, you did not criticize other cops.

If a person wanted touchy-feely, there were lots of other places to look for work. Because Sarah had come to believe that *one suspect* in her entire career was innocent, this did not make her a bad cop, a weak link. She'd prove that anytime she needed to. Abruptly she stood up. 'Hey, Marcel,' she said, 'suck that up. We're going back to the Point.'

Sarah had spent a lot of time at Hunter's Point in the course of her career. It was a rough place where over eighty-five percent of the adult population had either committed or witnessed a violent crime. At the McDonald's she suddenly realized that if they cruised the streets for a while in the neighborhood, she could find some somebody here she could break. And sure enough, there was Yolanda, coming out of one of the boarded-up establishments.

Marcel pulled up and Sarah was out of the car, badge out.

'Hey, I didn't do nothing. What you comin' at me for?'

'Just get in, Yolanda. We're going to talk.'

Now she had the twenty-year-old woman in the backseat of

their unmarked car. Marcel was in plain sight on the corner, not fifteen feet away, but they weren't going to good-cop, bad-cop this witness. Sarah was going to get some answers herself.

'I saw you at the jail the other day, didn't I, Yolanda? You were visiting Damon down there again, weren't you? How is Damon?'

Damon Frazee was a goateed weight-lifter who occasionally did some mayhem on citizens, as he had a couple of weekends before – a friendly little bar fight with a knife or two. Unfortunately, Damon was looking at life in prison now under California's three-strikes law. If convicted it would be his third violent offense and he would be gone from Yolanda forever. Sarah figured she could work this to her advantage.

'Framed,' Yolanda mumbled. 'Damon got hissef framed.'

'One of the brothers plant that knife on him, did they?'

A sullen nod. 'But I ain't do nothing. You got no business taking me in.'

'I'm not taking you in. I'm talking to you, that's all. I'm thinking maybe you can help Damon.'

'Ain't nothing gonna help Damon. You lyin' if you think so.' The poor mixed-up girl was shaking, biting at her nails. Her eyes were glistening with unshed tears.

Suddenly, Sarah leaned in close, snapping out her words like a drill sergeant. 'Get your fingers out of your mouth, child, and *don't you dare* call me a liar, you hear me?'

A sullen nod. Sarah slapped at the window by Yolanda's head. 'I said DO YOU HEAR ME?'

'I hear you.'

Sarah hated this kind of interview, but she'd done it many times before and knew she would again. Too bad – she was doing Yolanda a favor. But she was going to get what she came for.

'Now, listen, we got this shooting down here last Thursday, maybe you heard something about it.' She waited. 'That's a question, Yolanda. *Maybe you heard something about it?*'

Silence.

'What I'm thinking, see, if you remembered anything important, anything I can use, like who might have been in the car, something like that, who set it up, what you heard about it, anything, maybe I can do something about Damon.'

The eyes, almost more scared of hope than of anything else, came up. 'What you mean?'

'I mean we don't go for the strike, the third strike. He does some county time, he's back home for Thanksgiving.'

'If what?'

'What I said.'

Yolanda huddled down into herself. 'I give them brothers up, they come kill me.'

'What boys, Yolanda? You give me a name, *one name*, we start looking, maybe get enough evidence on 'em – hardware in the car's trunk, like that – we don't even need you to testify at the trial.'

This last was complete fabrication and Sarah knew it, but she wasn't lying about cutting a deal involving Damon. The cops would trade a third-striker for a gangbanger any day. As for Yolanda, she was right. If she did someday have to testify, she might very well end up dead. But Sarah was willing to take that risk for her.

It was a tough profession.

Yolanda looked up, waited as though for further guidance. It wasn't coming. People here in the projects knew that if they didn't take help when it was offered, it tended to disappear. And Sarah was right here, nodding at her. 'Just give me a name, Yolanda. One name.'

'Lionel Borden. He hang the World Gym most days. He was drivin'.'

Freeman was on the couch, thumbing through one of the Russo folders. Hardy, at his desk, had another half hour of work – he'd decided to try to leave the office at five-thirty so he could see his family – but he was glad enough for the silent company.

After getting back from dropping Graham at the jail, he'd put in two hours on Tryptech. Good work, too, he thought. Tedious as hell, but God was in the details. Checking his newly arrived records of past transom and conveyor failures at the Port of Oakland, he'd hit a vein in which there might be some pay dirt. It seemed that only seven months before the accident with Tryptech, the Port itself had sued the manufacturer who had produced the couplings for its transoms, alleging irregularities in their holding capacities.

It didn't exactly get him up and dancing, but he did call Dyson Brunel with the news, and spent another forty minutes with Michelle, outlining their follow-up.

Now – more necessary tedium – he was preparing the first of the binders he'd be living with for the duration of Graham's trial. It was mindless and pleasant work, labeling his tabs: *Police Report. Inspector's Notes. Inspector's Chronological. Autopsy. Coroner. Witnesses*. Beginning to organize the discovery he'd been given for Graham's defense.

By the time he got to trial, he'd have a dozen binders jammed with everything even remotely connected to his client, the victim, the trial. What he found scary was that he'd have memorized most of it. He looked up. 'I'm getting to *Publicity*, David. I'm going to need that folder.'

Freeman had his post-workday glass of wine at his elbow. He spoke calmly. 'You can't be considering change of venue?'

Hardy had to give it to his landlord – he was joined at the hip to the issues. But Hardy thought if anyone would want a change of venue in this case, it would be the prosecution. San Francisco, after all, was the town that had elected Sharron Pratt, possibly the only prosecutor in the entire world who was more interested in helping and understanding lawbreakers than in punishing them.

This was still the city that had accepted the notorious diminished-capacity 'Twinkie' defense when a supervisor had sneaked into a basement window in City Hall, shot the mayor to death, *reloaded*, walked down the hallway, and then slain another supervisor.

The jury's decision in that case? Boy! That shooter must have been pretty upset, and besides, he was on a sugar rush from all those Twinkies and couldn't really be held responsible for his actions.

So, as Freeman loved to say, it was a banner town for defense attorneys at any time, and now under Pratt even more so. Reasonable doubt had transmogrified here to any doubt at all. The slightest doubt about any issue in the trial would likely result in acquittal.

This was good news for Graham Russo, who would benefit from the city's knee-jerk liberal bias, so Hardy wanted the trial here. And Graham had an absolute right to be tried where the alleged crime occurred. Here they'd stay.

But Hardy resisted any tendency to feel complacent. The stakes were too high to take anything for granted in a murder case. 'No,' he told Freeman, 'I'm not going to ask for change of venue, but I'd like to file all that stuff and head on home, if you're finished reading it.'

The accordion folder bulged with newspapers, magazines, Nexis and Lexis printouts, everything Hardy had found in print to date about the case. 'I've got to just cut out the stuff about the case,' he said. 'It's going to be unmanageable if I throw in whole newspapers every day.'

Freeman was only half listening, back with another article. 'I wouldn't do that. I'd save it all. You never know.'

'You never know what?' Hardy didn't always agree with the old man, but he was always interested in his opinion. Freeman had forgotten more than many attorneys ever learned, and if he wanted to talk theories, Hardy would listen.

'Context.'

Hardy repeated the word. 'Meaning what?'

'Here's *Time*, right, your boy on the cover.' He started flipping the pages. 'I count at least eight related stories: assisted suicide, Kevorkian, Supreme Court, Ninth Circuit, states opposed and in favor. Here's a guy with Lou Gehrig's disease, wants to live forever. Pulling the plug.' He closed the magazine. 'It just goes on and on. Here's all your research for closing, if you decide to go that way.'

He reached up to the coffee table and grabbed a newspaper. 'Okay, forget that obvious stuff. Here's the paper reporting Sal's death for the first time. I myself noticed something in there, apparently unrelated to your client, that would arouse my curiosity. If you cut out the Graham articles, you'd never run across it.'

Hardy, intrigued, stepped over to the couch. Freeman handed him the newspaper, his eyes challenging. Could Hardy find it?

In a couple of minutes he'd scanned the entire first section. The story on Sal's death was near the back, but there was nothing remotely relevant there. A follow-up story on the enduring legacy of Hale-Bopp and the Heaven's Gate crusaders. A painter on the Bay Bridge had fallen to his death. Hardy closed the paper. 'I give up.'

Freeman was savoring his wine, enjoying that and his little puzzle. 'Front page.'

Another minute. A shake of the head. 'Nothing. I don't see it.'

'How about the bomb threat?'

Hardy reread the article. The new federal courthouse had been evacuated a little before noon after someone had called in a threat. 'I don't know, David. I don't think Sal had anything to do with that.'

'I don't either. But where is the courthouse?'

Freeman didn't need to explain any further. 'That's what I mean by context, son,' he said. 'You got a hundred or so people, maybe more, milling outside in the alley under your victim's window couple of hours before he's killed.' He shrugged. 'I don't know what it means, if anything. Maybe not, probably not. It just catches my interest, that's all.'

21

On its best day the third floor of the Hall of Justice was a study in controlled mayhem. Lawyers, cops, bailiffs, clerks, prospective jurors, relatives and friends of defendants or victims, the curious, law students, retirees, reporters, anyone with a legal or political ax to grind – these folks would congregate in the wide-open hallways.

Sometimes they didn't all get along.

Unlike the federal courthouse, with its renovated marble-arched interiors inspiring confidence and even awe in the majesty of the law, the Hall of Justice, with its green paint and linoleum floors, inspired nothing. It was a big, loud place where bureaucrats worked and deals got cut.

The minute Hardy arrived for Graham's arraignment, he was noticed. 'That's him!' he heard. 'There he is!'

The reporters were flies to his honey, shoving microphones into his face, shooting questions in their low-key and dignified manner, impeding his progress down the hall. A couple of minicams were rolling and the bright lights nearly blinded him.

His peripheral vision had picked up some placards behind the knot of reporters. There were a lot of bystanders today, even for the Hall. The show, after all, was about to start.

'No comment. Sorry. I really can't say anything yet. Please, I've got to get through here.'

He went through the special extra metal detector set up outside Department 22. He knew it was for his case, placed there to guard against the possibility that someone would try to kill his client to show the world that assisted suicide was wrong.

In the courtroom it was less frenetic, although every seat in the gallery was taken. The presiding Calendar judge, Timothy Manion, a youthful, dark-haired leprechaun with whom Hardy had tipped several glasses back when they'd both been assistant DAs, had ascended to the bench but appeared not to have called the first 'line' – a reference to the computer printout listing defendants and charges.

Walking up the center aisle and through the rail, Hardy breathed a sigh of relief. Graham hadn't even been led out into the courtroom yet. At the jury box attorneys waiting for their lines to be called could sit when there was an overflow gallery, and Hardy took one of the chairs, next to an older courtroom regular. 'This crowd here for you?' the man asked.

Hardy said he thought so and the guy passed a business card over to him. 'You need some motion work, background checks, anything, I'm available.'

Hardy nodded, friendly, but it bothered him. The hustling for clients, for work, it just never let up. He glanced at the card, then put it in his pocket. 'I'll keep it in mind, thanks.'

Finally, he got a chance to take in the surroundings. He hadn't been in Superior Court for four years and it hadn't changed in any way. High ceilings, no windows; the room was large and utterly bland. In front of the bar rail the gallery held about a hundred and twenty people on uncomfortable, theater-style seats of hard blond wood. There was also standing room for another forty or so.

Recognition was kicking in. Sharron Pratt herself was here, in the second row. At the end of the jury box Gil Soma conferred with Art Drysdale. Hardy checked for Dean Powell, but the attorney general was leaving it to his deputies.

Then the gavel came down and all eyes went to the bench.

To the judge's left a door at the back of the courtroom led to the defendant's holding tank, and as the fourth line was called this morning, that door opened and Graham Russo was brought in.

There was an audible hum in the gallery that Manion stilled with a warning glare. Hardy got up from his seat and went to meet his client at the podium in the center of the bullpen.

After his night in jail Graham looked wan and tired, and the orange jumpsuit reinforced that impression, but when Hardy asked him how he was doing, he said okay. Then, leaning across his attorney, he whispered at the prosecution table, 'Hey, Gil.'

When Soma looked over, Graham smiled at him. Keeping his hand behind the podium so the judge couldn't see, his body blocking it from the gallery's view, he flipped him off. Hardy, of course, saw it. He immediately covered Graham's hand with his own. But not in time.

'Your Honor.' Soma was up out of his chair. 'The defendant just made an obscene gesture to me.'

'Not obscene enough,' Graham whispered.

'Shut up,' Hardy ordered him. He didn't know what Soma hoped to achieve by bringing this little contretemps to the judge's attention, but Hardy knew Manion, and he wasn't going to react well to any grandstanding, particularly if it involved whining.

He'd been rearranging his papers, and now he raised his eyes. 'Mr Hardy,' he said simply, 'control your client. I don't want any shenanigans in here, is that understood? This is a court of law.'

'Yes, Your Honor,' Hardy said, and decided then and there to take a gamble, 'but for the record, Mr Soma may be mistaken.'

The judge, sensing a pissing contest, wanted to keep his busy day moving. He bobbed his head and said, 'Noted.'

Keeping his own expression under tight control, Hardy threw a look at Soma. The message, he was sure, got delivered. From now on every word counted. To every play Soma made, no matter how small, Hardy would fashion a defense. Best let Soma know he had a fight on his hands. Hardy would kick his ass in this courtroom if he could, every time he could. That knowledge might make the boy reckless. It might make him scared. If nothing else, Hardy had rattled his cage.

But the moment was just that, a moment. Hardy knew – indeed, most of the courtroom knew – what was coming next, and a stillness settled as the judge looked straight at Graham and intoned his name. 'Graham Russo,' he began, 'you are charged by indictment with a felony filed herein.'

The words were pro forma but they always had an effect on the gallery. There was a stir behind Hardy. Manion glared for quiet, but it didn't work this time. Some members of the gallery had come to make a stand.

'This wasn't any felony!'

'It wasn't even wrong!'

'Sal Russo had a right to die!'

The gavel. When relative quiet had resumed, the judge raised his voice so he could be heard all the way to the back of the room, but his tone was mild. 'I know a lot of you people have gone to some trouble to get down to this courtroom today, but I'm not going to tolerate this kind of disturbance. So all of you do yourselves a favor and do not interrupt these proceedings again. I will remove every one of you all the hell out of here. Is that clear?'

Apparently it was.

'Mr Russo.' Manion repeated the formula, continuing, '. . . to wit, a violation of section 187 of the Penal Code in that you did, in the City and County of San Francisco, State of California, on or about the ninth of May, 1997, willfully, unlawfully, and with malice aforethought' – and here the judge paused again, as if he himself were questioning the language. But he took a heavy breath and went ahead with it – '*murder* Salvatore Russo, a human being.'

Manion then had the clerk read the special circumstances alleged by the prosecution: murder in the course of a robbery. When he'd done, the judge nodded. 'How do you plead, Mr Russo?'

Graham spoke right up. 'Not guilty, Your Honor.'

'All right.' This wasn't any surprise. Manion consulted his computer sheet again. 'This being a special-circumstances case, bail will be denied. Mr Hardy, do you have a comment?'

'Yes, Your Honor. There is no way the prosecution can justify this as a special-circumstances case. My client should be allowed to post bail. Mr Russo voluntarily turned himself in to the authorities yesterday—'

Soma was on his feet. 'After hiding out for four days.'

Hardy turned to him. 'He left town before he knew there was an indictment against him.'

'So he says.'

The gavel came down. Manion wasn't yet angry – sometimes Calendar was so boring that these peccadilloes in courtroom etiquette were almost a relief to a judge who had to sit through eight hours of procedure – but he didn't want to lose any more control. 'Gentlemen,' he reminded them, 'all remarks get directed to me. That's how we do it.'

Hardy apologized. Soma sat down. Drysdale put a restraining hand on his arm and Hardy heard him whisper, 'Just listen!'

'All right, Mr Hardy, go ahead.'

Hardy made his case. 'Mr Russo will surrender his passport, Your Honor. There is no risk of flight. As I've already said, he voluntarily turned himself in just yesterday, as soon as he'd returned to the city after a few days away.'

Manion appeared to be giving his argument some thought. 'On the other hand,' he said, 'special circumstances precludes the possibility for bail. That's the law.'

'Yes, Your Honor, I realize that.' Hardy took a deep breath, glanced at Graham, nodded, and waited. This was more argument than he'd expected. He suddenly wondered if Manion subscribed to *Time*.

People started coughing as time stopped for a while.

At last the judge invited counsel up to the bench. Hardy got there first and to his surprise found that Soma had remained back at his table. Drysdale was standing next to him. 'The kid's a little excited, Judge,' he said quietly, referring to Soma.

'No sweat, Art, don't worry about it. But this bail thing.'

Drysdale nodded. 'There's no bail allowed. That's the law, Judge.' Apologetic. Really nothing Drysdale could do about it.

'I know the law. But it seems to me what Mr Hardy says here is true. There's very little if any flight risk, right?'

This was starting to make Drysdale uncomfortable. 'There's no bail allowed on specials, Your Honor,' he repeated feebly.

'But you do admit that this defendant is no danger to the community?'

'We can't be sure of that, Your Honor.'

But Manion was running out of patience. 'So there is no public policy reason to deny bail to Mr Russo? There's no risk of flight and he poses no danger to anybody?'

Drysdale didn't even try to answer this time.

'I don't suppose the People want to drop the specials?' Manion was giving Drysdale every opportunity to save face. Bail was permitted for non-special-circumstances murder. All Drysdale had to do was lower the charge; it would still be a murder case. But he was shaking his head. 'I can't do that, Your Honor.'

'In other words, your office is simply making me deny bail to Mr Russo because it *can*? Is that what I'm hearing?' The judge, disgusted, shook his head. 'Next time you see Mr Powell, Art, I want you to tell him he makes me proud to be an American. Would you do that?'

He turned to Hardy and offered a sympathetic smile. 'I guess we'll be denying bail, Diz.'

Hardy hadn't planned to have lunch with the Taylors – maybe a little snack at Lou the Greek's. But the arraignment had begun later than he'd thought and then dragged on. Getting his case called had consumed an entire hour, and before they'd finished, getting a trial date three months hence, another twenty minutes had gone away. After that it had taken Hardy the rest of the morning to see Graham in jail, where they had conferred for another twenty minutes or so.

In that time the bailiff had come up and conveyed the good news that the sheriff (no doubt at Manion's urging) was moving Graham to an AdSeg cell for the duration of his confinement. AdSeg, short for 'administrative segregation,' was most often used when an inmate was in danger of being hurt among the general population of the jail. In Graham's case, Hardy was sure, it was a courtesy.

So Hardy finally got back to the hallway outside Department 22 at a little after noon. Helen and Leland were sitting like statues, sharing a wooden bench with an Hispanic teenager who was breast-feeding her baby. As Hardy approached, they stood and made their introductions and then Leland, with the force of edict, had suggested lunch. His office was up on Market, top floor of the bank. He had his own private dining room, his own chef. They'd just take the limo.

It was not a particularly large room, but it was beautiful, with its hardwood floor, the antique sideboard with its stunning floral arrangement of iris and gladioli. The wall covering was a soothing green silk. Water had been poured.

Hardy was seated in an amazingly comfortable upholstered armchair with a view to the northeast – Alcatraz and Angel Island. There was chop on the Bay, a high covering of cirrus. In front of him the table had been set for three: white linen, crystal, china, silver.

The setting was meant to intimidate, although of course not obviously. It simply made clear the line of command.

Leland Taylor was in touch with his inner self. He knew who he was, what he wanted, how to get it, and didn't unduly concern himself with internal doubts or how his actions might appear to others. Hardy thought this might be one of the perks of being born to, and living a life insulated by, great wealth. Leland was in charge, an immutable fact of nature. His time was more valuable than Hardy's, his opinions more valid. His stepson's lawyer was, essentially, staff – a servant to do his bidding.

Evidently some unspoken rule dictated that chitchat precede business. Mrs Taylor – Helen – had been carrying the conversational ball for twenty minutes. She was good at it, but Hardy was relieved when they got down to tacks. 'My wife was gratified to see you'd never lost a case,' Leland said in his reedy voice.

Hardy sat back in his chair. 'I've only done two murder trials. I've been lucky,' he said modestly.

A dry chuckle. 'Let's hope it's not that. You seemed very sure of yourself in the courtroom. That bail business, what I heard. Is the judge a friend of yours? I gather that would be to our advantage, hmm?'

Hardy explained a little about the system. Normally, cases stayed in Department 22 until the day of trial, when they were sent at random to other courtrooms and the judges who would actually preside over the case. This one was important, however, and got assigned now for trial in three months to Judge Jordan Salter in Department 27. That way the judge, who knew it was coming – as well as the lawyers – could prepare for unusual or unique issues that might arise.

Hardy did not view the choice of Salter, a Republican appointee and an old buddy of Dean Powell, as propitious.

Taylor put a hand over his wife's. 'Do we know him?'

Helen shook her head prettily. Everything she did was done prettily. She was very attractive, Hardy thought, nothing like what he'd imagined a wife of Sal Russo could have been. Not that he imagined Graham's mother would be unattractive. It was more a matter of style. This woman fit her husband, Leland, to a T. Poised, confident, insincere.

'Anyway,' Hardy said, 'the judge can have some influence, of course, but it boils down to the case against Graham, which fortunately has a lot of holes.'

There was no immediate response to this, although glances were exchanged, some message conveyed. Finally, Helen spoke. 'Do you think Graham did this, Mr Hardy?'

'Killed Sal for money? No, I don't.'

'It's absurd,' Leland said. 'He could have all the money he wants by simply asking for it.'

'Which of course he won't do,' Helen added. 'I'm afraid he doesn't want to feel in our debt, which is I suppose noble enough, but I'm his mother. It would not be debt. Leland and I have discussed this.'

'But the fact remains,' Hardy said, 'he didn't feel comfortable asking, did he?' The dynamic, he saw, was transparent enough. There might not be monetary payback, but there would be strings. Lots and lots of strings. Behavior issues, how one acted. And if Hardy knew anything at all about Graham, he wasn't a string kind of guy.

'We did help him with law school.' These petty details seemed distasteful to Leland, but he wanted them on the table. 'Although that would appear to have been money ill spent.' A tepid smile. 'Well' – he brought his hands together – 'but that's not the point, either, is it? We were just rather wondering how Graham was intending to pay you. You're not doing this, what's the word, pro bono, I assume?'

Hardy smiled. 'No. Graham's paying me. But I can't really talk about those arrangements without his consent.'

'Of course not,' Leland said. 'I wouldn't suggest—'

A discreet knock on the door was immediately followed by a waiter bearing a tureen, from which he ladled a dark, clear consommé into their bowls.

After the waiter had gone, Leland tasted the soup to no comment or reaction. It was perfect – dark, intense, rich, perfectly balanced – perhaps the best soup Hardy had ever tasted in his life, and he had to say something.

'Thank you,' Leland said in response to the compliment. 'Yes, it's quite nice.' Conveying an air of 'What else could it be?' Then he went back to Graham, precisely where they had left off, on the money. 'But Helen would like to' – another glance at his wife – 'actually, *we'd* like to help out, monetarily.'

'I don't know,' Hardy began, only to have Leland cut him off.

'I have spoken to some of our attorneys here at the bank,' he said, 'and they tell me there's no ethical question. My understanding is that you would be free to accept remuneration from any source, so long as it was understood that Graham was your client, that you represented *his* interests, not ours. Is that correct?'

Hardy had to laugh. 'This question doesn't exactly come up every day. What you say sounds right, though. I'll check and make sure. I'd still want to talk to Graham about it.'

Helen reached over and this time put her hand over Leland's. This was evidently some preemptive-strike code they'd worked out. 'We'd expect that, wouldn't we, Leland?'

'Of course.' A pause. 'Sure.'

Leland Taylor wasn't a man who said *sure* very often, and from Hardy's perspective it came out stilted. But maybe not. Maybe everything just seemed a little bit skewed up here.

'Good,' Helen said. 'Now, Mr Hardy, if we may, can we ask how you plan to proceed?'

Hardy nodded. 'You can ask,' he said, 'but it's pretty early. I've barely begun looking at the evidence, so anything I say now wouldn't be set in stone.'

'We understand that,' Leland said. They were definitely two-teaming him. 'But certainly the general plan will be to play up Sal's illness, Graham's closeness to him, particularly at the end? You're shaking your head. You don't agree?'

'Actually, I do. Graham doesn't.'

'What do you mean?' Helen asked.

'He tells me he wasn't there. He wasn't any part of it.'

The waiter entered again during the ensuing silence, removed the tureen and the soup bowls, then set in front of each of them a little work of art featuring seared scallops, angel's hair pasta, some zucchini blossoms. A limpid bright orange pool of sauce. A bottle of Kistler Reserve Chardonnay appeared, was poured.

Hardy thought he might swoon from the first taste, but again, to Leland it was just grub. As soon as the door closed, he continued as though there had been no interruption. 'But isn't that Graham's best defense? That the killing was out of mercy?'

'It might be, sir, but he wouldn't even plead to that last week. Legally, that's still murder.'

Helen spoke. 'He's afraid he won't be able to practice law.'

Hardy nodded. 'That's right. That's what he tells me too.'

'He wasn't exactly tearing up the field to this point, though, was he, Helen?'

This seemed to invite some response from Graham's mother, and Hardy waited until it was clear none would be coming. 'The problem is,' he said, 'there are certain . . . irregularities. Somebody else may have been there. There might have been another motive. Sal might in fact have been murdered.'

'But not by Graham.' Helen was certain about this.

'No, but that's who's going to trial for it.'

'Wait a minute,' Leland said. 'I'm hearing all kinds of conflicting reports here, Mr Hardy. Do you believe Graham killed his father or not?'

Hardy thought for a minute. 'I guess I don't think he did.'

'Even out of mercy?'

'No.'

Helen blurted out, 'But all those articles, all this . . .' Winding down, she stopped.

Leland picked up the thread. 'That means you think someone else did it?'

Shaking his head, Hardy grabbed for his wineglass. A sip during the daytime wouldn't kill him and he wanted the extra second to think. 'I don't think it's out of the question Sal killed himself. The coroner didn't even rule it out. I might go that way.'

'I see.' Leland busied himself with another bite, thinking. 'What would happen, though, if you argued for assisted suicide and the jury believed you?'

'Graham wouldn't let me do that.'

'But if he would . . .'

'No one can predict what a jury is going to do.'

'I'm not trying to. I'm asking you a simple factual question. What would be the result if a jury decided Graham had assisted Sal's suicide, or helped him die in some compassionate way?'

This was in many ways a fascinating turn, and Hardy

considered it a minute. 'That's not a technical defense,' he said carefully, trying to be precise. 'A jury that followed the law *should* convict on murder.'

'Should?' Helen picked up the nuance, the wrinkle.

Hardy nodded. 'Except that this is San Francisco. Here you never know. Even a judge like Salter might not instruct the way the prosecution wants. Any given jury – if the defense can guide them right – might do anything.'

'If they concluded it was an assisted suicide?'

'They might.'

'You mean they'd find him simply not guilty?' Helen wanted to be sure she understood.

'Yes. Not guilty.'

'Well, then,' Leland concluded, 'that's your defense.'

Hardy demurred. 'It's not that simple. The prosecution is going to make sure the jury knows that assisting a suicide isn't a defense to murder, and the judge should instruct that way.'

'But might not.' Helen didn't want to let it go.

Hardy wanted to keep her hopes in check. 'But probably will. It's moot anyway – Graham won't let me do what we're talking about here.'

'So what's your mandate,' Leland asked him, 'to do what your client wants, or to get him off?'

And that, Hardy thought, was a hell of a good question.

They'd gotten to dessert – a cream puff stuffed with brûlée, fresh blueberries, coffee.

'All right' – Hardy put his cup down – 'now if you don't mind, I've got a couple of questions for you.' They both were listening. 'Sal broke into your house three times in the past couple of months, didn't he? Why didn't you press charges?'

The couple communicated in their wordless way, and Helen took it. 'We thought he needed help. We did contact the social services. They were, I believe, arranging something when Sal . . . died.'

'But it must have bothered you?'

Leland answered. 'It was very traumatic for Helen. We thought the best approach would be to leave it to the authorities. You can appreciate that we didn't want to become involved with Sal again.

Helen had already been through all that years ago. It was painful.'

Hardy kept his eyes on the wife. 'And you weren't concerned it might happen again?'

'I didn't believe Sal would hurt me. It was more sad than anything, really. Pathetic. He just seemed so confused.' Helen hadn't really answered the question. He would never have accepted it from a witness, but here there wasn't much he could do. She continued on. 'He really seemed to believe he still lived with me. At the Manor.'

'The Manor?'

A pretty, embarrassed smile. 'Our home.'

'He was that far along? With the Alzheimer's?' Hardy asked.

'I don't know anything about the disease,' she said. 'He wasn't malicious. He just didn't know where he was, where he belonged. I felt sorry for him,' she repeated.

'I didn't,' Leland interjected. 'I wanted him arrested. It's all right, Helen, I'm on the record with this. I thought he was a grave danger to my wife.'

'And George, your other son,' Hardy said to Leland, 'I gather he agreed with you?'

This question appeared to stun both of them. Their magic code seemed to fail. Finally, Leland took a sip of coffee, wiped his lips with his napkin. 'George isn't any part of this,' he said with finality. 'To answer your question, yes. What dutiful son wouldn't object to the father who'd deserted him coming back to harass his mother? But this is not a Taylor family matter. This is about Graham, not George.'

As if on cue – perhaps some button had been pushed under the table – the waiter reappeared. 'It's two o'clock, sir.'

Leland looked at his watch and made a face. 'Some oil leases,' he said apologetically. 'I've really got to run. Mr Hardy, you'll contact us after you've spoken to Graham, about what we discussed, helping him out? Good, then. Helen?' He reached out a hand to help his wife up from her seat. Lunch was over.

22

When Leland Taylor's limo dropped him back at his office, Hardy had a message from David Freeman asking him to come down. Something had come up with Dyson Brunel and Tryptech, and they needed to talk.

What now? Hardy thought.

But Freeman was – no surprise – in court for the afternoon. In the meanwhile a messenger delivered another box of discovery documents on Graham. This stuff kept pulling him along until nearly five o'clock, when he realized he had better try again to see what Freeman wanted.

The old man was buried in some legal text in the law library off the Solarium. He was chewing contentedly on the butt of a thick cigar. Three half-finished china cups of coffee told Hardy he'd been back in from court for at least an hour. But he showed no sign of impatience. Time didn't exist for Freeman – only the beautiful law.

Hardy pulled up a chair next to him. 'Dyson Brunel,' he said. 'What's happening?'

Freeman finished his paragraph, made a notation in ink in the margin of the book, marked his place with his cigar, and closed it. 'This dredging fee.'

'What about it?'

'Dyson's having trouble pulling the cash together to pay for it. Tryptech's running a little thin. He wants to pay you and Michelle in stock options for a while.'

Shocked, Hardy sat back in his chair. 'In stock options? For Tryptech?'

Freeman nodded. 'It's not unheard of.'

'I'm not saying it is. I'm wondering what I'm supposed to live on until I can cash them in.'

'I thought you'd wonder that, tell you the truth.'

Hardy didn't need this at all right now. Tryptech was his main source of liquid income, his salary. 'You'd tell me if you thought they were going belly up, wouldn't you, David?'

'I don't think it's like that, Diz. Brunel tells me the company's still very strong. I think I believe him. It's a cash-flow issue.'

'But they don't want to pay us in money? That's one way to keep the rest of the old cash flowing.'

'He says they're doing some restructuring, trying to make their cash outflows look a little leaner.' Freeman lowered his voice, implying a confidence. 'The annual report is coming up, Diz. They're carrying the eighteen-mil container loss forward on their books. And that, plus our legal fees . . .'

'Not exactly the national debt, David.'

'No, but all out of pocket. It directly impacts the bottom line.' Freeman held up a palm, cutting off Hardy's rejoinder. 'I'm just delivering the message here. I didn't think this up. Dyson says he's worried about his shareholders, who tend to notice these things. He's afraid the company won't look as good on paper as it could. As it is.'

Hardy heard his warning bells going off. 'And they're offering stock options?'

'No. Actual shares. I'm inclined to accept. I think we're looking at a large recovery down the road, and we'll do better than all right. The problem is, I won't be able to keep paying you for your hours, or at least not as many of them. Brunel might manage half-time hourly cash for one employee . . .'

'I'd call that a rather substantial problem, David. If I'm not paid, I can't work. What am I supposed to live on?'

'I know, I know. But even for a few months?'

'Jesus, I don't know, David. If it turns out to be worthless paper . . .'

'Yeah, well, Brunel's story is it could work out to be a very lucrative deal.'

'What else is he going to say? That it probably won't work? We'll all get stiffed?' But Hardy realized he was just whining. He might as well hear the complete proposal. 'So what's the offer?'

'They discount their shares to two and deal you twenty thousand to carry you through, say, September.'

'That's very generous.' The ironic tone was thick. 'What's the stock going for now, three?'

'And an eighth.' Freeman spread his hands. 'I know, it's low, but Dyson says that's all the better for us – we'd get more of them. It's been as high as nine. Maybe it's going there again, maybe higher. It could be worth a fortune, way beyond your billables. I'm keeping the firm in, if that's any consolation.'

'It's not a matter of consolation.'

And in truth – if the Tryptech ship wasn't going down the way its container had – Hardy knew that potentially this was a great deal. At today's price Dyson was offering him sixty thousand plus in stock, far more than he would make in the next four months. But he also knew that the operative word was *could*. Unfortunately, the stock market, like any given jury, was notoriously unpredictable. 'It's not that I don't believe it could be lucrative,' he said, 'but I'm a working stiff who kind of depends on a paycheck every month.'

Freeman was silent for a beat. 'You really might want to do this, Diz,' he said at last. 'As a long-run move it could really work out.'

Hardy's brow creased. As a matter of course he knew that David had run a Standard & Poors on Tryptech before taking them on as clients, and if David still thought the company checked out, it would probably survive. It wasn't the biggest manufacturer of computers and parts, but it wasn't the smallest.

But even David Freeman had been fooled before. And after having worked with him for the better part of a year already, Hardy was of the opinion that Dyson Brunel wasn't America's most honest man. The offer more than worried him. Could Tryptech have gotten to the point where it could no longer pay any of its contractors, not just its lawyers? If that was the case, they were dead, and soon.

Plus, *restructuring* was a scary word; it meant they were laying off employees. Hardy knew this had been going on at Tryptech with increasing regularity. Of course, as long as the company was in business at all, it would need legal help, but this late-in-the-day finagling to get his services, essentially for nothing, in exchange for stock that had been in free fall for months, struck Hardy as desperate.

'If they're strapped for cash,' he suggested, 'maybe we could talk about getting the Port to settle.' Hardy thought he could probably negotiate something like $10 million in a long weekend. Of course, Tryptech was hoping to get nearly three times that when all was said and done, but it might be bird-in-the-hand time.

'I don't think so,' David said. 'I suggested that to Dyson, of course. He's not ready to go that way. Not yet.' Another pause. 'He said he had all his people to consider. Customers, shareholders, contractors, everybody.'

Hardy chuckled. This, coming from a man who was laying off workers and probably dissembling – which was the lawyer word for lying – about the actual number of computers he'd lost in his container, struck Hardy as plain silly. 'Well, thanks anyway, David, but you'll have to tell Brunel I don't think so.'

A disappointed sigh. 'All right. But if you don't mind, I'm conveying the same offer to Michelle.'

Hardy left the room, shaken. Suddenly his main source of income looked good to be drying up.

'What drives me nuts is I go into this litigation game for the security of it—'

'There's your problem,' Frannie told him. 'There is no such thing as security. It is a pure myth.'

His wife knew whereof she spoke. Orphaned as a young child, she'd been raised by her brother, Moses. Then her first husband had been killed within a week of her discovery that she was pregnant with the baby who turned out to be Rebecca. 'This is why, my poor suffering husband, we should really really try to recognize and enjoy things when life is going well. Like now, for instance. This minute.'

There was a blanket under them and another one over them as they lay on the rug in the living room. The shades in the bay window were drawn, the kids were asleep, and the elephants on the mantel had circled and were at rest. Tony Bennett was on low, singing some Billie Holiday. A fire threw a flickering light.

'This minute isn't too bad,' he admitted. 'Why are we in the living room?'

'Sexual urgency,' she said.

'That was it,' Hardy agreed. 'I remember now.' He leaned over and kissed her. 'I love you.'

'Well, all right, if you must.'

'I must.' Her head was on his shoulder, a leg thrown over his. A long moment passed. 'And you're okay with all this?'

'With what?'

'All these changes coming up. It's going to be different.'

'You're still going to be here, right?'

'I'm considering it.'

'So nothing's really changed. You just think it might be changing, but you've been dying to get out from under Tryptech anyway . . .'

'I just worry,' he said.

Frannie went up onto an elbow, her red hair glowing in the firelight. 'You? You're kidding?' She leaned up against him. 'Dismas, everything changes all the time. Don't you think life would be pretty boring if it didn't?'

'Boring would be nice,' he said. 'I could live with boring.'

'You'd hate it. Your boredom tolerance is zero. You just want to guarantee everything.'

'And what's the matter with that?'

'Nothing, except you can't guarantee anything.'

'I hate that part,' he said.

'The good news, though, is you've got a client you believe in whose parents seem to want to throw money at you.'

'Which I'm not sure I can take.'

She was quiet for a minute. 'Let's play a game,' she said. 'I'll say something, and then you try to think of something positive to say about it, instead of how it could all come back and bite you on the ass.'

'Sounds like fun.'

'It is.' She kissed him. 'You should try it.'

Eventually they got to the bedroom. Hardy was in a deep sleep when the telephone rang next to the bed.

'Hello?' He looked at his digital clock – eleven-fifteen.

'Mr Hardy. I'm sorry to wake you up. This is Sergeant Evans. We need to talk.'

Adrenaline jolted in and suddenly he was awake, throwing off his blanket, grabbing a bathrobe. 'Just a minute,' he whispered, carrying the portable phone into the kitchen, closing the bedroom door behind him. He flicked on the light and pulled out a chair at the kitchen table. 'Is Graham all right?'

'He's fine. I just talked to him.'

Hardy tried to process this, but he must have been more asleep than he thought, because he couldn't do it. 'You just talked to him when?'

'Just now. He called me.'

'From jail?' He was asking stupid questions. Of course he'd phoned her from jail. That's where he was.

'We decided we had to tell you.'

Hardy's first thought was that Graham had confessed to the pretty young cop. She knew he'd be at his low ebb – lonely, depressed, and scared – and had gone back to nail him on his first night in the slammer. And succeeded.

'We're together.'

Again, Hardy's brain didn't seem to be accepting the data it was getting. 'You're together in what way?' he asked.

'I guess the usual way.'

Hardy's experience with murder suspects and homicide inspectors who got 'together' in anything like an interpersonal relationship was limited, if you didn't include one shooting the other.

'I'm in love with him.'

'You're in love with Graham?'

'Yes.'

'Okay.'

Frannie's words came back at him. Nothing was guaranteed. Nothing was predictable. It wasn't just the stock market or juries. It was everything. 'Okay,' he said again.

'I know it's a little weird.'

'I'll get used to it,' Hardy said. 'So does this mean you think he's innocent?'

'He didn't kill his father.'

'No, I don't think so either.'

'But somebody did.'

'Do you know that for a fact?'

'I'd bet on it. In fact, I *am* betting on it.'

'Do you know who it was?'

'No. If I did, I'd arrest him, get my man out of jail. But they've pulled us off the case. It's all politics. If they'd let us look, I'd find him. There's something, I know that. More than you've seen.'

'Maybe not,' Hardy said. 'I got another pile of discovery today.'

There was a brief silence, then Evans said, 'This won't be in any discovery.'

She outlined the efforts of both herself and Lanier: the fish supplier, Pio, who'd died within the same week as Sal; the fact that Sal had been a cash courier for some high-stakes gamblers. 'This guy Soma just hates Graham and decided to go get him. When he had enough for that, we got called off.'

Hardy was silent for so long that she said his name.

'I'm still here. I'm just wondering what you want to do.'

'I want to help Graham,' she said. 'It can be on my own time, I don't care. Find out where these other trails go. The only thing is, I can't . . . I'd have to come to you, not my boss. I couldn't go to him.'

'That would be Glitsky?'

'Yeah. You know him?'

'Jesus,' Hardy said.

'What?'

'Oh, nothing. Just a little late-night humor. Yeah, I know Glitsky. You could say that.'

'I think he'd fire me. No, I think he'd shoot me.'

'I think you're right.'

'So can we do that, me and you? Keep it between us. And Graham, of course.'

'Could I have a free investigator working with me to help my client? Could I do that? Call me crazy, but I think so.'

Sarah hung up the telephone in her kitchen and sat at the table with her hands shaking. She'd done it, joined the enemy.

She'd told Hardy she was betting on Graham being innocent, but that was putting it mildly. In reality she was risking everything on it. Her credibility, her career.

Over the past few days she'd tried to take the long view of the developing situation between Graham and herself. If she were a man . . .

This always stopped her, for of course she wasn't.

But if she were, she might be able to get away with having a relationship with one of her suspects. If she were a male cop, the old boy network would close in around her and though she might take a lot of grief about it, it would never become a public issue. Sarah had known three men on the force in her career who had 'dated' their suspects. If memory served, one of those had even been a murder rap. One of these liaisons – not the murder – got to marriage.

But if it came out about Graham and her, she had no illusions. She was going to be finished. Even if the Police Officers Association went to bat for her, Glitsky would see that she was reassigned out of homicide.

She hoped that by calling Hardy she was doing the right thing. Although she was no longer sure what the right thing was anymore.

Now wide awake, Hardy sat at his own kitchen table.

It had been an amazing day, Graham's hidden allies appearing with no warning. The parents wanting to help pay for his defense, Sarah Evans volunteering to help with his investigation.

Sarah's suggestion that someone else altogether might be involved widened the scope of things dramatically. It also provided him with a tactic that always played well for a jury: the so-called 'SODDIT' defense, an acronym for Some Other Dude Did It. Sarah wouldn't even have to find another suspect. If Hardy could point clearly enough to where there *might* be one, he might be able to churn up enough doubt to get to reasonable.

But the thought that really refused to leave his mind was David Freeman's magic trick with the newspaper of the other day – context, context, context.

Today's discovery documents included a listing of all tagged physical evidence so far in the case. Hardy would have lots of time in the coming months to go to the evidence locker and physically examine every item on the list, but the list itself had provided at least one important, or potentially important, bit of context.

He had already known that the $50,000 Sal had kept in his safe, the money in Graham's safety deposit box, had been bank-wrapped seventeen years before. What he hadn't really considered until now was the fact that he had an exact date: April 2, 1980.

Fifty thousand dollars was a lot of money now, and seventeen years ago it had been a fortune. Where had it come from? Had there been a bank robbery? A kidnapping? Something that might have been in the newspapers?

He didn't know, but the *Chronicle*'s archives would be open tomorrow, and he was going to find out.

23

He started six months before the date the bills had been wrapped, skimming the headlines. He didn't have to go very far. When he came to the first week of November, 1979, he figured he'd gotten what he'd come for, and stopped right there, nearly running out of the archives in his hurry to get to a telephone. 'Judge Giotti, please. Dismas Hardy. Please tell him it relates to Graham Russo.'

'This is Mario Giotti.' Hardy had never expected the judge to pick right up. You didn't just call a federal judge and have him come to the phone. But that's what Giotti had done. Maybe he had some personal interest.

Hardy introduced himself. 'I'm representing Graham Russo. I've got a few questions, if you could spare some time.'

'Of course. Sal was one of my oldest friends. I assume you want to talk about the condition of the scene when I found the body. I can assure you I didn't touch anything.'

Hardy knew there wasn't going to be any way to finesse it. 'Well, Your Honor, in fact what I'm curious about is the fire at your father's restaurant, the Grotto.'

For a long moment there was no answer. Then, 'You said this relates to Graham Russo?'

'I don't know if it does.'

'I can't imagine how it would. That was years ago.'

'Yes, sir.'

Hardy waited and the judge didn't let him down. 'If you're free for a while, why don't you swing by here? I'm not due back in court until one-thirty.'

Even after the long walk through the seven rooms that comprised the judge's law offices – half a city block long – Hardy wasn't prepared for the majesty of the judge's private chambers. He was used to the Hall of Justice, where the rooms were to human scale.

Here at the federal courthouse, deities reigned. Giotti's room measured about forty by fifty. The ceilings began halfway to the sky. There was an enormous fireplace, incongruously appointed with an artificial heating unit. With carved wood, exposed beams, inlaid marble, an entire wall of books, and three separate seating areas, the room underscored the power of the position: a federal judgeship was the job God wanted. Certainly His own celestial throne-room couldn't have been much more imposing.

As Hardy entered, Giotti had gotten up from his beautiful Shaker-style desk and was moving forward with an outstretched hand. 'Mr Hardy? Nice to meet you. Did my secretary get the name right? The good thief?'

'Dismas, that's right.'

'Also the patron saint of murderers, if I'm not mistaken?'

Hardy nodded. 'You're not, although Graham Russo's not been convicted.'

'No, of course not. I didn't mean to imply that.'

'And, perhaps more to the point, I'm no saint.'

A wider smile. 'Then we ought to get along just fine. I'm not much of a saint either. Cup of coffee? Would you like to sit down?'

Hardy said that coffee would be fine and chose the seating arrangement closest to the fireplace, with its space heater turned up. 'I know,' Giotti said, 'these enormous rooms. You can't heat them. With all these fireplaces – all of us judges have them, you know – and in this entire building only one of them is functional.'

'How did you decide among you who got it?'

'The same way we decide anything. Seniority.'

Hardy clucked. 'And we're always hearing how federal judges get anything they want.'

'We get eighteen percent more than average mortals, but that's the limit.'

'Another illusion shattered.'

'May it rest in peace,' Giotti intoned as the door opened and the secretary brought in a coffee service. After she'd gone, the judge sipped and sat back, balancing his cup and saucer on his knee. After making sure Hardy was comfortable, he moved along.

'You want to know about the fire at the Grotto? I'd be curious to know how it even came up.'

Hardy explained the admittedly tenuous connection. Out loud, it sounded lame.

'You're saying Sal had a great deal of cash . . .'

'Fifty thousand dollars,' Hardy said.

Giotti waved that off; the exact figure didn't matter to him. 'All of it bank-wrapped and dated, so you went through the *Chronicle*'s archives and ran across the Grotto fire five months before that date?'

'Yes, Your Honor, that's what I did.'

'And you surmise that there's a connection of some kind between these two elements?'

'I don't know,' Hardy said. 'This is the third time your name has appeared in this case.'

'The third?'

A nod. 'You found Sal, then the bomb scare earlier that same day, the day he was killed—'

'How did my name appear there?'

'Not your name precisely, Your Honor. Some connection to the courthouse here.'

'But then back to my name, my father's name in any event, with the Grotto fire?'

Hardy could understand it if Giotti grew impatient with this, although he didn't show any sign of it. He sipped his coffee again, a benign expression on his face, waiting for Hardy to tie together at least some part of these strings.

Which he couldn't do. Spreading his palms, he smiled sheepishly. 'I don't even know what I came to ask, specifically,' he said. 'There seemed to be some . . . some . . .'

'Connection?'

'Yes. I suppose so.'

'To what?'

'I don't know.' Hardy carefully placed his cup into his saucer, feeling very much a fool. 'I'm sorry, Your Honor. I'm wasting your time. Quite often I actually think before I roll into gear. Evidently this wasn't one of those times.'

Giotti didn't seem to mind. He gestured expansively. 'Don't feel like you have to leave, Mr Hardy. This might not be a waste of anyone's time. I'm curious as to how you plan to approach the overriding legal issue in the case.'

'Assisted suicide?'

The judge nodded. 'You know that here in the Ninth Circuit we expect to be in a bit of a war with the Supreme Court over this whole right-to-die question? It's not unlike what seems to be going on between Sharron Pratt and Dean Powell.' He leaned forward, placing his cup and saucer on the coffee table. 'We've already come down in *Glucksberg* on the side of the angels, but we're going to be overturned. At least that's my prediction. It's my hope the Court doesn't compel a blanket prohibition by the states, but they might.'

'On assisted suicide, you mean?'

'Yes.'

Hardy was extremely surprised – stunned even – that a federal judge would discuss such an issue with someone who might someday appear in his court as a litigant. He took his time framing an appropriate response. 'Are you among the judges in favor of it?'

Giotti smiled in a weary way. 'Let's say I'm against prohibiting it for terminal patients. In legal terms, and *Casey* agrees with me, it's a liberty interest issue, not too dissimilar to abortion. Provided, of course, you've got cruise control.'

'Cruise control?' Suddenly they were talking about cars?

Giotti laughed. 'Sorry. Jargon. Acronyms. CRUIS – competent, rational, uncoerced, informed, stable. You got a terminal patient on cruise control, he's got the right to take his life.'

Hardy ran through the litany and a question rose. 'Did Sal Russo fit your definition?'

'I think so, when he formed the original intent. Recently, no, I'd say not.'

'So you knew him pretty well?'

'Both for a long time and pretty well, and those are not the same things at all.' Giotti sat back and crossed his legs, comfortable. 'I talked with him at least twice a month, sometimes more often' – he pointed vaguely – 'out there in the alley. Once in a while in his apartment.'

'Selling fish?'

Giotti nodded. 'That's what he did. He was a great guy. Did you know him?'

'I met him a few times.'

Hardy wasn't sure where to take this. Giotti seemed to want to talk, perhaps reminisce, although it could be he was simply taking his lunch break and enjoyed talking to somebody. Hardy thought that his daily life here must be fairly isolated, proscribed. 'I know Graham a lot better.'

This brought a frown, quickly suppressed. 'Yes,' the judge said, 'I suppose you do. He's not the most popular man in this building.'

Hardy smiled. 'I'd heard some rumor like that.'

'You don't walk away from a clerkship. I don't think it's ever been done. It raised some hackles.'

'Yours?'

Giotti considered this. 'To be honest with you, yes. I had a lot of hopes for him. Through Sal. You know what I'm saying? Your friend's kids? You hate to see a terrible cycle repeating itself. I didn't want to see Graham turn out the way Sal had.'

'Although he was your friend – Sal, I mean?'

'Well, not like when we were younger.' Giotti let out a deep sigh. 'Sal failed. In life. I'd hate to see that happen with Graham, though that's the way it looks like it's going.'

'So what happened with Sal? He wasn't always a failure, was he?'

'No. When he married Helen . . . have you met Helen?'

Hardy nodded.

'Gorgeous woman, wouldn't you agree? Well, that needs no discussion. When Sal married her, the whole town envied him. He was a gifted athlete, had this wonderful personality, ran his own business, had three beautiful kids . . .'

'So what happened?'

'I don't know. Maybe he was living a lie, doing some high-wire act and pretending he could keep his balance until something gave him a good knock and he went over. On the other hand, Helen married Leland pretty quick – she might have cut his heart out. He disappeared for a few years. After he came back, he wasn't ever the same. He was beaten.'

With no idea what possessed him, Hardy played a hunch. 'And you helped set him up as Salmon Sal?'

Giotti shifted in his chair. His eyes sharpened. Then he broke a grin. 'Say what you will about lawyers, I love how their minds work. Yes, well, Sal was my friend. I felt sorry for what had happened to him. Although *set up* is perhaps a little too strong. Perhaps people were more willing to know Sal because I did.'

'And he never talked to you about the money?'

A cock of the head. 'What money?'

'Remember? He had fifty thousand dollars, so he didn't have to work. He had all this cash.'

'How do you know he had it back then? I know it's dated back then, but that doesn't mean it was in his possession.'

'You know, that's a good point.' Suddenly.

The bills had been wrapped and dated, but that said nothing about their history over the past seventeen years. In fact, maybe this was the money that Sarah Evans had suspected Sal had been delivering for one of her gamblers. Would Graham know anything about that? Did he suspect as much himself? Hardy would have to ask him.

And then, the horrible thought: Graham's retainer money. Where had that come from?

Meanwhile, he felt the judge's eyes on him, was pulled back by a comment. 'He was very sick by the end, you know. In a lot of pain.'

'But no longer, as you say, on cruise control?'

'That's true. The Alzheimer's was getting pretty severe. You couldn't miss it. He couldn't make his own decisions.'

'But you say that sometime earlier he might have told Graham he wanted to die, to take his own life when it got bad enough?'

The judge ventured another smile. 'Did I say that?'

'I'm his attorney. It might help to know if he did.'

'So you are going with assisted suicide.'

'We've already pled. Not guilty to murder one.'

Giotti blew out heavily. 'Murder one is ridiculous.'

A grim smile. 'That's my position too. I hope the jury agrees with us.'

'Get it in front of them and it can't fail. Not in this town. Not that I should comment on this at all.'

'I don't hear any comment,' Hardy said, making explicit their understanding. 'But I've got a problem with Graham, who won't admit to being there.' He didn't want to mention his other problem, that he was fairly certain Graham had not helped his father die at all, that he was telling the truth on that score.

'He was there,' Giotti said simply.

'That day? You know that?'

But Giotti backed away from that. 'I can't say that day for sure, but he came all the time. Sal told me he saw him a couple of times a week.'

'Graham says this wasn't one of the days.'

'Have him change his mind and he'll walk.' Meaning he wouldn't be convicted.

Hardy leaned forward, elbows on his knees. 'He won't admit anything, Judge. He is one stubborn fellow. He thinks they'll pull his bar card.'

Giotti considered that a moment. 'All right. So you admit it for him.' Now the judge, too, leaned over the coffee table and lowered his voice. 'It wouldn't be Graham's fault – there'd be no ethical problem with the bar – if the jury came back with "not guilty"; just bought assisted suicide and let him go. Graham himself would never have to admit anything. The bar couldn't yank his card if it was his attorney's argument, not his own testimony. All you've got to do, Mr Hardy, is keep him off the stand.'

This was, suddenly, as strange a conversation as Hardy could ever remember having: a federal judge counseling him on his defense. And it was a strategy, he realized, that had every hope of success, not too dissimilar to Leland Taylor's suggestion of the day before. If only he could convince his client.

'That might work, Judge.'

'If it doesn't, and again I am not commenting directly here' – Giotti waited and Hardy nodded his assent – 'at least then you've based your case on the constitutional issue, and I can assure you with reasonable confidence that this circuit would tend to look favorably on any appeal.'

The moment froze, Hardy struck with an almost surreal awareness. The white light out the window. The space heater suddenly clicking off. A portrait of some Native American chieftain on the opposite wall. If he'd heard it right, Mario Giotti had just told him that if Hardy lost Graham's case, the judge would see to it that the conviction was overturned on appeal.

He didn't dare ask if he'd heard it right. He had. Any more

direct confirmation would be collusive – downright indictable. Nodding like a puppet, setting the frame in his mind, he stood up. 'Well, Your Honor, I want to thank you. It was very nice to meet you.'

'My pleasure,' the judge said. 'It's not every day I get any personal time. I appreciate it.'

They were moving to the door when Hardy stopped. 'Can I ask you one more thing? Very fast.'

Giotti trotted out his smile again. 'You can ask it slow if you want. What is it?'

'You said Sal was unable to make a decision at the end.'

The judge corrected him. 'An informed decision.'

'And this was obvious to anybody who did any business with him?'

'Maybe not. But certainly to anyone who had known him.'

Hardy frowned. The judge asked him what he was getting at. 'I'm trying to get a picture of the last moments. If he was lucid one second, had made this decision, then in the middle of it changed his mind, that could account for the trauma they found around the injection site.'

The judge's eyes went to the corner of the room, the filigreed redwood moldings hugging the distressed drywall. Lips pursed, his eyes went dull for a long beat. 'He knew it was getting toward the time. He used to tell his bad Alzheimer's jokes, you know? Then lately he'd stopped doing that, which I took as a sign that he was getting serious about it.'

'But suddenly this tumor was going to end things quickly.'

Giotti waited. 'And?'

'And so he wasn't facing the same thing. Instead of a long, slow advance into dementia where he'd lose his dignity, his new reality was about dealing with pain.'

'Okay?'

'Which from all I've heard about him, he was macho as hell. I'm just trying to get to his state of mind. He wasn't going to let pain beat him, even great pain.'

Giotti took that in. 'That flies,' he said. 'I remember one time we were out on the *Bonus*. We'd just landed a salmon and he slipped on the deck and the gaff went through the palm of his hand, all the way through.'

'Yow!'

'No kidding. Sal gave one good yell, then just twisted the gaff back out and wrapped his hand in an old T-shirt. Didn't even head the boat back in. We fished the whole day and he never mentioned it again.'

'That's what I mean,' Hardy said. 'I don't see him deciding to die over the pain.'

'Maybe the combination,' the judge replied. 'That and the Alzheimer's. Whatever it was, something clearly got to him. It must have, don't you think?'

'Must have,' Hardy said. 'It must have.'

24

'He says it's an emergency.' Phyllis's clipped tones came over the speakerphone, filling his office.

Hardy was huddled with Michelle, catching up on the ever-fascinating world of stress tolerance in various metals. It was Wednesday afternoon, almost evening, certainly after five – at any rate, way too late for what he still had to do.

He hadn't even been to see Graham, who'd no doubt been languishing in his AdSeg unit all day, wondering what, if anything, his lawyer was up to. And he'd been working on Russo all day – after Giotti, over to the Hall for more discovery, a look at the actual evidence. The materials from the safe: the money, baseball cards, old belt. Then the syringes and vials with their labels stripped off.

He had a less-than-amiable chat with Claude Clark in the hallway, when Hardy had stopped him, honestly trying to help, perhaps to make amends about the blown deal with Pratt. He told Clark that Barbara Brandt was a liar. Not true, Clark had countered, and even if it were, Hardy made deals he couldn't keep. Clark would take a liar anytime – at least you knew where you stood.

He really ought to go stop in and see Graham, but it was three-thirty before he gave up waiting for another opportunity to apologize to Glitsky and began to brave the abysmal traffic back uptown to Sutter. He had had a two o'clock with Michelle which he'd rescheduled to three and then four, and he was going to be late for that too.

Even if someone hadn't parked in his space under his own building.

Staring at the unfamiliar car in the spot for which he paid a fortune each month, he marveled anew that anyone could oppose capital punishment. Surely, stealing someone's parking place was a death-penalty affront to civilization.

Just to add a certain je ne sais quoi of tension to the equation, he had a date with Frannie in less than two hours and at least another hour here with Michelle, so he'd told Phyllis no more calls the last time she'd put one through – a reporter. If it wasn't Dyson or Frannie, he couldn't talk to anybody. And now she'd buzzed him back, interrupting again.

He shook his head in frustration. 'Sorry, Michelle.' Then, out loud, 'Who is it, Phyllis?'

'A Dr Cutler.'

'I don't know him.'

'It's about the Russo case.'

'What isn't?' He asked it to himself, getting up to cross to his desk, but an answer came from an unexpected quarter.

'This.'

It was a flat statement from Michelle, with a harsh finality that nearly startled him. He suddenly realized that she wasn't thriving under his tutelage. She was doing fine with the details and strategy of the case, but since her interaction with him was constantly being subverted by Graham Russo, she was getting understandably impatient. He gave her an ambiguous gesture, picked up the phone, and said hello.

He heard papers rustling and turned to see her going out the door, closing it behind her, so he missed his caller's introduction. 'I'm sorry, could you repeat that?' He heard a sigh. Hardy wasn't making many friends.

'My name's Russell Cutler. I play ball with Graham.'

'My secretary said Dr Cutler?'

'That too.' There was a small pause, the sound of a breath being exhaled. 'I prescribed the morphine for Sal Russo. I've been trying to live with it and I'm not doing very well. I thought telling somebody might help.'

Hardy took a moment. 'It might.' But then another thought occurred to him, and it nearly turned his stomach. His client had lied again – to him, maybe to his lover, certainly to the police and to *Time* magazine. If this doctor played ball with Graham, then the medical connection to the morphine was not through Sal – as Hardy had reluctantly come to accept – but through Graham himself.

Jesus Christ! he thought. Would it never end?

Struggling for a calm tone, he fell back upon his job, his role. The lawyer. 'Have you mentioned this to anyone else? The police, for instance?'

'No. I thought it would be better if I told my story to Graham's side, you know?'

'That was a good thought,' Hardy conceded. 'Where are you located?'

Cutler told him he was a resident at Seton Medical Center in Daly City. He lived in San Bruno, had graduated from UCSF Medical School. He had played baseball for Arizona in college and had been 'drafted' by Craig Ising when he showed up in the city, playing haphazardly, but as often as he could get the time. He hit the long ball and it was great money. 'So Graham and I became friends and he kind of told me about Sal. He was afraid to go to public health because he thought they'd report him because of the AD. He'd lose his driver's license among other things. They'd put him in a home. You know the drill, the indigent sick? It's appalling.'

'I've heard,' Hardy said, although he was daily getting a new appreciation for how bad it must be. 'So you . . . what? With Sal?'

There wasn't any answer for a minute, although the connection hadn't been broken. When Cutler came back, his voice was muted. 'Look, I'm in the lounge here . . .'

'And you can't talk?'

A false cheer, the voice back to normal. 'Good. Right. Yeah.'

'So when can we get together?'

'This is always my favorite part.'

'It's why we're such a great couple,' Hardy said. 'You're always so eager to share the excitement.'

Frannie nodded. 'That must be it.'

Hardy felt that there hadn't been any choice, not that this was any consolation to Frannie. Nor had it been to Michelle, either, judging from the *Gone home* Post-it note on her office door when Hardy had finally stopped by to resume their stress-tolerance discussion. His trained legal mind intuited that she was displeased with him.

As was his wife now at his decision to meet with a witness at the Little Shamrock on Date Night. Her brother, Moses, having poured a round for a group in the front window, was back into earshot before Hardy was aware of it.

Hardy was trying to explain. 'It couldn't be helped, Frannie. The guy's got eight hours off tonight and then he's on call all the rest of the week. What am I supposed to do?'

His wife, nursing a Chardonnay, feigned pensiveness. 'Here's a radical concept, but what about waiting till next week? What do *you* think, Mose?'

A thoughtful pout. 'Never put off until tomorrow what you can do today?'

Hardy approved of this support. 'See? Pure wisdom. Your brother has a doctorate, you know. He must be right.'

Frannie cast a look between them. 'You know what they call the person who comes in last in the class in med school?'

'I give up,' Hardy said.

'Doctor.' Frannie smiled.

McGuire looked hurt. 'I'm not that kind of doctor, anyway.'

Hardy wanted to get back to the topic. 'Besides, Frannie, anything could happen in a week. What if my witness dies in the interim?'

Frannie histrionically slapped her palm on her forehead. 'Silly me,' she said, 'I forgot all about that possibility, which *is* pretty likely, I suppose. The guy's – what? – twenty-five? Thirty? Death must stalk him like a panther.'

'I didn't say it was likely. I'm trying to be careful.'

Hardy was sticking with club soda until he'd had a chance to interview Russell Cutler, who should be here any minute, he hoped. If he didn't chicken out. He was already fifteen minutes late.

Frannie suddenly put her hand over his. 'I'm teasing you. Mostly. But we *are* going out to a real restaurant later and eat real food that I don't cook, right?'

'Right.'

'We're in complete agreement?'

'Total.'

'All right. I'm with you, then.' She looked over her husband's shoulder at the doorway. 'This witness is a doctor?'

'Yeah.'

'I think he's here.'

Dr Cutler still wore his light green scrubs, maybe as a means of identification. If so, it worked. Hardy left his wife with her brother, and the two men shook hands at the door.

The Little Shamrock was San Francisco's oldest bar, established in 1893. Twenty feet wide from side to side, it extended back three times that distance. Antique bicycles, fishing rods, knapsacks and other turn-of-the-century artifacts hung from the ceiling, and there was a clock that had stopped ticking during the Great Earthquake of 1906. Tonight, Wednesday, at seven twenty-two, there were two dozen patrons, half of them at the bar. The rest were shooting darts or sitting at tiny tables in the front. The Beach Boys were singing 'Don't Worry, Baby' on the jukebox.

Hardy took Cutler to the back of the place. Here three couches were arranged sitting-room style. Tiffany lamps shed a feeble light. The bathrooms were behind some stained-glass screens, and people with a highly developed olfactory sense tended to avoid the area, at least until the place got rockin' and the beer smell overlaid anything else.

But Cutler didn't seem to mind or even notice. 'I have trouble believing I've let it go this long,' he began before he'd sat down. 'With all the articles, the media . . .'

'It's all right, you're here now. That's what matters.'

'You know why I told your secretary it was an emergency? I thought if I didn't get it out today, I never would.'

Frannie had been right. Cutler was between twenty-five and thirty. At this moment there were black circles under his eyes and the outline of stubble on his cheeks, but Hardy guessed that when he was rested and shaved he would be fresh-faced, even boyish. He was neither as tall nor as broad in the shoulders as Graham, but possessed that same athletic grace of movement, although his cropped black hair made him appear more a Marine than a jock. 'I'm a wreck about this. I don't think I've slept since Graham was first arrested.'

The first job would be to reassure him. 'Why don't you just tell me the level of your involvement with Sal? I'm not the police, you know. What you tell me doesn't necessarily have to go any farther.'

Cutler sighed. He kept opening and closing his hands. Finally, he linked them and leaned forward. 'Graham was kind of being Sal's caretaker toward the end, kind of waiting and watching. They had made some deal about the AD, and I think were both okay with it. Graham was going to help him die before he got . . . before he went to a home, I guess. But then Sal started getting these headaches.'

'The cancer?'

Cutler nodded. 'But we didn't know that at first. So I ran the CAT scan. We got a second opinion, then a third. There wasn't any hope. We couldn't operate. We were convinced the size and location of the tumor was increasing his intracranial pressure. That appeared to be what was causing the headaches.'

As the story came out, Hardy realized that it had been as he'd begun to surmise. Sal was actively fighting the pain, not obsessing about the progress of the Alzheimer's. 'So I wrote up a scrip for the morphine. We tried oral painkillers first, of course, but they became less and less effective.'

Over his head, Hardy faked a layman's understanding. 'Of course.' Added, 'But you finally got to the morphine so Sal could use it to kill himself?'

Cutler nodded. 'Eventually. Down the line.'

'But you wrote the prescription? So there's a record of it, anyway?'

This made Cutler's hands clench, but his voice was under control. 'Yeah, but . . . well, I wrote the prescription to Graham, in Graham's name. He picked it up at the pharmacy at Seton. I guess he thought it was out of the city, it wouldn't be as easy to trace.'

'Okay, but why the secrecy? You have a sick man. You're his doctor and you prescribe drugs. What's the problem?'

'There wasn't one, not by itself.' He shook his head. 'It's all so stupid, I shouldn't have done it the way I did, that's all.'

'What way was that?'

'I wanted to refer Sal to a pain management center, but he refused. They have more sophisticated techniques and medications that could have kept him from having to give himself so many injections.'

'But in the end you stayed with the morphine. Why was that?'

'Basically it was because the old man was a pain in the ass. We started with morphine a couple of times and it worked, and he wasn't going to take anything else.' Cutler looked imploringly at Hardy, as though he hoped for absolution. 'Look. I'm in the last year of my residency. I'm really not supposed to follow my own patients independently. I mean, it's not illegal, but it's frowned on in real life. *Strongly* frowned on. I'd be screwed. And after this many years it's kind of important I get to the end.

'See, Graham didn't want his dad in the system in any way either. Sal was just terrified that somehow somebody would decide he had to be institutionalized. So I did all this on my own.'

'What about the other opinions? How'd you get them?'

A shrug. 'That was easy. I got a tech buddy helps me with the scan itself, then a specialist gives me a curbside consult and verifies it's terminal and inoperable. There's nothing that can be done anyway, so what are we supposed to do? See?'

Hardy saw. 'So you knew, or thought, Sal was going to kill himself?'

'Let's just say we wanted to keep that option open.'

'And so Graham scratched your name off the vials? You're doing him a favor and in return he agrees to keep your name out of it so you don't get screwed at work?'

'Yeah, that's it. I figure it's bad enough if I follow a patient independently. If I even appear to assist at a suicide on top of it, then best case I'd be looking for another residency. Worst case they'd take my license.'

Hardy had to appreciate the similarities in the problems of the two young men. No wonder they became friends; their professional concerns were nearly identical.

'But you didn't help Sal kill himself?'

'No. I did prescribe the drug, though.' He shrugged. 'We should have just been up front with it, I suppose. Now I see Graham in jail charged with murder and he's still protecting me. I figure I've got to say something. Maybe it'll help him.'

And having said it, suddenly he appeared to grow calm. Sitting all the way back on the couch, he let out a deep breath. 'I bet they serve beer here. I could go for a beer.'

'I'll get it.' Hardy got up, went behind the bar, and pulled at the Bass tap. When he got back, Cutler thanked him for the beer. 'So what do we do now?'

Hardy sat across from him. 'When is your residency over?'

'Mid-July. Why?'

'Because the trial starts in September. As soon as I put you on my witness list, people are going to want to talk to you. But we ought to be able to keep it between us until then. You didn't break any law, did you?'

'Not that I know of.'

'Okay, then. And the police haven't asked the mystery doctor – that's you – to come forward, have they? No? So put it on hold, don't worry about it. My main concern, to tell you the truth, is that these are more lies Graham told.'

'But he was just protecting me.'

'I understand that.' Hardy wasn't going to go into it. Graham's penchant for benevolent falsehoods might well wind up hanging him. 'But back to you. I won't have to list you as a witness until just before the trial, so by the time any of this comes out, you'll be clear with your residency.'

'I shouldn't have done it,' Cutler repeated.

'I don't know about that. You did the right thing. The morphine helped Sal while he was alive, didn't it?'

Hardy could see he wanted to accept this, but still had doubts. He leaned forward and patted the young man's knee. 'This legal stuff, forget it. Nobody's going to bust you for what you did. You tried to ease someone's suffering. That's what doctors ought to do, don't you think?'

A sip of beer, a lopsided grin. 'I don't remember anymore. I used to think so when I had a life.'

Hardy patted his knee again. 'Believe it,' he said. 'Now enjoy your beer, then go get some sleep. And thanks.'

Hardy and Frannie stayed in the Avenues at the Purple Yet Wah, a Chinese restaurant not fifteen blocks from their house. Eating their way through the appetizers – pot sticker, calamari, egg rolls, paper-wrap chicken, barbecue pork rib, deep-fry shrimp, and half a dozen more dishes – they were back home by ten-fifteen.

Hardy had five messages waiting. Glitsky left his name.

Michelle was really sorry she'd snapped at him and left so abruptly. They had a lot of work to catch up on tomorrow. Maybe he could set aside a little Tryptech time?

Graham Russo had understood that Hardy would come by every day. What was going on? Why hadn't he come in? Was everything all right? His only visitor that whole day had been his mother. He'd been thinking, and maybe Hardy's decision not to mention Joan Singleterry – the phantom woman from Sal's past – was a mistake. Graham wasn't making her up. Sal had really wanted to give her the money. Please call. Jail is hell.

Graham again. Same thing. Going nuts.

The last call was from Sarah Evans. Ten minutes ago. She had talked to Graham again and gotten an idea and thought maybe she was on to something.

25

There was a muted tone even in the public areas of Baywest Bank. This would have been noticeable even if the building weren't located on such a blighted and vulgar thoroughfare. Since it was on Market Street, though, with its bums and garbage, its debris and stench, its fumes and pornography, the contrast was especially striking.

The other day when he'd come to lunch here with the Taylors, Hardy had passed right through the lobby to the elevators and had scarcely looked at the surroundings. Now his business was here and he took them in: polished floors, burnished dark wood, tinted windows to the outside.

There was nothing so obviously crass as a waiting line in the lobby here at Baywest. When you entered through the revolving front doors, you were greeted by a young man in a business suit and asked your business. If you needed to see a teller, of which there were only three, you were given a number and asked to have a seat in one of the upholstered chairs tastefully arranged around the lobby.

Hardy identified himself as Graham Russo's lawyer and said he would appreciate a few minutes with George, although he didn't have an appointment. It was nine-fifteen A.M. Mr Russo was at a meeting. Hardy said he would wait and was directed to another armchair in the back of the lobby.

The bank's officers lived in cages, as they do almost everywhere. The burnished-wood motif from the public area was carried over here in the back, creating half-high walls around each unit. The upper half was glass, and Hardy, getting to his wingback chair, looked into George's office for a quick glimpse.

Without the nameplate he could have picked him out from a hundred people. Dressed in a different style than Graham, sitting in a posture behind his desk that Hardy had never seen in Graham, George still bore a remarkable resemblance to his older brother.

As he waited, Hardy made a few notations on the yellow legal pad he'd begun carrying with him everywhere he went. There was so much to remember, so much to organize, and he only had three months before the trial – an absurdly short lead time that he'd argued bitterly against at the Calendar hearing. But his old colleague Tim Manion – the judge – though inclined to sympathy on the bail issue, had proved intractable in scheduling the trial.

After Hardy had argued for a couple of minutes, Manion had summoned him up to the bench and given him a little lecture. 'I understand you turned down a very reasonable settlement offer, Mr Hardy' – no 'Diz' on this topic – 'so I assumed your client would be anxious to tell his story and clear his name.'

'But, Your Honor, three months—'

The gavel. A tight smile. 'Unless you'd like to start in sixty days as the law provides.'

So Hardy had until September. He knew he had to explain this to Michelle pretty soon too. He moved her to the top of his list. He owed her that much. He'd worked for bosses who didn't tell him what they expected or what he could expect in terms of their support, and he had thought them cruel. He didn't wish to leave Michelle with that impression of himself.

But he didn't dwell on Tryptech. The grand jury indictment notwithstanding, he was actually going to file a nine-nine-five motion for dismissal that he would lose, but he felt he had to get on the boards with the fact that there was not enough evidence to justify holding Graham at all. There were signs that Sal had been murdered, perhaps, but no reasonable attempt to connect that murder to Graham by physical evidence.

So he'd try, make the point, get laughed at.

He made another note. Today he must remember to place ads to run for a month or more in the local newspapers, in the *L.A. Times*, the *San Jose Mercury*, and also – being thorough – in the various regional editions of *The Wall Street Journal*, maybe in *The New York Times Book Review*, asking anyone with information on a Joan Singleterry to come forward. He wouldn't risk introducing her before a jury. Graham's story about her, even if true in all respects, smelled bogus. But Graham was right: they would be unwise to abandon the search for her if she could shed some light on Sal, or on the money. If any part of Graham's story was true and Hardy could verify it, it could destroy the prosecution case, as least insofar as the special circumstances.

Then there was Sarah Evans and her pursuit of the gamblers and fishmongers. He had to coordinate that more closely. It wasn't merely a matter of his SODDIT defense. He didn't need Sarah's information so much for the jury as he might to get to the truth.

Which was why he was here now . . .

He raised his eyes. The door had opened and George was saying his name, a concerned look on his face. Hardy threw his legal pad into his open briefcase and stood up, tried a smile. 'Mr Russo, how are you? I'm representing your brother—'

'I know who you are,' he said. 'And how I am is busy. What does my brother have to do with me?'

The tone made it even ruder than the words. Hardy cocked his head, trying to get a read on George, but it didn't look like he was going to get much of an opening. 'I haven't seen my father in ten years. I don't talk to my brother. I'm not interested.' But his color was high. Like it or not, his emotions were engaged.

Hardy retained an even tone of his own. 'I understood you saw Sal when he came to your mother's house a month ago.'

'So what?'

'So you just said you hadn't seen him in ten years.'

George's eyes narrowed. It wasn't clear whether it was with fear or rage. He pointed a finger at Hardy. 'That's a lawyer's trick, turning my words.'

Hardy made the snap decision that he wasn't going to score any points here with sweet talk. 'Here's another one,' he said, '– where were you on the afternoon your father was killed?'

This stopped him dead. He opened his mouth to speak, thought better of it, closed it again. He glanced toward the lobby. Some customers had turned their heads, noticed the confrontation. Hardy pressed what he took to be his advantage. 'It might be more comfortable in your office.'

They were inside. Hardy pulled the door to behind them while George retreated behind his desk. He'd obviously had enough time to think by the time he got seated. 'I don't have to answer any of your questions, do I? You're not with the police.'

'No, that's right. Of course, I could go to the police and tell them you were uncooperative and acting suspicious, that you didn't have an alibi for the time of the murder and you had a great motive. Plus you look enough like Graham that anyone who thought they had seen him at Sal's might have been confused.' Hardy sat back and crossed his legs. 'Then you *would* have to answer them.'

'I had nothing to do with my father's death.'

'I didn't say you did.'

'You just said I had a motive and no alibi.'

Hardy shrugged. 'Maybe I'm wrong.' He waited.

George's tone shifted. Suddenly the arrogant banker gave way to a frightened child. 'What made you come here? I don't even know why you're talking to me.'

Sitting back, Hardy decided he'd played enough hardball. He could ease up a little. 'Your mother.'

A confused, betrayed look. 'What about my mother? She told you to talk to me?'

Hardy walked him through it, leaving out any reference to Sarah, his secret agent who'd been the conduit. 'Your mother went to see your brother in jail yesterday and told him, among other things, that she was worried about you. You'd blown up at some family gathering a couple of weeks ago, didn't you? You were so hateful to your father.'

'He was hateful to us. He just walked out on us.'

'Yes, he did. And you could never forgive him, could you?'

'Why should I?'

Hardy let that question lie. Instead, 'Your mother thinks it's possible that *you* killed Sal.'

'Jesus, what are you saying?' George took a handkerchief from his lapel pocket and wiped his forehead.

'You told your father you went to some client's but you didn't go there, did you?'

'How do you . . . how can you say that?'

'Your mother said it. She told Graham. He told me.'

'He's a liar.'

'Maybe it runs in the family. Where were you?'

George ran a hand around under his collar. Gradually, though, over ten seconds or so, he got himself back under control. 'I was at a client's on a confidential matter.' He checked his watch. 'And I am very busy. This interview is over.'

Hardy didn't move. 'Do you want me to go to the police with this? You think I ask hard questions, you should see them.'

But the younger brother had made his decision. 'I don't think you ask hard questions. And you can inform the police or not. I didn't see my father. I didn't even know where he lived.' He picked up the phone. 'If you're not ready to leave, I can call security.'

Hardy was sitting in the jail's visiting room and Graham was in his orange jumpsuit, standing by the window. Hardy had just told him about Helen and Leland's offer of financial help.

'Graham?'

Finally, he turned around. 'They want something, but I don't see how I can tell you no.'

'Maybe they want to help you.'

'No, they want to buy me.'

'They wouldn't even be buying *me*, only some of my hours. I made it clear: I'd be working only for your interests, not theirs.'

Graham eased himself onto the corner of the table. He wore a weary smile and was shaking his head. 'That's not how it works. Leland pays you and then eventually you come to see where your interests lie. I've seen it happen a thousand times.'

His hands crossed in front of him, Hardy met his client's gaze. 'I'll rise above the temptation.' Then, more seriously, 'I've thought a lot about this, Graham. A lot, believe me. It's the only way I defend you and not go broke, which of course I'd gladly do on your behalf, although not if I didn't have to. But I leave it up to you.'

Hardy watched the young man wrestle with it, family ties and financial bonds. He sighed. 'My mom sure puts the "fun" in *dysfunctional*, doesn't she?'

'I don't think she's dysfunctional. Confused, maybe. You interested in my call on this, really?'

'Sure.'

'She sees your dad in you. Apparently a lot of people do. It's her second chance that way. She wants to give you a chance to make your life turn out all right, to save yourself, and the only language she has is money. You don't do things her way, Leland's way, but something in her wishes that *that* way – *your* way – could work. She wants to help.'

'And what about Leland?'

'He doesn't have to matter if you don't let him.'

'All right,' he said. 'Take the damn money.'

Carefully keeping any elation out of his voice – this really was a critical decision that would keep them both afloat – Hardy felt his shoulders relax. He turned to his legal pad. 'Oh, by the way, I had a nice talk with your friend Russ Cutler last night. Funny how you forgot to mention him.'

Graham didn't shrink from it. Caught again, oh, well. 'I had other things on my mind. I tried to go off the record and tell Sarah. She wouldn't let me.'

'It's going to come out as more lies.'

Graham shrugged. 'I promised him I wouldn't bring him in. What was I supposed to do, betray the guy?'

'I don't know if I'd characterize it as betrayal, maybe telling your attorney, trust that he could keep a lid on it.'

Graham accepted the rebuke. 'You're right, I'm sorry.'

Hardy smiled. 'You gotta love a guy who's so consistent, but last night I passed a few pleasant moments plotting to kill you after I get you off.' He shrugged. 'It passed, but I really would love it if you had any other little secrets you've been keeping up to now. If you wanted to share them, this would be a good time.'

Still sitting on the table, Graham swung his legs under it like a child. 'Craig Ising's holding ten grand for me. My money.'

Hardy had to laugh. 'You are a piece of work.'

Embarrassed, Graham remained matter of fact. 'One way or the other, this thing's over in six months, I figure. I didn't want to lose my apartment, so Craig's keeping up on the rent. If I'm in jail, it doesn't matter. But if I win, then what?'

In spite of himself Hardy thought he had a point. In fact, he had wondered what Graham's plans might be regarding his wonderful place. It was human nature to protect his own hearth before he worried about Hardy's home and family, not that it didn't rankle just a bit.

'So that's it?' he asked. 'I realize we've got the proverbial loaves and fishes of falsehoods here, but maybe we keep at this long enough we'll run out. You didn't run off on your lost weekend and get married to Evans, did you?'

'No.'

'You don't know anything about your father's money except what you've already told me about Joan Singleterry, whoever the hell she is?'

'Right.'

'And you don't know who she is?'

'No idea.'

'And if I catch you in even the smallest fib, I get to stick an icepick under your kneecap?'

'Both of 'em.'

'You swear on your father's grave?'

This sobered him, as Hardy had meant it to. 'I swear,' he intoned.

This would have to be good enough and Hardy took it. 'Okay. Now let's talk some matters of law.'

Without naming Graham's stepfather as one source of the idea, Hardy outlined in some detail the suggestion that both Leland and Giotti had proposed as a defense. As a lawyer himself, Graham seemed to appreciate the distinction between admitting he'd done something and having a jury conclude he'd done the same thing. If he never admitted it, ever, to anyone, he would be legally blameless. He could resume his life with a clean slate.

They discussed the strategy until the lunch bell. Graham's acquiescence was a nice surprise, especially after his earlier refusal to plead to essentially the same thing. But, as Graham pointed out, they weren't the same thing at all.

Not in the eyes of the law.

Of course, there were great risks. Graham was charged with first-degree murder and, if convicted with special circumstances, would spend the rest of his life in prison. But Giotti's offer seriously mitigated that risk.

They left it unresolved, but kept the door open.

Driving back uptown, Hardy was going around with it. It was starting to look as though his defense would be to admit that Graham, who couldn't admit it himself, had committed a murder that in fact he hadn't committed. For a reason that he didn't have.

And this, if it worked, might set his client free.

The law, he thought, was a sublime and terrible thing.

Sarah Evans planned to take full advantage of yet another beautiful wrinkle in the system.

The city and county of San Francisco were physically coterminous; they shared the same geographic boundaries. This created interesting possibilities in the always complicated world of legal jurisdiction.

Practically, one of the results of this arrangement was that the jail was controlled by the county sheriff's office, not by the city's police department. Although it was directly behind the Hall of Justice, in what used to be part of the Hall's parking lot, the jail might as well have been on the moon for all of its official connection to police events at Southern Station, which was the city's name for the police presence at the Hall.

Sarah told Marcel Lanier she had some reports to catch up on after their shift – she'd hitch a ride home later. He left her working at her desk in the homicide detail.

At some time between six and seven the coming and going of other homicide inspectors slowed down, and Sarah cleared her desk, took the back steps out of the Hall, and walked around to the entrance to the jail, flashed her ID, and told the admitting deputy that she had to see Russo. She signed in, knowing that her bosses in the PD were unlikely to review the log. Attorney room B would be all right. She checked her weapon at the desk.

'I can't come here very often.'

They sat across the table from each other now, inspector and prisoner. Graham longed for her hands over the table, but knew he couldn't.

A silence settled. They simply looked at each other. Graham told her he loved her. She bit at her lip and found she couldn't respond. 'What's it like out there?' he asked finally. 'Outside.'

'Windy. I've got a game tonight, you know. Thursdays.' She sighed. 'How are you holding up?'

'Better now.' But he couldn't hide his uncertainty about it. 'I think I got the right lawyer.'

Sarah nodded. 'Did he tell you he talked to your brother? George won't say where he was.'

A shake of the head. 'Georgie didn't kill Sal.'

'Okay.' She didn't want to argue about it. She thought it was entirely possible, in fact, that George had killed Sal. Nothing Hardy had told her ruled him out in any way, and her training was to keep pushing until you got to something. 'But I wish I could talk to him. I'd shake his tree a little harder than he's used to.'

'So why don't you?'

'I can't. I've got no case. If I shake him down off duty and he complains, which he would, it's harassment and there goes my job. Hardy's trying to get my boss to move on it.'

'Your boss?'

'Lieutenant Glitsky – he and Hardy know each other. But it won't matter. Glitsky won't do it. There's nothing to move on, especially since Glitsky's already got a suspect in jail.'

'Don't remind me.'

'I am looking at the other things, Graham. Craig Ising's friends. The fish stuff.'

'I know.' Then, quietly. 'I know you are.'

She could see him being brave and it was tearing her up. Say what she would about his chances at his trial, the fact remained that he was locked up, a prisoner. He wasn't going out to play ball tonight the way she was. He was here, alone, scared. She felt like she had to hold him. He needed her. But she couldn't do that, although if she stayed any longer, she might. 'I've got to go,' she said.

The headache had been bad this morning and he'd gotten a call near dawn. He came right on down and gave Sal his shot. His father hated to shoot himself up. Hated it!

After that Sal slept and Graham read for a while, some magazine, passing the time, dozing a little himself. He didn't have to be in at work until midafternoon and had come to love these times with his dad, even to depend on them, difficult as they sometimes were. In his dad's presence he felt like he belonged somewhere. He was loved for who he was. He felt important, needed. It was as simple as that. He didn't feel that way anywhere else.

He heard Sal stirring in his room down past the kitchen and a minute later he appeared. 'Good boy,' he said. 'Still here. How about I take you down for lunch at the Grotto. I love their cioppino. Nobody makes cioppino better than Bruno Giotti.'

Halfway out of his chair, Graham sat back down, his stomach churning, and not over the mention of food. Since his father's headaches had started, the bouts of forgetfulness had become more frequent as well, but this morning was more than forgetfulness. This, to Graham, was new.

'Dad, the Grotto isn't there anymore. It's Stagnola's now, remember?'

Sal laughed. 'What kind of boy am I raising here? What are you talking about, you don't know your own backyard? Come on, get up, fish don't bite all day.'

To look at him there was no change. He'd even dressed, for Sal, with a degree of proper conservatism: tennis shoes and khaki slacks and a blue workshirt that had been pressed before he'd taken a nap in it. 'So we going or not?'

Graham was going to have to talk to Russ Cutler, he thought. He didn't know what to do, how to handle this – humor Sal or dig his heels in. He just didn't know.

'Yeah, we're going,' he said.

He'd stick with him until this passed, if it did.

In the alley, getting into the truck, Sal had another idea. 'Hey, why don't we swing by the Manor, surprise Georgie and Deb, take'em out with us? They love the Grotto.'

'They went out with Mom, shopping, remember?'

Sal didn't seem entirely sure, but said, 'Oh, that's right. Well, we can still go.'

'Sure. I'll drive, okay?'

Again, Sal hesitated before accepting this, but finally climbed up into the cab. 'That fucking Mario,' he said conversationally.

'Who?'

'Giotti.'

'The judge?'

Sal gave his boy a look. 'What are you talking about, the judge? No, I'm talking Mario Giotti, Bruno's kid.' He gave his son a hard whack on the arm. 'You been smoking something, bambino?'

'No. Sorry. What about Mario?' Graham was heading east on Mission, down to the old Embarcadero – now Herb Caen Way. He'd turn north at the Bay and head up along the piers to Fisherman's Wharf. Maybe by the time they arrived, Sal would know where he was. 'What about Mario?' he repeated.

Sal was smiling, remembering something. 'That fucking guy, he's in at work last night in his suit and tie, cutting garlic, tomatoes. Can't decide if he wants to stay and help his old man or go on in the law. I tell him stay and help his old man. Family, huh? That's what counts.'

Graham nodded, let his lungs go. 'Yeah. You went to the Grotto last night?'

'Yeah, shit, after work. Get some courage before I go home. Your mother . . . well, I won't say anything bad about your mom, but this life, me, you kids . . . it's the only one she's got, you know. Her mom and dad fucked her up so bad. Wasn't for me, she'd be some dried-up old society lady, only sometimes she forgets that and I gotta remind her.'

Sal was right, Graham thought. Helen never should have stopped loving him, no matter what Sal had done. Family counts. She should be here with them now, in this truck. She should see this, help them both. But she wasn't, couldn't be. Not now, not anymore. And Graham knew it was a tragedy for her as well.

He reached over and laid a hand for a moment on his father's knee. 'She loves you, Sal.'

'I know,' he answered breezily, this man who hadn't seen his wife in fifteen years. 'But I got to talk to her, straighten her out. She's all mixed up. We ought to go home maybe.'

They were getting to the Wharf. 'After lunch.'

It wasn't yet noon in midweek and there were plenty of places to park in the lot. The ferry had just disgorged a stream of commuters and Sal bounced out of the cab. 'We better shake it.' Graham hustled next to him to keep up. 'This crowd's going to beat us, we don't get a move on. Smell that cioppino. I love that smell, nothing better.'

They came to the door of Stagnola's and stopped. Sal's face dropped and he reached a hand out to Graham, as though he needed to be steadied. 'What's going on?' he asked. 'This isn't the Grotto.'

'I know, Dad. The Grotto's closed.'

'Well, that's just bullshit! I was here last night. Mario was in the kitchen in his suit cutting tomatoes.'

Graham said nothing. He put his arm around Sal, but the old man twisted away and walked out into the street, turning back to look at the building. He stood there a long time, squinting in the bright sunlight.

Graham walked out to him and put his arm around him again. This time his father leaned into him. 'This ain't the Grotto,' he whispered hoarsely, his voice skirting the edges of panic. 'What the hell's going on?'

Graham shot up in his cot, breathing hard. He'd almost been asleep, almost been dreaming, wasn't sure which.

In the jail most lights were out, but even here in his AdSeg unit there were always noises, always shadows.

Sal had slept in the cab again – another nap – and when he woke up he'd pulled out of it that day. Graham knew he should have done something right then. Sal had *told* him he would be going by the Manor, looking up Helen. He should have believed him. He should have done everything differently.

But he didn't want to believe it. It was too hard. It was easier to deny the progress of the disease, to believe that Sal wasn't quite gone yet mentally. He had more time. Graham had more time with him.

He lay flat on his back, his arm thrown over his eyes. He missed him horribly. This was the only time he had with Sal anymore.

Memories.

PART FOUR

26

Dismas Hardy checked his watch. Where was the judge? He was five minutes late. The bailiff had even pulled Graham from the holding cell and sat him next to Hardy, unshackled and in his trial clothes rather than the jail jumpsuit.

David Freeman was sitting at the defense table with Hardy and Graham, and doing it for free. He had joined the defense team – wheedling his way in. Hardy was grateful, not only for the legal assistance, but for the company.

They in were Department 27 in the Hall of Justice on a Monday, the third week of September. As in all of the courtrooms at the Hall, there was no hint of the weather outside, but the morning had been warm and still – unusual in the city for most of the year, but relatively normal in the weeks after Labor Day.

Graham's trial clothes were a pair of slacks and a sport coat. Freeman and Hardy had decided that a business suit would strike too formal a tone for the jury. They wanted to play up Graham's 'regular guy' image, so for the past week during jury selection, the defendant had appeared in court in a respectful coat and tie, anything but a stuffy three-piece lawyer's uniform.

Hardy was fighting his nerves. Freeman and Graham were talking quietly to his left. He was half turned away from them, peripherally aware of Drysdale and Soma at the prosecution table across from him on the other side of the courtroom.

He swiveled further to check out the gallery, now filled to bursting for the opening fireworks. Jury selection had taken nearly ten days, with the final juror selected last Friday, just before the evening adjournment. The trial proper was beginning any moment, with opening statements, the first evidence.

Hardy was damned if he was going to spend these last seconds reviewing his notes one last time. When his moment arrived, after he'd listened to Soma's opening statement, he was reasonably confident that the right words would come in for him. His notes were just that: key phrases, high points, several *don't forgets*. He never wanted to see the damn things again.

His eyes raked the gallery, rested for a second on Frannie, who'd surprised and delighted him by saying she wanted to come down to root for him, at least for his opening statement. The kids were back in school. She might bring him some luck. He gave her an imperceptible nod, touching hand to heart as though he were straightening his tie. She saw it and nodded back.

In front of Frannie, Graham's mother, Helen, who'd come to court for every day of jury selection, imitated a trompe l'oeil statue. Hardy stared at her for several seconds, during which time she did not so much as blink. Her ash-colored hair was off her face, hands clasped on her lap. A general murmur hovered over the courtroom – people talking, speculating, arguing – but Graham's mother was by herself, alone, self-sufficient. Neither her husband nor her other son was there, nor had they appeared last week.

Hardy recognized other faces on Graham's 'side' of the gallery, several staff from his office. These were Freeman's acolytes, here to see the show, especially the opening statements. Freeman had shamelessly pimped Hardy to these Young Turks as a master, and they'd come to see him work his magic.

He'd never lost! Freeman had told them all, and Hardy had rushed in with the clarification that he'd only fought twice. Never losing would have a lot more punch six or eight trials down the line. But they'd come anyway.

Conspicuously absent was Michelle, who had assumed much of the day-to-day responsibility of Tryptech. She was clearly resentful of the trial, of the way Graham Russo had come to consume her boss's life over the past months, but Hardy thought it was actually working out very well for all concerned. Never a trial lawyer, Michelle was superb in her new role as corporate litigator. Hardy's billings on Tryptech had dropped to about five hours a week, Brunel's limit on cash outlay, and Michelle was taking her pay in discounted stock. Hardy hoped that she wouldn't wind up impoverished by that decision, but she had made it on her own.

On his side also, and it surprised him, was Sharron Pratt herself. The newspapers had it that she planned to attend as much of the trial as her schedule allowed. Barbara Brandt, too, the perhaps-lying lobbyist – a redundancy? – whose face had become familiar, talked nonstop to her contingent by the back doors.

On the other side, behind the prosecution table, in the first row and far to the side, sat Dean Powell, the attorney general of the state of California. Like Pratt he was here to observe, to be a presence.

Hardy glanced over at Freeman and his client, still head to head, chatting amiably. Hardy was too tightly wound up even to feign listening. He blew out heavily, then stopped midway in the breath, lest any sign of his nerves get misinterpreted by the jury. He must forever appear confident, though not too. Grave, friendly.

Juror #4, Thomas Kenner, was looking at him, and Hardy met his gaze, nodding as if they had been acquainted for ages. Leisurely he took in the rest of the panel.

Jury selection had not gone well. In one important sense the final panel failed to be a representative cross-section of the citizenry of San Francisco – and that had been Hardy's primary goal. In spite of the jury experts he and Freeman had hired, they had nearly been unable to counter the prosecution's strategy. By the (bad) luck of the draw the jury pool had contained a huge preponderance of men, and though Hardy and Freeman had used their peremptory and other challenges to eliminate as many as they could, still the final panel had eight men, six of whom were white.

It was a generalization, but Hardy had no illusions: these working class men would not be as sympathetic as women would be. Soma and Drysdale had been shamelessly gender biased about wanting men on the jury – all men! Gender bias was okay if you won. Anything was okay if you won.

Of the four women, Hardy had a young Asian mother, an African-American thirtiesish schoolteacher, a divorced white secretary in her fifties, and a young gum-chewer with short hair dyed a bright carmine who read meters for the gas company.

Friday night after the adjournment, after the jury had been empaneled, Hardy and Freeman were having a consolation drink in one of the back booths at Lou the Greek's. Soma and Drysdale had come in and sat at the bar up front. They were in high spirits, raised their glasses and toasted one another. Hardy heard them clearly enough. 'Here's to the best jury in America!'

Freeman, his liver-spotted lugubrious face buried in his bourbon, raised it enough to nod knowingly. 'Good thing you're motivated by a challenge,' he'd said. 'I'd say you got one.'

Understatement. Freeman's forte.

Gil Soma's stridency at the bail hearing, his sharp-edged ironic tone when he'd been with Drysdale and first met Hardy, his obvious, vitriolic hatred for Graham Russo – these examples had all worked to convince Hardy that Soma's courtroom behavior would not help his case. Jurors would not warm to him.

But this appeared now to have been wishful thinking. Soma was neither arrogant nor stupid, and his easy manner in front of the jury showed that he was aware of his personal shortcomings and had learned to harness them.

Now, attired in his charcoal suit, his muted blue tie, his artfully scuffed shoes (for the common touch – an old Freeman trick), he stood quite close to his mostly male jury and spoke to them quietly, without histrionics, sincerely convinced of the justice of his position.

'Ladies and gentlemen of the jury. The defendant, Graham Russo, murdered his father for money.'

There was a minor stir in the courtroom at the drama of the words, but it subsided before Judge Jordan Salter had to intervene. Soma's eyes never left the jury box, calmly surveying them. 'In this trial, in the coming days and perhaps weeks, we'll be presenting a great deal of evidence, an *overwhelming* array of both direct and circumstantial evidence, that will prove to you, and prove beyond any reasonable doubt, that early on the afternoon of Friday, May ninth, the defendant, sitting right there at the table to my left' – and here he pointed as naturally as if it had been at a lovely sunset, meeting Graham's hard glance with a calm one of his own – 'came to his father's apartment, and while there, he killed his father with an injection of morphine, took money and property, and fled.

'There may be evidence that Salvatore Russo – Sal, the

defendant's father – was suffering from Alzheimer's disease and from brain cancer. No one disputes these facts. There may be evidence that on some days the defendant came to his father's apartment to administer morphine to help Sal deal with his pain. No one disputes this either.

'But on May ninth the defendant came not as a helper, but as a thief. Not as a healer, but as an assassin.

'The defense may suggest that Sal Russo was in pain, that he was dying anyway, that somehow the defendant Graham Russo was entitled to decide whether he should live or die. But whether through simple greed or some twisted sense of loyalty, Graham Russo took his father's property and his father's life. This the law calls robbery and murder, regardless of motive.

'We will introduce witnesses who will testify that the defendant was a trained paramedic, skilled in giving injections, that he had nearly constant access to and in fact provided the syringe that was used in this fatal injection, that he obtained, under his own name, a prescription for the morphine he needed to kill his father.

'We will bring before you a witness, Ms Li, a teller at the defendant's Wells Fargo Bank branch, who will testify that on the very afternoon of Sal's death, defendant placed into his own safety deposit box' – and here Soma paused and lowered his voice – 'fifty thousand dollars in cash and a collection of baseball cards from the early 1950s worth another many thousands more.'

Hardy had been worried sick about Alison Li's testimony. But Freeman had noticed a crucial failing in everybody's reading of Alison's transcripts. And they had the videotapes anyway.

But the jury wouldn't get to Freeman's argument, or to the tapes, for several days, and right now Soma's monologue was casting its spell.

Graham shifted in his chair. Subtly, Hardy moved his hand over Graham's sleeve, giving a little squeeze – a message that this was okay, they had known it was going to sound bad at first. Graham was going to have to keep himself under control.

Soma was smoothly proceeding. 'Sal Russo had his own safe, underneath his bed in his apartment. We will show you a letter from Sal to defendant, on the bottom of which is written, in defendant's own handwriting, the combination to that safe.'

Several of the jurors made eye contact with one another. Soma's rendering made an impressive litany of connection, Hardy had to admit. 'We will show you that defendant was in desperate need of money. He had quit one job and lost another in the space of a couple of months. His work as a paramedic did not begin to cover his monthly costs. He drove a BMW sports car. . . .'

The young attorney was laying out the case in textbook fashion to the jury, who gave every indication of believing him.

Soma paused. 'Finally, I'm going to ask you, ladies and gentlemen, to listen to police inspectors as they will recount for you the many, many times where they gave the defendant the opportunity to explain his actions, his motives, his behavior. And time and again you will be struck, as I was, by the defendant's absolute disregard for the truth. He has lied, and lied, and lied again. I will ask for your patience as I walk these inspectors through their interviews with the defendant, before he had even been charged with any crime, and you will hear lie upon lie upon lie.

'We will prove his lies. We will prove his actions. We will prove his motive. We will prove beyond a reasonable doubt that the defendant, Graham Russo, killed his own father out of simple greed – for the money and baseball cards in his safe.' Soma pointed to Graham one last time, his voice flat and uninflected, relating pure, rational, passionless fact: 'There sits a murderer.'

At the bench, in the hush that followed, Salter made a few notes, then looked up. 'Mr Hardy?'

Freeman leaned over around Graham at their table and whispered that they should ask for a short recess. Indeed, that's what Hardy felt like. Actually, he wanted a long recess – say two to three weeks to rethink everything he thought he'd had clear before.

Naturally, he and Freeman had rehearsed all the probable scenarios they could devise about Soma's opening statement. They had, in fact, nailed down a close approximation of what they'd just heard; after all, they knew the evidence, and that was all the prosecution was allowed to talk about.

Somehow, though, on this day, with Soma's low-key delivery (which they hadn't predicted), the case felt different. Suddenly the jitters gripped Hardy terribly – his stomach roiled with tension. The worst thing he could do, he realized, would be to delay. If he hesitated at all, his nerves would begin to throw off sparks, visible to the jury and his opponents. His doubts about his client and strategy would choke off his words, his throat, his breathing. Worst of all, the jury could use these precious moments to savor and digest the rich nourishment that Soma had just provided them.

In California the defense has the option of delivering its opening statement immediately following that of the prosecution, as a form of instant rebuttal, or waiting until later, at the beginning of the introduction of its own case-in-chief. Hardy had planned all along to deliver his opening right after Soma's, but suddenly it seemed even more crucial. He had to get up – now! To start.

Brusquely, he shook off Freeman's hand, not even seeing him really. He was on his feet, aware of a jelliness in his knees, a low-pitched roar in his ears.

At the same time he mustn't forget that this was performance. He had to appear loose, especially in front of all of these men. If they were like Hardy, and at least a few of them had to be, that's what they would relate to and respect.

He felt trapped in the endless psychic toll of maleness: weakness kills.

Anger, though, was all right, and was the closest Hardy could get to anything positive. Grim lipped, he got to the jury box and turned all the way around to face Soma. The message was controlled anger mixed with derision. A shake of the head. Hardy was disgusted by the untruth of what he'd just heard.

He was back facing the panel. He tore a page out of Soma's book, subtly mocking his opponent's only bit of flamboyance, pointing his own hand at his client. 'Graham Russo,' he began, 'cared for his father, protected his father, and loved his father. These are the primary facts in this case. It is an obscenity that he has been charged with murder at all. Here is the true version of what happened on May eighth and ninth of this year.'

In the course of the trial Hardy would call his client by his first name, much as Soma had referred to him only as the defendant. 'It's true that Graham was a regular visitor to his father's apartment. He went there to administer shots for Sal's pain, but he also went there to visit, to take his father to dinner, to organize and clean and help with the laundry. He did this regularly for nearly two years, and much more frequently in the last six months of Sal's life, as the Alzheimer's progressed and the cancer in Sal's brain became more debilitating.

'Over the last few weeks Sal had suffered some rather more serious bouts of forgetfulness. Sal was terrified of being placed in a nursing home. He didn't much trust the system. Incidentally, he passed that trait along to his son.'

Here Hardy risked an insider's smile, confident that at least some of these jurors would share the feeling that bureaucrats were perhaps not the earth's most exalted life form.

'So what have we got here? We've got a simple Italian fisherman who didn't want to end his life in lonely destitution. On May eighth he was lucid and spoke to his son. He had some money in the safe under his bed, money he'd saved for a long time. His son should take it and put it in a safe place so he could use it for pain medication, for Sal's rent, for private nursing care in his apartment if it came to that before the cancer killed him. Anything, Sal said, just don't leave him alone in a home to die.'

Freeman, Graham and himself had argued for hours over the entire Singleterry question, and finally had decided that Hardy's instincts were right. Twenty-two hundred dollars in ads all over the country had resulted in a whole lot of responses, but no Joan. Sal's request to Graham might have been genuine – certainly Graham seemed to believe it – but it wouldn't play here before the jury. So the defense team had reached a consensus: Joan Singleterry must have been someone in Sal's past, dredged up by the Alzheimer's, by now quite possibly dead. She wasn't going to get mentioned at the trial.

Hardy took a beat, realizing as he did that his legs were now firm under him. It was a relief. He looked up and down the panel, making some eye contact where it seemed natural.

'So, yes, Graham had his father's money. We will show you that it was on *that* day, May eighth, that Graham took this money and the baseball cards to his safety deposit box.

'On May ninth his father called him again. Twice. The pain was terrible. Could Graham come right over when he got the message? The dutiful and caring son, he did go to his father's apartment one last time.'

And, Hardy thought, here is where it gets tricky.

He took a deep breath. 'You're going to learn that Sal Russo died of an intravenous morphine injection. He had had a few drinks. Dr Strout, our city and county coroner, is going to tell you that his death was quick and relatively, if not completely, painless. Sal's doctor had earlier prescribed for him a form called a "DNR." It stands for "do not resuscitate." It's kind of like a "Medic Alert" bracelet that instructs paramedics to let a person die if that is nature's course. Sal had his DNR sticker out when he was found. He was a very sick man, in great pain every day, terrified that he was losing the last of his mind, afraid of being sent to a home. This was the man who died. The victim. His son Graham loved him.

'No murder for money was done here, no murder at all. The prosecution cannot and will not prove to you that Graham Russo killed his father. The evidence will not show that Graham is guilty, because despite all the prosecution's desperate rhetoric and their urge to make headlines, he is innocent.'

Hardy paused, nodded at the empaneled jurors, and realized that he was done.

'That little fucker's pretty good.' Freeman contentedly chewed his lo mein, his chopsticks poised for the next attack. They were sitting in the holding cell, the only place they could talk to Graham privately during recesses and lunch breaks. The cell was 'furnished' with two concrete shelves that served as benches built into the walls, and an open toilet. There was nothing for an inmate to steal or vandalize.

The place was littered with cardboard cartons from the take-out that Freeman had ordered up earlier in the day, as a special treat, from Chinatown. There were also containers of vinegar, Mongolian fire oil, packets of soy and other sauces, extra chopsticks, paper plates and napkins.

'Gil's not dumb. He was the star at Draper's.' Graham was dipping a duck leg into some plum sauce.

Hardy's own appetite had disappeared. Even without the stink of the holding cell, ripe and cloying, his opening statement had left his stomach hollow, unsettled. He couldn't imagine putting any food in it. Freeman noticed; he raised his eyes from his lunch. 'You all right, Diz?'

Standing at the bars, arms crossed over his chest, looking back toward the courtroom, Hardy lifted his shoulders. 'Nerves.'

'You did fine, laid out the boundaries, drew the lines.' Freeman popped a pot sticker, whole, into his mouth, chewed a moment. 'It's all Alison Li. There is no evidence that Graham put the money in the bank within months of Sal's death. That's it. We don't have to prove anything except that. They've got to prove what they've got no evidence for. And they can't do that.'

'Right.' Graham was all agreement, back to a carton he'd missed on his first pass. 'Can't be done.'

Hardy gave them both a weary smile. 'Well, then, that's settled. I think I'll go say hi to my wife.'

'Bring her in here,' Freeman said.

Hardy threw a quick glance around at the depressing cell. Shaking his head, Hardy was moving toward the door. 'I don't think so.'

She'd waited in the gallery, now nearly deserted during the lunch hour. Greeting him with a kiss on the cheek, she read his mood. 'Dismas, it wasn't that bad.'

He pulled down the seat next to her and sat. 'I can see the *Chronicle* headline tomorrow: "Russo Defense Not That Bad." '

'It was better than that.' She put a hand on his knee and squeezed it. 'You'll do fine. You're doing fine. But I notice our friend Abe isn't hanging around.'

Frannie knew about the original disagreement, of course, but the summer had intervened – the kids home all day, classes and camps and soccer and baseball – and she'd been assuming it had more or less blown over. 'Are you still in a fight?'

Hardy shrugged. 'I guess so.'

'You ought to go see him.'

'I've tried. I don't know what else I can do. He thinks I've sold out somehow, that I'm not the same person.'

'But you are.'

'No. I'm defending somebody he arrested not once, but twice. He really believes Graham's a killer, and not some kind of a mercy killer either. A bona-fide stone murderer. Which is, of course, how cops are supposed to think.'

'But he's always been a cop.'

'I know, and I've always gotten the benefit of the doubt. But now Abe thinks I've sold myself a bill of goods too – that Graham suckered me and I'm an idiot for believing him.'

Frannie crossed her arms and looked away.

'What?'

'Nothing. Just that I hope you didn't. You're not.'

Hardy shook his head. 'No way, I'm not.' He checked the courtroom, making sure it was otherwise empty. 'Look at Evans, she's a cop too.'

'But she's in love with him.'

'She wouldn't have let herself get there if she didn't think he was innocent.' He took in his wife's expression. 'I love that thing you do with your eyes when you think I'm full of it.'

Frannie smiled at him. 'All I'm saying is that she could have found herself attracted to him and because of that convinced herself that he couldn't have done it. That kind of thing has been known to happen. I fell in love with you, for example, before I knew everything about you.'

He grinned back at her. 'And now that you know? If you'd known back then?'

'It probably wouldn't have made any difference.'

'Which is my point,' Hardy said.

'No,' Frannie countered. 'It's *my* point. Sarah Evans is a cop and she loves him. She doesn't care if he's a murderer or not.'

'He's not.'

'I hope not, Dismas. I hope you're both right. But listening to Mr Soma, I have to tell you I'm not so sure.'

There it was, Hardy thought – an honest take on the respective opening statements, and from his own wife no less, who might have been expected to give Hardy's side the benefit of the doubt. If Frannie's reaction was anything like the jury's – and he had to assume it was close – he was in more trouble than he'd realized.

And he'd thought he'd been in it up to his eyeballs.

27

From his days as a prosecutor Hardy knew that one of the first orders of business in a murder trial, prosaic as it might seem, was to establish the fact that a murder had taken place. For this reason he predicted that Dr John Strout, the coroner for the city and county of San Francisco, would be the first witness Soma would call.

But he was wrong.

It was the first workday of the week. It was directly after the lunch recess. Drysdale and Soma's first witness was Mario Giotti. Apparently, even Salter had known of this arrangement; the two jurists entered the courtroom from Salter's chambers. Maybe they'd even had lunch together.

Hardy surmised that this timing had been arranged entirely for Giotti's convenience. He could come down to the Hall from the federal courthouse during his lunch break, testify immediately, say his piece for the record, endure a (hopefully) brief cross-examination, and be back in his chambers by two o'clock.

What galled Hardy was that he and Freeman had been kept ignorant while every other principal in the trial had known about this arrangement. But there wasn't anything he could do about it now. Giotti was on the stand, taking the oath.

Judge Salter had restricted the attorneys' access to the witness box. He didn't want either Hardy or Soma to intimidate any witnesses by getting too close to them physically. They were to ask their questions from the center of the courtroom. Soma stood there now.

'Mr Giotti,' Soma began, 'can you tell us your full name and occupation please?'

When he got to 'federal judge,' there was an audible buzz in the courtroom. Several members of the jury glanced at one another – a lot of juice up there. Soma, shamelessly obsequious, asked Salter's permission to address the witness either as 'Judge' or 'Your Honor.' Trying to make a gracious joke, Salter said he would allow it if the court reporter had no objection. He leaned over the podium and asked her approval. She wouldn't get confused? Everybody had a chuckle, the universe bending over backwards to be nice to the federal judge.

Hardy dared not object. What would he object to? It would alienate Salter and possibly Giotti, and it was better luck to be hit by a truck than to get a judge mad at you.

'Judge Giotti,' Soma began, 'on the night of Friday, May ninth, of this year, can you tell us what you did?'

Giotti knew a thing or two about how to give testimony, and he looked at Soma, then the jury, then sat back and told his story. Although technically witnesses weren't permitted to give long answers – the lawyer was supposed to ask a series of questions – Giotti evidently wasn't inclined to do it that way, and Soma let him go on.

'I went out to dinner with my wife, Pat, to Lulu's. After we finished, she took her car back home. She'd been downtown earlier in the day and I decided to pick up some papers that I'd left at my office so I could review them over the weekend. My office is at the federal courthouse on Seventh Street, which happens to abut the alley where Sal Russo had his apartment.

'Mr Russo and I had been friends for many years and I'd made it a habit to buy fish from the back of his truck on Fridays, put it in a cooler in the trunk of my car, take it home for the weekend. On this Friday, Sal hadn't shown up so I thought I'd go check and see if he was all right. I knew he'd been sick. I was in the neighborhood anyway.'

'And what did you do then?' Soma prodded.

The heavy brow clouded. Giotti didn't appreciate getting prompted. He knew what he had to say and he'd get to it. The scowl faded slowly as he went on. 'I walked up and knocked on his door. There was a light on inside, but no one answered, so I tried the doorknob and it opened and I saw him – Sal – lying on the floor in his living room.'

'He was lying on the floor?' Soma asked.

Giotti's eyes narrowed. Soma wasn't scoring points with the judge. 'I said that, didn't I?'

Trying to recover, Soma stammered. 'Yes, you did. I'm sorry, Your Honor. So Sal Russo was lying on the floor? What did you do next?'

Giotti had delivered his message to Soma. Hardy wasn't about to object. The judge went on without interruption for another couple of minutes. He'd called 911, waited for the paramedics and the police – first two uniformed officers and then the inspectors – noticed the DNR sticker on the table, the syringe and vial, the bottle of whiskey. He didn't touch anything; he knew the drill. So he just waited, then answered the police questions and went home.

Though he'd guessed wrong on the timing, Hardy had assumed that Soma would call Giotti as a witness at some point, not because of any real strategic reason but simply because it was natural that the person who first came upon the body would be a necessary step in drawing the picture of what had happened. Giotti would fill in that blank.

But that was not Soma's only rationale. After asking Giotti one or two innocuous questions – a chair had been knocked over in the kitchen; the syringe and empty vial were on the low coffee table – he got to some meat.

'Your Honor, you've testified that Sal Russo was lying on the floor, is that right?'

'Yes.'

'Was there a chair or something nearby he could have been sitting on?'

Giotti closed his eyes, visualizing. 'His chair. He had an old recliner he liked. He was on the floor in front of that.'

'In other words, between the recliner and the coffee table?'

'Yes.'

Soma went back to his table, grabbed a photograph passed to him by Drysdale, had it entered as People's Exhibit One, and asked Giotti if the picture captured the reality he'd witnessed upon entered the apartment.

'That's the way it looked,' he agreed. 'Sal was on the floor, on his side, just like here.'

The image was clear and damaging, its message undeniable.

If something benign had happened, wouldn't Sal have been sitting in his favorite recliner, at least? Wouldn't his deliverer have tried to make him comfortable in his last moments? Instead, the victim lay on his side, in a hump on the floor. As though he'd been poleaxed.

Soma left the jury to ponder all of these things. He'd gotten what he wanted, so he thanked the judge and sat down.

Hardy felt that he and the federal judge were basically on the same side, although Giotti was, technically, a witness for the prosecution. His testimony in a fair world – ha! – should have come a little later in the trial, and Hardy had been almost looking forward to it; he thought he'd be able to put some points on the board. But first, now, he'd have to undo some of Soma's damage.

'Judge Giotti,' he began, 'you were good friends with Sal Russo, weren't you?'

A nod, genial. 'I'd known him for years, although we didn't socialize much anymore. We were close acquaintances.'

'And as his close acquaintance, did you see him often?'

Giotti considered this. 'As I said, almost every Friday I'd pick up some fish when I wasn't traveling. Once or twice I'd gone up to his apartment and had a drink with him. End of the day, end of the week.'

'On your visits to Sal's apartment for drinks, did he sit in his recliner?'

'Sure. Yes.' Then Giotti threw him a bone. 'Sometimes.'

'But not always?'

'No.'

'Where did he sit other times?'

'Your Honor!' Soma spoke quietly, reluctant to intrude upon Giotti's testimony. 'This is irrelevant.'

But Salter didn't think so. 'Overruled.'

Hardy repeated his question about where Sal sat. 'He'd sit anywhere,' Giotti said. 'Sal was a free spirit. He'd sit on the coffee table, on the recliner, the couch, the floor. He'd move around.'

'So he could have been sitting on the floor when he received this injection and—'

'Objection!' This was Drysdale, citing speculation, and this time Salter sustained him.

Hardy turned back to his table, and Freeman was surreptitiously motioning him over, so he pretended he was getting a drink of water. 'What?'

Armed with Freeman's quick advice and the photograph, he returned to the witness. 'Judge Giotti,' he said, 'looking here at People's One, is the reclining chair in a reclining position?'

Freeman, of course, had spotted that it wasn't. In the picture it appeared to be straight up, and Giotti said as much. 'Now, to the best of your recollection, was it like this when you entered the room?'

Giotti closed his eyes again briefly. 'I'd say yes. I don't remember it being down. I would have had to push it up to walk around it, and I didn't do that.'

This was good enough and Hardy would take it. He could later argue that Sal's body had simply either fallen out of its chair or, better, that he'd been seated on the floor when the injection was given. In all, he was heartened. Giotti had helped him. The jury would at least have some possible alternatives to consider. He considered it was time to move to the other point he'd originally intended to bring up.

'Judge Giotti, you've testified that you were aware that Sal was sick. Did you know he had Alzheimer's disease?'

'Not for sure, no.'

'Did you know he had cancer?'

'Your Honor!' Soma was behind Hardy, objecting, his voice developing its telltale shrillness. 'I fail to see relevance.'

And of course, in a legal sense, there wasn't much. But Hardy felt he had to get some human feeling for Sal's pain into the proceedings. He had a sense Giotti would cooperate.

First, though, Salter had to be gotten around. And the trial judge seemed to agree with Soma; Hardy's questions were irrelevant and unnecessary. But Giotti's authority cut both ways in the courtroom, and when he looked up at Salter and told him he didn't mind answering – though this was beside the point – Salter acquiesced and overruled the objection.

Giotti turned back to Hardy. 'The headaches were evidently pretty horrible. Sal told me' – now Giotti looked over to the jury, speaking to them – 'half kidding, but you knew he meant it, that if I didn't see him for a few days, I should check his apartment.

He might be dead. If he didn't die from the pain, he might just kill himself.'

'And is that why you did just that on May ninth? Stop by his apartment?'

'Essentially, yes. I think he'd planted that seed.'

Hardy nodded, pleased that he'd gotten it in. 'He knew he was going to die soon, is that what you're saying?'

Drysdale: 'Objection, speculation.'

'Sustained.'

Hardy: 'I'll rephrase, Your Honor. Judge Giotti, did Sal Russo ever seriously tell you he thought he was near death?'

Drysdale again: 'Objection.'

But Salter overruled this one, and Giotti nodded. 'Yes. He told me he'd be dead within a couple of months.'

'He knew that?'

'He thought he did, yes.'

'Thank you, Your Honor. That's all.' He turned to Soma. 'Redirect?'

But the prosecutors realized that perhaps, for all their fawning, Giotti was not exactly in their pocket, and they passed the witness.

As soon as the judge had left the stand, before he was through the bar back into the gallery, Salter pointed down at Soma with his gavel. 'Your next witness?'

'The People call John Strout.'

The tall man with the Deep South accent moved from the gallery into the bullpen, took the oath, and went around to the witness chair. Strout testified about once a week in one case or another and was a recognized forensic expert throughout the country. He often traveled to other jurisdictions to render second opinions on ambiguous causes of death. So he sat back, legs crossed, languidly at home on the stand, while Soma got his name, occupation, experience, on the record, asked the first few predictable questions.

Then, 'In other words, Dr Strout, are you saying that twelve milligrams of morphine injected directly into the vein is sufficient to cause death?'

Hardy thought if Strout were any more relaxed up there, he'd be dead. Which didn't mean he wasn't paying attention. He corrected Soma. 'Twelve milligrams intravenous *could* be sufficient to cause death, especially if there were other factors such as alcohol.'

'And was there alcohol in the case of Salvatore Russo?'

'Yes.'

'How much?'

'Well, his blood alcohol level was point one oh.'

'And is that a lot, Doctor? Was Sal Russo drunk?'

'In California he was legally drunk, yes.'

Hardy didn't have any idea where Soma was going with all these questions about Sal and drinking, and that worried him. So what if Sal had been drunk? How did it relate to Graham? How could it hurt him?

'Now, Doctor, could the alcohol level in the victim's blood contribute to the effect the morphine might have?'

Strout took his time, wanting to be precise. After a moment he uncrossed his legs and leaned forward in the witness box. 'Yes, it could have.'

'In what way?'

'With that much alcohol aboard, the morphine would have caused his blood pressure to drop rapidly.'

'Almost instantaneously?'

Strout nodded. 'Almost.'

'And then what would happen?'

'Well, with no blood pressure, you get no blood to your head and you pass out.'

This was the answer Soma expected, and he nodded, pleased. 'But if Sal Russo injected himself and went unconscious, he would not have had time to remove the needle from his arm, is that correct?'

'Yes.'

'And in this photo' – Soma entered the Polaroid print into evidence – 'can you see the syringe on a table near the body with the cap in place over it, Doctor?'

'Yes.'

'Then, assuming that the needle was found as shown in the photo, and assuming further that Mr Russo did fall unconscious from the combined effect of alcohol and morphine, it is true, is it not, that this scenario is not consistent with Sal Russo having administered the morphine himself?'

'Yes,' Strout replied. 'Assuming those facts as true, this morphine was not self-administered.'

Hardy scribbled a note. He would hammer Strout with all of this 'consistent' and 'inconsistent' in his cross-examination, but he understood Soma's point, and he thought the jury would too. Soma made it sound as though Strout were saying that someone had killed Sal Russo. It wasn't a suicide.

But Soma, well on his way to establishing that, had more, and not in the category of maybe. 'Dr Strout, was there any evidence of trauma on the victim's body?'

Strout nodded, going on about the bruise to the head, behind the ear.

'Could this bruise have knocked the victim out?'

'Briefly. Yes, I think so.'

'Do you know what could have caused this bruise?'

Hardy objected, citing speculation, but was overruled. This fell well within the doctor's realm of expertise. 'Well, whatever it was didn't cause a concussion and left no imprint on the skull. I can say only that it was a relatively heavy blunt object without sharp edges.'

'Such as a whiskey bottle?'

'Objection. This *is* speculation, Your Honor.'

'Overruled.'

'Yes,' Strout answered. 'This would be consistent with the whiskey bottle at the scene.'

Soma kept at it, staccato style, barely taking time to draw breath between questions. 'How about the injection site? How did that look?'

'Well, there was trauma there too.'

'What do you mean by trauma?'

'In layperson's terms the skin and muscles were slightly torn as the needle was coming out. Like a deep scratch.'

'Not as the needle was going in?'

'No. Definitely not.' A small but important point, since a skilled shot-giver like Graham wouldn't have botched the injection itself, whereas a jerk or a struggle after the needle was in could happen to anyone.

Soma thanked Strout and walked back to the prosecution table, where he glanced at some papers on the desk. Hardy was ready to pounce with objections should Soma, as he expected, try to wrap it up.

The picture, Hardy thought, was clear enough. Somebody loaded the victim up with alcohol, then hit him on the head, knocking him out long enough to get the shot in the vein, in the middle of which Sal jerked, either in spasm or waking up.

All of that would be speculation on Strout's part, and not admissible.

But Hardy didn't get his opportunity to object. Soma simply turned to him, amicable and professional for the jury's benefit. 'Your witness.'

Hardy took it right to him. 'Dr Strout, did Sal Russo kill himself or did somebody kill him?'

Crossing his legs to get more comfortable, Strout settled in the witness chair. 'Well, from the pure forensic evidence, it could have been either.'

'Are you saying there is no way to tell, from a strictly medical standpoint, whether Sal Russo killed himself or someone else killed him?'

'Yes, that's what I'm saying.' Strout waited. An experienced witness, he wasn't about to lead an attorney so he could be interrupted and made to look unprofessional.

Hardy nodded, apparently intrigued with these unearthed truths. 'Is there anything in the forensic evidence, Doctor, that would lead you to think one is more likely than the other?'

Strout thought this over briefly. 'No.'

'What about this bruise on the head we've heard about? Did that contribute to Sal Russo's death in a medical sense?'

'No.'

'Not at all?'

'No, not at all. It was possibly enough to knock out Mr Russo, but it had nothing to do with his death.'

Hardy feigned a small surprise, bringing in the jury. 'Doctor, did you just say that this bruise was *possibly* enough to knock out Mr Russo?'

'Yes. It could have.'

'And are you saying it might *not* have?'

'That's right too.' Strout was showing a hint of impatience. 'I said it wasn't very serious.'

'Yes, you did, thank you, Doctor. Essentially it was just a bump on the head, isn't that right?'

'Yes.'

'Now, was the head trauma suffered before or after the injection?'

'I can't say.'

'So Sal Russo might have injected himself, fallen over, and hit his head?'

'Yes.'

'And if the head injury happened before the injection, can you tell how long before could it have happened?'

Strout thought for a moment. 'Only from the bruising, within a day or two.'

Hardy feigned shock and disbelief. 'Doctor, do you mean you can't even say that Sal Russo got the bump on his head on the same *day* as his death?'

'Not for sure.'

'Not for sure. Well, then, Doctor, is it correct to say you don't know if this bump on the head has any connection at all to Sal Russo's death?'

'Yes, that would be correct.'

'Good.' Soma had wanted to use Strout's testimony to prove that a murder had taken place, but Hardy didn't think it was going to work. He started hammering at another nail. 'You've also told us about a trauma at the injection site. You said it was consistent with someone injecting Sal with the morphine. Yes?'

'Correct.'

'But it's also consistent with Sal Russo injecting himself, isn't it?'

'Yes, that's true too.'

'Sal Russo might have jerked as he was injecting himself, mightn't he?'

'Objection!' Soma stood, which Hardy took as a good sign. The trial had barely begun, and already the younger attorney's placid demeanor was showing signs of turbulence. 'Speculation, Your Honor.'

This was overruled. Hardy tried to keep his face neutral. Strout said he was correct: Sal might have jerked as he was injecting himself.

Hardy nodded genially and pressed on. 'Doctor, there's one last point I'd like you to clarify. Didn't you tell Mr Soma that Sal Russo had a blood alcohol level of point one oh, and that because of this, he might have become unconscious while the needle was still in his vein, and therefore not have been able to withdraw it?'

'Yes, that's what I said.'

'You said this scenario was consistent with your finding, didn't you?'

'Yes.'

'But consistent only means it *could* be true, not that it *is* true. You can't rule out other scenarios, can you?'

'No.'

'So even with Sal Russo's elevated blood alcohol, might this just as easily *not* have happened?'

'Yes.'

'In other words, Doctor, just to be perfectly clear about this, there is nothing in your findings or testimony that indicates that Sal Russo did *not* kill himself. Would that be an accurate statement?'

'Yes.'

'This could be a simple suicide, couldn't it?'

'Yes.'

Salter was frowning and Hardy liked the look of it. When you get a coroner saying you don't necessarily even have a crime, an overworked judge might find himself wondering why he was presiding over a murder trial.

Hardy thanked the witness, but before he'd gotten back to his table, Soma was up on redirect. 'Dr Strout,' he said, 'you're not saying that this *was* a suicide, are you?'

'No.'

'And why was that?'

Strout shrugged, a drop of impatience finally leaking out. 'There was just no way to tell, one way or the other.'

Hardy went home for dinner, stayed for most of two hours, kissed his little darlings good-night, then headed downtown again, first to the jail to keep Graham company and discuss the day's events and their ongoing strategy, then back to his office for a more critical postmortem with David Freeman.

When he got back home at eleven-fifteen, he was ready to collapse and not altogether thrilled to find Sarah Evans at his dining-room table, talking with Frannie over coffee cups. 'If that's decaf,' he said, 'I'll have some, though I'm philosophically opposed to the idea of it.'

His wife offered a cheek for a kiss.

In the past months Evans had become Sarah. The midnight phone calls gave way to the occasional meeting here at the house. She and Frannie, close to the same age, had interests in common. Sarah was talking about getting married, having babies; Frannie now about joining the police department. Both wanted all this to happen in the future sometime. They'd had some good discussions. Frannie said, 'Sarah and I have decided that when the kids are gone, I should be a cop. Not a family counselor after all.'

Hardy pulled up a chair. 'Good idea, I mean it. Fast times, great benefits. A really swell clientele. You'd enjoy it. But do you want to hear my idea about after the kids are gone?'

'Okay, what?'

'You travel the world and go to exotic ports with your retired husband and be his love slave.'

Frannie put a hand over his. 'The reason I love him,' she said. 'It's that wacky sense of humor.' Frannie patted his hand. 'He's had a long day.'

Mentioning Hardy's day brought them all back to reality, but especially Sarah. It was why she had come over. As a witness she wasn't allowed in the courtroom. She'd worked in the field all day and by now was a wreck, needing to know how it had gone. Hardy was honest with her. 'It's Soma's turn. He gets to lay out his case first. Later I show up and slay him.'

Not amused, Sarah sighed. 'I just don't feel like I've done enough.'

'You've done more on this case than any cop I've ever heard of, Sarah.'

'It still doesn't feel like enough. If they've only got one suspect and that's Graham, then all Soma's got to do is make the murder and there's no other option.'

Hardy knew that this was mostly true, and it wasn't much

comfort to him either. And he didn't even want to start on his fears about the jury. Putting a good face on it, he kept his tone light. 'He won't make the murder.'

'But, Dismas, it *was* a murder. You and I both think it was a murder.'

'You do?' Frannie suddenly asked.

Uh-oh, Hardy thought. He hadn't consciously been trying to hide anything from Frannie, but neither had he wanted to burden his wife with all the ins and outs of the case. She had her own life she was handling here on the home front, and much more efficiently, he felt, than he was handling many parts of his.

He had outlined for her the general theory of his defense and told her that he honestly believed that Graham hadn't done it, but not that someone else had.

One of Frannie's main complaints about her husband being involved with murder trials was the fact that he would be working with someone who had killed someone on purpose and thus had a slightly better-than-average chance of doing it again, perhaps to his attorney and/or attorney's family.

Now Hardy shrugged. 'It could have been. We knew that.'

Frannie played with it for a while, then balled a fist and brought it down on the table. 'Shit,' she said. 'Just shit.'

'What?' Sarah asked. 'Didn't we know it?'

'We knew it,' Hardy assured her. 'Frannie didn't.'

Sarah reached a hand over the table. 'That's what I've been looking for all this time, Fran. Who killed Sal.'

Her flat, stunned gaze went from one of them to the other. She let out a deep breath. 'I'm going to bed.' And she was up and out of the room.

Sarah started to rise, to follow her. 'Let her go,' Hardy said. 'It's all right. I'll talk to her.'

She sat back down, arms crossed. 'I'm sorry, I thought . . . I should go.'

'No,' he said sharply. 'I want you to understand that we've got an outstanding defense going here. Even David Freeman thinks it's good, and he's Mikey as far as I'm concerned. It's going to work. I believe it will work.'

'And what if it doesn't?'

He didn't answer. There wasn't an answer.

Sarah had her elbows on the table and blew into her steepled hands. 'I could just quit my job,' she said. 'I could work on it full time.'

Hardy shook his head. 'You're better inside.'

'I'm no good. I haven't found anything. Sal wasn't carrying anybody's money that I can find. Hadn't for years. Not even a sniff of it. Nobody killed what's-his-name for his fish business.'

'Pio,' Hardy said, hating his damned memory.

'I should go strong-arm George, Graham's brother. Shake him down. Find out where he was.'

'And get fired?'

'It doesn't matter. If he did it . . .'

Hardy reached across the table and touched her elbow. 'Slow down. Slow down. Take a breath.' He waited. 'Listen, this is always the worst, after you're committed and you don't know how it's going to go. You just got to believe you made the right decision, that's how it's going to work.'

'But I can't just sit here! I can't!'

'Graham's just sitting there.'

This seemed to hit home. She took a breath, let it out heavily. 'So? What then? I can't believe we've got a righteous suspect with no alibi and nobody's even—'

'No, we don't. Who's that?'

'George.'

Hardy shook his head. 'George is not any kind of suspect. He doesn't need an alibi. Nobody saw him near Sal's, ever. There's no prints, no medical background, no real knowledge of his father's situation, even. If he was going to kill Sal out of rage, he would have done it differently. If he knew he was going to die soon anyway, why would he do it at all? Besides, he wouldn't let his brother go to prison for the rest of his life.'

'I bet he would if it came down to either Graham or him.'

Hardy pondered a moment. 'Look, Sarah, it wasn't Graham, right?'

'Of course.'

'He really didn't do it? That's what you think?'

She stared at him. 'You do?'

'No, as a matter of fact, I don't. He didn't do it, so I'm going on the assumption that they can't prove he did. That's the system.

I've got to believe in it.' In fact, Hardy had serious doubts about the system, and supposed that Sarah did, too, but this wasn't the time to air them. 'Look,' he said, 'if it makes you feel better, use some police magic and see if you can find out where George went, get some hard evidence: maybe he used a credit card, made a phone call.'

'I wish Abe—'

Hardy shook his head, stopping her. 'Abe's got a suspect in custody. How is he going to justify continuing an investigation?'

Sarah sighed. 'I know,' she said at last. 'I know. It's just so frustrating.'

'And you're on the list for tomorrow, right?' Meaning the witness list – she would probably be called the next day. 'You ought to get some sleep. It'll look better with a little rest.'

She sighed a last time and stood up. 'Do you want me to go in and talk to Frannie?'

'That's all right,' Hardy said. 'We'll work it out.'

Frannie was asleep, lying on her side facing away from his half of the bed. Her breathing was neither regular nor heavy, but she was asleep.

That was her story and she was sticking to it.

28

Hardy's official workday the next morning carried over the tension from his kitchen. He'd finally fallen asleep after one o'clock and was up at five-thirty, going over his notes, trying to second-guess what would happen in the courtroom that day.

Frannie did not get up to make his coffee.

He was out of the house – he *had* to be out of the house – by seven-thirty, just as the kids and his wife were getting to the breakfast table. Kiss the kids good-bye – all he was doing anymore with them. Eyes from Frannie, no words in front of the children. Tonight maybe.

Then, at the Hall, waiting and waiting for his partner and costrategist, David Freeman, who hadn't arrived by the time the bailiffs brought Graham into the holding cell, surfer hair combed back neatly. He was putting on his civilian coat and tie at a few minutes after nine o'clock.

'Where's Yoda?' Graham had christened Freeman after the Star Wars gnome. Hardy thought it a fairly astute characterization.

'I don't know. Probably doing a little cold-fusion work, keep his hand in.' Studied nonchalance. In truth, though, Freeman's absence left him with a low-voltage sense of unease – a good-luck charm misplaced. As though he needed any more bad vibes. But there was no point harping on it. Other matters pressed.

Hardy looked around behind him, lowered his voice. 'You talk to Sarah this morning? She came by my house last night. She wants to go after your brother.'

'I know. We talked about it.' Graham's massive hands were making confetti from the edges of a yellow legal pad. 'I don't think it's a bad idea.'

'You don't? You did last time I asked.' In the early days, when

Hardy was gearing up for his 'some other dude did it' defense, he'd questioned Graham about George's motives and opportunities. Graham had laughed at him; there was no chance his brother could have been involved. Now he was singing a different tune.

Graham looked as though he'd eaten some bad cheese. 'Maybe I'm finally getting pissed off. I've been thinking about me, you know, my situation here' – he motioned toward the door to the courtroom – 'all this. But you know what?'

The eyes seemed to reach all the way into his soul. This was no act, or if it was, it was one Hardy hadn't seen before in nearly five months of daily contact.

'What?' Hardy asked. 'But quiet, okay?' He raised his eyes, suddenly aware of voices from the courtroom, from the jury box, which was haphazardly filling up.

Graham leaned in toward him. 'Somebody did kill Sal, Diz. That's the thing. With all this concentration on getting me off, we kind of pushed that under the rug. Now I think about it, I want the son of a bitch, I don't care if it's Georgie.'

'And you think it is?'

'I'd like to make sure it isn't, let's put it that way. You know what I think? You know how I told you if Leland pays you, he gets something for it?'

'Yeah.'

'What he's getting here is keeping you off his favored son.'

Maybe on more sleep, with Freeman at his side and his wife not mad at him, Hardy would have reacted more coolly. But he felt a rush of blood, heard a pounding of it in his ears. He clipped it out. 'I hope I'm not hearing you say you think I'm in Leland's pocket.'

'Easy, Diz. I don't think you meant to be.'

'I'm just too stupid to see it, right?'

Part of it, of course – suddenly clear – was that it could have been true, and Hardy in fact hadn't seen it. By paying Hardy's bills for Graham's defense, Leland Taylor had effectively defused any investigations Hardy might have otherwise considered pursuing within the Taylor family.

Graham shrugged. 'It's an obvious stone and it's unturned.'

'There's no way to turn it.' Hardy's voice echoed in the holding cell. 'Glitsky won't look at it. Sarah risks her job if she . . .' He shook his head. 'You know this. There's no way.'

Graham remained calm. For one of the very first times Hardy got a glimpse of the legal mind that had gotten his client his federal clerkship. 'There's no way without alienating Leland, that's true. And he's set us up so we won't. It's subtle and it's sweet, and that's the way my stepfather works.'

'You think he's protecting George?'

Another shrug. 'I know from Mom that he doesn't know where George was. I know it worries the shit out of him. And Leland thinks a couple of other things.'

'Like what?'

'One, there's bettable odds you're going to get me off, so there's no real risk anyway, just a few more months of my already wasted life. I'm a pawn he'll risk losing to save his bishop.'

'What's the other one?'

'Sal's death wasn't any great loss. He was old and feeble and a pain in the ass. If Georgie killed him, it wasn't like a *real* murder. More like putting down a dog. Sal was a nonentity when he was alive. He didn't count, not to Leland. And he would be dead anyway in a couple of months. What does it matter?'

Hardy sat back in his chair, ran a hand through his hair – shades of Dean Powell.

'Tell him,' Graham said. 'See what he does.'

'Tell who?'

'Leland. Tell him you're going to be looking into George's alibi. See if he cuts off the money or, even better, offers you more if you don't. Then at least we'll know.'

'We won't know about George.'

'But we'll know for sure why Leland's in. This is money, after all, thicker than blood. Georgie's the heir apparent to the bank. If he killed Sal – hell, any scandal . . . good-bye line of succession.'

'I'll tell him,' Hardy said. He dug his thumbs into his eyes, a wave of exhaustion washing over him. He suddenly wondered if he wouldn't be wise to plead some kind of personal crisis – toothache, migraine, chest pains – and ask Salter for a one-day continuance.

But this was only day two of the marathon that was the trial proper. It was unimaginable, but he knew he'd be more fatigued than this before it was over. If he was going to beg a day off – highly frowned upon – it should at least be when the danger of dropping dead from exhaustion was a real possibility.

But he couldn't give in to any of this – it was the devil. 'I might as well tell him we're looking at Debra too.'

'My sister?'

'Debra's a big reason you're here.'

Graham shook his head. 'I don't think so.'

'Believe it,' Hardy said. 'I was reading Sarah's reports this morning getting ready for her testimony. First phone call she made on the case was to Debra.'

'And what did Debra say?'

'She told Sarah you were probably lying. You couldn't be trusted. She was the one who brought up the baseball cards, before anybody even knew about the money. She got Sarah looking at you, Graham. That's what started it.'

'She's so stupid,' he said flatly.

'She also works at a vet's, right? She gives shots to animals? My guts tell me a lethal injection is more a woman's way to kill than a man's. Debra needs the money more than anybody else.'

Graham had his head in his hands. 'No no no. That's not it. It's nothing like that.'

'What's it like, then? You tell me.'

Sitting back, crossing his arms, Graham came back to Hardy, his voice low. 'Deb and I were close until I was out of law school. She didn't buy into the Taylor magic the way Mom and Georgie did, so we were on the same team. Then she married Brendan.

'So two years after she's married I'm at this nightclub and I look over and here's Brendan flossing the tonsils of some babe who is not Debra. So I go over a little closer, make sure. Yep, it's Brendan. He's cheating on my sister.

'So what do I do, the good brother? First I kick Brendan's ass, then I go tell her.' He let out a long sigh. 'So she's got two options, right? She either believes me and confronts Brendan, or she wimps out and tells herself some other story, like her brother's lying to her instead of her husband.'

'But why would you lie to her?'

'I never liked Brendan. I didn't think he was good enough for her, which, P.S., he isn't. I'm trying to ruin her marriage.' He spread his palms. 'So anyway Brendan got home before I went to tell her and made up his own story first. He told her I'd been drunk and just teed off on him for no reason. So she blew up at me for beating up the son of a bitch, threw me out of her house, called me a liar. I wasn't happy in my life and couldn't stand it that she was.'

'So that's it?'

'That's it. I'm a liar. Brendan's a good husband who loves her. End of story.'

Promptly at nine-thirty Salter pointed again at Soma, and he rose at his table. 'The People call Sergeant Philip Parini.'

David Freeman still hadn't made his appearance.

This was the first Hardy had seen of the Crime Scene Investigations specialist who'd drawn the Russo case, although he'd read his reports. The man himself was slight of build and precise of movement. His tailor had done a very good job on the dark blue suit. Parini parted his wispy crown of black hair in the middle of his head. A ramrod in the witness box, he rested his folded hands on the wooden railing in front of him.

From the middle of the courtroom Soma was ready once again to try to establish that a murder had taken place. 'Sergeant Parini, was your unit the first to arrive at the scene – Sal Russo's apartment at the Lions Arms?'

'Oh, no, not at all. Judge Giotti was there. We also had paramedics, a couple of uniformed officers who had secured the scene, and inspectors Lanier and Evans.'

'And can you tell the jury what you found there?'

Parini cleared his throat, but there was no sense that it was out of nerves. He wanted to be clearly understood, that was all. 'First, I double-checked with the officers that nothing had been disturbed. The paramedics had arrived a few minutes after the officers and had been apprised of the DNR situation. The victim was clearly deceased. The lead EMT told me that the body had already cooled perceptibly by the time they arrived.' This was hearsay, but Hardy didn't object; it wasn't the issue.

'And would you describe the body, then, as you found it?'

Parini ran his pro-forma description, which he then verified against the photograph that was People's One.

As this was going on, Freeman pushed open the swinging section of the bar rail, patted Hardy on the shoulder, and sat down at the defense table, on the other side of Graham. Hardy shot him a questioning look and Freeman mouthed, 'Later.'

Soma, in the center of the courtroom, didn't even notice the minor interruption. He was back at the witness. 'So, Sergeant Parini, based on your training and experience, did the position of Sal Russo's body look like a suicide to you?'

'Objection.' Hardy remained seated. 'Speculation.'

From his bench Salter was a bit of a ramrod himself. 'No, this is informed opinion, Mr Hardy. Your objection is overruled. Sergeant Parini, you may answer the question.'

Parini nodded. The drill of the witness stand had its own rhythm, and the sergeant was familiar with it. He waited while the court reporter reread Soma's question and then picked it right up. 'Yes, my initial impression, from the body – not just that it was on the floor. Its position was unnatural.'

'Unnatural how?'

'It seemed to have been dropped there.'

Soma did some light pantomime, sharing the import of this fact with the jury. 'Did you find anything else, Sergeant, that led you to conclude that this was a homicide?'

'Yes, I did. There was a whiskey bottle – Old Crow bourbon – on its side on the floor under the table. Its cap wasn't on tight and quite a bit of the whiskey had seeped out onto the floor.'

'And what was the significance of that, in your opinion?'

Hardy thought he could object, but he'd be overruled again. In the view of the criminal courts Crime Scene Investigations inspectors – so long as their training and experience was ritually invoked – had nearly the authority of expert witnesses. They were allowed a wide latitude in what would otherwise be speculation.

So Hardy kept quiet and listened to the words, all the more damning because he thought the theory they supported was what had, in fact, happened.

It just hadn't happened with Graham.

Parini went ahead with the confidence of someone who'd thought it all through carefully. 'I think the most reasonable explanation was that it was either knocked over in a struggle or perhaps kicked over in an assailant's haste to get out of the apartment. It was still dripping slowly when I got there.'

'Did you find the syringe, Sergeant?'

'Yes. It was right there on the top of the coffee table, capped, along with an empty vial.'

'In other words, the needle was not in the victim's arm, was it?'

'No.'

'And what did you do with this syringe and vial?'

'I bagged it and sent it to the lab for analysis, fingerprinting, and so on.'

'And can you tell us, Sergeant, what the lab found?'

'That the vial had contained morphine, and that there were fingerprints on both it and the syringe.'

'And did you identify these fingerprints?'

'Yes, we did. They belong to the defendant, Graham Russo.'

Parini stayed on the stand for the better part of two hours. He described the chair on the floor in the kitchen, the scratches on the cabinetry, the safe, Graham's fingerprints all over the place, even on the DNR tube. Soma entered the vial, the syringe, the bottle of Old Crow, the tube and sticker, into evidence. It all took time, and Salter called a halt for lunch before Hardy could begin his cross-examination.

Hardy gathered his papers, asked Graham what they wanted to order for lunch. Freeman was uncharacteristically silent, brooding, leading the way for the three of them back to their holding cell behind the courtroom. When they got there, Freeman waited and let them both pass, then told Hardy that maybe he ought to sit down.

Graham took off his coat and was twisting his body back and forth, exercising. Hardy cricked his own back. 'I've been sitting all morning, David. What's up?'

Freeman shrugged. It had to come out anyway, and if Hardy wanted to stand, so be it. 'I got a call at the office. One of the associates in crisis.' He paused. 'Michelle, as a matter of fact.'

Hardy made a face. Some kind of blow-up with Tryptech had been bound to happen sooner or later, they'd been in wait-and-delay mode for so long, some judge had probably decided enough was enough and set a hearing date in the next couple of weeks. But then another thought occurred. 'Why didn't she call me?'

Freeman blew out a breath. 'Well, she feels a little awkward.' Graham stopped his calisthenics, listening. Something in Freeman's tone . . .

'You know Ovangevale Networks?'

This was like asking Hardy if he'd heard of Disneyland. Ovangevale had come from nowhere and grown like ragweed in the last five years with its internet applications. They were the new kids on the block and a powerhouse in the industry.

Hardy swore. 'They stole her, didn't they?'

'Not quite.'

Graham looked over at Hardy. 'I love the way Yoda strings it out, don't you? You want to go out for the sandwiches, David, let us have a guessing game till you get back?'

'What?' Hardy asked simply.

Freeman rolled his eyes. 'They're buying Tryptech,' he said.

'No, they're not. That's impossible.' Hardy flatly didn't believe it. 'Not with this lawsuit hanging, they'd—'

'Their own lawyers did some back-door contingency deal. They got the Port of Oakland to go along if Tryptech would settle for twelve five.'

'Twelve five!' Hardy's voice echoed in the tiny space. 'We can get close to thirty and they're—'

Freeman held up his hand. 'It's an albatross, Diz. They don't care about the short-term loss, they just want it out of the way. Get on to new business, move ahead.'

'So how long has Tryptech known about this?' He whirled with nowhere to go. 'I've got to call Michelle. Why didn't she call me?'

Although he knew at least one reason why: he hadn't been there for her over these last months.

'Well, that's the other thing,' Freeman said. He took in a breath. 'The tender offer's at fifteen a share. She'd been getting paid now for four months in discounted shares, as you knew.'

'Yeah, I knew.' Hardy's head was going light. He'd turned down the same offer, but Michelle didn't have a family to support. She could afford to take the risk. He found himself sitting down finally on the concrete bench.

Freeman was going on. 'One and a half,' he said.

'One and a half what?'

'The discounted share price. The original talk was two, you remember, but it finally went out at one and a half. Michelle's got over forty thousand shares.'

Hardy was still trying to make sense of this. Sluggishly, his brain tried to compute the numbers, but the zeroes slowed him up and Graham had him by several seconds. 'That's six hundred thousand dollars,' he said.

Never looking more like Yoda, the infinitely kind, infinitely wise, infinitely sad Freeman met Hardy's eyes. 'She feels really bad about this, Diz. She wanted me to break it to you.'

A sense of unreality hung over the afternoon. One part of Hardy realized that of course he was standing in the middle of the courtroom in Department 27, asking Parini questions. Most of him, though, felt as if it were floating somewhere in the ozone, disembodied, the precious silver astral cord snapped forever.

Six hundred thousand dollars for four months' work!

'Sergeant, does the fact that you found Graham Russo's fingerprints on many surfaces in the room mean that he had been there on that day?'

'No.' Parini remained an eloquent robot. Although police inspectors tended to be witnesses for the prosecution, he was answering the defense counsel with the same cooperative efficiency. 'Fingerprints are oil based. There's no real time limit. A fingerprint on something only means that sometime the finger came in contact with it.'

'So are you saying that Graham might not have been in his father's apartment on that day at all?'

'Yes. There would be no way to tell.'

'All right.'

Nothing's all right! He could have had that money! He'd be free!

'I'd like to ask you a question about this whiskey bottle, if I may. Dr Strout has already testified that Sal Russo was legally drunk at the time of the injection. Was the bottle under the table within reach of his arm?'

'Yes, I'd say so.'

'So that, as Sal was lying there, he could have reached for the bottle and knocked it over? Would that have been possible?'

'Yes.'

'And yet didn't you tell Mr Soma that the bottle had probably been kicked over or knocked over during a fight?'

'That was a surmise,' Parini said.

'There might not have been a struggle at all, is that what you're saying?'

'That conclusion isn't inescapable from the whiskey bottle, yes, that's what I'm saying.'

Hardy put on a smile. *Who could smile at a time like this?* He included the jury. 'Good. A last question about the bottle. Did you find anything on it that indicated it had been used as a weapon of any kind? To hit Sal behind the ear, for example?'

'No, we didn't.'

'None of his hairs? No blood?'

'No. Neither.'

'Any fingerprints that weren't Sal's?'

'No.'

'But you did find Graham's fingerprints, did you not, on the vial of morphine and on the syringe?'

'Yes, we did.'

Hardy thought this was clear enough. Certainly it would be absurd to believe that Graham had come in wearing gloves against leaving his fingerprints, picked up the bottle and knocked his father out with it, then taken off his gloves to administer the shot.

It was time to move to the next point. 'Now I'd like to ask you about the kitchen, where the chair was on its side. How wide is this room?'

'Not wide at all. Eight feet or so.'

'And where are the stove and refrigerator?'

'They're both against the right wall.'

'And is there a sink and counter?'

'Yes, a sink at the end and a wraparound counter against the opposite wall.'

'So are you saying there is a kind of corridor between the sink's counter and the stove and refrigerator?'

'Yes, that's the way it was set up. With a window at the end, over the sink.'

'It must be a narrow corridor, isn't it?'

Parini knew that *narrow* was open to interpretation. He clarified it. 'Four feet, maybe less.'

'But wasn't there a table in the kitchen, too, set into this corridor?'

'Yes, there was.'

'And did it appear to be in its normal position in the room?'

Parini gave this question a bit of thought, as though the idea hadn't occurred to him. Perhaps it hadn't. 'Yes, it was centered, about where I'd expect it to have been.'

'So are you saying that it didn't appear to have been knocked sideways or in any way out of position in this purported struggle in the kitchen that was so violent, it knocked over the chair and scratched the cabinets?'

'No. It was in the center of the corridor.'

'And besides the chair and the scratches in the cabinetry, were there any other signs of struggle in the kitchen?'

'No.'

'Just a chair lying on its side?'

'That's all.'

'Were there dishes on the drain? Cups, glasses, plates?'

'Yes there were.'

'And had any of these been knocked over by this supposedly violent struggle between two large men in the relatively tiny enclosure of the kitchen?'

Soma was up behind him, objecting. 'Leading the witness, Your Honor.'

But on cross-examination the defense attorney is allowed to do just that. Salter knew this and correctly overruled Soma.

'Was there anything you saw in the kitchen, Sergeant Parini, that would rule out the possibility that Sal Russo, drunk as he was, could just as easily have staggered against the chair, knocked it over, and simply left it there?'

This was the crux and Soma knew it. He objected again on grounds of speculation, and Hardy waited in suspension for Salter to rule.

Hardy was coming back to the present, though still sick in his heart. Walking an invisible tightrope between very close interpretations of the same evidence, he thought he'd phrased the question well. For his purposes all he needed was doubt about the struggle. Someone else could have been with Sal, could have helped him die, but there must not appear in the minds of the jurors that there had been any fight.

The judge finally spoke. 'No, the question stands. I'll overrule the objection. Sergeant, you may answer.'

The reporter read it back, and Parini gave it a reasonable amount of time. 'No,' he said. 'He could have stumbled against it just as easily. Nothing ruled it out.'

All at once his frustration over Michelle's Tryptech treasure gave way to enthusiasm to plumb the vein he'd hit with Parini. In the midst of these emotions Hardy made a cardinal mistake. Forgetting one of the first precepts of cross-examination, which is never to ask a question for which you don't know the answer, he said, 'In fact, Sergeant, isn't it true that there was *nothing* in the apartment that pointed to a struggle between Sal Russo and some purported assailant?'

'Well, no, that isn't true. There was the position of the body.'

Covering quickly, Hardy strolled back to his table and, stalling, took a drink of water. 'That's right, Sergeant, the position of the body. You said earlier that it looked like Sal Russo got dropped, do I have that right?'

'That's right.'

Hardy was moving to the exhibit table. Having dug himself this hole, he remembered that the Chinese used the same word for *disaster* and *opportunity*. He picked up People's One. 'Do you mean that the victim was not in the same position as shown here?'

Parini glanced at the photo. 'No. That's how he was.'

'And to your mind, does that look like he was dropped?'

'Yes.'

'Or fell after being hit? Knocked out?'

'Yes. He was sort of crumpled.'

Hardy knew where he was going and he picked up the pace. 'Looking now at People's One, Sergeant, where the victim is lying sort of crumpled as you put it. By this do you mean his legs are curled up under him? Not stretched out?'

'Yes.'

'As they might have been, say, if he'd been sitting on the floor and then collapsed with loss of consciousness?'

Parini did not answer. The unflappable witness darted a quick glance toward the prosecution table. Hardy didn't wait for him. 'Isn't it true, Sergeant Parini, that Sal Russo's position is exactly consistent with a collapse from a sitting position?'

'Well, it would—'

'Yes or no, Sergeant. Isn't that true?'

'Yes, I suppose so.'

'And having collapsed in this unnatural position with his legs under him, might his arm have fallen in such a way to knock over the whiskey bottle we've heard about that was under the table?'

'It might have, but—'

'Is that a yes, Sergeant? Yes, it might have?'

Parini hated it, but he nodded. 'Yes.'

Hardy took a breath. 'All right, one last point. You've testified that the syringe and vial were left sitting on the coffee table. Would you describe for the jury in what way, if any, these implements show any evidence of a struggle, or haste, or violence?'

Parini studied his lap for a moment, then met Hardy's eyes. 'There was none.'

'And the lamp in the room, Sergeant, had it been knocked over?'

'No.'

'Had the glass been knocked off the table?'

'No.'

'Was the table itself knocked over?'

'No.'

Hardy nodded, walked over to the exhibit table, and picked up a handful of Polaroids. 'Sergeant Parini, as we've seen, these photos show dozens of objects in this room, do they not? Was any one of them broken, or out of place, or disturbed in any fashion that you could tell?'

Parini's scowl was profound. 'No.'

'So would it be fair to say that your opinion that this scene shows a struggle is based entirely on the position of the body and a whiskey bottle out of the place on the floor?'

Parini hesitated, but couldn't think of anything else to bolster his testimony. 'That's right, I suppose.'

'You suppose, I see. And you've already said that both the position of the body and the whiskey bottle can be explained without reference to any alleged struggle, isn't that true?'

Hardy felt he couldn't have scripted Parini's reaction any more perfectly. The sergeant crossed his arms over his chest and leaned back in the witness chair. Intransigence incarnate. Or, Hardy thought, bullheaded stupidity.

'Well, counselor, it's my opinion there was a struggle.'

'Precisely,' Hardy said. 'That's your *opinion*.'

Hardy hadn't said a word about the safe, about all the evidence of Graham's presence. There were a dozen areas into which he could have wandered, but only one that did his client any good. He'd damned well rebutted the argument that two grown men had left any sign of a struggle in the apartment.

This didn't mean that Sal Russo hadn't been cold-cocked from behind with the whiskey bottle and fallen like a lump – which Hardy believed was what had transpired – but that there was no evidence to support that theory. He'd leave it at that.

29

Sarah was next.

The prosecution might have a secretly hostile witness in the female inspector, but she couldn't do anything about the cards she held. They were excellent for Graham's enemies. Directly after the midafternoon recess, after stretching and coffee or cigarettes, the men on the jury were especially unlikely to lose interest with a pretty woman on the stand.

She wasn't in one of her cop suits, which were purposely formless and without style. Knowing that she'd be testifying, Sarah thought she should look as good as she could. So she was wearing a red silk blouse that showed no skin but shimmered tantalizingly over her breasts with each breath, with the beating of her heart. A short combed woolen skirt and low pumps flattered her good legs. Her hair was off her face, falling to her shoulders.

When she came through the bar rail, Hardy put a hand over his client's arm, squeezed hard enough to draw blood. 'Look down,' he whispered. 'She catches your eyes, you're both done for.'

Inexplicably, perhaps ominously, Art Drysdale rose and walked to the center of the courtroom. Hardy caught a worried glance from Sarah but, like his client, could make no sign that it meant anything. He looked across to Freeman, who shrugged again, but beneath the nonchalance Hardy detected a note of concern. Could they have found out? Would Drysdale, in his homespun way, hang Sarah out to dry?

If so, there was no immediate sign. Drysdale quickly introduced himself to the jury and to Sarah and started in. As he was going along with it, Hardy began to see the logic behind choosing Drysdale for this witness. Endlessly affable, he would remain the same calm and reassuring inquisitor as he drove home lie after lie after lie.

Soma, on the other hand, by about the fifth lie, would have his adrenaline running. Unable to stop himself, he would speed up. And this was evidence to be savored, lingered over.

This was a lovely young woman putting stake after stake into the heart of a handsome man. It would have been a very difficult Q & A, even if she'd had no feelings for him, and no one would suspect that she did. The more her answers seemed wrung from her, the more devastating they would be.

'Inspector Evans, you've had a great number of opportunities to interview the defendant personally, have you not?'

Sarah nodded, then spoke, her voice a tempered contralto. 'Yes, sir, I have.'

'When did you first speak with him?'

'At his home, on the day after' – she paused and searched for a neutral phraseology – 'the victim's death.'

'That was a Saturday, was it not?'

'Yes.'

'And did you ask the defendant if he'd seen or talked to his father the day before?'

'Yes, I did.'

'And what did he say?'

Sarah looked over at Graham. Hardy thought he saw a flush creeping into her complexion, but in a moment she was back at Drysdale. 'He said no. He hadn't seen or talked to his father the day before.'

And so it began. To get to most of the answers Drysdale had to use the same approach he'd used on the first question. 'Did you ask?' 'What did he say?'

Throughout, Sarah managed to retain her composure. Hardy had coached her that her testimony would not ultimately affect the verdict. She should tell the truth, and he'd explain the falsehoods in his closing statement.

But Hardy had to admit that listening to this almost unbelievable litany of lies was more than disheartening. He prayed that the jury would buy his version of why Graham had lied, but perhaps he'd underestimated how much people valued the truth. He saw it in the eyes of almost all the jurors.

Say what one will about evidence, juries were often helped along in their deliberations by a perception of the kind of person who was charged with the crime. And Graham, with this testimony, looked very, very bad.

Under Drysdale's patient and meticulous examination, the jury learned that Graham had lied to the police about being close to his father, about knowing what was causing Sal's pain, about the number of phone calls he'd received from Sal, about the morphine supply and the doctor who'd supplied it. He'd lied about giving the shots themselves.

He'd lied to his own brother about the existence of the money, to his sister about the baseball cards.

He'd denied knowing about his father's safe, professed ignorance of his own bank, to say nothing of his safe deposit box, denied that he and Sal had ever talked about money to pay for doctor bills.

It was four-twenty and Drysdale had to be getting to the end. Hardy couldn't even remember any more lies that Graham had told *him*, although he was sure that given time he could come up with some. Finally he heard those magic words, 'Your witness.'

Freeman reached over, around Graham, and touched Hardy's sleeve. 'Let me take her,' he whispered.

Graham, joking, poked him with an elbow. 'She's mine,' he said, and Hardy told him to shut up again.

Freeman didn't let go. 'I can undo it. Soma sat down for her and let Drysdale do it. You can sit down and let me.'

Hardy wasn't sure what Freeman had in mind, but the old man had a well-deserved reputation in the courtroom. He shook things up, often with great success. Indeed, this was precisely the reason Hardy had agreed to let him sit in with them. And now he wanted to play.

Hardy nodded. 'Go for it.'

Freeman wasted no time. He stood up at his place at the table and, as Drysdale had done, introduced himself and began. 'Inspector Evans,' he asked, 'in your opinion, and based on your training and experience as a law-enforcement officer, is the defendant here, Graham Russo, a man that you can trust?'

There was a long, dead pause of shock in the courtroom.

Freeman had obviously given this question a lot of thought during the ninety minutes or so that Drysdale had kept Sarah on the stand and Hardy thought it was perfect – pure Freeman. He would never had thought of it.

Of course it was inadmissible. It was speculation. It wasn't based on evidence. It was, from any legal perspective, a just plain dumb question.

But Hardy had a sense – and Freeman probably *knew* – that neither Drysdale nor Soma would object. After all, they had a police officer up on the stand who had just recounted what seemed like a million lies the defendant had personally told her. What was she going to say? How could she possibly say that, yes, she trusted him?

Sarah bit her lip, looked at Drysdale, then Graham, finally Freeman. Hardy threw a look up to Salter, who seemed to be waiting for the objection that did not come.

'Yes,' she said.

In the room itself order of a sort was restored in time for Salter to call an end to the day's proceedings.

But as the gallery began filing out, the orderly queue trying to get through the double doors dissipated into pushing and name-calling. The fireworks picked up out in the hallway and over-flowed out the back door – the legal professionals' exit from the building.

Hardy went with Graham back to the changing room; the defendant would be sleeping, as usual, in his jumpsuit. Pleased that Freeman had so beautifully undercut Sarah's damaging testimony, Hardy's mind nevertheless kept going back to Michelle and Frannie and what in the world he was going to do with the rest of his life.

So twenty minutes later, accompanied by the bailiff and Graham, he was surprised when they got to the corridor behind the building on the way back to the jail and were stopped by the gathered crowd of at least eighty people.

The reaction to Sarah's testimony.

Pratt was in the thick of it. The district attorney had been in the courtroom and had raised her fist and said, 'Yes,' very audibly, right after Sarah had uttered the same word.

Now, back behind the hall, it was a mob scene. Hardy saw Freeman standing over by Drysdale. Barbara Brandt was there, Soma, a bunch of cops in uniform, tons of press.

In nearly twenty years under a great variety of stresses and burdens, Hardy had never before seen Art Drysdale really lose his temper. But he'd lost it now with Sharron Pratt, the person who'd fired him a few months ago.

'I'll tell you what you are, Sharron.' His voice carried all the way back to where Hardy stood with Graham and the bailiff at the doorway. 'You are an absolute *disgrace* to law enforcement. In fact, you're not in law enforcement at all. You're in social engineering.'

To Pratt this was a badge of distinction. 'You're damn right I am! The people elected *me*, Art. You know why? They were tired of the letter of the law, and the spirit be damned! They were tired of deals getting cut in back rooms.'

The bailiff decided he ought to get Graham back into the jail, to his cell, but Hardy stopped him. 'You're going to want to hear this, Carl.' So they stayed, flies on the back door.

Cameras were rolling. Microphones were pointed. Hardy saw Sarah next to Marcel Lanier, inside the knot of acrimony. She hadn't been the grenade, but she was the pin that, once pulled, had led to the explosion.

'We didn't cut any deals in back rooms.' Drysdale was raving, standing on a concrete planter box. He stormed at the crowd. 'This woman has *no clue*! Doesn't anybody see that?'

Pratt shot back at him. 'You put Graham Russo on trial for murdering his father when you *know* he didn't. That says it all.' The DA played it for the crowd, raising her own voice. 'Anybody out here think this wasn't an assisted suicide? Anybody think this was a murder? I'm waiting.'

Hardy didn't miss the irony in the fact that the defense team and Sarah were probably the only ones who *did* think Sal had been murdered. But this wasn't the time to bring it up.

Taking his cue from Pratt, Drysdale struck again. 'Ask your friend Barbara Brandt, Sharron. Ask her if she's ever met Graham Russo. I'll tell you what – she hasn't! We checked her out, Sharron. It's all made up.'

Brandt yelled out, 'That's a damn lie. That's—'

Drysdale shouted her down. 'But don't let the truth get in your way. It never has before.'

Suddenly, even Sarah was in his sights. He turned to her and pointed. 'And while we're at it, what reward are you giving Sergeant Evans for her testimony today? You going to let her be your chauffeur?'

Freeman, in the unaccustomed role of peacemaker, reached a hand up to Drysdale. 'That's out of line, Art. Come on down.'

'This is a travesty. This is a goddamn travesty.'

The climax was over. Hardy heard Pratt say something about 'sore loser,' loud enough for the crowd, but the public face-off wasn't good politics, and evidently this had finally occurred to her. Drysdale was pushing his way, Soma in tow, to the back lot.

Suddenly Abe Glitsky was standing at Hardy's elbow. 'What's going on? What was Art doing?'

Hardy looked over. 'Evans went sideways. Art thinks Sharron had something to do with it. He's a little worked up.'

'How sideways?'

'Not much,' Hardy lied.

Shackled next to them in his jumpsuit, Graham wasn't intimidated. 'She said she believed me.'

The scene shifted for Glitsky, registered. 'How special for you,' he said. Then, to the bailiff, 'Carl, what's this guy still doing here?'

Carl could take a hint. He was moving with his prisoner before the question was over. 'He's on his way to AdSeg.'

In front of them the crowd had thinned. Part of it – some reporters and supporters and David Freeman – had followed Soma and Drysdale. Pratt, enjoying the photo op, had led another group off on a different walkway.

Evans and Lanier stood by themselves, alone, arms folded, and watched as Graham was led by them.

'All politics aside, Abe, you'll be happier in the long run if you look into George Russo's alibi,' Hardy said. 'Graham's brother?'

'I know who he is.'

'You know where he was when Sal bought it?'

'I don't need to.'

'Well, don't say I didn't try.'

But neither of the men moved away. Hardy had his hands in his pockets, wondering if Sarah was going to come over and say something. Glitsky, his jaw working, the scar white through his lips, stood with his arms crossed, feet planted. Eventually, his chest heaved. 'Evans said on the stand she believed your man?'

'She said he was trustworthy.'

'How did that come up? How'd the judge let it in?'

'Freeman. The guy's a wizard. It was just one word. Drysdale objected afterwards and got sustained, but who cares? The jury heard it.'

'How'd Freeman guess about Evans?'

Hardy shrugged, unable to divulge what he knew. 'Instinct, I suppose. He was right.'

'I've got to talk to her. She doesn't think Graham did it?'

'That's the impression I got.'

'Why not?'

'I don't know.' Lies, lies, lies. He wanted to tell Abe, but didn't dare. The higher priority at the moment was protecting Sarah – and Graham. He wasn't happy about it, but felt he had no choice. 'You'll have to ask her.'

Frannie's saving grace was that she didn't carry a grudge. In this way she was the polar opposite of her husband, who could nurse a slight for decades if the stars were aligned just right.

Beaten down or not, and Hardy felt utterly tromped upon, it wasn't his style to slink. He let himself in his front door, put down his briefcase, walked into the living room, and stood in the middle of it. After a few seconds, letting out a long breath, he went over to the mantel and moved the elephants around.

He smelled baking bread. He heard the kids in the backyard, several neighboring youngsters out there with them. He'd come directly home. There wasn't any point in going by his office and checking up on Tryptech, talking to Freeman, reviewing anything. He wanted to be with his family. Everything else was truly out of his control.

The weather continued warm. A breath of sea-scented air wafted through the open front windows.

Frannie's arms were around him from behind. 'Why did you marry such a ball-breaker?' she asked.

He turned, his arms around her. 'I didn't mean to keep anything from you. There was just so much going on, I forgot.'

Leaning into him, she was barefoot, wearing cutoff jeans and a blue tank-top, no bra. 'I was tired. Maybe jealous of all the time you spend with Sarah. Both of you knew something I didn't.' She shrugged. 'I'm really sorry, Dismas. It just hit me wrong.'

Kissing her, he said he'd punish her later. 'Meanwhile, want to hear a fun story about Tryptech? Maybe you'll want to sit down.'

They were in the living room again, but four hours had evaporated into the children's routines. Taking that essential half hour to brief Frannie on Michelle and Tryptech and his lost fortune – never mind any emotional reaction to it – had cost them all of their potential down time.

And because they hadn't called their children in early from the backyard, the games with the neighborhood kids went on until well after six. Late dinner. Brush teeth. Pajamas.

Then, for an added bonus, Vincent remembered that he'd forgotten his homework. He had to write a poem – at least sixteen lines and it had to rhyme and his parents weren't allowed to help him except that he needed his dad to approve every word, but not give him any of his own.

'Daddy, no help allowed.' Eyes overflowing, the glare. 'It has to be mine. You don't think I can do anything myself!'

Frannie had earlier decreed that this would be a bath night too. Rebecca decided to take a shower, no more bath with her little brother – more weeping and gnashing of teeth from Vincent. It wasn't fair. Everybody hated him. Rebecca got everything she wanted.

Vincent hated everybody and was going to run away and live with the wolves or Balto or somebody who cared about him.

Finally, nine-thirty, Hardy pulled the windows down, drew the blinds against the darkness. A chill evening breeze had freshened, the breath of autumn. 'Well, that was a good time.'

With an exhausted sigh Frannie dropped onto the couch in the front room. 'No kidding. I am going to drink a glass of wine,' she announced. 'Perhaps two. Would you like to join me?'

'Gin,' Hardy said. 'Three fingers. One ice cube. No olive.'

* * *

The television was all over it. The war between the prosecutors. Cops divided among themselves. Sharron Pratt and Barbara Brandt and social engineering. Art Drysdale and David Freeman with their sound bites on Sarah.

Drysdale: 'Sharron Pratt's wrongheaded policies have so permeated the system that good cops don't even know what the law is anymore.'

Freeman: 'Inspector Evans knows the truth in her heart. Graham Russo loved his father.'

Hardy hit the remote, killing the picture. 'God bless David.' The gin was nearly gone. 'He's got his lines and he rides 'em like a racehorse.'

'But Sarah's in big trouble, isn't she?'

'That could be, although in today's climate, if Pratt's got anything to do with it, she might get a medal.' Hardy sighed.

'It's serious down there, isn't it?'

'As bad as I've seen it. It's civil war – brothers against brothers, sisters against sisters. Everybody hates everybody. I've got one last problem, too, fairly serious.'

She looked over at him sympathetically. 'Not a new one?'

He smiled wearily. 'This one's almost ancient – seven, eight hours. Leland Taylor.'

'He hasn't stopped paying you? Not now?'

'No,' Hardy said, 'but he might.'

He told her about his morning discussion with Graham, that he really should tell Leland he was going to be investigating the family. Leland would cut him off. 'And if you're doing the math, my love, you'll realize that he's my last regular source of income.' He tipped up the glass of gin, the last drops. 'I can't tell him, not after today.'

'Do you need George?'

He shook his head. 'I tell myself no, but that's just what I want to hear. If we found out he killed Sal, then Graham's free and we won. So of course we need him. I've got to find out about him and if I even start to look, I'm dead.'

Suddenly there was a knock on the door. Hardy looked at his watch: ten-fifteen. It must be Sarah, he thought, wrecked over her testimony today, needing more counsel and comfort.

Hardy's day had begun at five-thirty after last night's late one and the tension with Frannie. He'd actually considered asking Salter for a continuance this very morning for fatigue, and that was before he learned he'd missed out on more than half a million dollars, before the long day in the courtroom, the marathon with the children.

It had to stop, he thought. He couldn't continue like this.

But if Sarah needed him, he had to be there for her. She was doing so much work for him, and doing it well. He couldn't abandon her now and wimp out. Willing himself out of his chair, he got up and opened the door.

'We've got to talk.' It was Glitsky.

30

Sarah thought the car ride into town was about as free from tension as a dentist's waiting room.

Marcel was driving, silent. He'd turned up the squawk box, which he never did. The dispatcher was sending squad cars to Potrero Hill for a domestic disturbance. There was a robbery in progress at a fast-food store down by San Francisco State. A couple of backup units were needed at a fire site in Chinatown.

Finally Sarah reached over and turned the thing down. 'Get over it,' she said. 'I've always told you he didn't do it.'

'Not the point,' her partner said. 'We're on the stand, we are *with* the DAs. They might fuck up our cases, they might be assholes, but they're *our* assholes.'

'Maybe yours, not mine. And Glitsky finally woke up.'

Lanier cast her a disgusted glance, quick, then brought his eyes back to the road. 'What else's he gonna do, you rub his face in it? Makes him look like a horse's ass for not pursuing it sooner, even though there was no way he could have done it. I'll tell you—' He stopped, biting his tongue.

'What?'

'Nothing. Doesn't matter.'

'Nothing, doesn't matter,' she mimicked.

He set his teeth. 'Maybe it does, then. I'll tell you something, Sarah. You're the first woman we got here in homicide, and if you weren't one you'd be out of it. So don't tell me Glitsky's your pal now. You showed him up, and he's covering his ass.'

'I didn't make it here on some kind of gender quota, Marcel, if that's what you're saying.' He was silent and she raised her voice. 'Is that what you're saying?'

'I'm saying a man pulling that shit on the stand would be directing traffic out in the Taraval.'

'I was right.'

'Yeah, well, join the crowd. Pratt thinks she's right too. Always.'

Sarah had an arm resting on the open windowsill and stared out at the grimy Tenderloin streets. 'Look, Marcel, what if we go out now with Glitsky's blessing and find a killer here? What if the wrong guy's in jail and we put him there? That bother you at all?'

'I'll tell you what bothers me, Sarah. What bothers me is you're my backup, and suddenly I'm seeing you're not there for me. That's what bothers me.'

'How am I not there? One word yesterday?'

They were at a red light and it afforded him the opportunity to turn and face her. 'It's a team game. Yeah, one word puts you on the other side.'

Her lip quivered, but she was damned if she was going to break. 'I'm not on any other side. I've *always* said Graham Russo didn't kill his dad. I've always told you that.'

'That's me, here, privately. That's in the family. A witness stand's a whole different thing.'

'What about you looking at Tosca? What was that all about? You're telling me that's different?'

'That was on my personal time, doing a favor for the AG. Yeah, it's different.'

'So we don't care about getting the right suspect?'

'Yep. We do.'

'All right, so?'

'So. We got him.'

'My name is Blue. I work as a model.'

'I'm sorry,' Soma said. 'Your full name, please.'

'Blue is my full name.'

Sal Russo's downstairs neighbor stared at the young prosecutor as though daring him to ask her again. She was dressed in a black leotard and a black sweater. She was leaning forward, resting her hands on the rail at the front of the witness box, tapping her metallic blue, inch-long fingernails.

In the morning's session, at the hands of Art Drysdale, Marcel Lanier had run through the kind of grilling that Sarah had gone through yesterday. He'd recounted Graham's lies again for the jury, definitely leaving the strong impression that at least one of the investigating officers – the man, the guy who identified with the jury as a working-stiff cop – did not find the handsome young defendant trustworthy at all. Hardy and Freeman had let his testimony go without cross-examination.

But Blue was going to be different. Blue's testimony was about the struggle that had undoubtedly occurred, which Hardy had to keep her away from connecting to Graham.

'Now, Ms . . . ?'

Soma had talked to Blue a minimum of half a dozen times in preparation for her testimony today, but apparently he was having a hard time with the concept of formally addressing a one-named witness on the stand, and this worked to Hardy's advantage. Blue was Soma's baby and he was making her impatient and cross with him from the outset.

'Just Blue,' she snapped. 'Blue is my legal name. I had it changed like five years ago.'

'All right, Blue, I apologize.' Soma gathered himself, tugged at an ear, cleared his throat. 'Can you tell us your address, please?' She did. 'And where is this apartment in relation to the deceased's apartment? Sal Russo's apartment?'

Soma's tongue was tripping him up. Hardy thought he must have done far better in moot court appearances during law school or he never would have gotten selected for his clerkship. This was not his finest hour and Hardy thought it couldn't have come at a better time.

'Right underneath it.'

'One floor below?'

Another exasperated expression from Blue. What the hell else did *right underneath* mean if not one floor below? But she answered him. 'Yeah, my ceiling was his floor.'

'Good. Now on May ninth, the day Sal Russo died, were you in your apartment during the afternoon?'

'Yeah. I had a session. Modeling.'

'One session? All afternoon?'

Again, Soma – trying to make it crystal clear to the jury – was stomping on her toes. Blue stiffly pulled herself up straight. 'Yes, sir.'

'And did you hear any unusual noises from Sal Russo's apartment?'

'Yes, sir.'

'Can you tell the jury what they were?'

With obvious relief Blue turned in her seat and faced the panel. 'I heard some stomping around, then Sal yelled out, "No, no, no," like that' – she did a good impersonation of it herself, waking up anybody who'd been dozing – 'and then there was this bumping, which I guess I heard was like a chair getting knocked over—'

Hardy stood. 'Objection, Your Honor. Speculation.'

Salter overruled the objection, and Soma nodded, then continued. 'You heard a loud thump?'

'Yes.'

'And voices?'

'Yes.'

'Did you hear other voices besides Sal's?'

Again, Hardy stood. 'Objection. Speculation.' He knew this would be overruled, but he thought it would be important to focus the jury right away on his position that there was no way Blue could be sure that voices came from Sal's apartment.

Salter knew what Hardy was doing: making unfounded objections to argue his case to the jury. He didn't like it, and as expected, he overruled him.

Blue got the question again, and nodded. 'Yeah, there was somebody else there.'

'And this other voice, was it a male or female voice?'

'Objection.' Hardy might be alienating her and the judge, but so be it – he had to try again. 'Your Honor, the witness could not possibly know for a fact that these voices came from Sal Russo's apartment, much less that it was Mr Russo's *voice*. Similarly, she couldn't know for a fact if the voice belonged to a male or female.'

Salter's tone was brusque. 'Mr Hardy, that's why we have cross-examinations – you know, the part where *you* ask questions. I'm sorry, Mr Soma, proceed.'

Soma asked about the upstairs speaker's gender again.

'It was a man.'

Hardy was up again. 'Objection. The witness couldn't possibly be sure it was a man, Your Honor.'

Blue's insistence upon her career as a model got shaky. She shot back at Hardy, across the courtroom. 'I know men's voices, sugar.'

This brought a little titter to the gallery, quickly squelched by a look from Salter, who then took off his glasses and tapped them on his podium. 'Blue,' he said, 'please don't talk to the attorneys out there on your own. Let's have counsel approach the bench.' He waved them forward.

Hardy got up with Freeman. Drysdale walked forward with them and met Soma at the podium.

Salter leaned down. 'Mr Hardy, I've already ruled on your repeated objections. Let's move along.'

'I guess I'm asking you to reconsider, Your Honor. Blue may well have heard voices and they may just as well have come from Sal's apartment, but she can't state that as fact.'

Freeman, true to form, stuck in his two cents. 'As a matter of law, judge, he's right. Ask Art, he'll tell you.'

The judge glared down at him. 'I don't need him to tell me, David, or you either.'

In a murder case the specter of a verdict being overturned on appeal due to judicial error hangs like a scimitar over the neck of every trial judge. Salter put the ear ends of his eyeglasses into his mouth and considered carefully.

By repeating the objection over and over, Hardy had bullied him into second-guessing himself. 'On reflection, I believe Mr Hardy has a point. I'm going to sustain his objection, and reverse my decision on the previous objection.'

Soma threw his hands wide. 'But, Your Honor . . .'

The judge stopped the histrionics with a pointed finger. Drysdale helped, laying a soft hand on his partner's sleeve. Salter's first ruling *had* been right, but having already changed his mind once, he was never going to change it back. Hardy had stolen one. Salter put his glasses back on. 'All right, gentlemen, thank you.'

When the attorneys had all returned where they belonged, the judge turned to the jury. 'You will disregard Blue's statement that she heard voices from Mr Russo's apartment, or the gender of those voices. Back to you, Mr Soma.'

The prosecutor went back to his table for a sip of water, trying to buy himself the time to think of another tack. He took a deep breath, threw a look at the ceiling, then turned back to the witness.

'Blue,' he said, 'have you ever seen the defendant before?'

'Yes, sir,' she said.

'Would you please tell us where?'

'Oh, lots of times. He come by the apartment, be out in the alley with his dad, like that. Lately he be there all the time.'

'And did you ever talk to him?'

'Couple of times. Say hi, like that. Nothing really to speak of.'

Soma was about to ask another question, perhaps in this same vein, but Drysdale had a small coughing fit and raised his hand, asking the judge if they could have a couple of minutes recess, which was granted.

When, after five minutes, court was called back to order, Soma announced that he was through with this witness.

She'd given him nothing.

But she was going to give Hardy quite a bit. He knew why Drysdale had had his coughing fit. Soma, flustered by the reversal on Salter's objection ruling and floundering while he thought up another line of questioning, had asked a question for which he didn't know the answer, and it had opened a door for the defense. The coughing fit had tried to slam that door shut, but it hadn't come in time.

'Blue.' Hardy wasn't going to go formal on this woman, get hung up over nomenclature and make her mad. He smiled at her. 'During the many times you saw Graham with Sal, did you ever see them fight?'

'No. Nothing like fighting.'

'What do you mean, nothing like fighting?'

'Well, they was always laughing, more, you know. Most the time. Sometimes they just be sitting on the back of his truck, talking. Mostly that's when I see 'em. Just talkin', laughin'. Sometimes in the lobby, the halls like.'

'So you would say they acted as though they liked each other, is that right?'

'Objection! Conclusion.' Soma knew he had brought this on himself. By degrees his vocal register was going up. His objection was sustained, but Hardy didn't care.

He smiled at the witness again. 'Blue, during the time you lived below Sal, did you ever hear any other bumps, things falling over, stuff like that?'

'Sure, sometimes, maybe he bump into some lamp, something like that.'

'Did you ever go to his apartment?'

She showed her teeth. 'Not on business.' Another ripple of laughter. 'Couple of times, he told me he had some good salmon, I could come and get it. I love that salmon.'

'Me too,' Hardy said. 'And during those times you went to his apartment, did you notice if Sal was a good housekeeper? If the place was clean and uncluttered?'

'Lord, no,' she said. 'There was magazines and boxes and stuff everywhere.'

'Any of which he might have tripped over as he was walking around, isn't that true?'

Soma objected again, got sustained again. But Hardy felt he was making his point to the jury and pressed on. 'All right, Blue, now I'd like you to try to remember the day Sal died and you heard this noise upstairs, like something falling. Do you remember that?'

'I said I did.'

'That's right, you did. Then you told Inspector Lanier that sometime later you heard the door upstairs closing, isn't that right?'

'That's right.'

'Now, to the best of your recollection, how much time passed between this bump you heard and the door closing?' Hardy wanted to establish a temporal distance between the two events. The longer the lag between the bump and the door closing, the less likely there was any causal relation between the two. Therefore, a struggle became a less likely scenario.

Blue sat back in the witness stand, pulling her hands off the rail. Methodically, she began cracking her knuckles one at time. Her eyes were far away. 'I hear the bump. I hear him kind of moaning, "No, no, no." Pretty good amount of time, I 'spect.'

Hardy pounced on this. 'While you were hearing these noises upstairs, you were having a modeling session? Is that what you're saying?'

'That's right. That's why I don't go up there, see what's the matter, when I hear this bump and him saying, "No." '

'All right, Blue. Now, this "pretty good amount of time" you've just referred to, could it have been more than a half hour?'

'Could have been.' She paused, obviously nervous that she'd get caught in a lie. So she decided to come clean. 'I fell a little asleep.' She leaned forward now, looked at the judge, down into her lap.

Hardy played the card he'd picked up from Sarah. It had not been on any of the transcripts, but Lanier had mentioned to Sarah his feeling about the smell emanating from Blue's place. 'Blue, did you smoke marijuana this day? Is that why you fell asleep?'

Cornered, Blue's eyes were all over the room. 'It wasn't that long,' she said ambiguously.

'You mean that you were asleep?'

'And afterwards, after he was gone, I went up, but nobody answered.'

'You didn't try the door?'

'No.'

'Do you clearly remember that the sound of the door closing was after you woke up from your doze?'

'Yes.'

'And was the scraping or bumping before?'

'Yes, sir. It was.'

'So it might have been as long as an hour between the scraping and bumping and the entirely separate sound of the door closing, is that right?'

Another objection, this one overruled. In Salter's view this last point wasn't speculation. Blue could make a reasonable estimate of how long she'd been asleep. She told Hardy he was right: the sounds weren't really all that close together.

'Thank you, Blue. That's all my questions.'

Soma got up on redirect and tried to repair some of the damage. 'Blue, I've got here a transcript of your interview with Inspector Lanier. It says, and I quote, "I hear the door open, then the ceiling creaks, somebody else there." '

'That's right.'

'Good. Now, continuing with the transcript, you told Inspector Lanier – well, maybe you can read what it says here. Would you do that?'

Blue took the paper and read the highlighted text. ' "And then some other noises." '

Soma patiently nodded, leading her through it. 'In other words, Blue, aren't you saying here that the noises occurred after this someone arrived upstairs?'

Her face took on a pained expression. 'No, I don't mean that.'

'But didn't you say "then some other noises"?'

Blue was shaking her head. 'But I don't mean *then* like meaning *after*. I mean *then* like *next thing I thought*.'

This was bad news for the young attorney, who hadn't given much thought to the woman's syntax. She'd said *then*, which to him meant *after*. In this context that's all the word meant to him. To someone with a little less education than Soma, however, the word could be almost endlessly fluid.

As Hardy had discovered when he'd talked to Blue, preparing for his cross.

But Soma couldn't leave it. It struck him as unfair. He had the right meaning and he was, somehow, wrong. He turned to the jury, including them, his voice getting that familiar stridency. 'But then *means* after, Blue. Isn't that the meaning of the word?'

Hardy could have objected that he was badgering the witness, but Soma was shooting himself in the foot anyway and Hardy thought he'd let him do it. Blue pulled herself up. 'Sometime it might. But that's just not what I meant.'

During one of the afternoon recesses a uniformed police officer stuck a note in front of Hardy. Glitsky wanted to know where he could meet Hardy in moderate privacy after he got off today. Hardy thought a moment, then scribbled his reply and sent the officer on his way.

Glitsky had saved Hardy's bacon.

By authorizing Sarah to look into George and Debra's possible connection to Sal's murder, he'd relieved Hardy of any obligation to tell Leland that his money was being used to investigate his own family. It was a police matter now.

Hardy and Glitsky hadn't said a lot of words the previous

night about their ongoing feud. It was behind them, leaving its slightly bitter residue. Instead, they mostly talked about the lieutenant's long interview with Sarah Evans, which had led him to reconsider his earlier decision to drop the investigation.

The rest of Hardy's afternoon was taken up by four witnesses, various other residents of Sal's building, people who'd seen Graham in the vicinity. Hardy asked each of them the same questions: had they ever witnessed anything like a fight between Sal and Graham? Did they see or hear a struggle of any kind in or around Sal's apartment on May 9?

They all said no to everything.

The breeze was stiff out of the west, bending the cypresses in the Park as the lieutenant headed west along Lincoln. A fitful sunlight struggled through the intermittent cloud cover and, when it could, cast long shadows. Traffic was heavy until he turned on Masonic, winding his way back up to Edgewood.

He parked and got out of his car. There was no sign of any wind up here, though in the sky some angels had raked the cirrus into neat rows. He crossed the street and walked up to the address Hardy had given him.

Hardy was leaning against his car, his arms crossed over his chest. 'You said private. I thought you'd like it here.'

The lieutenant threw another look all around. 'What is this place?'

'Graham Russo lives here.'

Glitsky nodded. 'I wish I did.' Then, 'Evans and I had another talk today. We didn't do this right.'

'I know that.'

'You know about Tosca and this guy Ising?'

'Graham's mentioned them both.'

'You didn't hire an investigator? Find out what they've been up to?'

Hardy told a fib of omission. 'Money's tight, Abe. I'm barely breaking even.' He shrugged. 'I can't worry about who did it. It's my job to get my client off.'

'What I hear, you might be doing that.'

Again, a shrug. 'It could happen, though we got a bad jury for it. So what are we doing up here, me and you?'

'This time of day there's lots of eyes at the Hall.' Glitsky looked around the quiet street as though checking for spies. He took his time answering. 'I wanted to let you know we're going to keep looking. Evans wants to go and question the brother and sister directly, but that gets squirrely. We'd have to give them a reason, and then what?'

'I've had the same problem.'

'And these possible money angles.' Glitsky shook his head. 'Contrary to popular belief I don't want to ace the wrong guy.'

'Time's running out, Abe. It might be too late already.'

'I know,' Glitsky said. 'But for the record.'

There was only a slim chance it would do much good in the time he had left. Still, it was a grand gesture for a professional cop and administrator. 'For the record,' Hardy said, 'I appreciate it.'

Frannie was asleep by nine.

Hardy tossed until eleven, then got up and turned on the news. After yesterday's human-interest bombshell with Sarah and the fallout from her testimony, the trial was back to hot copy. Hardy learned that evidently he'd done well with Blue today; the newscaster reported that one of the prosecution's major witnesses had failed to establish that any struggle had taken place in the apartment between Sal Russo and his son.

'But tomorrow is Alison Li, the bank teller who—'

Hardy hit the remote and decided to give sleep another try.

31

This wasn't possible, Hardy was telling himself. Could it be that his own stupidity was going to cost him the case?

It looked that way right now. The four attorneys were in Salter's chambers talking about the admissibility of the videotapes. Freeman might believe that the defense didn't need them, that the entire money/bank issue was beside the point, but to Hardy they were the equivalent of a smoking gun for the defense. If the videotapes were admitted after Soma had gone to great lengths to prove that Graham had, for whatever reason, come to the bank on Friday, Hardy had *proof* that he hadn't. It would devastate the prosecution's argument.

But now it was looking as though it wasn't going to happen. Drysdale and Soma hadn't questioned the tape's admissibility in any of the pretrial hearings, but now, with Alison Li coming up next, they'd requested this hearing in chambers, charging that Hardy couldn't lay any foundation for the tape – what it was, where it came from, how it was relevant. It should be ruled inadmissible.

'Judge' – Hardy was on his feet in front of Salter's desk – 'I got this tape months ago. It was in my discovery that I shared with the prosecution. Mr Soma and Mr Drysdale have had every opportunity to review it. It clearly shows that my client didn't go into the bank on Friday, which is one of the cornerstones of their case.'

If Hardy wasn't so hot himself, he might have been concerned by his partner, David Freeman's, posture. The old man was in a corner of the room, seated, arms crossed, keeping out of it. A bad sign in itself.

Drysdale, too, had recovered from his explosion of the other afternoon. He was low-affect here, and he did most of the talking.

Soma stood next to him, barely concealing his smugness. Drysale was talking: 'We have no problem with the original tape, Judge. Our problem is with Mr Hardy's copy.'

'All right, so let's use the original,' Hardy said, giving up a point far too quickly. The greatest enemy in any trial was surprise, and Hardy had just opened himself up for another one.

'We were told the original's been erased.' Soma couldn't keep the note of triumph out of his voice.

Hardy had no idea how long Soma had known this, or for how long he'd been planning his ambush, but he was obviously enjoying the hell out of it now.

Hardy turned to him. 'It has not been erased.' But even as he said it, he knew it had to be true. Soma wouldn't have any reason to bluff. 'I asked the bank to save it.'

He had figured he had the copy. He'd even copied the *copy* to give to Soma and Drysdale. The efficient and personable Ms Reygosa, the manager, had assured Hardy that the bank would keep the original as backup.

With his infuriating calm, Drysdale was back at Salter. 'Naturally, we wanted to review the original for accuracy after we'd seen Mr Hardy's copy, Your Honor. Evidently the bank misinterpreted Mr Hardy's request and thought that once the tape had been copied, they would be free to reuse it.'

Hardy pressed his fingers against his temples. This could not be happening. It was completely his incompetence. He couldn't believe it, and there was no one to blame but himself. 'Your Honor, I have the copy and it has remained unedited and in my possession—'

Soma cut him off, shaking his head in disagreement. 'The copy could have come from Blockbuster, Your Honor. There's no date or time on it. It could be anything.'

'I'll get Ms Reygosa to testify it is a complete and accurate copy of the original that's been erased, Your Honor. That's sufficient foundation.'

'Alas, Mr Hardy' – Soma's dramatic reading made Hardy want to punch him – 'Ms Reygosa didn't make the copy. The copy was made by one Juan Xavier González, who has returned to his native Honduras after somebody took a hard look at his immigration status.'

'You son of a—'

'Look, Diz.' This was Drysdale, serious now, cutting Hardy off before he talked himself into a contempt fine. 'Technical inadmissibility aside, your tapes are supposed to cover three working days, right? Twenty-four hours.'

'We all know this,' Hardy said.

'Except they're only a little over twenty-two and a half hours long. There's an hour and a half missing.'

Hardy well remembered his day of fast-forwarding the videos to the good parts. Evidently Soma hadn't let his own boredom make him sloppy.

Drysdale went on. 'This guy González not only erased the originals. He *couldn't* have given you full copies.' He turned to Salter. 'There's no foundation, Judge, and more to the point, these tapes don't prove a thing.' Drysdale didn't have the gloating tone, but the words alone were enough.

Unnoticed by Hardy, Freeman had pulled himself out of his chair. Hardy felt a hand on his shoulder, reassuring.

Salter had heard enough. The tapes were inadmissible.

Gil Soma started on each witness with an enthusiasm that Hardy found daunting, especially so after the defeat he'd just suffered in chambers. No videotapes! After all of his effort to procure them. What a fool he was.

Now, on Thursday afternoon, Soma was approaching the end of his case in chief. From his self-confident demeanor it was clear that he barely, if at all, felt any of the wounds that Hardy had inflicted.

Alison Li started out as nervous as she'd been at the bank on the day Hardy had first interviewed her. Soma was gentle with her, leading her through the standard witness questions – name, place of business, and so on – gradually getting to the meat. 'Ms Li, do you recognize the defendant here' – pointing – 'Graham Russo?'

'Yes, I do. He's a customer at the bank where I work.'

Pleased out of all proportion, Soma slowly walked back to his table and picked up a piece of paper, and entered it into evidence. 'Now, Ms Li, I'd like you to look at People's Fourteen here and tell us if you recognize this document.'

She took the paper and scanned it quickly. 'Yes, this is a sign-in form for customers holding safe-deposit boxes.'

'And did you see Graham Russo, the defendant, sign this document?'

'Yes, I did.'

Now Soma put his enthusiasm to good use. 'Ms Li, aren't customers supposed to sign in *and date* this form?'

'Yes.'

'But, as we see here, Mr Russo didn't do that, did he?'

'No.'

'Did you ask him to do it?'

'Yes.'

'And yet he didn't?'

Hardy wanted to break up the rhythm, so he stood up. 'Asked and answered, Your Honor.'

Perhaps Salter was sympathetic to Hardy's despair. This wasn't much of an objection. Still, the judge nodded. 'True enough. Sustained. Move along, Mr Soma.'

But Soma had a knack for the small and telling variation. 'Did the defendant give a reason why he wouldn't put the date on this form?'

'No. I didn't notice. He said he would and I thought he did, but he didn't.'

And so it went.

By the time Hardy stood to begin his cross-examination, Alison Li had drawn the picture clearly. Graham Russo had come in sometime that Friday afternoon and deposited something in his safe deposit box. He appeared nervous. He was in a hurry.

They thought they'd have the videotapes to fall back upon, and without them Hardy was forced to bring David Freeman's argument into play. The defense team had prepared extensively for it, and Hardy was possessed of a near ethereal, desperate calm as he walked to the center of the courtroom.

He brought a smile forth and showed it to the witness. 'Ms Li. You have testified that Graham Russo brought a briefcase with him on the afternoon in question. At any time, did you see the contents of the briefcase?'

Alison's nerves were back in play. She shifted in her chair, looked at the jury, then at Soma, finally back to Hardy. 'I never said I did.'

'I didn't say you did either.' Hardy kept any threat out of his voice. They were having a conversation, that was all. 'But I am asking you now. Did you see what was in the briefcase?'

'No.'

'Not at any time?'

'No, never.'

'So you don't know what was in the briefcase, or in fact if *anything* was in the briefcase, isn't that true?'

Hardy took the moment to get a read on the jury. Obvious as this question was, it did what Freeman had predicted: poked a hole into one of the prosecution's main assumptions, its scenario of the day of Sal's death. He saw several members of the jury sit up, digesting this.

Alison Li nodded her head and told him that yes, it was true. She didn't know what was in the briefcase.

Hardy was making the point that Graham had not necessarily taken the money and baseball cards from Sal's apartment and essentially hidden them in his safe deposit box. There was no *proof* that Graham had deposited the money or anything else within months of Sal's death.

In fact, Hardy believed Graham's version completely: he had had the money and the baseball cards in the briefcase, and he'd put them into his safe deposit box on Thursday. But the truth here did not serve the ends of justice – Hardy was beginning to wonder if it ever would in this case – so he jettisoned the truth without a backward glance.

Hardy continued. He was going to nail this down. 'Did you, personally, Ms Li, ever get a chance to see the contents of Graham Russo's safe deposit box?'

'No. Customers generally go into a private room.'

'So to your own personal knowledge, do you know how long the baseball cards and money were in Mr Russo's box?'

This slowed her to a stop. Her mouth opened and closed a couple of times and she looked at the jury as though asking for help. 'I don't know.'

'Could it have been weeks?'

'Yes, possibly.'

'Months?'

'I don't think so.'

Hardy had gotten what he wanted. To the jury, he'd gotten to reasonable doubt about whether Graham had killed Sal and then taken the money and run it to the bank to hide it.

His own confidence was beginning to come back, and he still had another point to make. 'Do you remember talking to me at your bank last May sometime?'

At this line of questioning Alison's eyes took on a defiant glow. 'Of course.'

'And during our discussion, didn't you tell me you thought that Graham Russo had come in to make his deposit on Thursday?'

'No. I said I wasn't sure. I thought it might be Thursday or Friday.'

Hardy tried again. This was either an outright lie or a faulty memory. 'You don't remember telling me it was Thursday?'

'No.'

He took a breath, pausing. 'All right, Ms Li, so you say it was Friday that Graham came in, is that right?'

'Yes. It *was* Friday.' Evidently she'd spent enough time repeating it to the police that she'd come to believe it.

'Do you remember that clearly?'

'Yes.'

'All right, then, Ms Li, since you remember it so clearly, perhaps you can remember what time it was on Friday. Can you tell us that?'

She thought a couple of seconds. 'It was the afternoon.'

'The late afternoon? Early afternoon? When?'

He didn't much like to do it, but she was defensive and still defiant and he could play that against her. She was starting to snap her answers out at him. 'Later.'

'After three? After four?'

'It seemed like it was near the end of the day.'

That's because it was, Hardy thought. But it was Thursday, not Friday. He had her. The jury would know that Graham had been working on Friday afternoon.

'You're sure it was near the end of the day?'

'I just said that. Yes, I'm sure.'

'After three?'

'Definitely, at least.'

'After four?'

'It seemed like it. Maybe. Yes.'

'On Friday, was it?'

She almost screamed in her anger. 'Yes, on Friday. That's what I said, didn't I?'

Hardy smiled at her now, a genuine smile. 'Yes, you did, Ms Li. Friday, late in the afternoon. After four. Thank you, no further questions.'

Salter nodded, pointed to the prosecution table, whose inhabitants looked a little glum, asked for redirect.

Soma stood up. 'No redirect for this witness.' He leaned over and conferred a moment with Drysdale. 'The prosecution rests, Your Honor.'

Hardy had shown them. His adrenaline had kicked in after losing his videotapes, and he'd turned it on them. He dared half a grin at Soma, flashing on a sign he'd seen affixed to a motorcycle outside a bar someplace: *This Harley belongs to a Hell's Angel. Fuck with it and find out.*

'That was pretty sweet,' Graham was saying. They had adjourned for the day and had gathered in the holding cell. 'Friday I was at work after three. I can prove it. You got her.'

'I think I did,' Hardy agreed.

'Not that it matters,' Freeman grunted. He had boosted himself up onto the table and was swinging his feet.

'Yoda unhappy,' Graham said. 'Yoda sad.'

'I'm not unhappy. It was a good show, but I'm saying it doesn't matter. If I were Soma – no, I don't want to be Soma – if I were Drysdale, I would simply amend my story. It's not too late if the jury's leaning toward him anyway.'

'To what?' Hardy asked.

'Oh, I don't know, pick one. How's this? Graham has the combination to the safe and, thinking Sal never even looks in it anymore, he waits till his dad's out of the room and takes the money – it doesn't matter when – and puts it in his own box at the bank. So on May ninth Sal happens to check the safe and sees it's gone. *That's* why he makes the two calls to Graham that morning. That's why Graham rushes over. That's why he has to kill him.'

Hardy had had little enough to celebrate this week. He didn't need to get his parade rained upon right now. 'There's no proof of any of that.'

Freeman twinkled. 'Exactly right. My point. There's no proof of anything. There is no physical evidence. Soma's just drawing you both into a pissing contest. Don't go there. You don't need it.'

Graham let out a deep sigh. 'I just enjoyed watching Mr Hardy here kicking a little butt.'

'Don't get me wrong. Nobody likes fireworks as much as I do, Graham, but that's not what it's about. It's about evidence. Keep focused on that. Diz, you've got to write your eleven eighteen. Get it to Salter tonight, argue it tomorrow morning.'

Freeman was referring to a motion routinely made by defense counsel after the prosecution has rested, under Section 1118.1 of the California Penal Code. It is nearly always rejected by the trial judge. The motion – called a directed verdict of acquittal – asks the judge to dismiss all charges against the defendant on the grounds that the prosecution has failed to provide probative evidence sufficient to justify a guilty verdict.

Hardy had considered it, of course, but it seemed a waste of time in this case. He turned to his old partner. 'It's not worth it, David. Salter's going to turn me down anyway. He couldn't direct a verdict, not with all the big guns out.'

Freeman nodded. 'He sure could. I don't think he will, either, but stranger things have happened.'

'When?' Graham asked, joking.

Freeman slid off the table. 'We can't get complacent. To quote the great Yogi Berra, it's not over till it's over, and sometimes not even then.'

'That wasn't Berra who said that, was it?' Graham asked.

'The first part, I think. Wasn't it Berra?'

Hardy picked up his briefcase. 'You titans work on that one. I'm going to write the damn motion.'

It was after five o'clock on a Thursday night and he came up through the main office, past the reception desk where Phyllis, answering telephones, ignored him. He looked in at the Solarium, hoping to see someone, but all of the associates were in their cubicles, working.

Or maybe avoiding him. They'd have heard about Michelle's coup, or his idiocy, and in his mind they pitied him or had decided he was a terminal loser. Either way, no one stepped out and greeted him and he trudged up the stairway to his office, carrying the briefcase that, from the feel of it, was where he kept his barbells.

Dust had settled heavily over every smooth surface. The window hadn't been opened in a week. He turned on the desk light – a green-shaded relic from the days when what was now Rebecca's room had been his office at home – then turned around and threw up the sash. From Sutter Street wafted the smells of diesel and coffee and, more subtly, patchouli and crab. The city.

The letter from Michelle was centered in the middle of his desk. Sitting in his chair, he opened the envelope and gave it a once-over. No new news. He got halfway through his second pass on it before balling and throwing it toward the wastebasket. It missed.

Running his palm over the wide expanse of his desk, he cleared away a path of dust, then put his feet up.

He had no idea how much time went by. He wasn't thinking in the sense of having discrete thoughts. Nor was he relaxing, not precisely. He was on 'charge,' listening or feeling for something that . . .

He wasn't sure.

Maybe just letting the mass of facts settle: the stratagems, issues, distractions. Something, the weight of all of it, had simply stopped him. Was he missing something?

Of course, you always did. He couldn't *see* the killer of Sal Russo, and someday he would need that. This he knew on a level beyond reason – he was kidding himself if he denied it.

He would need the closure.

Even if it didn't help Graham's verdict, and in spite of the mass of detail he had internalized, he knew he needed more facts. And worse, some sense told him he already had access to what he needed to know; he just didn't recognize it.

So he shut down, the cogs locked. He wouldn't be able to move until one of them shifted slightly.

It had gotten measurably darker and he hadn't noticed. He spun his chair so he could see out the window. Above the street, through the canyons of the buildings, the sky burned a dark turquoise. The line of traffic below had disappeared.

His green banker's lamp threw a pool of light onto his desk, the only light in the room. He stood and walked around to the dartboard, pulled the three darts, and began throwing in the semidarkness.

Sarah always prided herself on being far too tough to cry, but the past two days – since she'd told the world she believed in Graham – she'd felt like it often enough.

It wasn't just her partner. She'd worked hard for some grudging acceptance among the men in the detail and thought she'd made inroads. Now all of that had vanished.

After 'The "Yes" Heard Round the City,' as Jeff Elliot had called it in 'CityTalk,' Sarah got called into Glitsky's office. He appeared to listen to everything she had to say, though it ran counter to the company line.

She told him she'd come to the conclusion that while Sal had been murdered, it hadn't been his son who'd done it. She admitted that she had talked to him personally – the softball connection, the *Time* magazine moment in his apartment – and thought she had some sense of who he was.

All of Graham's lies, she explained, misguided as they might have been, were reducible to one impulse and then, as lies will, they'd had to multiply to cover each other. He hadn't killed Sal. Somebody else had.

Glitsky had sat back slumped, elbows resting on the arms of his chair. He spoke so quietly, she could barely hear him. 'If this turns personal, Sergeant, or *is* personal, and anybody finds out, you realize you screw your partner, me, the whole department. You know that?'

Sarah had felt sick. Glitsky knew. She was dead meat. But he didn't go that way. Instead, he drew a deep breath and sat himself up. 'Okay, you want to find your killer?'

If she did, he'd turn her loose on it.

* * *

Glitsky had approved hours for Sarah on the Russo case, though they would be billed to administration. Now at least she was getting paid for what she'd been doing anyway.

But her lieutenant had severely restricted her movements. Glitsky wasn't about to get his rear end put in a wringer by Dean Powell's troops if word got out that now, with the trial almost concluded, the police were checking witnesses, maybe looking for another suspect.

She started with George Russo. When she'd first revealed herself to Hardy and begun helping him, she'd gone to George's Bush Street Victorian half a dozen times, on random nights. George, she'd concluded, had no life. It might be that he was genetically wired for rage at his natural father. He could have rushed out at lunch one day and killed Sal over the imagined slight to the honor or peace of mind of his mother. That, Sarah thought, was in the realm of the possible.

But whatever else might be going on, George kept his nose clean. He was the heir apparent to a banking empire, and his role transcribed his life. He did not party with anyone outside of his ordered little universe. Stalking him, she was convinced, was a waste of time, and she'd stopped.

But tonight, with nothing else substantive to pursue, she was going to try again. Marcel had been only too happy to dump her off early at the Hall, and she'd taken her own car up to Baywest Bank on Market Street and waited.

As always, George was a dream to tail. He was big and dressed handsomely. In spite of the relative warmth of these September evenings, he sported what she thought was an enormously affected homburg over a cashmere overcoat.

At a little after six he had left the bank on foot. Hands in pockets, he'd strolled purposefully a few blocks, never slowing or looking behind him, through the Tenderloin district – pimps and whores and derelicts. She wondered about the route – this wasn't George's turf by any stretch – but the question resolved itself when he turned into a small, expensive French restaurant on Polk, where he sat in the window and ate his dinner, alone.

There was nothing for her to do but wait for him to come out and see what he did next.

Now it was almost eight-thirty and she was sitting in her car alone and suddenly the tears threatened. Exhaustion was killing her. She hadn't been alone with Graham in over three months. She hadn't had time for any exercise. She'd almost forgotten the physical connection between her and Graham. Had it been as real as it felt? Or would all this have been for nothing? Would their love still exist when he got out? *If* he got out . . .

This was the specter that haunted, that she tried to ignore. Graham might not get out, not ever. Hardy and Freeman and – admit it – she herself might fail him.

Graham had a very real opportunity to spend the rest of his life in jail. And then what of her? How could she continue to be a cop, knowing that the system she was sworn to uphold had ruined her life? Glitsky hadn't told her anything she didn't already know: she was way over the line. And if she couldn't be a cop, what would she become?

She was saved from further introspection when George exited the restaurant and walked by his earlier route to Baywest, where he retrieved his car in the parking lot. Sarah was ready to follow him back to his home, when he turned right off Market, surprising her, back into the lower Tenderloin.

By now it was full dusk. The few streetlights that still worked in this part of town had come on. George drove slowly up Eddy to Polk, hung a right, then another one, and started back uptown. He turned right again. And again. Going in a circle.

Suddenly, her pulse beginning to race, Sarah knew what George was doing. He was cruising.

Reaching for her handheld, she put in a call to her dispatcher. 'I need an Adam unit' – a black-and-white patrol car – 'ASAP for backup at . . .'

When George pulled over and the woman got into his car, she was ready. She waited until he had pulled into an alley, then told her Adam to roll.

She was right behind the squad car and so had a bird's-eye view as the two uniformed officers came up to George's car and knocked on the windows, one on either side, shining their flashlights down, illuminating what was going on inside.

Finally, a wedge.

* * *

The two uniformed officers took the prostitute over to the black-and-white car, fifty feet up the street. Sarah kept George back by his car. It was doubtful he would have recognized her in any event, but clearly now, in darkness and in terror, he didn't know who she was except trouble. He'd taken off his coat for the business and now he was visibly freezing in the wind. She thought it was good for him.

Sarah had his wallet in her hands, was ostensibly checking over his ID. 'George Russo. Do you know it's illegal to traffic in prostitution?'

He decided to try a ridiculous bluff. 'I don't—' Stopping. 'She's a friend of mine.'

Sarah smiled at him and yelled up the street. 'Hey, guys! This john says he and the girl are friends. Ask her if she knows his name.' She turned back to him. 'I'm betting not, George. You know *her* name?'

George had the eyes of a spooked horse. He glanced out behind Sarah as though searching for something – salvation, maybe. Sarah gazed levelly at him. 'Linda, Julie, what?'

From the other car one of the officers called down. 'She says he can go to hell. She doesn't know him.'

'Look at that,' Sarah said. 'I won my bet.'

'All right, so what now? I pay some fine? What?'

Sarah could waste a lot of time putting him through hoops, but she knew exactly what she wanted, and the best way to get it. She told him a lie. 'You know we've got a new program to cut down on this vice traffic, George. It's really getting out of hand, and you johns tend to just walk away. So you know what we're doing now? We're putting names and pictures in the paper.'

'You don't do that.'

She nodded. 'We do now. It's a new program. Didn't I say that?'

'I can't have that.'

'You don't get to choose.' She hardened up her voice, put her hand on her gun. 'All right, come on along with me.'

'Where are we going?'

'To my car. I'm parked right behind my friends there. Then we all go downtown. Where do you think?'

'Are you saying I'm under arrest?'

Again, she gave him nothing and he stammered into the breach. 'Look, I can't let this happen to me. I cannot get arrested for prostitution. I don't care what that girl says – she's a friend of mine. I've got to call my lawyer.'

'If you're going to call your lawyer, you can do it just as well from the Hall of Justice.'

He lowered his voice. 'Look, what if . . . I mean, can't we take care of this here? Maybe we can—'

She cut him off. 'Don't make it worse, George. Attempting to bribe a police officer is a crime too. Maybe you didn't know that. Let's pretend that for now, huh? Now let's go.'

He was cracking. 'No, look, please—'

She raised her voice again. 'Hey!'

One of the officers stopped what he was doing and began trotting down to her. 'Everything all right, Inspector?'

She held up a hand, keeping the officer out of earshot distance. 'One minute, thanks. Stay close.'

She looked back to George. 'Turn around,' she said. 'Put your hands behind your back.'

The officers wanted to put him in the black-and-white, where there was a screen and no handles on the back doors. But Sarah was a homicide inspector – the top of the hierarchy – and they knew it from the call number the dispatcher had given them: 14-H. She told the uniforms they could drive the hooker around the corner and let her go. The john was a witness in a homicide investigation and she was going to squeeze him now. In her car.

He was in the backseat, handcuffed, shivering with fear or cold or both. She got into the front seat and spun around. 'I'd like to make you a trade.'

A born trader himself, George narrowed his eyes at the unexpected gambit.

Sarah didn't let him get an answer out. 'My real interest is your brother.'

'Graham? What's Graham got to do with this?'

'This is going to make you tell me where you were when your father got killed.'

'Fuck you. Why should I?'

Sarah looked flatly at him for a minute, then turned around and started the car.

'Wait a minute, wait a minute!'

'We can talk downtown.'

'No, no. I was just . . .'

'Being an asshole?'

'Yeah. Yeah. I'm sorry. What do you want to know about Graham?'

She turned the car's engine off. 'I don't want to know anything about Graham. I want to know about you. Graham didn't kill your father.'

'My father isn't dead,' George said. 'I work with him every day.'

'Sal.' She clipped it. 'Don't get even slightly cute with me one more time or this discussion's over. Understand?'

George didn't give much away, but he did nod. 'Okay, Graham didn't kill Sal. So what?'

'Okay, so somebody else did. I'm eliminating suspects.'

He leaned back, the haunted look in his eyes giving way to something else. Shrewdness, a deal in the making. 'You can't think I had anything to do with that. I didn't even know where Sal lived.'

'That's what you've said, but I don't know it's true. You wouldn't tell Graham's attorney or anybody else where you were that afternoon.'

'Why should I? It's nobody's business. You cops never asked.'

'Well, it's my business. I'm asking now. You can tell me where you were and I'll go away and that'll be the end of tonight's little adventure. Or not, and I can write you up, fill out an incident report, you get to see your name in the newspaper.' She leaned forward. 'Look, all I want to know is where you were. You don't tell me, I'm going to become a lot more interested in you as a murder suspect. Every minute of your last year is going to get a profile.'

'I don't—'

'On the other hand, you tell me where you were and if it's got nothing to do with your father, then this moment tonight, your girlfriend, everything – it all stops here.'

'You don't write it up? Or whatever it is you do?'

'I won't do anything.'

'My father, especially. He can't know.'

This phraseology slowed her momentarily until she realized George was talking about Leland, not Sal. 'He won't.'

Infuriatingly, as she was closing in, he skittered away again. 'How do I know I can believe you?'

She smiled. 'Well, the truth is, George, you can't. Either way, you're no worse off than you are right now.' Her voice became conversational. She knew the battle was hers if she kept it cool. There was no need for the heavy artillery; enough hits with the light gauge would accomplish the same thing. 'Look, George, it's simple. You've got nothing to lose. Just tell me.'

He closed his eyes and swallowed, then mumbled it out. 'Mitchell Brothers.'

'What?'

He repeated it. The Mitchell brothers had been San Francisco's kings of pornography for years until one of them had shot and killed the other one, which threw a damper on their partnership. Still, the original Mitchell Brothers Theater – five or six blocks from Baywest Bank – continued to thrive under the original name.

In terms of sexual provender, it went a good deal farther than the titillating nudity of the North Beach tourist shops. Featuring hard-core live sex shows, private booths, one-on-ones, and kinkiness of every imaginable kind, it was as raunchy a place as San Francisco could provide.

'It's my rotten luck.' George was slumped now, going on. 'The one day I do anything, the one *hour*, that's when Sal dies and everybody wants to know where I am, where I was. And if Leland finds out where I was . . .' He shook his head. 'He'd cut me out, too, like Sal did. Then it would really be over.'

'What would?'

'My life,' he said. 'My career, everything he's raised me to do.'

She had to ask. 'So why did you risk it? Why'd you have this girl tonight? Why don't you get yourself a girlfriend?'

This was torture. 'There's no . . . Leland wouldn't . . .'

'Like any of them? Approve?'

He shook his head. 'I can't make any mistakes.'

She tried to understand. George blamed himself for being abandoned; if he had been better or more lovable or something, it might not have had to happen. He might never understand the way it had formed him, but now he was an adult with an adult's needs and desires, and, stunted by the fear of rejection, he was afraid to pursue them. Legitimately.

It saddened her, so she spoke gently. 'I'm afraid you're on the wrong planet for no mistakes, George. Everybody makes them here on earth. They're allowed.'

'Not to me. You don't know.'

But the defenses were coming back up. He straightened in the seat. His eyes narrowed again, seemed to focus more sharply. The slackness went out of his face. 'So anyway, that's where I was,' he said. 'Is that what you wanted? Do we have a deal?'

'Yes.'

'You won't tell my father?'

'That's right. But sooner or later, you know, something else like this is going to happen. He's going to find out.'

'No,' he said. 'It's going to stop.'

Just what he needs, she thought, as though he weren't already one of the most repressed young men she'd ever met. But she wasn't his counselor. She'd tried, even – against her instincts – cared for a moment.

Someday he'd change, or he would implode. Or he might stay the same and live a miserable, pinched life of money and toys. Either way, Sarah wasn't going to have anything to do with it.

She didn't know how she could check it out, but for the moment George had given her a believable alibi. And this solved one of her immediate problems.

But it hadn't solved Graham's.

32

Hardy smelled bacon and felt the soft touch of his wife's lips against his cheek. 'I turned off the alarm and gave you an extra half hour.'

'You're my savior.'

'I know. Come eat and get dressed after.'

It was five forty-five. He stepped into a pair of jeans and threw a jersey over his head. Out their bedroom window he could discern the outline of the Oakland hills, so the sun must have been somewhere behind them, but it hadn't marched into the sky yet.

His coffee was poured in an oversized mug. Eggs were scrambled and steaming on his plate with six fat strips of bacon, English muffins, and marmalade. He loved marmalade and for some reason never thought to eat it.

He sat down. 'Did I already mention the savior thing?'

She smiled. 'What time did you get in?'

'Twelve-thirty, one, something like that. I finished the motion. Salter might—'

She stopped him, putting her hand over his. 'Later. Trial later.' She pointed. 'Breakfast now. Eat.'

He closed his eyes and nodded, smiling. She was so right. 'Good plan,' he said.

'Everybody needs one.'

At seven-thirty A.M. the sturdy jogging figure appeared in his running clothes at the end of the alley. Hardy, waiting at the automatic gate to the parking lot behind the federal courthouse, was dressed for court in a dark suit and blue tie.

With a good sweat worked up, Giotti didn't stop until he was almost upon him. He didn't expect any interruptions on his morning run through the downtown alleys, certainly not from a lawyer on business.

'Morning, Judge.'

Giotti was breathing heavily, but managed a half-smile of welcome. He took a moment – recognition not quite there. 'Mr Hardy. You're up early.'

To Hardy it felt like high noon. 'I've got to deliver a motion at the Hall before eight. I wanted to catch you first. I remember you said you jogged most mornings.'

'Not enough.' He indicated the gate behind them, which had somehow swung open – a guard watching for the judge? a remote switch in his pocket? 'You want to go inside?'

'No. Here's fine. I've only got a minute.'

'Okay, how can I help you?'

'Do you know if Sal knew anybody named Singleterry? Joan Singleterry?'

This was the cog that had slipped for Hardy last night. He and Graham had spent hours in the past months surmising about Sal's early life, the mysterious Singleterry woman, and had come up with nothing. But suddenly, in his open-vessel state at his office, Hardy remembered that Giotti had actually known Sal Russo during those early days, had fished and worked with him, played ball and partied with him.

Hardy was starting to have a feeling that Joan Singleterry might have a bigger role here than he'd understood, and Giotti could be the key to her identity.

Did he imagine it? The judge's clear gaze seemed to flicker for an instant. But then he was back as he'd been, still catching some breath, thinking about it. Dashing Hardy's hopes. 'I don't think so.'

'She wasn't an old girlfriend, before Helen, maybe?'

Giotti pondered some more, shook his head no. 'I'm sorry. Is it important? What's this about?'

Keeping it vague, Hardy said it was just a name in discovery that led nowhere. He was starting his defense today and needed everything he could lay his hands on. If this Singleterry woman was a source of the money – something like that – it might lead to another suspect.

He must have betrayed a little of his disappointment. The

judge gave him a manly pat on the shoulder. 'I don't know if you're going to need any suspects. I've been following the trial pretty closely. It seems to me it's going pretty well.'

'It'd go better if I could produce a killer.'

Giotti appreciated the sentiment. 'Well, that, sure. But you kept the struggle out pretty good, I thought.'

'I meant to thank you for that. The idea.'

The judge shrugged. 'I just told the truth. There was no physical proof of any struggle. Since I know your strategy, I've got an inside track, but I get the feeling Soma and Drysdale don't have a clue what you're up to.'

Hardy allowed himself a small smile. 'Well, wouldn't it be pretty to think so?'

Giotti broke a true grin. 'Hemingway allusions, yet. You're a well-rounded human being for an attorney, Mr Hardy. When this is all over, if you don't appeal' – again, the reminder – 'we ought to have a drink sometime.'

'You could probably twist my arm.'

The judge nodded. 'I might do that.' A kind of wistful look came over him. 'I just remembered how I miss Sal. Isn't that funny?'

'How is that?'

Perhaps he shouldn't say. His mouth tightened, his body language briefly saying 'No, never mind,' but then that pose broke and he smiled sheepishly. 'Do you have a lot of good friends, Mr Hardy?'

Hardy shrugged. 'A few. I'm lucky with that, I suppose.'

'I used to be too. That's what they don't tell you about this job.'

'What's that?'

'Well, to get it – and don't get me wrong, it's all I've ever wanted. But to get it you've got to – how can I put it? – develop friendships. You make real friends when you're on the rise, some would say on the make. You give parties, go to them, hobnob. You impress people with your brains – your legal knowledge and learned opinions and quick wit. It's heady.'

'I'd imagine it would be.' Though Hardy had no idea where Giotti was going with this, or why he was divulging these intimacies to him.

'Then you get appointed.' Giotti's expression said a lot about disappointment, the alternate roads not taken. 'It all ends. You're cut off. Some of the more cerebral judges, they do fine. Others miss the friendships, but friendships aren't on the docket. Too much opportunity for conflict of interest, see? And these are the very people who put you here. Suddenly you can't fraternize anymore, certainly not the same way. You wind up pretty much alone.'

Hardy suddenly understood. 'Except Sal?'

'The last one of my old friends. I could go up and just' – he instinctively looked around for other people, other ears – 'and just *bullshit* with him. I think it must have been you digging up that Hemingway just now. That was Sal. He knew a lot, he was funny, I could be who I was around him.'

Hardy motioned behind him, toward the federal courthouse. 'You brethren don't play a lot of practical jokes on each other in there, huh?'

The judge's voice rasped. 'It's a serious life, Mr Hardy. Don't let 'em tell you different.' Giotti gave himself a last beat of reflection, then put it behind him. He was too busy for any more of this. 'So someday maybe you and I, we'll go have a drink somewhere. I'll call you Dismas, how's that sound?'

'I'll still call you "Your Honor." '

Giotti laughed out loud. 'That's what I mean,' he said. 'That's just what I mean.'

Hardy handed his directed-verdict motion over to Salter in his chambers and sat in exquisite suspense while the judge read over the five pages.

This was a murder case. Discussion of Hardy's motion would be on the record. So over by the judge's window, Soma, Drysdale, and Freeman quietly kept up the flow in the mighty stream of law gossip. They'd all previously read Hardy's motion out in the hall and made informal small talk about it before the judge had them come into his chambers.

The court reporter sat in the chair next to Hardy, ready to catch any precious pearl, should one fall.

Hardy thought he had done a more than competent job on his motion, clearly laying out each factual allegation made by the prosecution, and then demonstrating in turn how they had failed to prove any of them: they hadn't placed Graham at the apartment, they couldn't prove a struggle, they couldn't even get the coroner to state unequivocally that it had been a homicide. There was no temporal connection or relevance to the money or the baseball cards. Alison Li's testimony was meaningless.

The prosecution had nothing.

By contrast, Judge Salter had a lot. He had a multi-photo-op hot-potato case of the very first order, hand-delivered to his courtroom by his good friend and political crony Dean Powell. He had an indictment by the grand jury that had brought things to this pass. He was privy to the backstage maneuverings of the attorneys, the motions here in his chambers, the lies of the defendant. He also had social relations with Federal Judge Harold Draper, Graham's old boss – not quite enough to compel him to recuse himself from the case for conflict, although Hardy would make that argument should it come to an appeal.

None of these were matters of law. All of them, taken together, mattered more than the law.

Hardy had no doubt that one day Salter would leave the bench to pursue a political career. He had the bland good looks, the social connections, the inoffensive public personality. He was unfailingly polite, even friendly in an impersonal way.

Now he had finished reading Hardy's motion and he took off his glasses, squared the pages on his desk, and laid them there. The frown that meant 'I'm in deep thought' gave way to the smile that said, 'We're friends here.'

'Gentlemen.' He motioned the other attorneys over, then gave his attention to Hardy. 'This is one hell of a well-written motion, Diz. I mean it. You make a very colorable argument.'

Colorable, Hardy thought. Uh-oh. He exchanged a look with Freeman, who shrugged. It was expected, and it was over.

But Salter was observing the niceties. 'Do you want to add any oral argument?'

'They've failed to prove anything, Judge. Certainly not robbery, which is why we've got the specials. There's no causal relation between the money and the death. There's no paper showing when Graham got the money or the cards. The boy was taking care of his dad. He loved him.'

Out of the corner of his eyes Hardy could see that Soma was moved to comment, but Drysdale laid a hand on his sleeve, cutting him off before he began.

Salter let a small silence build. It wouldn't do to reject such a well-written, *colorable* motion out of hand. An important ruling such as this one, although almost foreordained by its very nature, demanded at least some minutes of cogitation.

La politesse.

'I don't know, though,' Salter finally admitted. 'I'm still very concerned about all the lies.'

'I think I've covered them, Judge. He panicked and then had to backfill.'

'But why did he panic if he had done nothing?'

'Homicide coming to his door. He freaked. It happens all the time.'

This was all pablum, totally irrelevant, and everybody knew it. Salter was going to turn him down because Hardy didn't have enough to *compel* him not to. He didn't have the murderer. He didn't have Strout saying it was definitely a suicide. Anything less wouldn't get it done.

Salter paused again, then drew in a lungful of air and let it out. Another smile among friends. 'I think we're going to have to let the jury decide, Diz. I'm going to deny the motion.'

'I want you to visualize something,' Freeman said. They were waiting for Salter to enter the courtroom. Graham sat between them at their defense table. Behind them the gallery was its usual din before court was called to order, although the noise was so familiar by now that no one noticed it. 'No, I mean it. Close your eyes.'

'If I close my eyes I will be asleep when the judge comes in. I guarantee it. I've done experiments.'

Graham looked back and forth between them, settled on Hardy. 'Better what Yoda says do. Otherwise he use Force. You die.'

Part of Hardy was relieved by Graham's tendency to keep things light. He rolled his eyes, then closed them. 'See, what did I tell you? I'm asleep.'

'You're talking,' Graham said.

'In my sleep. Happens all the time.'

'Diz.' He heard Freeman's voice. 'You're on a diving board, a high one. You're going to try a one and a half forward flip. You with me?'

'I'm there,' Hardy said.

Freeman kept on. 'Think the dive through. *Commit* to it. You're going all the way around and then halfway around again, a long time in the air. All right?'

'Ready.'

'*Think it!*'

Hardy forced the image.

'All right, now jump! Tuck hard, spin, you feel it? Don't pull out. Don't pull out.'

Hardy rolled with the dive. It was a long way around, but he held his tuck, entered the water cleanly, opened his eyes. 'Okay.'

'You get around?'

'No splash,' Hardy said. 'Cut it like a knife.'

Graham looked from one to the other again. 'You guys are crazy,' he said.

But Freeman had a valid point. This morning Hardy would open the case-in-chief for the defense. He would be calling his defense witnesses, and this was where their strategy could not waver. It would seem that they were hanging in the air, spinning, for a good deal of the time.

They weren't going to try to get the judge to instruct on lesser included offenses; the jury *would have no option* to convict Graham of manslaughter as a compromise. Graham wouldn't take the stand to appear sympathetic and likable. There was going to be no chance for a couple of years in prison and a life resumed. It was to be murder or nothing – life or freedom.

This was the agonizing crux of it. As it stood now, some members of the jury might still believe that Graham had had no part in his father's death. After Hardy presented his case-in-chief, however, no one would doubt Graham had done it, an 'it' that the law defined as murder: the deliberate taking of a human life. What the defense needed to do was to polarize the jury to convince them that if they did *not* believe Graham had killed his father for money, then they should acquit rather than convict on a lesser offense.

The prosecution had emphasized the financial motive for the

killing to bolster their charges of a first-degree murder conviction. Hardy's gambit was going to make the game winner take all – first or nothing.

This course was fraught with tremendous risk, although they all agreed that it was their best chance for acquittal.

But it would destroy the defense if Hardy forgot even for a moment and began to pull out of the spin before he reached the end. He could not allow himself the luxury of bringing up his possible 'other dudes.' He had one and only one story and he had to commit to it now, before he began, or they would lose.

Dr Russ Cutler was the young man Hardy had met and questioned for the first time at the Little Shamrock. Back then he'd been unshaven and exhausted, draped in his medical scrubs and his guilt over not having come forward about prescribing the morphine. Now he had finished his residency and gone into private practice. He had also spent a good deal of time rehearsing his proposed testimony with Freeman and Hardy.

In a tan linen suit and maroon tie, well rested and confident, he took the stand and swore to tell the whole truth and nothing but.

'Dr Cutler, would you please tell the court your relationship to Graham?'

'We play softball together on the same team. I consider myself his friend. I was his father's doctor.'

At these last words the white noise in the courtroom went away. Hardy's voice cut into the silence. 'Now, Doctor, as Sal Russo's physician, did you examine him in the last six months before his death?'

'Yes, I did. Graham told me that he had a sick father, and asked if I would look at him.'

'And would you tell the jury what you found?'

Cutler was happy to. Hardy thought him the perfect witness for his male-dominated jury. First, he was a guy himself, neither too young nor too old. He was dressed neatly enough for authority, but not much more. With solid features, he wasn't quite handsome, though he showed a lot of teeth when he smiled. Easy and approachable, that's what Cutler was.

Even better, Hardy realized. He cut nearly the same figure as

Judge Salter, except that he was twenty years younger, and he was sincere.

'And when you discovered what you thought was a brain tumor on the CAT scan, what did you do?'

'Well, then I went to an MRI.' With Hardy's nudging, Cutler explained a little about magnetic resonance imaging.

'And what did that reveal?'

'What I had suspected and feared – that the cancer had advanced beyond any ability to treat it. It was terminal.'

Behind him Hardy heard Drysdale's voice. 'Your Honor, excuse me, may we request a sidebar?'

Hardy didn't like this at all. 'Your Honor, I'm in the middle of something here.'

'It relates to what Mr Hardy is doing, Your Honor.'

Salter gave it about three seconds, then motioned the attorneys forward to the bench.

Once in front of the judge Drysdale wasted no time either. 'Your Honor, the prosecution will stipulate that Sal Russo had terminal cancer and perhaps Alzheimer's disease. He was going to die soon. All these questions by Mr Hardy aren't addressing any evidentiary issues.'

Freeman spoke under his breath. 'Neither did your case in chief.'

Salter glared him quiet. 'Mr Hardy?'

'Your Honor, it's our intention to show how the deceased's physical condition might have driven him to want to die.'

Soma's high-pitched voice rang out. 'So what? It's still murder.' The attorneys all turned to him at the outburst. Salter remained calm. 'Address your remarks to the court, all of you. That's me, Mr Soma. Mr Freeman.' He stared to make sure his point had come across. 'Mr Hardy, are you getting to some kind of mental defense? Are you going to be asking for manslaughter based on some theory?'

Hardy didn't answer directly. 'Your Honor, I'm getting to the relationship between Graham and his father. The prosecution is contending that he robbed from Sal, although they couldn't prove it, as you yourself noted this morning.'

Salter rebuked him. 'That's not entirely accurate. I did deny your motion, however close I thought it was.'

But Hardy kept at him. This was crucial to his case and he couldn't let it go. 'Nevertheless, Your Honor, Dr Cutler's testimony bears on the motive of the defendant. Graham Russo would not have stolen from his father. He loved him.'

The judge chewed on his cheek, slipped on his reading glasses, took them back off. 'Motive?'

'Yes, Your Honor.' Hardy had to have it, but it was another huge risk.

Salter thought another moment, then delivered his judgment. 'I'm going to allow it.'

Hardy let out a breath of relief. The attorneys returned to their tables. 'Dr Cutler,' he began again. 'You've just told us that Sal Russo's cancer was terminal. Did you have a prognosis on how long he would live?'

'Yes. Six months to a year.'

'And what about the disease itself, the tumor? Was it painful?'

'Indirectly, from the increased pressure in his head. This produced horrible headaches and began to cause visual changes and motor weakness.'

'And over the next six months or a year, would these symptoms grow progressively worse?'

'Yes.'

'There would be great pain, is that what you're saying?'

'Yes, unbearable pain.'

'Unbearable.' Hardy nodded and went back to his table to get a drink of water. There he was stunned and somewhat pleased to see his client, usually a devil-may-care wiseguy, with his jaw hard set, apparently blinking back tears. Hardy didn't want to draw attention to the moment – it would appear staged – but he noticed some of the jury had followed him over. He could only hope that they would see and draw the proper conclusion from it.

Back at the center of the courtroom Hardy began again. 'During this diagnostic stage, Doctor, all the tests and second opinions and so on, did Sal come to see you often?'

'Two or three times a week for a couple of months.'

'And did he come alone?'

'No, never. Graham always came with him.'

'Graham Russo came every time?'

'Yes, sir.'

'And these visits and tests, how did Sal pay for them? Did he have insurance?'

'No. That was one of his main problems.'

'And how did he solve that problem?'

'Graham paid for everything out of his pocket.'

The defense side of the gallery came alive now, and Salter had to gavel for quiet.

'Can you tell us more specifically what Graham paid for?'

Cutler remained completely at ease, talking to the jury, who were rapt. 'He paid for everything. The visits, the CAT scans, the MRI, the prescription.'

'Thank you, Doctor. We'll get to the prescription in a minute, but how can you be sure that this was Graham paying you personally, and not just handing you his father's money?'

Cutler crossed one knee over the other. Again, he brought it right to the jury. 'Graham and I play softball on a semipro team. After the games we'd collect our pay and he'd hand me his money. I'd take it in and pay his bill.'

'All right. Now referring to the prescriptions you wrote for Sal. Was one of these for the "Do Not Resuscitate" form?'

'Yes, it was.'

'Could you please tell us about that?'

'Sure.' Cutler had already been on the stand awhile, and Hardy's questioning would go on a little longer, but the doctor was still enthusiastic and, Hardy noted, he was holding the jury. 'It's pretty self-explanatory' – he had an almost apologetic tone – 'but Sal didn't want any extraordinary measures done to keep him alive. If the paramedics found him apparently dead, they were to leave him that way. He was pretty adamant about it. He had a lot of dignity.'

'And did he ask for the DNR himself?'

'Yes. Graham was there, but Sal wanted it in case he decided to kill himself.'

Hardy heard the susurrus sweep the gallery, but he kept it moving. 'Did Sal specifically tell you he planned to kill himself?'

Cutler, bless him, chuckled. 'Not exactly. We discussed his options. That was one of them.' He turned to the jury, explaining. 'That's the way these things go.'

'What do you mean by that, Doctor?'

'Well, you've got a patient who is going to die soon in great pain. On top of that, in Sal's case, you had his fear of the progress of Alzheimer's disease. So there was a lot of subtext, a lot of backwards questions.'

'Backwards questions?'

Cutler contemplated how to rephrase it. 'Okay. On the morphine, for example, Sal asked if twelve milligrams could be a lethal dose. "I don't want to kill myself by mistake," he said. But what he meant was "Can I kill myself with this if I decide to?" '

'Your Honor! Objection. Speculation. Dr Cutler can't know what Sal Russo meant by his question.'

Salter started to sustain, but Cutler had had enough of lawyers telling him what he, as a doctor, could or couldn't do. 'I know *exactly* what he meant,' he blurted out. 'He asked me how to kill himself, would it be more effective with alcohol, and I told him that if I answered his question I could lose my license and even go to jail. So we played this game where—'

Salter stopped him. 'Doctor, please. Confine yourself to answering specific questions. That's how we do it here.'

A tense silence settled over the courtroom. But Cutler had made the point and the jury would understand: terminal patients were often driven by the law to speak in code. The communication was clear on both sides.

Salter finally spoke again. 'Go ahead, Mr Hardy.'

Hardy nodded. 'This discussion about suicide, Doctor, was Graham there when you had it?'

'Yes. He was always there.'

Hardy took a small break, another sip of water. Graham had recovered his composure and gave him a nod. Cutler's testimony had clearly registered with the jury. Several of the men were taking notes. No one appeared distracted. They were waiting for his next sally. 'Dr Cutler, you knew that Graham worked as a paramedic, did you not?'

'Sure. Guys get hurt playing ball, Graham and I were the two medical people. It's how we got to know each other.'

'And to your personal knowledge, did he give his father morphine injections?'

'Yes. The first time or two during visits. It makes a big

difference with drugs whether you give them into the muscle, which is called IM, or the vein, which is IV. Initially, I recommended higher doses to be given IM. These could be lethal if injected IV. Later, Sal began to have breakthrough pain, so I instructed Graham on IV dosing guidelines. I wanted him to be especially clear on it.'

The jury had already heard this, but Hardy didn't think it would hurt them to be reminded. Graham had known what they knew.

'So Graham could have given these injections IV or IM without Sal's knowledge that he was doing anything unusual or different?'

Hardy heard Drysdale's voice. 'Your Honor. Objection. Relevance?'

'Mr Hardy?' In spite of himself Salter seemed to have gotten interested and was giving him wide leeway with Dr Cutler, but he thought Drysdale might have a point here. Where was this going?

Hardy was delighted with the objection, since it gave him a chance to explain. 'Your Honor, Mr Drysdale and Mr Soma have gone to some lengths to try to leave the impression that Graham hit his father behind the ear with the bottle of Old Crow so he could administer this shot without his father objecting. Though they haven't proven it, my question to Dr Cutler clarifies whether Graham would have had to do that in any event.'

Salter considered and then overruled the objection. The question was relevant. Cutler had it read back to him, and then told the jury that an experienced person such as Graham could have injected Sal IV or IM with complete impunity.

Which made clear to the jury, Hardy hoped, that Sal would never have had to suspect a thing. There would have been no struggle or need of one, not if Graham had been there.

Which he hadn't been, of course. But that was no longer the point.

Tactically, Hardy thought Soma and Drysdale made a mistake letting the younger man take Cutler's cross-examination. The two men were polar opposites, and Graham's friend the doctor was far more likable than the strident prosecutor.

Of course, both the men were fast-track urban professionals

and almost by definition had to possess Type-A personalities to have gotten where they were. They probably were – deep down inside – more similar than not. It was a matter of style more than anything, but style counted here, and played into Graham's hands. At least at first.

'Dr Cutler, you've said that you consider yourself a friend of the defendant. Have you known him for a long time?'

Cutler shrugged. 'About two years.'

'And you play baseball with him, is that correct?'

'Softball, but yes.'

'Outside of softball, do you see each other socially?'

This struck Cutler as funny. 'Outside of softball I don't have a social life.'

Humorless, Soma clucked. 'That would be no, Doctor, wouldn't it? You didn't see defendant socially?'

'Right,' Cutler agreed.

This answer, simple as it was, frustrated Soma. 'Your Honor,' he said to Salter, 'the question calls for a negative and Dr Cutler has answered in the affirmative.'

Salter huffed, 'So ask clearer questions, Mr Soma. Let's move along.'

Obviously swallowing his bile, Soma turned back to the witness box. 'Doctor, one more time, outside of softball, did you see defendant socially?'

Hardy wondered what Soma hoped to accomplish by this display. He was coming across as unusually petty and foolish, and to get what? That Cutler and Graham didn't party together? Who cared?

But the doctor just smiled, unruffled, and answered as bidden. 'No.'

Stiffly, Soma intoned, 'Thank you.'

'Don't mention it.'

A ripple of laughter in the gallery. Even Salter seemed to be suppressing some amusement. Soma finally seemed to get it. He forced a little smile of his own. 'Did defendant share with you any of his motives for accompanying his father?'

'Yes, of course. The obvious ones. I thought they were pretty obvious, anyway.'

'You did?' Soma raised his eyebrows and brought in the jury.

He'd started roughly, but had picked up a scent. He knew what trail he was going to follow now. 'You thought it was obvious why Graham brought his father down?'

'Yes, that's right.'

'Did you think it was obvious that he was being the dutiful son?'

'Yes.'

'And do you know for how long he had been this loving son?'

Hardy stood up. 'Objection, Your Honor.'

'Sustained.'

'We've heard testimony in this trial that the defendant hadn't seen his father for the previous fifteen years. Is that what you'd call being a loving son, Doctor?'

Again, Hardy was on his feet, objecting.

Soma fought back. 'Your Honor, the jury doesn't have to buy the defendant's late attack of altruism.'

The judge sustained Hardy, but Soma's attack continued. 'On any of these visits, was Sal Russo difficult to attend to?'

'What do you mean, difficult?'

'Well, doctor, here is a man with Alzheimer's disease, sometimes he doesn't know where he is, he doesn't know who *you* are, he's got a tremendously painful cancer in his brain. Surely he was a little cranky from time to time. Would you say that was the case?'

'Yes, sometimes.'

'And did the defendant ever mention to you that his father was being burdensome or difficult to take care of?'

'Well, he was—'

'Yes or no, Doctor?'

'Yes.'

'And maybe he was getting a little tired of it?'

'Objection! Hearsay. Speculation. Badgering the witness.'

But Soma whirled, flashed a malevolent glance at Hardy, spun back to Salter. 'I'm asking the witness what he heard with his own ears, Your Honor. It's neither hearsay nor speculation. And I'm not badgering. I'm trying to get straight exactly what he heard.'

Salter allowed the question, overruling Hardy, and was about to ask the recorder to read it out again, when Soma delivered it word for word. 'And maybe he was getting a little tired of it? Did Graham Russo ever say that?'

'All right, maybe he did.'

'Maybe he did. Yes. Now, let's move to these medical bills and doctor's bills and so on that the defendant was paying. They must have been expensive. Were they expensive?'

'Yes.'

'Very expensive? In the hundreds? Thousands? Ten thousands?'

'Say the high thousands.'

'All right, let's say the high thousands. Did the defendant ever mention to you that this was becoming difficult? This was a financial burden he could do without?'

'No.'

'No? He was paying thousands of dollars to keep alive a man who was near death anyhow, and he never mentioned any frustration about that?'

'No. That never came up.'

'It never came up. Perhaps that's because he wasn't spending his own money.'

Hardy stood again. 'Your Honor—'

But Soma stepped in again. 'Your Honor, Dr Cutler has told us he received money from Graham for these bills after softball games, and now we learn it was thousands of dollars.'

'Proceed,' Salter intoned.

'Are we to believe, Doctor, that the defendant makes thousands of dollars playing *softball* and that every time he paid you for medical services you witnessed the source of the money?'

'Not every time—'

'Ah, so the defendant would sometimes bring money from, apparently, another source?'

Cutler threw an apologetic look across the courtroom to Graham and Hardy. What could he do? 'Yes, sometimes,' he said.

'And that source was his father, isn't that so?'

'Objection! Speculation.'

But Soma kept right on, his voice rising in pitch and volume. 'And maybe that source was drying up, wasn't it, Doctor? And there wasn't as much money anymore as defendant—'

'Your Honor! I object.' Hardy was forced to raise his own voice.

For nearly the first time in the entire trial Salter banged his gavel. 'Mr Soma, please! Get yourself under control. Another outburst like that and I'll find you in contempt. You hear me?'

'Yes, Your Honor, I'm sorry.' But he looked neither diminished by the rebuke nor sorry for what had caused it. He was drawing some rich blood.

'Doctor,' he continued, 'did the defendant ever indicate to you that he was entitled to something for all the trouble he was going through?'

'No. He was—'

'Did *Sal Russo*, defendant's father, did Sal ever complain about how much these visits were costing?'

'Yes, sometimes he would—'

'Did it ever occur to you that he meant to ask how much it was costing him, not Graham?'

'No, it wasn't—'

'Do you know it wasn't his father's money?'

'No, but—'

'Do you know his father didn't pay back even the softball money as soon as they got back to his apartment?'

'No, but I—'

'Your Honor.' Hardy had to try to break up this rhythm. 'The witness is entitled to explain his answers.'

'They're all yes-and-no questions, Your Honor.' Soma was really on a roll. He didn't want to give the judge time to make any ruling on the objection. The jury would remember what he'd gotten, not how. 'I'll watch it, Your Honor.' Which was easy to say – he was finished. He'd gotten what he'd come for. 'No further questions.'

'I have one.' Freeman the wild card came up and around the defense table for redirect. He hadn't even cleared it with Hardy, so he must have been sure he was on to something. 'Dr Cutler, at any time in all of your treatments of Sal Russo, did you, Sal, and Graham ever frankly and fully discuss the possibility of assisted suicide?'

There was a collective gasp in the gallery. This was the kind of question Soma might have asked. To hear it from the defense table was shocking.

But Freeman had done it and it was now on the record. Cutler, shell shocked anyway from Soma's assault, now looked stunned. 'Yes, many times. He asked me if I'd help kill him if he got too far gone. I said I couldn't.'

'And was Sal Russo lucid during at least some of these discussions?'

'Yes. Many of them. Most.'

'It was brilliant, if I do say so myself, and I do.' Freeman was in the holding cell defending himself. Hardy and Graham were both having trouble appreciating his genius. 'We got assisted suicide in the front of everybody's brains now.'

'We did before, David. It was more subtle was all.'

'Subtle schmuttle.' Unwrapping his Reuben sandwich, Freeman scoffed at the idea. He took a juicy bite, leaned over so the bag would catch his drippings, swabbed his thick lips with a napkin. 'Listen up. Graham didn't say that he was thinking of killing his dad, *for any reason*. Remember, we're loving this assisted suicide defense, but it's still illegal, my sons.' He pointed at Graham. 'Even if it's going to get you off.'

Graham was unconvinced. 'Yoda better that clearer make.'

Freeman motioned over to Hardy. 'That's for this silver-tongued devil in closing.'

'How can I thank you enough?' Hardy asked.

Freeman grinned and took another bite. 'No charge.'

33

Thursday afternoon, all day Friday, Monday and Tuesday of the next week, was a long, slow waltz for the defense. Hardy had to get the jury to hear about the progress of Alzheimer's disease, about Sal's relations with the rest of the estranged family, about the places and times Sal and Graham had been together in public. So he called Helen and George and Debra and the young Dr Finer, who'd first examined Sal at the county clinic. He called the owner of the U.S. Restaurant, where they had frequently eaten.

Keeping up on the motive issue, he brought up many of Graham's past co-workers and associates. One at a time Hardy called as witnesses several EMTs – three male, two female – who'd crewed with him over the past two years, all of whom had nothing but good to say about his compassion, bedside manner, cooperative spirit, medical knowledge, punctuality, and general competence. He'd made no enemies within his ambulance company.

Besides Russ Cutler, three other members of Graham's softball team, the Hornets, testified that he'd brought his father to games, introduced him around, went out for food afterward. He was a solicitous and dutiful son.

Especially effective was Roger Stamps, who'd been with them in Fremont after a game a year or more ago when Sal had wandered away from the softball field. He and Graham had driven the darkened streets for over an hour before locating Sal in the coffee shop of a bowling alley.

Graham had paid his father's tab, got him belted into the car, and drove him home. He'd never shown impatience or anger. Stamps hoped that when he got old he could have a son as devoted as Graham.

Craig Ising was a guy's guy and hence a good call for this jury, but there was a risk to calling him as well. In Hardy's mind there was a very real legal question as to whether Graham's knowing participation in the high-stakes softball games, even leaving aside the question of claiming his income from it, constituted a felony.

In the end they decided to call Ising as a witness anyway. He, better than anyone else, could put a positive spin on Graham's apparently irresponsible defection from Harold Draper's courtroom, as well as explain the intricacies of his motivation to be a replacement player: that Graham had correctly predicted the end of the baseball strike, had wanted another look from the major league clubs, wouldn't play as a scab, and so on.

If Graham wasn't going to testify, somebody else had to make the jury aware of his state of mind, and Ising was the best choice. Graham hadn't acted like a selfish flake – he was a man in pursuit of a dream.

Soma and Drysdale kept a low profile. The occasional objection would come up over a witness's characterization of one of Graham's actions, but generally the prosecution seemed happy to let Hardy call his people and let them talk.

None of the witnesses were rebutting the evidence that had been presented. What could there be to worry about?

On Wednesday morning at seven-thirty Hardy sat behind the closed door of Abe Glitsky's office with David Freeman and Sarah Evans. They were reviewing all the leads that, as Sarah had independently discovered over the past four months, had gone nowhere. Hardy and Freeman were contemplating calling one more witness and then they were going to wrap up the defense, Hardy getting to tie the pieces of his story – Graham's story – together at last.

The early confidence he felt in their strategy had completely disappeared by now. Not that the trial hadn't gone as well as he'd hoped, but a jury was always a crapshoot, and this one particularly. Hardy had been in the air with his dive now for most of four court days, and it was all he could do to hold his tuck for the next hours.

He hadn't rebutted any prosecution evidence in his own case

in chief. Oh, yes, he'd done his best to discredit witnesses on the issue of whether there had been a struggle, but that had been about the extent of his arguments. He had presented an affirmative defense that was simply an alternative explanation of the same facts that the prosecution had used.

It was going to come down to a matter of what the jury believed. Or whom they believed. In that sense it was good that no one had found any 'other dudes' to point at.

And now they were all committed. Hardy's defense was really the only possible one left. But he couldn't shake his intense discomfort over the fact that it was, basically, a cynical lie. A lie that served justice, he believed, but still a lie.

Freeman was not being his most endearing self. He appeared to have slept in his suit and certainly hadn't showered – obvious in the cramped room. He had consumed a healthy, well-rounded breakfast of peanuts and had piled the shells in front of him on Glitsky's desk. 'Look, Lieutenant, we can go down to Judge Salter right now and get ourselves a month continuance, and I think we ought to do it and investigate the hell out of this gambling connection.'

Hardy tried to rein his partner in. 'He'd never do that to the jury, David. Not at this stage. And it's not about any gambling, anyway.'

Freeman paid no mind, breezing along, jawing at Glitsky. 'We know that Craig Ising is in cahoots with at least two dozen other gamblers downtown, most of whom used Sal Russo to run their money around—'

'A long time ago,' Hardy put in.

'– some of which might have been the wrapped bills in this case.'

'There's no evidence of that,' Sarah said.

Freeman snapped, 'None that you've found.'

Sarah's eyes flashed at him. 'That's right. None that anybody could have found.'

Glitsky sat up. 'Hey, hey, nobody has to get accusatory. Getting mad isn't going to help anything.'

'I'm not mad.' Freeman appeared genuinely surprised. He was simply arguing his position, for him a function of drawing breath. How could it offend?

Evans, however, had some color in her cheeks. 'I interviewed Craig Ising twice, Mr Freeman.' Actually it had been four times, but Glitsky had only known and approved of the last two of them, so she went with that. 'I told him we weren't interested in his gambling, only in Sal. He said to his knowledge no one had used Sal in at least two full years.'

Freeman scoffed at that. 'He says . . .'

'Graham corroborates it,' Hardy said.

Freeman looked from one of them to the other. 'Here's the deal,' he said. 'Sal had memory problems. This ring a bell, Pavlovs? He might have stumbled upon this opportunity to deliver a bag of cash and forgot he even did it.'

'To who? From who?' Glitsky asked.

'Abe means *whom*, David. To whom, from whom.' Hardy favored Abe with a smile.

Abe looked over. 'Whom this, Diz.'

Freeman ignored the exchange. 'That's your job, Lieutenant. Find that out.'

Like Freeman, Glitsky wasn't angry. He admired Freeman's persistence, but he realized that he was fishing and had nothing. 'Point me to any evidence, any direction, David, and we're on it. I'm not saying it couldn't have happened. I'm not even saying it didn't happen. But I've got a suspect on trial for what we'd be asking these people about, if we could find out who they were.'

'What about the cooperative Mr Ising?'

Hardy had to speak up again. 'He's *our* witness, David. He's been nothing but a help.'

Freeman waved a hand. 'That's old news. What's he done for us lately?' Back at Glitsky. 'Look, you call Ising in, rip him a new asshole over all this gambling, tell him you're giving him up to vice if he doesn't give us the name of every one of his cohorts, and then you call all of them downtown and find where their stories don't coincide. Does he have a sheet?' Meaning a police record.

Truly amused now, Glitsky rolled his eyes at Sarah, turned to Hardy. 'Anything else, Diz?'

'I think you went a bit over the line, David. Suggesting we arrest the entire young generation of the city's power elite, I don't know, maybe that didn't seem reasonable.'

'Glitsky could do it.'

They sat at their table in the empty courtroom. Freeman had tried another ploy, suggesting on round two that this time Glitsky arrest Dan Tosca and somehow squeeze him for information on the multimillion-dollar fish-poaching trade. But again, as Glitsky and Sarah had pointed out, there wasn't even any smoke around Tosca. Why should they go looking for a fire?

'The point is *not* that he could do it, David, but that he'd have to explain *why*, and there wouldn't be any good reasons.'

The old man shook his head. 'Picky picky picky.'

'Besides,' Hardy continued, 'I thought we'd decided to stay in our tuck.'

'That was you,' Freeman said. 'Me, I'd go to any lengths to keep a verdict away from a jury. If a judge would give me a five-year continuance, I'd take it on general principles.'

'Spoken like a true defense attorney.'

'Which, I might remind you, is what I am.'

'And you'd let your client rot in jail?'

'Absolutely.'

Hardy had to laugh. 'Were you born with this great compassion for your fellow man or is it something you've developed over the years?'

'Both. But all right, Glitsky washed. Now we're back on Plan A. We calling Brandt?'

They'd beaten this decision to death but were pretty clear with what they should do. On the one hand, Barbara Brandt would be a stirring defender of assisted suicide and would put the issue right into the collective faces of the jury. But Freeman had already done just that on redirect with Russ Cutler. Only a moron – and Hardy hoped there were none on the jury – could avoid some sense of the real issue in this case.

On the other hand, Brandt would swear that Graham had killed Sal. She was probably a liar and certainly a loose cannon. Hardy didn't know what, if anything, Drysdale and Soma had discovered about Brandt's lie detector test, but the polygraph expert's name was Les Worrell and he was on their witness list.

Hardy had questioned Worrell and believed that Brandt had in fact passed the test. But he'd also read newspaper and magazine reports opining that Barbara Brandt had been coached in how to pass the test. What Hardy didn't know was if Worrell had been implicated in that collusion, and he was loath to ask about more things he didn't know. The whole polygraph issue was inadmissible, but Hardy and Freeman thought they knew a land mine when they saw one.

'I'm going to let my instincts decide,' he said finally.

'Go with what you feel, huh?' Freeman asked.

'Right.'

'Dumbest idea I ever heard.'

Hardy shrugged. 'You do it all the time.'

'But I'm the incredible David Freeman.' It wasn't clear whether he was kidding or not.

'I'm going to win them over, David. I'm going to make them see it.'

'Without Brandt?'

'Probably, now that I think of it. She can't tell the jury anything they don't already know from other sources.'

Freeman seemed to buy this. 'So? You got a plan?'

Hardy cracked a craggy grin. 'The outline's a little vague. A little smile, a little dance, a little seltzer in my pants.'

Drysdale, Soma, and the big boss himself, Dean Powell, were having their own meeting in the state attorneys' offices on Fremont Street. Though a day or so of the defense's testimony had gone by before they'd seen it, they were no longer unaware that Hardy was conducting his portion of the trial on a different plane than they had.

They had a big decision to make and weren't in precise accord about how to proceed. Dean Powell had the floor, which in this case was the head of the long functional state-issue table in the conference room. His face was set, and under the mane of white hair his color was high. 'I don't care about any face-saving strategy, Art, we're not backing away from the specials.'

'All I'm saying, Dean' – Drysdale's tone was mild – 'is that we don't want to let this boy go free. If the jury's only choice is to convict on robbery murder or acquit, they might just acquit, and then what's all this been for?'

'All this has been to bring a murderer to justice.' Powell wasn't entertaining other suggestions. 'That's what all this has been for. It's what it's always been for. Besides, they're not going to acquit.'

Fearless, Soma waded into it. 'We just want to drive a stake into the heart of that possibility, Dean. Give them another option to consider. Ask for manslaughter as a possible lesser verdict.'

'Hardy's leading them in that direction, Dean,' Drysdale added. 'Gil and I just want to cut him off.'

'God damn it,' Powell clipped, 'are you boys listening to me? Am I speaking some foreign language? We have charged our man Russo here with robbery murder. Don't you think I understand the implications of that? I assure you I do. And I'll tell you something else: if we back off, if we even *appear* to back off, we'll be broadcasting the news to the jury that we didn't prove the case. And then they *will* acquit.'

There was that familiar bubble of silence that succeeds the moment when a boss swears at underlings. Drysdale took a breath. 'How about this, Dean? We don't argue assisted suicide—'

Powell: 'Damn straight we don't.'

'– but we give it to Salter in our jury instructions?'

The dilemma they faced was a real one. In the same way that Hardy and the defense had gone into their tuck, vowing not to pull out of it until they had presented their entire argument, so, too, the prosecution had avoided muddying the murder waters by never alluding to the possibility that Sal's death was less than murder. Assisted suicide was still, both technically and in fact, a crime in the state of California. It might not be first-degree murder, but it was at least second, and no way less than a long prison term.

Drysdale was admitting the validity of Powell's position – that they might open themselves to ridicule (and acquittal) if they switched over and added the assisted-suicide argument at this point. But if they did do that, they would vastly increase the odds that the jury would not set Graham Russo scot free.

Drysdale believed that he could persuade Judge Salter to direct the jury that assisted suicide was still murder. Then, the jury could return with a verdict of first- or second-degree murder and Powell could still claim some sort of victory.

But the attorney general was adamant. He wasn't doing that. His team wouldn't play on that field. 'We picked this fight six months ago, Art. We get him on robbery murder or we let him go.'

Tempers were fraying and Soma cracked under the pressure, slapping his palm loudly on the table. 'Shit.'

Powell snapped back, the strike of a snake. 'Don't you give me that attitude, Mr Soma. You'll find yourself unemployed in a fucking heartbeat. You hear me? You afraid you didn't prove the case?'

Soma raised his eyes. 'We proved the case, sir.'

Powell stared him down. 'Let's hope you did. Because I don't want to hear one word in your closing about assisted suicide except to say it's no defense to a murder charge. Our boy killed his father for his money. That's what he did and that's why he did it. If you've got any kind of problem with that at this stage, either of you' – he paused, glaring – 'well, that's just too damn bad. You're going to have to live with it.'

Sarah's early-morning meeting with Hardy and Freeman in Glitsky's office was ancient history as she and her partner decided not to wait for the elevators and took the stairs on their way down to the lobby. On the second-floor landing Sarah glanced into the hallway and saw a pregnant woman, feet spread and planted, sitting on a bench alone outside of Graham's courtroom. Now, on a hunch, she asked Lanier to wait a minute and walked over.

'Are you Debra McCoury?'

The woman's face was blotched and she appeared to be near tears. She nodded. 'Who are you?'

Sarah sat next to her, introducing herself. 'I'm the one who arrested your brother. I don't know if you remember, but we spoke on the phone when I first—'

'I remember.' The face closed up.

'I've called since a few times. You've been a little hard to get in touch with.'

'Well, I work.' And evidently hated the fact.

'But you're here now?'

'And the other day too. I was a witness. I got time off,' Debra said. 'Without pay. They said they're doing the closing arguments today. I wanted to be here.'

From Graham, Sarah had learned quite a lot about Debra.

Like her mother had with Sal, she had married below some perception of her station in life, and it was playing the same kind of havoc with her. Graham felt nothing but sorry for her. She didn't have be so miserable, to keep herself looking so plain. Certainly, she didn't have to remain in a relationship with a cheating husband.

But it was the same as the case with George. Sal's abandonment had brought with it a nearly paralyzing loss of her self-esteem, along with a bitterness that soured everything in her world. Debra believed in her heart that she wasn't worth loving, that no one would ever truly love her. Sarah thought one look at her revealed her story. And now she was going to have Brendan's baby and life was going to get more complicated, sadder.

'So why are you down here?' Sarah asked. 'You told me you didn't like Graham, that he couldn't be trusted.'

Debra swallowed with some effort. 'He *is* my brother.'

'And what does that mean?'

'That means I don't want to see him sent to jail.'

'Do you think he killed your father?'

The blotches rose on her heavy neck. 'I don't know.'

'But you *do* think he stole this money?'

'I don't know that, either, anymore. I was here and heard that bank person. Nobody seems to know what happened about that. What did you want to see me about?'

In fact, she'd called Debra for the most part because Dismas Hardy had asked her to do so before they had finally left the 'other dude' phase of the investigation. Not that she or Hardy had thought Debra would lead to anything substantial.

Still, when she'd made herself unavailable, Sarah had wondered. 'I was following up on some other questions. You told me about the baseball cards. You also gave me the impression that you knew Sal had more money stashed away somewhere.'

'Which, it turns out, he did.'

'True, but that's not my point. My point is how did you know it?'

'I don't know. Maybe I wasn't sure of it. I guess Graham told me.'

'But I thought you hadn't talked to Graham in a couple of years.' Debra moved her hands over her belly, her face a brown study. There was a glint of moisture in her eyes. 'You also said Sal kept the baseball cards in his apartment. Had you been there? To his apartment? How did you know he kept them there?'

She was shaking her head. 'No. I just assumed . . .' Suddenly she whirled on Sarah. 'What are you asking me all of these questions for? I didn't do anything.'

'I didn't say you did.'

'But you're—'

'I'm just asking you to explain how you knew some of the things you told me about.' Lanier grew tired of waiting in the stairway. He came across the hall and stood in front of the two women. 'This is my partner, Inspector Lanier,' Sarah said.

Lanier nodded. 'Everything all right here?'

Sarah kept up the press. 'I'm sure you remember where you were on the afternoon that your father was killed. You wouldn't forget that.'

'No. I don't forget it. It was a Friday, wasn't it? I was at work.'

'All day? You didn't take lunch?'

'Yes. No. I think so. I don't remember. Probably.' Debra's hands massaged her stomach. 'Look, I don't like this. This is making me feel sick.' Perhaps because of Lanier's looming presence she made no effort to rise. 'Sal always had the baseball cards, from when I was a kid,' she said. 'I mean, he *had* to still have them. And the way my mother talked, she always said he had other money. That's why I thought that.'

'So why did you tell me Graham was hiding something and couldn't be trusted?'

Sarah knew the real answer to this question, but she wanted to hear the way Debra got around it. Finally, her eyes spilled over. She dug in her purse for something to wipe the tears away. 'He's not bad,' she said.

'Who isn't bad, Debra? Graham?'

But she was shaking her head from side to side, snuffling. 'I just don't want them to send him to jail. He didn't kill Sal for any money. I know that.'

'How do you know it?'

'I just know him. He wouldn't have done that.' She looked pleadingly at Sarah and Marcel. 'I don't care about the money either. Not anymore. I don't even want my share. I don't care about it. Brendan wanted—' She stopped.

'Your husband? What about your husband?'

'He's the one who wanted the money, who was on me to get the money.' She sobbed once. 'I didn't mean to get Graham in trouble. I just want our family back again, the way it was. Anything the way it was. Why can't it be that way anymore?'

The tears were falling freely now, and Sarah finally touched her shoulder, then stood up and motioned to Marcel that they should go.

34

Two days later Hardy rested the defense case without calling Barbara Brandt, or Graham Russo. Gil Soma spent a moment conferring quietly with Art Drysdale at the prosecution table. They were disappointed, but not surprised, that they wouldn't get a chance to hack at Graham.

They'd spent a full day in chambers arguing jury instructions. Salter had been very uncomfortable about not giving manslaughter instructions – not giving the jury any choice but murder or acquittal. But neither side wanted manslaughter, and that seemed to be a correct reading of the law, so Salter shrugged his shoulders and wished both sides good luck.

Now Hardy flashed a look behind him at the courtroom, which was filled to overflowing. It was reminiscent of day one, with Pratt and Powell and their respective acolytes in attendance, one team on each side. There was Jeff Elliot, the 'CityTalk' columnist from the *Chronicle*. And Barbara Brandt – bravely camouflaging her disappointment at being snubbed – surrounded by her entourage. Helen Taylor was in the first row behind Hardy. Graham's very pregnant sister, Debra, who'd evidently had an emotional morning, was next to her mother.

But Soma was up now, commanding all of Hardy's attention, that of all the courtroom. First he would give his closing argument, then it would be Hardy's turn. Finally, Soma would get the last word and Salter would give the jury their instructions. Then, at last, the jury would go into deliberation.

Hardy leaned over and whispered to Graham, asking him if he was all right, telling him this might get rough, he should stay calm, try not to react.

The young man smiled gamely, grabbed Hardy's arm, and gave it a squeeze. 'No fear.'

'Easy for you to say.'

After a lunch break when he hadn't been able to force a bite, Hardy was back with David Freeman and Graham Russo at their table in the courtroom. Soma had borrowed the low-key approach he'd used to such good effect in his opening statement and in about an hour had told the by-now familiar story in a straightforward and plausible manner. Reflecting Dean Powell's decision, he'd made no mention of assisted suicide as a reasonable second interpretation of the evidence for the jury, and this had been a huge relief for the defense.

Hardy and Graham now thought they had a chance. David Freeman was of the opinion that it was locked up; they would get their acquittal. And because Freeman had no sense of superstition and little of decorum, he'd kept repeating it during the recess, making the other guys crazy.

Graham had snapped at Freeman. 'You ever heard of not mentioning it when you're in the middle of a no-hitter, David? You don't tell the pitcher.'

'Why not?' Freeman asked.

Saying, 'Never mind, don't try,' to Graham, Hardy had left the holding cell.

Now he stepped out in front of his table, closer to the jury box than he'd been when talking to witnesses. He paused to slow himself down, gave a confident nod to Graham and Freeman, took a deep breath, and began.

'Ladies and gentlemen of the jury. I told you at the beginning of this trial that Graham Russo loved his father and I'm telling you that again now.'

He moved a step closer to the jury box. 'Sal Russo lived in a world that was closing up on him, a world of murky memories and ever-increasing pain. For years and years he'd been estranged from all three of his children, but about two years ago he reached out to one of them, to Graham, his oldest son.

'At the time Graham was having troubles of his own, troubles that I'm sure many of you have experienced as you've tried to get settled in your jobs and your life's work.'

Hardy had to get this jury, and in particular these men, to recognize the common ground they shared with his client.

'He had quit the prestigious appointment he got after law school to pursue his dream of playing major-league baseball, but then that dream, too, had fallen apart.' Hardy humanized it a little more. 'He just couldn't hit the curveball. I'm sure many of us know how that feels.' He got a chuckle or two.

'When he came back to San Francisco, resigned now finally to being a lawyer, he found that he couldn't find any work, that the people he'd thought were his friends in the yuppie world of the law had abandoned him.' These were calculated words, designed to move these mostly working-class men into Graham's corner.

Hardy continued. 'This is when he reconnected with Sal. We've also heard the members of his family – his mother and brother and sister – testify that it's also when Graham discovered that his father was having problems with his memory. He was in the first stages of Alzheimer's disease. Occasionally he would forget where he was, what he needed to do. Graham was the only one who would help.

'But he did more than simply help. He became his father's companion and friend. They went out to dinners together, to ball games. They drove around the city, talking, laughing together, reconnecting. Until finally, as we learned from Dr Cutler, Sal began getting these terrible, unbearable headaches.'

Hardy paused for a moment. He was going to change his direction now and confront the prosecution. 'You've heard Mr Soma and Mr Drysdale make assertions that Graham resented his father, the time he spent with him, the money he spent for his treatment. Let me remind you that no one in this trial has ever, not once, presented any *evidence* in support of these assertions. And you know why that is? Because they aren't true.

'Graham never got tired of helping his father, of nursing his father. Judge Giotti told you that Graham visited Sal several times a week to make sure he was comfortable, was taking his shots, right up until the end. Blue, Sal's downstairs neighbor – a witness for the prosecution – told us the same thing. Graham never wavered in his devotion. He loved Sal.'

Another pause. Hardy walked over to his table for a sip of water. He glanced at the yellow pad on his desk, on which were written only three words: *Love. Evidence. Close.* He'd barely touched on evidence yet, the burden of proof, the usual smorgasbord. He had to give it its due now. Tearing a page from Soma's book, he came right to the jury rail, talking to them now not in a speech, but human to human.

'Some of you may have noticed that I've spent very little time trying to rebut the evidence that the prosecution has presented. That's because there is precious little evidence. No one ever saw *or even said they saw* Graham treat his father other than as a friend and companion. The famous fifty thousand dollars? The baseball cards? Did Mr Soma or Mr Drysdale prove anything to you about them, other than that they once were in Sal's possession, and later they were in Graham's?

'Isn't it more reasonable to assume that Sal knew he was losing his reason and wanted his son, who was his caretaker and friend anyway, to hold his valuables so that, at the least, they wouldn't get lost or misplaced? Or so that Graham could use the money and proceeds from the cards to help defray some of the costs of Sal's treatment? From what you've heard about Graham Russo, doesn't that make a lot more sense than that suddenly, one day, Graham struggled with his father and stole his money? It's ridiculous. It didn't happen.

'Similarly, there was no proof of any struggle. Let me tell you something, and Judge Salter will repeat it to you when he gives you his jury instructions: the prosecution has to prove Graham's guilt to you beyond a reasonable doubt, and I don't have to prove anything. The burden of proof never shifts; it is always on the prosecution, and unless they can prove something, as far as you must be concerned, it just didn't happen.'

Salter cleared his throat and interrupted. 'Mr Hardy, I'll be instructing them on the law when you're finished.'

Hardy took it calmly. Salter was right. But it wouldn't hurt for the jury to see his passion. He turned back to the panel with an apologetic smile.

'As it turns out, you have heard quite a lot of testimony about Graham's character, about his relationship with Sal, about the kind of person he is. But even if you had none of that or didn't believe it, even if Graham sat there friendless and alone with no one to speak up for him, the prosecution has presented nothing to support their theory. That's all it is – a misguided theory with no facts, no evidence, no proof, to support it.

'Then how did it get to here, all the way to trial? I know you're all asking yourselves that question, and I don't blame you. So I'll tell you.

'It got here for one reason, and one reason only.'

Really there were two, and he hoped the jury had read the newspapers or talked to family members or somehow had discovered the personal connection between Gil Soma and Graham Russo. Freeman had bitched about Soma's involvement to the press on many occasions early on in the proceedings, and then Hardy had alluded to it in a couple of discussions with his reporter friend Jeff Elliot, who printed it in his 'CityTalk' column. It couldn't be admitted at trial, of course, but sometimes you got things to juries any way you could.

But Hardy, now, had to get to the lies. It was unpleasant and dicey, but he had to address the issue. 'Graham panicked when the police came to talk to him. He didn't panic because he thought he'd done anything morally wrong' – and here his phraseology had to be precise – 'but because he'd been close to someone who had taken his own life. He'd shown him how to use the syringe. He'd even on occasion administered the drug himself. He'd comforted and counseled him when nobody else would. And he knew he might be condemned for it. He knew his kindness and compassion might be twisted by those more interested in politics than in justice, more eager to exact a pound of flesh than to do the right thing.

'Graham Russo knew the world was full of bureaucrats, small men and women who live to control the lives of others. Men and women who like nothing more than to tell men like Dr Cutler what medical advice to give and tell us all what medicine we can and cannot take to ease our pain.

'Graham knew that these petty people weren't content to control only our lives; they seek even to control our deaths as well. Sal Russo finally was beyond their control now, but Graham Russo was not, and he was afraid. That is why he lied.'

Another pause to let it all sink in.

'As a licensed attorney in the state of California, Graham was faced with the very real possibility that, guilty or innocent, he would lose his ability to practice law. He might be disbarred. He could then never work in the profession for which he'd spent three grueling years in school and thousands of dollars in tuition. He couldn't let that happen.

'So he lied to police, and then he lied to cover his earlier lies. I wish this weren't the case, and believe me, so does he. But he did, and it's put him here. And let me add that even Sergeant Evans, who heard all of Graham's falsehoods firsthand, has told you she thinks Graham is a trustworthy person, not a liar.'

Hardy took a breath, relieved. He'd expected to be interrupted by objections at every second, but the closing argument was just that, an argument. He was making his case and evidently keeping within the bounds of specificity. That was going to change in a minute, but for the moment he was on safe ground.

'Graham knew that it looked like Sal had committed suicide. Indeed, Dr Strout, the coroner, is still not able to say it wasn't suicide. Perhaps Graham knew better. Perhaps he knew about the DNR sticker that was out for the paramedics when they arrived. Perhaps he knew that his father's pain had become unceasing, that life had become truly unbearable, that Sal was ready to die. That death itself, when it came, would be a peaceful and blessed relief.'

Hardy scanned the jury box, resting on several jurors. He wasn't offering any challenge, just telling them what he believed, what they had to believe.

He lowered his voice to a near whisper. 'Graham is a trained paramedic. He got two calls from his father on the morning of his death. He went to the apartment, where his father was in blinding pain. Perhaps Sal, sitting on the floor by his coffee table, had a last drink or two for courage. An intravenous morphine shot is – as Dr Strout has told you – instantaneous and painless. There was no struggle at any time. And for Sal Russo, there would be no more pain, no more confusion as the past inexorably slipped away from him, no loss of dignity. There would, finally, be peace.'

He met the eyes of every juror, one by one. It seemed to take forever.

'I tell you that Graham Russo has committed no crime. No murder was done here, no injury to society that requires retribution. This is an innocent man. Legally, factually, and, above all, morally innocent. You must find him not guilty – for all of our sakes.'

CityTalk, by Jeff Elliot

The hottest ticket in town on Thursday was Department 27 at the Hall of Justice, the courtroom of Judge Jordan Salter. There, to an SRO crowd comprised of most of the state's legal powerhouses, including California Attorney General Dean Powell and San Francisco District Attorney Sharron Pratt, euthanasia lobbyists, citizens' groups, and media representatives, the murder trial of lawyer/athlete Graham Russo closed in a flurry of rhetoric from both sides.

This reporter's view has always been that this trial was less about the murder of Salmon Sal Russo than it was a kind of grudge matchup between Gil Soma and Graham Russo, both of whom served a few years ago as clerks for Federal Judge Harold Draper. Soma hated Russo for leaving him a big workload, and here was the chance to pay him back.

Petty? You bet.

Defense Attorney Dismas Hardy took a bold stance and ignored the great majority of evidence presented by Messrs Soma and Drysdale for the prosecution, and instead painted his own picture of a devoted son who found himself in the agonizing dilemma of his father's terminal illness.

The jury evidently believed him. After deliberating only one and a half hours, at about three-thirty yesterday afternoon, as all the country now knows, they returned with a verdict of acquittal. They didn't say that Graham Russo assisted in his father's suicide. The way the law is written, that's just not an option.

Instead, they had to say that Graham did nothing wrong.

I think they were right.

PART FIVE

35

He was halfway across the lobby at Freeman's office – the sun was bright in the Solarium – when Phyllis called out from the reception desk. 'Oh, Mr Hardy.'

Turning on a dime, he marched to her desk. 'Oh, Phyllis.' He stared down at her as she looked up at him. 'Someday you're going to smile and I'm going to catch you and tell everybody.'

This wasn't the time, though. The phones were ringing all over the switchboard and she pointed vaguely off behind her. 'Mr Russo's in his office. He wants to see you.'

Yoda figured that proximity to his own august self during the four months of the trial preparation had been proper training to turn Graham into his very own Jedi knight, and after a week off to reacclimatize to civilian life, the ex-defendant had come in to work at the Freeman Building as one of David's associates. So much for Graham's worries about being unhirable in the law.

Hardy took a scintilla of pleasure from the fact that Freeman had given Graham Michelle's old office. The usurper was gone, and with her the memory (well, most of it) of what she'd done, what he hadn't.

Remaining for a moment at the reception desk, Hardy was deciding if he should go upstairs first, check his answering machine. He was out hustling jobs now, had been all morning, all the past couple of weeks since the trial had ended. The endeavor had not been entirely unsuccessful.

Since the conclusion of Graham's trial Hardy had reacquired a bit of star status in town. He'd gotten a lot of press, and calls had come in. He was looking forward to facing some of Dean Powell's minions again; the attorney general had decided to save face with his constituency by prosecuting some (but not all) of the doctors who'd admitted to being involved with their patients' deaths. Two of these doctors had come to Hardy. He wasn't sure he wanted assisted suicide to become 'his' issue, but on a case-by-case basis a lawyer could do worse – and at best find himself on the side of the angels.

He was still billing far less than he needed to live on, although he had a few months' reprieve. Hardy had a second time broken the first rule of defense law with Leland Taylor. Confident that he would win with Graham, and therefore that Leland would be favorably disposed to pay, he'd allowed him, after a generous retainer up front, to make monthly payments for Graham's defense. His trust had been justified and the checks had been coming in every month. There was no reason to suspect that the next one wouldn't arrive in a couple of weeks.

Since Hardy made three times his normal hourly rate when he was in court (though he'd told Graham it was only double), it looked to be a substantial payment, able to hold him over for a while. But Leland's payment would come to an end after that, and he'd need more steady work lined up by the time it did. Freeman would probably try to throw something his way again, but all in all he'd prefer now to go it alone, get his own practice into high gear. It was about time, and perhaps some of that work was waiting upstairs.

But his feet took him to Graham's. He knocked once and tried the door; associates didn't lock doors in the Freeman Building.

Graham wore a light blue suit and had cut his hair so it just brushed his ears. He looked absurdly young, fit, and handsome, obviously sleeping better than he had for the past six months. The bags had disappeared from under his eyes. But close up Hardy could still discern a sallowness, leftovers from the jail pallor. And something else – a sense of lingering fatigue, or a new worry.

Hardy closed the door behind him. 'Our dear Phyllis said you wanted to see me.'

'Oh. Yeah.' Two separate words. He blew out sharply. 'Sal's stuff is ready to get picked up.'

He gestured meaninglessly, but Hardy thought he knew what he meant. Sal's 'stuff,' both from the evidence locker and the storage bin where the city had moved it, was another emotional hurdle in the marathon that was the aftermath of a murder trial.

Picking up the last of his father's remains, going back to the Hall of Justice, where for so long he'd been in chains.

Hardy considered for about two seconds. It would probably take him most of the afternoon, but this personal stuff was more important than business. At least, he thought so – he was sure it was among his greatest failings. 'Okay,' he said. 'Give me five minutes to check my messages.'

His voice mail had seven calls.

The third one was from a Jeanne Walsh, who said she was calling about the Joan Singleterry advertisement. She left her number, which Hardy tried immediately, although no one replied.

One of Graham's first concerns after the verdict – and it endeared him to Hardy – was the distribution of the money to Joan Singleterry's children if they could find her with one last advertising blitz.

George and Debra had been as skeptical as Hardy would have predicted about the existence of a Joan Singleterry, and Sal's directive to give her his money.

But realizing that it was probably their best chance to get their hands on Sal's money without a legal battle, the siblings had told Graham they would let him give Joan Singleterry one last good try if he would split up the funds should it fail. Graham knew that any litigation to preserve the money after that would only eat up most of it, so he finally agreed.

But their last run at Singleterry was to be a good one. Instead of going nationwide with a tiny classified ad in the personals column of thirty or forty publications – Hardy's earlier strategy – they decided to take out a three-inch box in the sports sections of five of California's largest newspapers and, for good measure, a two-inch box in *The Wall Street Journal*. The advertisement, paid for by most of the money Graham had stashed with Craig Ising, would run for one full week. That week had passed on Sunday, two days before.

For Hardy, getting a call on the Singleterry question did not automatically give rise to soaring hopes. He'd received half a dozen similar replies that had proven worthless before the trial. Nevertheless, it did get his blood going. The trial was over, but the failure to achieve any sense of closure had kept him up several nights since the verdict had come in.

Someone had killed Sal Russo and gotten away with it. He couldn't shake the feeling that this connected somehow to Joan Singleterry. And, of course, it didn't escape him that if Singleterry were connected to a murderer, she herself might already be dead, murdered. The advertisement itself might, in fact, subject her to mortal danger. For this reason they had kept the ad as simple as possible. The name Joan Singleterry, Hardy's phone number, reward. No mention of Graham, Hardy, Sal. It would either work or it wouldn't.

Since it was on the way to the Hall of Justice and its evidence lockup, Hardy and Graham stopped off at the facility where the city had put up the rest of Sal's goods – what there was of them.

Now, within the past few years, with the Moscone Center and plans for the new Giants Stadium in China Basin, the South of Market area had developed pockets of hope, change, life. But a great deal of the real estate between Market Street and the Hall of Justice, and this included the Lions Arms, remained as it had been for decades: seedy, scabrous, and sad.

Graham punched his combination into the box by the cyclone fence and they pulled into the forlorn and soulless monthly storage rental facility. Peeling yellow stucco walls, rust-red corrugated iron doors. They drove slowly down one long row, around a corner, back up another one.

'Nice place for a party,' Hardy said. 'Couple of balloons, maybe a tuba band. A little imagination and you could really have a good time here.'

Hardy had picked up the key to the unit from the city custodian over a week ago. He was to return it when they'd finished cleaning it out. Sal's leftover goods from his apartment were in it, and Graham hesitated one last minute in the car – perhaps steeling himself against the weather, perhaps against a more powerful psychic storm – before opening his door. The wind was up in the midafternoon, sending grimy clouds of dust, soot, flotsam, swirling around the car. 'Gotta do it,' he said, almost to himself.

Hardy waited in the car while Graham worked the heavy padlock and threw the door all the way up.

The unit was tiny – six feet deep and maybe four feet wide,

and even so it wasn't nearly filled. With a minimum of talk they started a chain gang, lifting things and putting them into the open trunk of the BMW. Five or six boxes of books and bric-a-brac, kitchen and bathroom utensils, photo albums, a small closet's worth of Salvation Army clothes. None of this had been tagged as evidence or figured as part of discovery, and Hardy realized with a stab that he'd never before seen any of it.

Not that he'd needed it, he consoled himself. He'd won. But still, it rankled. Graham reached down and passed him a rectangular piece of plywood.

'Why'd they throw this in?' Hardy asked. 'I think I saw a Dumpster by the gate.'

Graham's expression went from hurt to anger, then dissolved when he realized that Hardy was looking at the back, obviously thinking that one of the movers had thrown a random board onto Sal's pile of junk. 'Other side.'

Hardy turned it over.

The light was right and the painting leapt out at him through the grain of the plywood: the boat by the wharf with the small boy fishing with a broken pole from the flying bridge. 'What is this?' he asked.

Graham shrugged. He was holding another box, waiting for Hardy to put the painting into the trunk and resume loading. 'One of Sal's.'

'Your dad painted this?'

Graham put his box down and came over, looking at the painting. 'He was pretty good, wasn't he?'

Hardy thought so. But more, he was interested in the background. 'Where was this?'

'His berth at the Wharf. When he still had the *Signing Bonus* – that's his boat, there. You can still make out the name. See?'

'What's this, then?' Hardy was pointing at the burned-out building in the background.

'The old Grotto. Right after it burned down.'

'Is that when he lost his boat? Did it get caught in the fire or something?'

'No. I think he sold it for parts a long time later. It just wore out.'

'But it looks worn out here, in this picture. Which would have been at the same time.'

A gust of wind came up, nearly pulling the board out of Hardy's hands. Graham was shaking his head, placing something. 'No,' he said, 'I know he painted it after the fire. We were in the Manor. He did it out in the garage.' He stared at it for another beat. 'He always loved that painting.'

'And obviously it was hanging in his apartment?'

A nod. 'Over the couch.' Hardy was still mesmerized. 'What?' Graham asked.

'It's just a powerful image.'

Graham agreed. 'Sal was pretty good. Maybe I'll hang it in my place. You want to grab that last box?'

The evidence lockup was in the bowels of the Hall, a huge room that smelled like an old library where people would occasionally change their oil. With its gray-green paint and interior cyclone fence, its bare-bulb lighting and cacophonous resonance, it had all of the building's usual institutional charm and then some.

Sarah was waiting by the sign-out counter. Out of force of habit Hardy had brought along his lawyer's briefcase and leaned over to place it at his feet. When he looked up, he was initially shocked by the casual kiss of greeting that she and Graham gave each other. Then he realized that the duty officer down here probably wouldn't recognize Graham anyway, and even if he did, why would he care? Graham was a free citizen again – he could kiss a cop if he wanted to.

It only took a couple of minutes. There was some paperwork that Sarah, as arresting inspector of record, had to sign.

'So where's Marcel?' Hardy asked.

Sarah gave him the bad eye. 'I took the afternoon off,' she said, which answered his question. The ostracism over her involvement with a murder suspect was, he suspected, just beginning. In the week after the trial the story about her and Graham had hit the press with a fury.

Hardy didn't think anyone here today wanted to pursue it, so he turned back to the counter. There were three cardboard boxes: two filled with the miscellaneous papers from Sal's apartment, and the third, the smallest one, with the contents of the safe, carefully labeled *S. Russo. #97-0101254, Safe. Evans/Lanier, Homicide* in indelible black marker.

Graham opened this last one first and peered inside, then looked up and nodded, a shaky smile in place.

'Still there?' Sarah asked.

'Most of it, at least.'

Sarah spoke to Hardy. 'I told him it wouldn't get stolen out of evidence. He didn't believe me.'

'She has a trusting heart,' Graham said.

'Lucky for you.' Hardy pulled back the flaps and started laying the money out on the counter – stacks of hundred-dollar bills. 'But it couldn't hurt to check before we leave.'

Under the bulging eyes of the duty officer, who asked if they had arranged for a guard out of the building, Hardy took out the tightly wrapped bundles, ten of them.

Next he reached back in and pulled out a shoe box, blew the dust off, opened it. The baseball cards didn't even fill it; newspaper was stuffed in at the end and on the sides to keep them from shaking around. Hardy reached in again and picked up the second shoe box and Graham put his hand in and rummaged around.

'How about if we put the money back in?' Sarah asked.

Hardy nodded. 'How about if we put everything back in? It's all here. Take it somewhere safe.'

'That's our plan,' Graham said. He lifted out the old belt and dropped one end to let it hang, then put it around his waist. 'You think I could find somebody to put a new buckle on this thing?'

Obviously, Graham was thinking of a memento of his father, although perhaps this belt wasn't his most stylish option; it was of unfinished black leather, heavy and thick. Graham held it around his waist. 'Little big for me, though.' He sucked in his washboard stomach. He smiled, turned to Hardy. 'It might fit you. You want to try it?'

Hardy iced him a smile. 'I'd respond appropriately except that there's a woman present.'

In the back lot they loaded the boxes into the backseat of Graham's BMW, the trunk having been filled at the storage place. With Sarah as armed escort Graham planned to get himself a new safety deposit box ASAP, then they'd take the rest of the stuff to his place up on Edgewood and decide what they'd do from there.

Graham had asked if he wanted a lift back uptown, but Hardy wanted to call his Joan Singleterry connection again. He had not told Graham about the call; no sense in getting his hopes up if it was a dead end.

The Beemer was idling and Graham and Sarah were ready to go. Hardy couldn't stop himself from asking, 'What have you found out about the cards?'

'I'm checking out the trade shows. It looks like they're going to bring in forty or fifty.'

'And you're splitting that with George and Debra too?'

Graham gave him a shrug. 'Without Singleterry, I'm afraid, it's their money. What can I do?'

Sarah leaned over from the passenger side. 'He's even thinking of declaring his softball earnings.'

Hardy deadpanned. 'Whoa! Don't get all carried away on me now.'

'I've reformed.' Graham was dead serious. 'I'm reporting every cent of income I make for the rest of my life. I'm going back and filing amended returns. I am never ever under any circumstances spending one more night in jail.'

Hardy nodded. 'Here's a perfect example of the beauty of our criminal system. You go to jail for a few months, you come out a better person.'

Back at his office he punched in the number again, and this time it picked up on the second ring.

'Hello, Jeanne Walsh?'

'Yes.' A young woman's voice. The crying of a baby in the background.

'You called me in response to an advertisement in the newspaper?'

'That's right, I did. What's this about? Do I get the reward? I could seriously use a reward.'

'It's possible,' he temporized. 'Actually, though, we were trying to find Joan Singleterry herself. Do you know her?'

'Of course. That's why I called. Joan Singleterry was my

mother.' The past tense sprang up at Hardy, immediately amplified. 'She died about four years ago.'

'Would you mind answering some questions about her?'

'No. I don't mind at all. Can I ask who I'm talking to, though?'

Hardy apologized. 'My name is Dismas Hardy. I'm a lawyer in San Francisco.'

'San Francisco? That's a long way away.'

'Where are you?'

'Eureka.'

Hardy had been doodling on his legal pad. Now he decided to take a couple of notes. Eureka was an old lumber port, the county seat of Humboldt County, California, three hundred miles up the coast.

'And did your mother live there, too, in Eureka?'

'Yes.'

'Did she always live there?'

'Just a second.' She was gone from the phone and he heard her scolding. 'No, no, no. Don't put that in there, Brittany. Mommy will be off in a minute, okay?'

Hardy could relate. Jeanne came back to the phone. 'I'm sorry, where were we?'

'Did your mother always live in Eureka?'

'Mostly. She was born here, then lived in San Francisco for a while, and then moved back. But her name wasn't Singleterry when she was down there. It was Palmieri, Joan Palmieri. Then back up here she married Ron Singleterry.'

Hardy's heart sank. 'But when she lived in San Francisco, your mother's name was Joan what?'

'Palmieri.' Jeanne spelled it. Hardy wrote it on his pad.

'Do you know a man named Sal Russo?'

'No. I don't think so.'

'Do you remember if your mother ever mentioned him?'

'Sal Russo?' She was silent a minute. 'No, it doesn't even ring a tiny bell. Was she supposed to know him? Does this mean I don't get the reward? Brittany, don't!'

Reward or not, the child was commanding more than half of Jeanne Walsh's attention. Hardy should let her go and get on his own horse. This, finally, was a definite link to Joan Singleterry and a new name with which to conjure. Palmieri.

He thanked her and told her he'd get back to her, this time unable to entirely suppress the rush of excitement. His hunch was becoming a certainty. He didn't know the exact mechanism, but Joan Singleterry was going to lead him to Sal Russo's killer.

36

The whole family pitched in making chili, quesadillas, and tacos. Pico and Angela Morales came by with their three children. Young and old ate together at the same table.

The law went undiscussed.

The kids went down to sleep before eight-thirty, five of them on the floor in Rebecca's room. When Pico and Angela woke up their clan to go home three hours later, Hardy and Frannie still had some energy and didn't let it go to waste.

This morning he made his four-mile jog and walk with something approaching ease. The city had turned cold by California standards – the high today would be 55 degrees – so he brought wood up from the cord of oak underneath the house. While Frannie baked bread, he cleaned his fish tank.

With all the domesticity he didn't arrive at the office until nearly noon. Among his messages was a call from another of the doctors who'd signed the published admission that he'd helped one or more of his patients die.

Hardy could see a groundswell developing here. Yesterday, he'd forgotten to return the padlock key for the storage unit to the city custodian, and he decided to use that as an excuse to go to the Hall.

The door to Glitsky's office was open. He sat at his desk and appeared to be buried in paperwork. Hardy walked in with his briefcase in one hand and some hot tea in the other, and the lieutenant sat back and graciously accepted the offering. The two men hadn't talked since the day of the verdict, and Sarah and Graham had not hit the gossip mills yet by then. Now, of course, they had.

Abe carefully sipped at the scalding liquid. 'Why don't you get the door?' he asked conversationally. 'God, I love the sound of that.' When they were good and alone, he took another sip. 'I guess you didn't know about Evans and your client.'

Hardy kept a straight face. 'What about them?'

Glitsky moved some paper around. 'I suppose you thought that if I'd known they were an item, I might have been a little skeptical about her professional opinion regarding his guilt or not. Might not have sent her out to investigate other innocent civilians with my blessing.'

'George wasn't all that innocent. Besides, Graham wasn't guilty. The jury said so.'

The lieutenant went to his tea, decided to say a few more words. 'She was a good cop. She had to be to get here. But you don't sleep with your suspects.'

'I never have, but I'd agree it's good advice.'

Glitsky nodded again. This was pointless. What happened between Evans and Graham Russo hadn't been Hardy's doing. It was galling that Hardy had possibly – hell, probably; hell, *definitely* – known all about it for months and hadn't mentioned a thing to Glitsky.

But then Glitsky realized that a part of it, perhaps the biggest part, was his own fault. It wasn't Hardy who'd cut off the communication they'd always had – it was himself. He sipped more tea, settled back into his chair. 'And this visit today is about?'

'I honestly thought you'd never ask.'

'Surprise,' Glitsky said. 'It's a cop tool.'

'Hey, that reminds me. Knock, knock.'

Glitsky shook his head. 'No.'

'No, really, come on. Humor me. One time. Knock, knock.'

Glitsky hesitated another second. There was no getting around Hardy. He'd just sit there with his shit-eating grin and keep repeating 'Knock, knock' until he got an answer. He growled it out. 'All right, Jesus, who's there?'

'Interrupting cow.'

'Interrupting co—'

'Mooo!'

In a major victory for the defense Hardy got Glitsky to crack a tenth of a smile. 'All right,' the lieutenant said, 'that wasn't bad. I see you're playing with your kids again. How are they? I ought to bring Orel by.'

Actually, with the trial over now and the first hectic weeks of school out of the way, his kids were giving him a period of joy. Last night, good as it had been, was becoming almost typical. Vincent actually preferred that Hardy tuck him in nowadays rather than Frannie, and miraculously, he'd been home a lot of nights to do just that. It seemed to make a difference to the boy, Dad being around with some regularity. Rebecca continued to be his darling.

'Anytime,' Hardy said. 'They love Orel. But now, to the singular purpose of this particular business call.' He grabbed his briefcase and pulled it up to his lap, unsnapping the clips. It was the first time he'd opened it since he'd left Graham and Sarah in the parking lot yesterday afternoon.

He couldn't help laughing. Somehow – probably while Hardy was busy helping with loading the boxes yesterday in the parking lot – Graham had slipped Sal's belt into his briefcase.

'What?' Glitsky sat forward in his chair, wanting to know. Hardy was just a bundle of laughs today. It wasn't natural.

He pulled it out. 'Among the contents of Sal Russo's safe.'

'What is it?'

'It's a belt, Abe. What's it look like?'

'In Sal Russo's safe?'

Hardy nodded. 'We just got it out of the evidence lockup yesterday.'

'What's it doing in your briefcase?'

Hardy avoided that. 'You wouldn't believe the stuff I accumulate in here.'

Glitsky held out his hand. Hardy stood and passed the belt over the desk. 'You want it?' he asked, keeping the joke running. 'Maybe it'll fit you.'

The lieutenant wasn't smiling. 'What was this evidence of?'

'Nothing. We never used it.'

'Though of course you checked it out?'

Hardy cocked his head. Suddenly Glitsky was interested and that made *him* interested. 'Of course. Before they tool belts they call them blanks. This is one of them. Anyway, there's no tannery mark, except that E-2 punch in the back. Nobody I talked to knew what that stood for, not even Freeman, and Freeman knows everything. Best we could come up with was a friend of Sal's was going to make him a belt and the old man picked out the blank, then the other guy never got around to it.'

Glitsky stared across at him. The scar had gone pale across his lips, a sign of tension. 'It might not be anything,' he said, 'but North Beach Station – all their stuff, they punch E-something on it, just like this. North Beach Station is E-2.'

'The North Beach *police* station?'

'No.' Glitsky shook his head. 'Fire.'

A line drawn from the Hall of Justice to Hardy's office on Sutter Street would almost intersect the administrative offices of the main fire station on Golden Gate Avenue. Hurriedly grabbing a cab uptown, Hardy couldn't help but notice, and thought it provocative, that that same line would probably cut through both Mario Giotti's chambers and the living room in Sal Russo's apartment.

Escaping his attention until this moment – it was, after all, an imaginary line – now he couldn't shake the conviction that this might be the axis around which the Russo case revolved.

It had gotten late, he wasn't sure how. He did finally return the storage-room key, then ran into some attorneys outside the municipal courtrooms who wanted to talk about the case, buy him some drinks, which he refused.

Then Jeff Elliot appeared outside the reporters' room on the third floor of the Hall and another forty minutes or so went away. He tried to keep a lid on what he was thinking, knowing that unless you wanted to leak something specific or start a rumor, and that wasn't his intention now, it wasn't a good policy to speculate to newspaper reporters.

Now, somehow, it was nearly five o'clock. He was relieved that he had made it to the building before the main fire department offices would close.

A bright sun flirted with the tops of Twin Peaks, but the day itself continued truly cold. The biting wind of the previous afternoon had picked up steam and an attitude coming across the Sierra Nevada mountain range, erasing the last memories of Indian summer.

Hardy hurriedly thrust some bills at the cabbie. Briefcase in hand, he half ran two at a time up the wide steps leading into the building.

In the lobby the late-afternoon glare against the polished right-hand wall was blinding. Shading his eyes, he found the office he wanted on the opposite wall and walked in.

For a city office the place appeared to run very well. Hardy was approaching the counter when a uniformed young black woman saw him, stood up at one of the desks, came around it, and asked if she could help him.

'This might be unusual,' he said, 'but I'd like to know if you can identify something for me.' He took out the belt and placed it on the counter.

Picking it up, she turned it over once or twice, noted the E-2 stamp on one side, put it back down. 'This is a hose-and-ladder strap,' she said as if she saw one every day, and maybe she did. 'We use 'em to wrap up gear on the trucks. This one's stamped by North Beach station. Where'd you get it?'

Hardy kept it vague. 'A friend of mine had it,' he said. 'He gave it to me. I thought I might make it into a belt.'

The woman laughed. 'This old thing? You'd have to cut off half of it first. Repolish it. Get it tooled.'

This had been Glitsky's second point, which Hardy felt he should have seen much earlier. The 'belt' was far too big for Graham or for Hardy, and Sal had been a wiry old man. What had made Hardy think it would fit him, that it was a belt in the first place?

The woman was turning it in her hand again, then snapped it a time or two. 'Besides, it's pretty brittle,' she said. 'Your friend must have had it a long time. Did he say where he got it?'

'I think he found it left behind at a fire scene,' Hardy said. 'Forgot to return it.'

She gave him another smile, obviously assuming that Hardy's 'friend' was himself, that guilt over the stolen strap had finally caught up with him. 'I don't think North Beach would use it anymore. You might as well hang on to it. Or I could just throw it away here. It won't make much of a belt.'

'I'll bring it back to him,' Hardy said. 'Maybe it's got sentimental value.'

She gave him a dubious look, handed the strap back to him. 'Maybe. Is that all you need?'

'I think so. Would North Beach know where they lost this? Or when?'

‘I don’t know that. You could go and ask them. Maybe they keep some kind of inventory of losses, something like that. Stations do things differently. But that thing is old. I’d be surprised.’

Hardy was wrapping it around his hand. He slipped it off and put it back into his briefcase, snapping the clips. ‘Me too.’ There was nothing else to say. ‘Well, thank you. You’ve been a big help.’

He walked back out into the lobby, took a few steps, and came to a stop. For a moment he considered turning around and going right back down to Glitsky’s office. Since Graham’s release Sal Russo’s death was again an unsolved homicide, and in theory Abe ought to be interested in any evidence related to it.

Except that now, thanks to Hardy’s efforts, the entire city believed the story that Graham had killed his father out of mercy. Nobody – except possibly Graham himself, Sarah, and Hardy – nobody was looking for a killer anymore. The case, although technically still open and unsolved, was concluded to everyone’s satisfaction.

Even to Glitsky’s.

Subliminally aware that people were beginning to stream out of the elevators and offices around him at the end of the workday, Hardy felt strangely rooted to where he was. He didn’t want to lose his train of thought. If he was going to bring up anything about this case with an eye to another suspect, he would need a lot more than this hose-and-ladder strap.

But he did have an idea where he might get just that. First he’d go back down to the *Chronicle* and re-examine the archives related to the fire at Giotti’s Grotto. It might have been months before the date on the wrapped money, but months, after all this elapsed time, was close enough. Without the strap any connection between that fire and Sal was a tenuous stretch. With it Hardy thought he had a causal link that was compelling. It was damn near conclusive of something. He just couldn’t put his finger on exactly what it was.

He would turn Sarah loose on it too. She wouldn’t share any of Glitsky’s reluctance. Whoever had killed Sal Russo was her enemy, her man’s torturer, and Sarah was going to bring that person down if she could.

Could it have been Giotti? Hardy visualized the affable and brilliant jurist. He could, though it was a big 'maybe,' imagine the judge helping Sal kill himself, as Hardy had argued that Graham had. Try as he might, though, and much as the symmetry appealed to him, he couldn't see Giotti *murdering* Sal. Not struggling with his oldest friend who was now a feeble old man, then knocking him out, fatally injecting him with morphine.

And that, Hardy reminded himself, is precisely what had happened, regardless of the story he'd made so convincing to the jury, to the city at large.

Far to the west the sun finally kissed Twin Peaks, then abruptly dropped below them. Downtown fell into shade as though somebody had drawn the blinds; the glare that had been bathing the lobby off the polished wall vanished. The startling sudden dimness, the transformation in the feel of the cavernous room, pulled Hardy, blinking, from his thoughts.

Automatically it seemed, his eyes went to the wall – etched marble with gilt inlay. Here were the names of those who'd died fighting fires in the city since before the Great Earthquake and Fire of '06.

The lobby had mostly cleared. Echoing footsteps from behind him, muffled voices carrying from a great distance.

Hardy stood transfixed, a premonition tickling at the edges of his consciousness. He moved a step closer to the wall, focusing down from his wide angle.

Another step, *feeling* it somehow before he recognized anything. It was here.

And then, suddenly jumping out, appearing as out of a Magic Eye poster, there it was.

He blinked again, now forcing himself to slow down. To make sure of what he was seeing.

R-A-N-D-A-L-L.

One letter at time, he told himself. Don't miss one and get it wrong. Not now.

G.

Okay. Stop and make sure. He raked the name slowly, left to right.

P-A-L-M-I-E-R-I.

* * *

It was just a name on a wall. But he knew that it was more, much more: it was the key to everything.

Randall Palmieri could have died in 1910 or 1950 for all Hardy could be sure, but he was certain that wasn't the case. His bones and heart *knew* that Palmieri had died in November of 1979, fighting the fire that had burned down the Grotto.

He retraced his steps back to the fire department's door, but it was closed now, locked up.

Timing, he thought; life's little reminder that you couldn't control a damn thing.

He looked at his watch – five-ten. He was furious at the efficient office he'd admired fifteen minutes before. He bet the fire department opened punctually at nine too.

All but running now, he descended the front steps and hailed another cab.

Insane frustration.

The *Chronicle* archives were also closed for the day by the time he arrived there. From a pay phone across the street he placed a call to Jeff Elliot, who he hoped would be working late in the basement. Jeff always worked late. He worked early. He worked all the time. Hardy's plan was that he would give Jeff the scoop first. The columnist would be satisfied with that. It was the way things were done.

But, of course, Jeff wasn't in. Hardy didn't even leave him a voice mail message. He wanted answers *now*. He'd waited long enough.

Without giving it much thought he got the number of the federal courthouse – another government office sure to be closed – and found that it was. He got a recording.

Which didn't mean that no one was working in the building. All right, perhaps the receptionists and some secretaries had gone home, but Hardy knew the law business and it was an absolute certainty that the judges' offices at the federal courthouse were little beehives of activity even as he stood here shivering. Graham had told him that while he'd been clerking for Harold Draper, there had been times when he hadn't gone outside the building for three days in a row.

So someone was there.

His instincts were telling him to slow down now. Fate was lobbying to make him stop. Nobody was around. The message was loud and clear: This wasn't the propitious moment. It wasn't meant to be. He should stop and think about the implications of all his discoveries and hunches and methodically follow things up tomorrow and the next day and the one after that.

But he was so close. So close. He felt it. Suddenly he couldn't wait. It was *right here* and it would escape if he gave it the chance. He couldn't do that.

Rather than fight for another parking space, he legged it down Mission a couple of blocks, freezing now in the stiff gale. Jaws clenched, he told himself that all his working out over the past months was finally paying off. He made it to the courthouse in under five minutes.

This time he was unmoved by the immensity of the building, the solid bronze doors that extended to over twice his height, the iron lanterns that had come from some Florentine palace. These doors, as he'd expected, were closed. But there was the other entrance by the gate to the parking area, in front of the Lions Arms, in the alley.

The security guard had seen it a hundred times. Here was some frantic lawyer who'd missed a deadline, waving him over, wanting to get into the building, perhaps have his brief accepted although it was half an hour late. The odds of that, he knew, were slim and none.

'Is Judge Giotti still in? I'd like to see him.'

'Business hours are over, I'm afraid.'

'This isn't strictly business. It's not court business.'

'Is the judge a friend of yours?'

The lawyer seemed to think about it. Maybe he was a friend of the judge's and didn't want to presume on it. 'No,' he said. 'He asked me to keep him up on the progress of a case of mine. I've got a few things to tell him about.'

The guard looked Hardy up and down. The rule was 'When in doubt, don't'. The judges got a lot of their work done after the formal workday, and all of them hated being interrupted. But if this guy was a friend of Giotti's . . .

Of course, if he were a friend, he'd have a private number. On the other hand, he wasn't pushing, really, though he was cold right at the moment and probably wouldn't mind being inside. 'You want to wait a sec, I'll go check with his office, see if anybody's there.'

'They wouldn't even take a message?' Graham didn't have a high regard for the denizens of the federal courthouse in any case, but even he was surprised that no one had come down to talk to Hardy.

'Apparently they were busy.'

Hardy had cooled off, figuratively, since striking out with Giotti's office too. He was back on Sutter Street, at his desk. Graham had come up on his summons. It wasn't much after six in the middle of the week, and the gristmill was humming along nicely. Hardy's original inclination was to get Graham to help him do some research on this ancient fire situation. He could use Sarah's help too.

But in the middle of venting his frustrations Hardy had changed his mind. He wouldn't be giving anything else away in this case until he'd narrowed it down somewhat. If the fire had been important in Graham's life, Hardy would give him the opportunity to talk about it. But if it hadn't, he didn't want Graham and Sarah asking around indiscriminately, raising warning flags for whomever he was hunting.

This investigation now, finally, was something Hardy felt he had to keep under his own close control. The outline of what he sought was still fairly nebulous. He reminded himself that Jeanne Walsh had never heard of Sal Russo; her mother, Joan Singleterry, had never mentioned him. Perhaps, even, Graham's Joan Singleterry had never been Joan Palmieri. He had to get all that straight first.

Graham had picked up his darts and threw the first one. Bull's-eye. He almost didn't seem to notice. 'Why'd you want to see Giotti?'

Hardy kept it vague. 'That painting of Sal's. It got me thinking. I wanted to ask him again about the Grotto fire. Do you remember much about it?'

Graham shook his head. 'I was fifteen. If you couldn't bat it or throw it, it didn't exist for me.'

'The fire obviously made an impression on Sal.'

'That's just the way he was, Diz. Things affected him.' He threw another dart, got another bull's-eye. 'That painting, to me, it's the loss of innocence in general. The fire's just another symbol. The ruined boat in the foreground, the boy with the broken pole. You notice all the garbage in the water? He's painting the thing out in the garage while he and Mom are breaking up. Think about it. It's impressionistic. It's his whole world breaking up.'

'You're probably right,' Hardy said.

After Graham left, he tried calling Jeanne Walsh again. She hadn't bought an answering machine since yesterday, or if she had, she'd neglected to plug it in.

It wasn't his night. He was going home.

When he opened the door to his house, it was almost eerily silent and he listened for a minute, then called out. 'Frannie!'

Furtive noises from the back of the house. 'Frannie. Kids. Dad's home.'

In seconds he was in the kitchen. 'Anybody here?'

Muffled giggling – at least recognizable as benign – from farther back. He walked through the master bedroom and into Vincent's, which had been transformed into an impenetrable maze of blankets, pillows, ropes strung from bed to chairs to bookshelves. He lifted up one of the blankets and looked under. 'Hey, guys.'

Rebecca held a finger to her lips. 'Shh!'

'Where's Mom?' he whispered.

'I don't know. Shh!'

This was not Hardy's favorite answer, but since a game was obviously in progress he didn't want to be a spoilsport, so he stood up and turned around.

'Mr Hardy? Hi.'

It took him a moment. This was Mary, their baby-sitter, having come out of hiding from wherever. What was she doing here? 'Is Frannie all right?' he asked foolishly.

The girl's face was all confusion. 'I guess so. Weren't you meeting her someplace? That's what she said.'

It was all coming back to him. It was Wednesday night. Date

Night. He was picking Frannie up at the Shamrock at seven. His mind, in its dance of frustration and speculation, had spun that little fact out of its galaxy. He'd not so much forgotten as absolutely misplaced the information.

He looked at his watch – seven-twenty – and gave Mary an apologetic grin. 'Sorry to break in on you like this. My brain's turned to mush. I've got to use the phone.'

They were at Stagnola's. Hardy and Frannie *never* ate on the Wharf, although the food was often wonderful. It was just such a tourist place, with traffic hassles and exorbitant parking rates. There were dozens of other spots offering great food in the city. Tonight, though, Hardy felt as though he needed to be here.

He also felt like he'd traveled a hundred miles in the past three-plus hours – from the Hall of Justice to the fire department main office, back to the *Chronicle*. Then the jog to the Federal Building and back. His office. Driving his own car all the way across town to his home in the Avenues, almost to the beach. Now halfway back downtown to the Shamrock to meet the long-suffering Frannie.

Until at last he was settled at his table, Chianti poured, tucking into an antipasto plate – pepperoncini, salami; mortadella, provolone, artichoke hearts, olives, caponata. Hot sourdough rolls by the basket. Heaven.

She'd given him several rations of grief since he'd finally arrived to pick her up. 'No, I understand, lots of times I'll get caught up in things around the house and forget that you exist too. Then I'll snap my fingers and go, "Oh, that's right, Dismas." ' Et cetera.

Since Hardy felt he basically deserved it, he'd let her go on. Except now it had all wound down, she was holding his hand over the table, glad they were together. He had to tell her, bounce it off her, see where he didn't have it right.

She listened carefully, then went another way. 'I think you should turn it over to the police.'

'What, exactly?'

'Whatever you've got. Let them go with it. Give it to Abe. This is what he does, Dismas.'

But Hardy was shaking his head. 'No, it's not. He's got to have a murder, a case.'

'How about Sal Russo? Doesn't he count?'

'Sure, he counts. But I don't have any proof of anything that would get him involved. All I've got is this hose-and-ladder belt, a fire in this place eighteen years ago, a dead fireman who might or might not have been at this fire.'

'And fifty thousand dollars.'

'So what? Nobody stole that from Sal, as a matter of fact. He had it when he died. Or Graham did, which is the same thing.'

Frannie sipped wine. 'But you think they're related?'

A nod. 'They've got to be. I've just got to find out where a few things connect.'

'Just.'

He shrugged.

'All I'm saying is you might want to run it by Abe. Have him look up this Palmieri, call the woman in Eureka—'

'Hassle a sitting federal judge.' He knew Abe, knew he didn't have enough. 'Abe won't do it, not yet, maybe not ever.'

Frannie's point was well taken, though, and in a day or two, after he'd secured his inferences, that's exactly what he'd do. He had no desire to get close to cornering a murderer. That *was* police work. It could be very unhealthy.

But he didn't yet think it was Giotti. Or rather, he didn't *want* to think it was Giotti, although he was convinced that the judge had some information that would move things along. Information that, whether he knew it or not, he'd somehow kept out of Hardy's scrutiny. That's all he needed – to talk to him.

The waiter had earlier introduced himself as Mauritio. He was one of those personable, talk-your-ear-off, swarthy and handsome older men in a tuxedo that you're either in the mood for or not. Now he came up to ask them about their dinner.

Hardy broke his most disarming smile, squeezed Frannie's hand gently, cueing her to be cool. She gave him a warning look; as if she wouldn't be. 'Does Judge Giotti still eat here all the time?'

'Oh, yeah. They're in here a couple of times a week for lunch, he and his wife. You a friend of the judge's' – he pointed at the Chianti – 'that bottle's on the house.'

'I don't know if he'd call me a friend. I'm a lawyer. But he's a good judge. He raves about the food here.' Hardy motioned down at his empty plate. 'This antipasto, he's right. He's a great guy.'

'The best,' Mauritio replied.

'Did I hear this place used to be in his family?'

'Yeah. Long time ago. Used to be Giotti's Grotto.' Mauritio's tired face took on a little more life. 'Believe it or not, I used to bus tables back then.'

Hardy shamelessly flattered the man. 'Before they had child labor laws?' Frannie squeezed his hand – don't pile it on too thick. 'So you must have known Sal Russo too?'

Mauritio's brow darkened briefly, but cleared when Hardy explained that he was the lawyer who'd gotten Sal's son off.

'Well, damn,' Mauritio said, 'that bottle *is* on us. That was good work. Poor Sal. Pray to God my son could do what his son did, I ever need it. What's your name again?'

They went through the introductions. Then Hardy asked if Sal had been around during the Grotto years.

'Oh, yeah. He and the judge, they were like this.' Two fingers together. 'Salmon Sal.' A shake of the head, a wistful tone. 'What happened to him, huh? But at least it was over fast. Any more time on the street, something worse might have happened.'

Hardy shot a look at his wife, went back to Mauritio. 'What do you mean?'

'Oh, you know, at the end, the last few months, the guy was a real pain. Last time I snuck him a lunch here, back in the kitchen, he wound up wanting to fight me over some bet we must have made twenty years ago. I didn't even remember it, something about Roberto Clemente, for Christ's sake. So I break him the news that Roberto's been gone awhile and suddenly he's all over me, I owe him a large one, he's gonna kick my ass.' Mauritio smiled over at Frannie. ''Scuse me the language.'

'It's all right.' Her brilliant smile. 'If I hadn't heard it before, I wouldn't know what it meant, would I?'

Hardy figured Mauritio was halfway to abiding love for his wife. He was going on. 'Anyway, the poor guy. He makes a scene, I kick him out, so he's yelling at me by the back door, says he gonna tell all the guys I'm a welsher. And I just made the guy a free lunch.' He shook his head in commiseration. 'You knew he couldn't help it. You couldn't hold it against him, but you didn't want him around. It was probably better he went out when he did. His boy did him a big favor.'

After dinner, a couple more questions.

'So the Grotto, it burned down or something?'

'To the ground. Saddest night of my life. Nobody could believe it.'

'Why not?'

He shrugged. 'I mean, the old man, the judge's father – fire was what scared him most. We had more hydrants and safety systems than anybody. Then the one time we need 'em, they don't work worth a damn.'

'It's a universal law,' Hardy said. 'Where'd it start?'

A sigh. 'Kitchen, they think. Then just took off. One of the fireman died, even. Horrible. Well' – he clapped his hands lightly – 'hey, enough of this. You folks eat good? I see the judge, I'll tell him you came by.'

37

As soon as Frannie had taken the kids out the door to school, he was at the kitchen table. With his wide-ranging if temporary amnesia yesterday, he was almost surprised that he'd remembered to throw Jeanne Walsh's telephone number into his briefcase. But he had.

She picked up on the second ring. There was no baby noise in the background, and she sounded more relaxed. 'Mrs Walsh, this is Dismas Hardy again. The lawyer from San Francisco?'

'Sure. The reward. I remember.'

Might as well feed her the sugar first. 'That's what I'm calling about. The reward may not be out of the picture. I'd like to ask you a couple more questions, if I may. Do you have a minute?'

'I hope so. Brittany's down for a nap. She's really pretty good most of the time. I don't know why she was so cranky yesterday. Maybe she's teething.'

Hardy was right back with her to the days of infancy, when there was nothing else in life but your child and its health and habits. Even the prospect of a reward, while possibly interesting, couldn't hold a candle. 'I'm sure she's wonderful,' Hardy said, 'but I did want to ask you about your mother. You said when she was in San Francisco, she was Joan Palmieri? Was that her maiden name, or was she married before?'

A nervous laugh. 'Didn't I say that? No, I guess not. Yeah, she was married to my dad. My natural father, not Ron.'

Hardy was getting confused with all the names. 'Ron?'

'Ron Singleterry.'

'But Palmieri?'

'Palmieri was my own maiden name.'

Okay, he thought. Getting there. 'And was your dad's first name Randall?'

'Randy, yes. How did you know?'

'And he was killed in a fire at Giotti's Grotto in 1979?'

'Yeah, that was my father. I was just a baby then. Well, four or five I must have been, but I don't really remember him. That's why we moved back up here. Mom wanted to start over, I think. It was probably a good idea. It worked out pretty well for her. Ron was a good guy.'

Hardy had been taking notes, writing it all down. 'But you still don't remember anyone named Sal Russo?'

'No. I thought about it all last night, I tell you. I even called my sister, but she didn't remember it either.'

Hardy was closing in on it. Sal had referred to Joan Singleterry's children – plural – not to her child. And now that was confirmed. 'Do you have other family, Jeanne?'

'No. Well, I mean my own family, Johnny and Brittany. But otherwise there's just my sister Margie. Margie Sanford now.'

'Okay, one or two more, if you don't mind. How about Mario Giotti, that name? Do you know him?'

She laughed. 'I will if we need to.'

'You don't need to. You're doing fine. The reward doesn't depend on you knowing Mario Giotti.'

'That's a relief, because I don't.'

'Never heard of him?'

'Nope. Sorry.'

Me, too, Hardy thought.

But he'd gotten a lot more than he'd have dared hope for even a couple of days before. He ran more names at her. Brendan or Debra McCoury. Graham Russo. George Russo. Leland and Helen Taylor. Everybody he could think of – he almost said David Freeman. You just never knew. She didn't know any of them.

He told her to hang tight. She appeared to be the child of the Joan Singleterry they were seeking. He'd get back to her.

But what was the connection? How had Sal known Joan? He poured himself a cup of espresso, working the possibilities.

Randy Palmieri had been killed in the fire at the Grotto. The Grotto had been owned by the Giotti family until a few months after it burned down. A mysterious fire that had eluded a state-of-the-art detection and sprinkling system started in the kitchen and wiped out the whole place. Sal Russo had kept a memento of that fire with him until he died, as well as fifty thousand dollars in cash, wrapped and dated a few months later.

On the personal side, Sal's marriage had ended at about the same time. He no longer felt noble or special or whatever it was he'd always felt, no longer had the heart to stand up to the forces represented by Leland Taylor. He didn't deserve Helen and their wonderful children anymore. She was right to cast him off. He wouldn't even try to see his children anymore.

He had more than failed, he had fallen.

And in the present, Sal was more and more living in his past – where now perhaps he could undo his past sins, repay his past debts, reclaim his old love. It was happening now, all of this, his life.

And it made Sal, as Mauritio had said, a pain in the ass. Perhaps more than that as his mind slipped away, as he forgot what he was supposed to keep hidden and secret, as he remembered what he'd promised to forget.

Perhaps Sal had become a danger.

At the fire department office the same efficient woman helped him. 'The hose-and-ladder strap was something else, wasn't it?'

Mild chagrin. He'd been caught in his fib. 'I really hate to admit this,' he said, 'but the truth is that I'm a lawyer. I was trying to be slick. It's an occupational hazard.'

It rolled right off her. 'So it wasn't your friend's belt?'

'No.' He got serious. 'I found this out since last night. I believe the strap came from a fire that killed a man, Randall Palmieri. He's on your wall out there. I wondered if I could talk to your Widows and Orphans person, find out a little how that works.'

'You can just keep talking to me,' she said. 'I'm the information officer.'

'I want to verify the identity of the man's offspring. There's a substantial reward involved. I think maybe they could use it. If a fireman dies on the job, I suppose there's some kind of pension or settlement?'

The woman nodded. 'Palmieri?'

Hardy nodded and spelled it for her. 'Randall G.'

'I'll be right back.'

He waited at the counter for about five minutes, at which time she returned with a black binder. 'Sorry that took so long,' she said, 'I wanted to ask my boss how confidential this stuff was.' She shrugged. 'I can't give you addresses or anything without a court order, but if you give me a name, I can tell you if it's here. That's all you said you needed?'

Hardy would have to take what he could get. 'Essentially, yes. Randall Palmieri,' he repeated.

She opened to the page and waited.

Hardy didn't need his written notes. 'His wife's name was Joan and she moved to Eureka and married a Ron Singleterry. She had two children, Jeanne and Margie, since married with different names.'

The woman nodded. 'That's what I have.'

'Do they still get the pension, the daughters?'

'No. The benefit ends with the death of the spouse.'

'So they're not getting any money anymore, any help?'

'Not from us.' The woman was still looking down at the page, then came up at him. 'I don't see how this could hurt. If you want more information, there's a trust listed here, cross-referenced. The Singleterrys may have been getting money from it, too, on top of the pension. Maybe they'd be free to tell you more about it.'

'Okay, thanks. Where's this trust located?'

She read it out. 'It's called the BGG Memorial Trust of 1981. It's administered, let's see . . . oh, it's only a couple of blocks away, at Baywest. You could probably walk right over.'

He didn't want to see anyone, least of all either David Freeman or Graham Russo, but both of them were hanging around the lobby when he got to his building at a little after eleven. There was no avoiding them, but he could try to keep it short and sweet. He put on his best harried air, ostentatiously looked at his watch.

'I'm running through here, guys, on the way to someplace else. I've got an appointment at lunch. Big dollars, David, you'll be proud of me at last.'

Phyllis looked disapprovingly over her bank of phones. Too much noise. Hardy ignored her. 'But, Graham, you might want to call your brother and sister, advise them not to go spending their inheritance money. We've got a real lead on Joan Singleterry. I'll tell you all about it later.' He kept moving toward the stairs, climbing.

Graham tailed behind him. 'But that's what I wanted to tell you.'

Hardy stopped, turned. Graham was brushing by him, two steps at a time. 'I left it in your office.'

Feigned outrage. 'You broke into my office?'

At the top of the stairs Graham grinned back down at him. 'It'd be harder if you locked it.' The young man was excited; clearly he'd found something. 'We would have called you last night but it was after nine-thirty. We figured you old guys were already asleep.'

'Get out of my way.'

Graciously, still beaming, Graham let Hardy open his own door. He crossed to the desk and in the middle of the blotter found a large article, stapled together, from an old copy of the *Chronicle*. Nineteen eighty-eight.

While he read, Graham was filling him in. 'So we had all these boxes, mostly just junk and paper, taking up room. Sarah thought we ought to go through everything in them, page by page, throw away everything we didn't want. Clean the place up.'

Hardy glanced up at him. 'And I think I live a wild life, going to bed at nine-thirty and all.'

'I didn't say it was all we did. Anyway, Sarah found that.'

It was one of those follow-up stories the papers sometimes run: 'What Happened To?' or 'Life After . . .' This one concerned the patched-together lives of six women whose husbands had been killed doing their jobs in the prime of their lives. A construction worker, two cops, a race-car driver, a charter pilot, and Randy Palmieri, fireman.

'This guy's wife, Joan Palmieri,' Graham was saying, 'she moved to Eureka and married a man named Ron Singleterry.'

'And her husband, I notice, was killed in the Grotto fire.'

'She's got to be our Joan Singleterry,' Graham said.

'She is.'

Graham went mute for a beat. 'You know about her?'

'A little. That's what I wanted to tell you about.'

'The only thing is,' Graham said, 'I called information in Eureka, she isn't listed. There's no Singleterry there, no Palmieri either.'

No, Hardy thought, but there's a Walsh and a Sanford and you don't need to know that right now. 'Well,' he said, 'it's someplace to start. Look, I've really got to run. We'll get to it later.'

But Graham, this close to something, didn't want to let him go. 'Wait a minute. What did you find?'

'Same thing, different story. *Chronicle* archives. I'm going to see if I can talk to Mario Giotti today, see how Sal was connected to the fire at the Grotto. If he was.'

'You don't think Sal started it by mistake, do you? Got drunk or something?'

'No,' Hardy said honestly. 'No, I don't think that.'

But at last he now knew the mechanism by which Sal had come to know Joan Palmieri's married name. He knew, as he would say, how it was all connected.

'Mr Hardy.' Judge Mario Giotti had not shrugged himself out of his robes, although he was alone, reading in his chambers. Hardy didn't think this was an unintentional oversight. The trappings of power and authority. 'You said it was an emergency.'

'I am sorry to bother you, Judge, and thanks for seeing me. I know you're busy.'

'If I didn't see people when I was busy, I'd never see anybody.' The strong smile. 'You want to sit down?'

Hardy went to the seating arrangement by the ornate fireplace, with its electrical heater purring within it against the bitter day. The wind had brought in a low blanket of cloud cover and as Hardy, in a trench coat, had been walking from his office to Giotti's, it had started to mist.

He got right to it. 'Judge, I've got a big problem.'

'I'd assumed that. What is it?'

Hardy considered his response. He wanted to blurt out, 'It's you,' but he had to restrain his tendencies. He had to box him in until there was no escape.

'I'm afraid it's about the fire at your restaurant again. I've come upon some information that leads me to think Sal had something to do with it.'

Giotti leaned back in his wing chair, fingertips templed at his lips. 'Go on.'

'You remember that morning I stopped you on your run out back here in the alley and asked you if you knew anybody named Singleterry?'

'Of course.'

'At that time I was hiding some information from the public, keeping it out of the trial because it seemed so inherently not credible.'

'And what was that?'

Hardy outlined Sal's request to Graham, that he give the money to this Singleterry woman. 'Since we didn't have her, I didn't believe anyone in the courtroom would believe the story. So we decided not to bring it up.'

'It does seem like a reach,' Giotti agreed. 'Now I gather you've found her.'

'Almost,' Hardy said, '– her daughters.'

The judge took that in. 'That would be good, then, wouldn't it? You could find out what you need about Sal?'

'That's true. I've done that. Joan Singleterry's first husband was Randy Palmieri.'

Giotti's face seemed by degrees to be growing darker now, the black circles under his eyes becoming more pronounced, the jowls heavier as his chin went down, resting on his chest. He let out a long breath and came back to Hardy. 'The man who died in the fire.'

A nod. 'That's right. You knew him?'

'Who he was, of course. The name's forever burned into my memory. It was a tragedy. How could I not know it?'

'I don't know. I don't suppose you could. But then, by the same token, I'm afraid I don't understand how you could forget the name Singleterry.'

'But Singleterry wasn't her name. How would I—?'

Hardy couldn't make himself listen to it anymore. He had to cut him off. 'Because, Judge, your trust – the BGG, that's your trust, isn't it? Bruno Giotti's Grotto Memorial Trust? It sent her money for seventeen years. I'm just having a hard time seeing how that could have slipped your mind.'

Giotti was nodding repeatedly, his eyes on the middle distance between them. After a long minute he got up and crossed the room back to his desk, stared above it out the window into the gray mist. 'I remember thinking I liked the way your mind worked, Mr Hardy. Maybe that was misguided. Now you're implying I had something to do with that fire, aren't you? With arson and murder.' Finally he turned around. 'I'm afraid I'm too busy for this. It's arrant nonsense.'

'I'd be glad to hear your explanation.'

Giotti's nostrils flared. 'I don't need to give you any explanation, Mr Hardy. Like everyone else in America I am innocent until proven guilty. If you've got some proof of these outrageous accusations, why don't you bring it to the attention of the police? Right now this interview is over.' He pointed at the door. 'You know your way.'

Hardy stood up, but instead of moving toward the door, he assumed an at-ease position in front of his chair. 'I don't think so.'

Clearly unaccustomed to anything less than immediate obedience at any display of his authority, Giotti stiffened. 'I said get the hell out of here!' He reached for the telephone. 'I'll have you removed.'

'You don't want to do that,' Hardy said calmly. 'I'm not talking about a twenty-year-old fire. I'm talking about Sal Russo.'

Giotti gently replaced the receiver. 'What about him?'

'The fifty thousand dollars.'

The judge waited.

'Somehow it came from the fire. I don't know exactly how it got into Sal's hands, but the police are going to want to find out. They're going to see a connection between you and Sal's death. Maybe a motive for you to have killed Sal. I don't have to tell you this.'

'You think I killed Sal?'

'I don't think Sal was ready to die when you injected him. That makes it murder.'

'You're out of your mind.'

Hardy didn't care about the judge's transparent denial. 'I want to know what happened. I don't have to go to the police. This is for me. I'm not going away until I find out.'

'No, I don't suppose you would.' Giotti went around behind

his desk, pulled out his chair, and sat down on it. 'This Palmieri person died in a fire at my father's restaurant. We've helped take care of the family.'

'You denied knowing the name. That's consciousness of guilt.'

The judge shrugged. 'We like to keep our charity anonymous. Perhaps you see a crime there. I don't think many other people would. Certainly not the police.' He picked up the telephone again. 'Now do I call security or do you leave on your own?'

This was high-stakes poker and the judge was calling his bluff. But Giotti had already tipped his hand – Hardy wouldn't still be here if he didn't have winning cards. He did, and he knew it. Now he was going to raise. 'You'd better call in the troops,' he said. 'I'm not going anywhere. Not on my own power. After everything you've already put me through, you think I'm going to let this go?'

Giotti's eyes were a black glare. 'You son of a bitch.' His hand was still on the telephone.

Hardy kept his voice low, calm. 'Security comes here, they'll have to file a report. It all gets official. We're not there yet, though, are we?'

The glare never wavered. 'What's stopping it?'

'Me, that's all.'

'And you're offering me some kind of . . . what?'

'I'm not offering you anything, Judge. I want to know what happened. I'm an officer of the court. If I have to go to the police, I will. If I don't have to . . .' He left it unsaid.

Giotti glowered another moment, then picked up his telephone, and Hardy feared he had lost. Giotti would call in some political chits among the honchos, the police would at best cursorily look into Hardy's information and decide that a respected federal judge had done no wrong. Hardy was yet another unscrupulous, meddling defense attorney looking for more headlines, ready to slander a beacon of the legal community if it would get him a few more clients.

'And then, of course, there's the newspaper,' he said.

Giotti took in the last warning, made his decision, and pushed a button on the telephone.

He waited, then asked his secretary to hold his calls. Replacing the receiver, he looked across at Hardy. 'Do you want to know what happened, or do you want to go to homicide? You're not going to get both, not from me. And whatever happens, it looks as though I'm going to need some legal counsel.' Giotti reached under his robes, took out his wallet, and pulled a bill from it. 'Do you want to be my lawyer, Mr Hardy?'

Giotti was offering him a five-dollar retainer. If Hardy accepted it, every word between them would then be subject to the attorney-client privilege. He could never take it to the police.

This was, Hardy thought, truly Faustian. He reminded himself, though, that in the eyes of the law, justice had already been done. No one else was looking for the murderer of Sal Russo. He had to know.

Still, he hesitated.

Giotti's voice, though he never raised it, cut at him. 'Do you honestly think you're going to find physical proof of a fire that occurred almost eighteen years ago? Proof that would stand up at trial? The insurance company looked pretty hard before they paid out, you can believe me.'

Again, the tone shifted. Impatience? Command? 'Now, you can come over and take this bill or you *can* walk out of here. One way you'll know and the other you won't. It's your call.'

Hardy crossed the room. Giotti, still seated, watched him all the way. The bill was lying on the desk between them and Hardy picked it up and put it into his pocket.

'All right, counselor,' said the judge. 'Now sit down and let me tell you a story.'

'Let's say the Grotto was having a tough time, tourism was down, the restaurant business is always skin of your teeth anyway. Then let's say one day we get a notice from the state about inadequate handicap access. We've got to build a ramp, renovate the lobby . . . to make a long story short, we've got to lay out, say, forty-five thousand dollars to bring the place to code or they're going to shut us down.

'Now let's also say the owner's son is a young attorney with political aspirations. But he still works in the kitchen sometimes – he loves it back there. He's all conflicted about his career, where it's going, what he's doing. So he keeps his hand in at the restaurant, and then suddenly it looks like the business is going belly up, because there's no place the owners are going to find thirty or forty thousand dollars for handicap upgrading.

'So this smart kid, he comes up with this smart idea. If there's a small fire – controlled – starts, say, in the kitchen, does a little damage, but basically it's so the insurance can cover the renovation. Let's say the young attorney has a good friend – his oldest and best friend – call him Sal, who owns a boat moored right out behind the place. And these guys are out fishing together – night fishing, they do it all the time – when the fire starts. They don't get back in till the skyline's ablaze.

'The attorney's thinking it's impossible the fire could spread. The place is rigged so it could never burn up. There's backup systems on the backup systems, but maybe he didn't figure on the grease in the kitchen, maybe it got too hot too fast . . . anyway, whatever, the place goes up.

'But a guy dies. A fireman, by mistake. Sweet-faced young guy, two little kids, pretty wife.

'There's no evidence of arson. It looks like one of the pilot lights caught some grease that had dripped down. One of the service staff must have left an apron near the stove. And, not that anybody's really asking, but the two friends alibi each other. They weren't anywhere near there all night. They were out under the bridge, knocking down the halibut. They got a boatload of fish to prove it.'

Giotti was leaning back in his oversized chair, his hands crossed over his middle. He sighed wearily. 'Let's say something like that happened, counselor. You going to try and take that to trial?'

Hardy was too wired for any games. Although he knew Giotti was absolutely correct: there was no evidence here anymore. Murder might have no statute of limitations, but to convict you still needed more than he'd ever be able to produce.

Any physical evidence of the fire was long gone. Sal's rock-solid alibi, and Giotti's, went that way to the grave with him. Joan Singleterry was dead. Even the insurance company's investigators had found no wrongdoing. There was no chance. No police department would waste a minute on it.

But there was more Hardy felt he needed to know. 'How do you think somebody like Sal could have gotten ahold of fifty thousand dollars in cash?'

'In this scenario it could have been part of the insurance money.'

'A payoff, you mean, to keep quiet.'

'A show of gratitude maybe. Maybe a little of both.' Giotti shrugged. 'Life's complicated.'

'And Sal couldn't handle the guilt, could he? He killed somebody, an innocent man, a guy just like himself, wife and kids. And it ruined him.'

Another shrug.

Hardy dug into his pocket and removed the bill, placed it on the desk. 'We're out of hypothetical now, Judge, and you're not my client anymore. You killed Sal, didn't you?'

'No, I didn't do that.'

'Because he'd started talking about it, didn't he? He was back in the past, telling people about the fire, wasn't he?'

'I didn't kill him,' Giotti repeated.

'I don't believe you.'

The judge pulled the bill back toward him, centered it in front of him. 'I don't care what you believe, Mr Hardy. Sal was my best friend. He saved my whole life, my career, everything, and he suffered terribly for it – really lost everything. You think after that, after all he went through for me, I'm going to reward him by killing him?'

'I don't think you had any choice.'

'Well, you're wrong. The fire was a tragedy, an accident, a mistake. I've tried to make it up to that poor family as well as anybody could. To Sal too. We stuck together, even if he sometimes made it a little hard on me. I *never* would have killed him. Don't you understand that? Never, under any conditions. I'd have gone down myself first.'

38

He didn't get out of Giotti's until after three and then, unable to refocus, he'd walked to the *Chronicle* building, gone to the archives, and read every story he could find on the fire, on Palmieri, on Giotti.

By now the rain was falling steadily, and he had walked back uptown to his office in the thick of it. There he discovered that in the past two days he'd collected twenty-one call slips and his voice mail ran to over ten minutes. There was no question, Graham Russo's trial had given his career a shot in the arm, even if at the moment he couldn't imagine that anyone would want to pay for the services of a bumbling moron such as himself.

Where had he gotten everything wrong? What had he missed?

He had to put that – all of it – out of his mind. The day hadn't been a total failure. He had found Joan Singleterry and her connection to Sal Russo. Her kids were going to get the money. Whoopee.

His biggest problem – he had trouble even phrasing it to himself – he didn't quite disbelieve Mario Giotti. The judge's vehemence and passion at the end of their discussion about Sal's role in his life had struck a resonant chord, and suddenly Hardy had lost the conviction that Giotti was lying.

Killing Sal was beyond Giotti's pale. He had never intentionally killed anyone. He had been trying to make moral restitution to the victims of the one accidental death – technically a murder, but certainly unintentional – he'd been involved with. He was not a cold-blooded man, a man who would kill with premeditation, even if his victim was already on the verge of death. That distinction would be critical to him. His life's work in the law could never let him forget it.

So who had killed Sal?

His office had grown dark and he flicked on his green-shaded banker's lamp. Guilt over his unanswered messages didn't just gnaw at him, it was taking huge bites. He was going to have to miss dinner, get caught up. Frannie would deal with it, possibly would relish some time away from his intensity. Besides, they'd had a date just the night before, a wonderful family dinner with friends at home the night before that.

He had to do some billable work, business development, something worthwhile.

Frannie had been able to tell from the tone of his voice that he needed to feel as though he'd accomplished something before he came home; it almost didn't matter what it was. She told him she'd be fine, she'd wait up. She had a book she was loving. She'd kiss the kids for him.

And, oh, she almost forgot, some potential client had called a little earlier and Frannie had said Hardy would be working late in his office. She'd given his office number, so he might expect a call.

But now, nearly three hours later, there hadn't been one. He wouldn't wait around for it. It would come later or it wouldn't.

Over the past few hours he'd been subliminally aware that the associates downstairs were going home. Their muffled voices carried up the stairs as they passed through Phyllis's lobby in twos and threes on their way out.

By a little after nine-thirty he'd made all of his return phone calls, mostly to various answering machines, although he had held the hand of one of his prospective new doctor clients and flatly turned down handling two divorces.

He was now doing some substantive preparation, taking notes on a stack of recent briefs that had been filed in various federal courts on the right-to-die issue.

Because he preferred his banker's lamp to the overheads, he was working almost completely in the dark. The green glass shade cast a soothing pool of light over his desk. Somehow it helped his concentration.

He sat back in his chair, closed his eyes briefly. The building was quiet. Outside, the wind gusted and threw some raindrops against his window, reminding him that it was still coming down. He got up, stretched, crossed back to his window, and looked down on Sutter, nearly deserted at this hour. One dark car was parked directly across from him, but otherwise the curbs were empty. The rest of the street shone darkly, streetlights reflecting off the wet surfaces.

He returned to his desk, pulled his yellow legal pad toward him, grabbed a copy of another published brief, and stopped.

He really ought to go home. He could do this note-taking anytime. It was late on a miserable night. He felt he'd finally paid himself back for the wasted daytime hours, although he couldn't say he'd accomplished much.

The building's night bell sounded. This in itself was mildly surprising, since the only people who would normally be coming to the office at this hour would be night-owl associates who had their own keys. It was unlikely that it was a client, especially since Hardy was all but certain that he was the last person in the building. Probably, he thought, it was one of the city's homeless who'd wandered up the small stoop to get out of the rain, pressed the lit button by mistake.

But it sounded again and he decided he'd better go check. The lighting in the hallway outside of his office was on dim. On the stairway, the same thing. The cavernous lobby ceiling had a few feeble pinheads of light. It was dark as a movie theater.

Hardy descended the curving main staircase and got to the circular marbled alcove at the bottom. Turning the dead bolt in the heavy wooden doors, he pulled the door open.

No one was there.

He stepped out onto the sidewalk to look. No one. Squinting through the rain at the car parked across the way, he couldn't see anybody in the front seats. The back windows appeared to be darkly tinted. He couldn't make out anything through them.

Enough of this. He was going home. First back upstairs to his office, where he'd pack his briefcase, and then out of here, out the front door again, down to the parking garage under the building. Home.

The back door to the Giottis' car swung open. It had been essential to ring the bell to find out if anyone else was in the building, also to be sure that the third-floor light was Hardy. It didn't look as though there was anyone else still working, but at a time like this one couldn't be too sure. There were no lights left on in the lower-floor offices.

When the bell rang the second time, the person working upstairs got up, came all the way down, opened the front door, and stepped out onto the sidewalk. It was Hardy, all right, though not exactly the well-dressed version that he presented to the court, whose picture had been all over the newspapers, his sound bites on the news. This was the working attorney, tie undone, coat off, collar open. But even from across the street there was no mistaking him.

There were shadows now, moving in his office. He'd gone back up there. Now the thing to do was ring the bell again, wait for him this time, until he opened the door again.

Then do the thing.

Hardy was just going to finish these last three pages. Otherwise, he'd have to go back and reread the first twelve again to catch up to his place in the brief, to where he was now, if he wanted to reboard the paper's train of thought. Now, the opening pages were still clear enough in his memory, the syllogistic rhythm of the argument unbroken. He went right back to the spot where he'd left off, picked up his pen, read a few words.

There was a sound.

His head came up and he listened carefully. There couldn't be a sound. There was no one in the building and he'd locked the door behind him.

Or had he?

Suddenly he couldn't remember if he'd turned the dead bolt back. It didn't matter, really, since he was going back down almost immediately, but maybe . . .

No, he'd locked it. He was pretty sure. He'd be done here in two minutes anyway.

And he was.

He'd heard no other noise, although lost in his reading, hurrying now to finish, scribbling the odd note, he was not likely to have heard one anyway.

Finally, he finished the brief, closed it back to its cover, put down his pen, and leaned back in his chair.

He looked up.

A silhouette was outlined in the doorway to his office.

39

'Mr Hardy?'

Hardy's hand was over his heart. 'Jesus Christ!'

'Did I startle you? I'm sorry.'

'No, that's all right. As soon as I land I'll be fine.'

'Your wife said you'd be working late. I thought . . .'

'It's all right.' His breath was coming back. 'How'd you get in here? Was that you who rang the bell?'

'Yes.'

He took another lungful of air. 'Where'd you go?'

'Nobody answered, so I went back to my car. Then – I must have looked away for a minute – I saw the front door closing behind you, then you moving around up here through the window, and I got out to try again, but this time the door was open.'

'Okay,' Hardy said. 'Okay. But I'm afraid it's a little late. I was just finishing up here, going home. I'm sorry. I can walk you back down, and we'll make an appointment for tomorrow. How's that?'

She stepped into the room. Hardy noticed that the strap to her purse was around her neck and that she was holding her purse in front of her with both hands. Or rather, that one hand was in the purse, the other holding it. 'I'm afraid that won't do.'

Hardy started gathering his papers, pushed away from the desk, started to stand up. 'Well, I'm afraid it's going to have to—'

'Sit back down, please!'

Something in her voice. He looked back up.

She'd moved another step closer and pulled the purse away, down to her side. Her other hand held a small gun, and she trained it levelly on him. 'You don't know who I am, do you?'

'No, ma'am, but you've sure got my attention.'

'My name is Pat. I'm Judge Giotti's wife. I'm really sorry to be meeting you like this.'

You're sorry? Hardy thought. But he said nothing.

Pat Giotti made some clucking sound. 'You and Mario had a long talk today. He told me all about it.'

'Yes, ma'am, we did. But he hired me as his lawyer, he may have told you, and I can't repeat anything he said to me. It's attorney-client privilege.'

A dry, mirthless chuckle. 'I know all about that, Mr Hardy. I also know it has no real teeth. I know all the ways it's been abused.'

'I wasn't planning to abuse it.'

'No, I'm sure you weren't, not now. But something could happen. Someday. The point is I can't be positive about it and unfortunately, that's what I have to be.'

Hardy's brain was on fire, trying to find a way out in a last desperate spurt of mental energy before it was silenced forever. But no ideas came – other than to keep her talking if he could. 'Were you this polite to Sal before you hit him?'

Her voice was tight with tension. 'I don't think rudeness serves any purpose. I didn't want to hurt Sal. I don't think I did hurt Sal.'

No, Hardy thought, only killed him.

But she was going on. 'But *he* would have hurt us. He would have ruined everything. Nobody seems to understand that. Even Mario didn't, always saying Sal was harmless, Sal was his old friend, a good guy. Well, let me tell you, Mr Hardy, Sal was out of control. He wasn't going to stop on his own. Somebody had to stop him. And it didn't matter, that was the amazing thing. He only had a few months anyway. He was dead in a couple of months at the most.'

'I know,' Hardy said. 'So what happened that you had to do anything?'

Keep her talking. Think. *Think!*

'You really don't know? Mario didn't tell you this?' A bitter laugh. 'It's so typical. He's always doing things like this, leaving it for me to clean up after him.'

'Tell me,' Hardy said.

In her calm hysteria she kept the gun trained on Hardy's chest.

Her body shifted, its language terrifying. He thought she would pull the trigger now, that it was over. He sucked in a breath.

'There was that bomb scare, that day, Friday. A little before lunchtime. You knew about that, of course.'

He nodded.

'When they cleared the building, the courthouse, Mario was out in the alley with his staff. Suddenly Sal is there, pulling him aside, all in a panic, telling Mario he's got to get the money together, the money isn't in his safe. He's thinking Mario took it back somehow. He tells him if he doesn't get it back, he's going to spread the word about the fire. He won't keep quiet any longer.'

She lowered her voice, but not the gun. 'Don't you see, Mr Hardy? He would have destroyed Mario's name. Which is all we have, all we've worked for all these years, Mario's reputation with his peers. And to let that senile *bum* threaten it? No, he had to be stopped. I couldn't let him bring Mario down. Sal wasn't anybody. He was dead anyway.'

'So your husband called you after he went back inside?'

She nodded. 'He thought Sal had simply misplaced the money – taken it out of the safe, put it somewhere else and forgotten where. So he went back up to Sal's room with him, to look for it. Can you believe the risk he took doing that? Anyone might have seen him and remembered. Then, when Mario couldn't find any money, Sal went off at him. Mario yelled back.'

Another tumbler fell into place: Blue's testimony, *before* her nap, the male voice in Sal's apartment. It had been Giotti after all.

But his wife was going on, the gun still trained on Hardy's chest. 'After he got back to his chambers, he called and told me what had just happened. And *still*, he tried to tell me it was all right. Sal was just having a bad day. How could he believe that? How could he not see?'

'So what did you decide to do?'

'I didn't know exactly. Not when I left to go there. Something, though. I was going to stop him. I brought this gun with me, just in case, but then there was the morphine out on the table. So much quieter and cleaner. I knew how to administer injections. One of my children is diabetic – I knew to put it in the vein. There was this heavy whiskey bottle. Sal never felt anything. I just knocked at his door and he let me in and we talked a minute, just like you and me now. And everything was there, laid out for me. As though God wanted me to do it, wanted to help me.'

With a jolt of terror Hardy realized that he'd led her to her moment. God had provided in this case as well: the building empty except for him. The open door. The cover of darkness for her escape.

It would be her second perfect crime.

He thought of a final question. 'Does your husband know?'

It wasn't really a laugh. It was too derisive. 'Mario? How could I tell him? He's a good man, a judge. He believes in justice. He doesn't understand that sometimes you have to act, not pass some abstract judgment.'

'So what does he think happened? That it was just his good luck?'

'He believes it was Graham. I think you convinced him. For which I thank you.'

This was her closing statement. Hardy could feel it.

The notion came to him – an instinct, far less than a thought or an idea. There was no time to analyze how good it was. In despair, his last effort, trying not to give it away with his upper body, he moved his foot under the desk and kicked a leg of it, producing a wooden thud.

This was going to have to be fast if he was to have a prayer.

'What was that?' She had to take her eyes off him for an instant. If he could make her do that . . .

'Maybe you forgot to lock the downstairs door behind you too.'

Her head began to turn, and only slightly. It was going to have to be enough. Hardy lunged for his banker's lamp as she fired. He went rolling with it over, then off, the desk. The lamp crashed to the floor, plunging the room into darkness as the sound of more gunfire exploded in his ears and he knew in the blinding flash of pain, God, he'd been hit.

A third shot. Another.

It was his leg, below the knee. Here came another shot. She wasn't wasting any time. He felt her steps on the floor, the vibrations through it. She was coming toward him as he lay.

The only light now with the lamp broken, and it wasn't much, came from the dimmers in the hallway outside his door. Fighting the shock and pain, he pulled his back up against the wood and the cover the desk barely provided. When he looked up, her form was there above him. Even in the darkness he could see the arm coming down. He was on his side, his back pressed against the side of the desk.

With no hesitation she fired again. The lick of flame across his belly.

He didn't want to die like this.

Aiming for a last shot to finish him, she finally made a mistake, coming too close. She was now within his reach, and he grabbed for her near foot, catching her at the ankle, bringing his other hand up around her leg.

He pulled as hard as he could, twisting her foot as he did. She screamed and fell in a heap next to him.

The gun hit the floor and went off again. He couldn't risk letting go of her leg, even for a second, but began pulling himself up her struggling body, arm over arm. He could feel a weakness spreading in him, but he couldn't give in to that. He had to manage to hold on to her.

She was pounding her fists on his head and shoulders, screaming at him. 'No! No! No!' Rolling over onto something hard, he felt the gun and grabbed for it, getting it into his hand, then rolling away.

'I've got the gun,' he said. 'Don't move. It's over.'

'No!' She kicked out in his direction. It wasn't over for her. She wasn't going to let him take her, not alive. The shadow of her came at him with all her strength, hit him full in the chest, knocking him backward again, grabbing for the gun.

His leg, as he tried to kick her off him, wouldn't do what he asked it to. When he twisted to get at her, his stomach stabbed at him. He screamed involuntarily at the pain, but she was a wild animal over him, scratching at his face, lunging for the weapon in his left hand.

He had no other option, his strength and mobility were ebbing away. He snapped the gun up, feeling it connect with flesh and bone – the side of her head. It stunned her briefly and without any reflection he brought the gun up again, connected with flesh and she collapsed to the floor.

He had to get to a light, a phone, get some distance on her. With all he had left, he pushed her off him.

Then wasn't sure he could get up at all. His leg wasn't responding. His stomach prevented any turning of his torso.

But he had to.

Pulling himself up by the corner of the desk, he finally got his dead leg pulled over to his doorway and hit the light switch. Pat Giotti was already moving again, coming to.

'Don't. Don't move!' he gasped at her.

She was wearing black spandex leggings and a black nylon windbreaker and there was blood – his blood, he realized – all over her. He couldn't get a breath. Hyperventilating, he kept the gun trained on her as he hobbled his way across to the desk again. Knocking the receiver off, he pushed 911, picked the receiver up again.

'Stay back!' It was all he could get out.

But she'd gotten to her knees now, again, less than five feet from where, shakily, he stood.

He had the telephone receiver in one hand, the gun in the other. When the operator answered, Hardy started to say his name. Consciousness was fading. He gasped to try to fill his lungs.

At that moment she leapt at him again, for the gun, over the desk.

He'd been wounded twice and had lost a deal of blood already, and she had only been stunned and now seemed to have regained all of her strength. With the adrenaline driving her, it was considerable.

When she hit him full body across the chest, he collapsed again under her. Both of her hands were on the gun now as she struggled to wrest it from him, twisted it back and got hold of it. She swung it around.

Hardy saw the black hole of the barrel center on his face.

A last, desperate grip, going to her wrist, bringing his other hand up, trying to slap it away, all the way around.

The gun fired and she screamed, her body arching back. 'You've shot me! Oh, God, I'm shot.'

The hand holding the gun went to her shoulder, but she managed to keep hold of it. Falling forward onto Hardy to keep him from moving, she jammed the weapon forward into the flesh under his jaw.

She pulled the trigger.

Click.

Again. *Click.*

An anguished groan and Pat Giotti's body, already collapsed on top of him, went limp. Hardy pushed to roll her off him. She'd been hit in the shoulder. She wasn't going to die from it.

He struggled. Got himself up. To the telephone.

He mumbled something, tried to get out his name and address. It sounded funny, though, indistinct. He tried again.

Shooting.

Fading fast. Darkness closing in.

Hurry.

He blacked out.

40

Sarah stood before Glitsky's desk, the door closed behind them. She was waiting for the boom to be lowered. Since the verdict on Graham, and then with the attack on Hardy and the resulting rumors and revelations about the Giottis, the Russo case continued to enthrall the public.

The feeding frenzy for the tiniest bits of news surrounding the principals had continued unabated. Over the weekend a television reporter, trying to make the connection between Craig Ising and Graham's income, had interviewed Ising and stumbled upon the information that Sarah had been with Graham at his softball tournament on the weekend after he'd been indicted. This had made the news last night and her lieutenant had summoned her into his office first thing this morning. The last straw.

'I don't have any excuse, sir. I did it. I was there.' Glitsky sat behind his desk, looking up at her. He didn't want to hear this. Not only was it grounds for dismissal from the force, but harboring a fugitive was a felony. 'All I can say is that I was sure Graham hadn't committed any crime. And I didn't harbor anyone. I had him turn himself in, didn't I?'

'Turn himself in? You had a man wanted for murder and you decided not to arrest him. That's not your decision to make, Sergeant.'

'Yes, sir, I realize that. I was wrong.'

'The grand jury had indicted him.'

'Yes, sir.'

She didn't have to go on about the political circus surrounding that indictment; Glitsky knew it as well as she did. Now he opened his desk drawer, thought a minute, slammed it closed. 'The POA' – Police Officers Association – 'doesn't want you fired, of course. They're telling me they'll sue the department.

First woman in homicide, all that crap. I hope you realize that if you were a man you'd be out of here.'

Evans stuck out her chin. 'With all respect, sir, if I were a man, this wouldn't be news. It would never have come up. It would have gotten buried.'

Glitsky snorted. 'You really think that?'

'Yes, sir. No offense. I've seen it happen several times.'

The lieutenant took that in. 'If you wanted to step down on your own, you could save everybody a lot of trouble.'

'It would make a lot of trouble for me, sir. I've worked hard to get here and I deserve to be here.'

Glitsky looked long and hard at the sergeant's face. She had made a tremendous error in judgment, but she still had the spine, independence, and intelligence that made a great cop. He considered his words with care. 'You know, Sergeant, this detail – homicide – it's not heaven. You don't get here and then stop.'

'I didn't say—'

He held up a hand. 'You said you deserved to be here, you earned it. Well, that's true, you did. But you don't just earn it and that's the end of it. You continue to deserve to be here, every day. Every single day, or you leave. That's the gig.'

Sarah took the rebuke stoically. 'He was found innocent, Lieutenant. He didn't kill anybody. Nothing like this is ever going to happen to me again. Graham didn't even get disbarred.' She paused, considering, then added, 'We're going to be married.'

Glitsky opened the drawer again, looked down at the scratch he'd prepared and signed off on – the formal charges he'd planned to send to the chief. All at once he realized he wasn't going to do that.

He pushed the drawer closed and brought his eyes up to hers. 'I'm happy for you,' he said.

There were days in the next few weeks, before he finally found out for sure, when Hardy wondered if it had all been worth it. He had had to know what had happened with Sal Russo, and the knowledge had nearly killed him. The gash that the second bullet had traced across his middle was a constant reminder of how close it had been. Another inch and a half and the slug would have ripped through both lungs and his heart.

He knew he still wasn't finished with the nightmares; the last *click* under his jaw was burned into his psyche. He would jolt awake, as often as not drenched in sweat, and lie there in bed next to Frannie until he finally gathered the strength to rise, to limp through his darkened house. Look in on both children. Rearrange the elephants.

Sit in the chair in his living room in the dark.

And still, with everything he'd suffered, he'd been lucky. The leg wound had passed cleanly through his calf muscle. His doctor assured him that he'd be able to jog his four-mile loop again within six months, although his long-jump career was probably effectively over.

Concentration, although improving, was still a problem. He would be sitting with Frannie or the kids and suddenly go blank, seeing the gun leveled at him, the perfect black little *o*.

He saw it now, at nearly noon on a Tuesday in the middle of October, and he jerked his head up. He was in the Solarium trying to follow an article in one of the law journals about some new 'natural death' hospice care facilities that were apparently operating within the law in Oregon and Montana and maybe several other states. He was making notes on arguments that might help his doctor clients here in San Francisco, although it was beginning to look as though Dean Powell was going to accept very reasonable nolo pleas – fines and light community service, which Hardy's clients were doing anyway – for most of them.

Hardy had checked with the licensing board and already had a promise that the doctors would be allowed to continue to practice. Freeman had told him that under the circumstances, Hardy might even do better. 'Hell,' he'd said, 'you could probably get a letter of apology.'

But neither Hardy nor his doctors, some of whom had recently discovered that political grandstanding had consequences in the real world, were willing to push their luck.

Hardy liked to think that the trial of Graham Russo had made the attorney general rethink his hard-line position on assisted suicide. If nothing else, Powell had come to realize that his earlier push for prosecution of these doctors was politically unpopular. And if it wasn't going to win votes, the AG wasn't interested in it.

Hardy was sitting up straight with his back against his chair. He told himself that the bandages around his chest were good for his posture. Any slouching was intolerable. There was a comforting and familiar buzz in the lobby behind him – associates coming and going, phones ringing. He looked out through the glass into the enclosed garden area where some pigeons were enjoying the sunshine.

Hardy was going to be all right, except that now his chest was an agony of itching from where they'd shaved him, where the last scabs were falling away. He tensed his calf and felt the familiar stab of pain. It, too, was healing, he supposed, but it wasn't done yet. He went back to his article.

David Freeman, brown bag in hand, knocked at the Solarium lintel, walked right in, and began unpacking. He pulled out a couple of wrapped sandwiches, a large bottle of Pellegrino water, little plastic glasses, and a jar of marinated artichoke hearts. 'I took the liberty,' he said, unwrapping the white butcher paper. 'Mortadella, sourdough, provolone. Brain food.'

Hardy pushed his journal to the side. 'I thought that was fish.'

'Fish too,' Freeman said. He had finished unwrapping the sandwich, spreading the paper out under it, making it neat. Pushing it over in front of Hardy, he poured some Pellegrino into one of the glasses and placed it in front of him too. This kind of solicitude from Freeman was unusual, and Hardy glanced over at him. 'What?' he said.

'What what?'

'Don't give me that, David.'

Freeman left his own sandwich unmolested, still wrapped in front of him. He sat back. 'They cut a deal with the judge's wife. Pratt accepted a plea.'

Hardy threw a disbelieving glance at the old man. 'What do you mean, she accepted a plea? What plea?'

'Manslaughter on Sal Russo, three years. Assault with a deadly weapon on you, three years concurrent, no additional time for the gun.'

For a second the room tried to come up at Hardy.

'Diz?'

'Assault with a deadly weapon? It was attempted murder, David, she tried to kill me. She *did* kill Sal Russo. And what do you mean no additional time for the gun?'

Freeman let out a long breath, cracked a knuckle. 'It seems Mrs Giotti's been under a lot of stress lately, imagining that Russo was a threat to her husband's career and that you somehow were part of this giant conspiracy.'

'Imagining? She *told* me her husband and Russo had started a fire that killed a fireman. She *told* me she'd killed Russo to shut him up. She *told* me she was going to kill *me* so I couldn't talk about it.'

Nodding, Freeman went along with him. 'Yes, indeed, my son. Quite mad, wasn't she, imagining all these terrible things about her husband and some fire?'

'But Giotti—' Hardy stopped himself. He couldn't say, and that realization choked him.

'What? The judge denies everything and her doctors confirm that she's imagining it, so we all know it never happened. Except, of course, for some nasty-minded columnists.' Freeman eyed Hardy shrewdly. 'Unless someone knew something admissible that could actually pin the arson on Giotti. You wouldn't know anybody like that, would you, Diz?'

'No.'

'I thought not. If you did, I'm sure at the very least you'd want to tell your old pal David?'

But Hardy knew he could never tell Freeman or anybody else what Giotti had told him under the seal of the attorney-client privilege. It had been the worst five dollars he'd ever earned. 'I don't know anything, David.'

The old man nodded. 'I believe you. But you know, with Pratt not exactly being in love with you to begin with, the fact that you couldn't provide any more information on Giotti didn't make her want to throw the book at his wife. After all, the judge still has some influence. You cross him at your peril. Pratt knows that. You're lucky she didn't charge *you* for trying to kill *her*.'

'Maybe the fact that it was her gun, that she brought . . .' Hardy made a face. 'Never mind that. What about Powell? Won't he do anything?'

Freeman shrugged. 'Why would he? And anyway he can't. Double jeopardy's still a no-no. Both crimes – you and Sal – they both happened in Pratt's jurisdiction and she's charged and prosecuted them. End of story.'

Fingertips to his temples, Hardy was trying to make his headache go away. 'So what's she going to serve, Giotti's wife?'

Freeman shook his head in commiseration. 'You haven't heard the best part. The judge has just stayed her delivery to the prison system, postponed it.'

'I know what *stayed* means. But how, for how long?'

'Indefinitely. She's going to do her time in the county jail, close to home.'

Hardy finally exploded. 'Jesus Christ, David! This wasn't some shoplifting spree! No judge could do that!'

'Well, this one must know Giotti, and he just did, and since Pratt thinks it's a swell idea, no one's going to object.'

'Well, I damn well object.'

'But you, my son, are the proverbial person that nobody asked. I hate to mention it, Diz, but you've made a few enemies. You're not even the player to be named later.'

Hardy took it stoically. It wasn't too great a shock. But he was curious about Pat Giotti's sentence. 'So how much time you really think she'll do?'

'A couple of years plus or minus . . .' Freeman trailed off. 'She's going to be a model prisoner, get an early release.'

'So what about all this?' Hardy vaguely indicated himself. 'What did I do this for?'

Freeman took a huge bite of his sandwich and chewed awhile thoughtfully. He drank some Pellegrino water. 'You won your case. Your client's free. You got yourself a passel of new work.'

This wasn't much satisfaction. Hardy had to ask. 'So I'm shot twice and almost killed and the person who did this gets a few months in the country club? That's it? What happened to justice here?'

Freeman nodded, took another sip of water, shrugged. 'Justice? I think it went on vacation.'

Stagnola's was packed with the Thursday lunch crowd.

October was high season for tourists in San Francisco and Fisherman's Wharf swarmed with them, getting off the ferries, walking up from Pier 39, down from Ghirardelli Square.

Mario Giotti had been overwhelmed with his wife's legal troubles over the past weeks. It had shocked and dismayed him to learn that she had killed Sal, but certainly once it became clear that she had, the next order of business was damage control. Which, given his influence and connections, hadn't proved too difficult.

The community, his brethren, had closed ranks around him, as he knew they would. Pat – and thank God she was still alive – had even come to agree with his decision about their story. She'd been under too much stress with the accusations Sal had been making against her husband and had cracked under the pressure.

There had been a fire at the Grotto, certainly, but nothing like a cover-up, nothing that could come back to haunt the judge and mar his reputation. In fact, if anything, the judge's anonymous contributions over the years to the family of Randall Palmieri were signs of his generosity and beneficence.

Throughout his attorneys' negotiations with Sharron Pratt, Giotti had feared that Dismas Hardy would step up and ruin everything, but evidently he'd put the fear of God into the man. Should he take it upon himself to abuse the attorney-client privilege, the state bar would rise in righteous indignation and lift his license to practice law. Giotti never considered that Hardy was simply a man of honor – that he had entered into a contract and would keep his word.

Giotti did wonder if Hardy had leaked something of their privileged discussion to the columnist Jeff Elliot, but he had no way to prove it, and no way to accuse Hardy of anything without implicating himself. Elliot had come pretty close to what had happened, but hadn't gotten it exactly right, and that in turn made Giotti think that Hardy had kept it close to the vest after all.

The reporter had dug and gotten lucky, but didn't have all the pieces. So the rumors had flown for a few days, but they died down. He hadn't even deigned to issue any kind of formal denial.

Everything was going to work out fine. This was his city; he belonged here. People loved him and always would.

And now here was his old friend Mauritio at the front door, greeting patrons as they filed in. Because of all the troubles, then having to decide some cases on the circuit in Idaho and then

Hawaii, Giotti hadn't been to his old psychic home, back to his roots, in nearly a month.

Now he arrived at the door.

'Hey, Mauritio!' His hale and voluble welcome.

His old friend – his old employee – drew himself up. The smile fled from his face. 'Good afternoon, Your Honor,' he said formally.

Giotti cocked his head to one side – a question. He still wore his smile. 'Mauritio. What's the matter? You look like you seen a ghost.'

'Maybe I do, Your Honor.'

Giotti knew it felt wrong, but tried to make a joke of it. 'Well, invite him in. He can sit at my table with me.'

'I'm sorry, your table?'

'Hey, my table.' He started to push his way by, but Mauritio stepped in front of him.

'You got a reservation, Your Honor? We got a packed house in here today.'

Giotti raised his voice. 'What do you mean, you got a packed house? I'm talking my table, what do you . . .?'

He noticed that people had started to gather behind them, to notice. He couldn't have that. He calmed himself. 'No. I don't have a reservation.'

Mauritio clucked. 'Hey, I'm sorry, Your Honor, maybe some other day. Maybe you call first, couple of hours ought to hold one. Meanwhile, you might try next door, but they're pretty crowded too. In fact, Judge, maybe you gonna have trouble finding fish anywhere on the Wharf. Since Sal Russo died, maybe you gonna have trouble finding good fish anywhere around here.'

Stiffly, Giotti stood a moment. Then he nodded and turned away.

Behind him he heard Mauritio barking to a knot of tourists. 'Hey, how you folks doin'? Come on in, come on in. We're saving a table just for you.'

The wind was high off the ocean, rushing up the cliffs and inland across the peninsula, bending the cypresses nearly to the ground. A chill autumn sun was sinking into the water out at the horizon, and a young couple stood before a grave site at the ridge of the

Colma cemetery. The man wore a baseball uniform.

Graham had played in the season's last tournament down in Santa Clara during the day. The Hornets had gotten beaten on their third game, so Graham was finished early. He and Sarah had decided to drive over to the coastal town of Santa Cruz and have a late lunch, then up the coast on Highway One. And then, suddenly in Colma, they'd made the turn into here.

Graham had distributed the proceeds from the sale of the baseball cards and the fifty thousand dollars to Jeanne Walsh and her sister in Eureka, and in spite of the reactions of his brother and sister, felt he'd discharged a debt of honor. He'd gotten a letter from Leland's lawyer on behalf of the other heirs telling him he couldn't give away their inheritance and that the Singleterry offspring had no legal claim. Graham had told them to go ahead and sue him and distributed the money in cash anyway.

It was perhaps something neither Debra nor George would understand, but that was going to be their problem and their burden. Afterward, to her credit, Debra had called to tell him it was okay – she wasn't going to be part of any lawsuit George might bring. Graham saw hope here.

He had no similar illusions about his brother or his mother. George and Helen would live and die in Leland's camp at a level of physical comfort and social constriction. That was their choice.

It wasn't his. He went to one knee and smoothed at the grass over where his father's remains were buried. He'd taken his spikes up with him, wearing them over his shoulders with the laces tying them together. Now, as though they were a holy necklace, he removed them, over his head, and placed them by the headstone on the grass.

'Don't say *mañana* if you don't mean it,' Sarah said softly. She was quoting from an old Jimmy Buffett song, one of the cuts on a CD they'd been playing ever since the verdict: 'Cheeseburger in Paradise,' 'Cowboy in the Jungle.' Themes of freedom and rebellion, rum and sunshine. After his time in jail, the tunes seemed to help Graham with normalcy. He'd get there.

But hanging up the spikes was a different symbol, a different type of commitment. He stood looking down for a last moment. 'I mean it,' he said.

Hand in hand Sarah and Graham turned to walk down the hill. Sarah sighed. 'There's one thing I still don't understand, even after all of this.'

'What?'

'All the paper, the notes, the names.'

'What about them?'

'Well, I must have made a hundred calls, maybe more, following up, checking addresses, trying to break the code. I reached maybe half a dozen people who remembered your father at all. And none of them were involved in fishing or baseball or gambling or anything else that related to anything. I just don't get it. All those names Sal wrote down, all those numbers.'

They'd gotten back down to the parking lot, and Graham's steps slowed, then came to a stop. Sarah waited.

'It was everybody he ever knew. He didn't want to forget.' The wind gusted, stinging his eyes. 'He thought if he wrote it all down . . .' He stood motionless, overcome with emotion.

Sarah took a tentative step and put her arms up around him.

Sal sat at the kitchen table, writing furiously in the margins of the newspaper in front of him. One of the obituaries was Earl Willis, and the name had started a trail of connection. Sal had already been to see Finer and he knew what was coming. He wasn't telling anybody what he knew. He wasn't going to have anybody pity him, no, sir.

The kid who'd sat next to him in third grade was named Earl Willis. Was he the guy that had just died? A non-Catholic. Earl Willis, that was his name.

Sal remembered. Now who sat behind Earl? He had to remember, what was her name? Dorothy something, that was it. Blake. Dorothy Blake.

Closing his eyes, he tried to envision his old classroom – the map of the world tacked above the blackboard. Miss Gray! That was it. His teacher, Miss Gray. Now, how about his other teachers? He wasn't going to forget those names. He was going to have them right here, written down, in case anybody asked, in case he forgot.

And his assistant coach on Graham's Little League team – the Jaguars? Yep, Jaguars. Sal remembered the guy: smoked like a chimney, always had a cigarette tucked in his ear, a pack in the arm of his T-shirt. What was that name? He knew it. He knew he knew it, it just wasn't coming, but he had that pad of paper by his bed in case it came to him tonight. He'd write it down then. No one would know that he was forgetting. He'd have it all right here.

But wait. What about the other kids on Graham's team? He remembered the shortstop, Kenny Frazier, good glove no hit.

He was out of newspaper margin – Miss Gray, the other teachers, the Jaguars. But, aha! – here was a brown bag from the grocery store. He pulled it over, writing fast. His and Helen's first phone number – the house on Taraval. He had to get that down.

But then the rest . . .

The rest of everything.

The afternoon sun poured in over him and he scribbled until the light was gone, thinking that if he wrote it all down – everybody and everything from the beginning – maybe he would be able to retrieve it all when he needed it. Maybe his life wouldn't all go away.

Maybe he would live forever.

Render up the Body

Marianne Wesson

Cinda Hayes no longer believes in the legal system the way she used to. She's left her job as Chief Prosecutor of the Sex Crimes Unit in the DA's office to become Director of the Boulder County Rape Crisis Center. But she hasn't been long in her new position when she finds herself agreeing to defend a death row murderer – who's also been accused of rape.

Though Cinda abhors the crimes he's committed she abhors the death penalty more. And her client Jason Smiley's claims of innocence are so persuasive that she starts to wonder if he is the victim of a gross miscarriage of justice. But the more she becomes involved in his case the more the rest of her life starts to go awry . . .

'An excellent debut' *The Sunday Times*

'A very fine achievement' *Independent*

'The story is gripping throughout, with a shocking final twist. This is a remarkable debut' *Sunday Telegraph*

0 7472 5769 8

HEADLINE
FEATURE